BARRIE DAVIES is a member of the Department of English at the University of New Brunswick.

The original 'At the Mermaid Inn,' one of the most notable literary endeavours in Canada, was the result of the combined efforts of three poets: Wilfred Campbell (1858-1918), Archibald Lampman (1861-99), and Duncan Campbell Scott (1862-1947).

A Saturday column that ran in the Toronto *Globe* from 6 February 1892 until 1 July 1893, it covered a wide range of material – original poetry and prose, book and music reviews, articles on philosophy, politics, poetics, religion, and writings on a myriad of other matters. Critics have often referred to the column in general terms, but until now it has been unavailable in book form for detailed study. This careful transcription of the entire series offers a fresh perspective on three of the most important Canadian literary figures of the late nineteenth and early twentieth centuries.

Here are three major Canadian poets as prose writers. Lampman writes essays about nature and poetry; Campbell provides controversial views on many subjects, especially religion and poetry; Scott writes book reviews and scholarly essays on music and a variety of Canadian matters. 'At the Mermaid Inn' gives a fascinating glimpse into the literary and social concerns of the day. This volume brings to new light one of the most readable and vital documents in Canadian life and literature.

Literature of Canada

Poetry and Prose in Reprint

Douglas Lochhead, General Editor

At the Mermaid Inn

Wilfred Campbell, Archibald Lampman, Duncan Campbell Scott in *The Globe* 1892-93

Introduction by Barrie Davies

UNIVERSITY OF TORONTO PRESS
TORONTO BUFFALO LONDON

Toronto Buffalo London
Reprinted in paperback 2015
ISBN 978-0-8020-2299-8 (cloth)
ISBN 978-0-8020-6333-5 (paper)

Canadian Cataloguing in Publication Data

Main entry under title:
At the Mermaid Inn

(Literature of Canada ; 21)

ISBN 978-0-8020-2299-8 (bound) ISBN 978-0-8020-6333-5 (pbk.)

I. Campbell, Wilfred, 1858-1918. II. Lampman, Archibald, 1861-1899. III. Scott, Duncan Campbell, 1862-1947. IV. The Globe (Toronto, Ont.) V. Title. VI. Series.

PS8365.A8 C818'.4'08 C78-001326-3
PR9197.7.A8

This book has been published with the assistance of a grant from the Ontario Arts Council.

Preface

Yes, there is a Canadian literature. It does exist. Part of the evidence to support these statements is presented in the form of reprints of the poetry and prose of the authors included in this series. Much of this literature has been long out of print. If the country's culture and traditions are to be sampled and measured, both in terms of past and present-day conditions, then the major works of both our well-known and our lesser-known writers should be available for all to buy and read. The Literature of Canada series aims to meet this need. It shares with its companion series, The Social History of Canada, the purpose of making the documents of the country's heritage accessible to an increasingly large national and international public, a public which is anxious to acquaint itself with Canadian literature – the writing itself – and also to become intimate with the times in which it grew.

DL

Wilfred Campbell, 1858-1918

Archibald Lampman, 1861-99

Duncan Campbell Scott, 1862-1947

Barrie Davies

Introduction

'At the Mermaid Inn' is a work of great importance and fascination because it is a complex record of three writers' involvement in the special problems not only of their time and place, but perhaps ours; for tendencies and reactions initiated in the nineteenth century have persisted with an increasing sense of anxiety and crisis into our own time. The column, which ran for almost eighteen months in the Toronto *Globe*, from 6 February 1892 until 1 July 1893, is one of the best guides we have to prevailing intellectual tastes and currents at the same time as it rivets our attention to peculiarly Canadian complexities.

With the exception of 27 May 1893, 'At the Mermaid Inn' appeared every Saturday. Each contributor received three dollars a week. Archibald Lampman with eighty-seven entries made the most contributions. Wilfred Campbell and Duncan Campbell Scott wrote about the same number, respectively sixty-seven and sixty-six. Unlike those of the other participants, however, Wilfred Campbell's articles appeared erratically, several one week being followed by none for several weeks. Campbell and Lampman provided the more outspoken and controversial pieces. Scott tended to hold aloof from contemporary issues and his voice is more arcane and monotone. He left it largely to Lampman and Campbell to discuss contemporary concerns, the tone of their writing modulating from anger, indignation, and urgency to sadness and rueful bewilderment.

The column ended abruptly in July 1893. Because this fact has never been explained, perhaps cannot be explained, some speculation is worthwhile. Ten days after the first appearance of the column in *The Globe*, that is, on 16 February 1892, Lampman wrote to E.W. Thomson:

> One of my next door neighbours is the poet William Wilfred Campbell. He is an odd fish. His first impression is unsatisfactory, and does not inspire confidence, but I find myself gaining in respect for him as I know him better. His mind is erratic and slovenly, but there is some good stuff in it, which comes out now and then in an accidental and unexpected kind of way. Campbell is deplorably poor. In comparison with him I am a small Croesus. Some members of the Government lured him here last summer under promise of doing something for him, and all that it has amounted to so far is a

> temporary clerkship at $1.50 a day. Partly in order to help his pockets a little, Mr Scott and I decided to see if we could get the Toronto *Globe* to give us space for a couple of paragraphs and short articles weekly, at whatever pay we could get from them; they agreed to that; and Campbell, Scott and I have been carrying on the thing (several weeks now).[1]

On 18 May 1891 Campbell had become a temporary clerk in the Department of Railways and Canals, where he remained until he joined the Department of Militia and Defence on 1 June 1893, at a salary of eleven hundred dollars a year. A month after he had thus achieved greater security and doubled his income, 'At the Mermaid Inn' ended. On 6 June 1894, in a letter to Thomson about Campbell, Lampman stated: 'I have reason to believe he regards me as an enemy, assisted by emissaries who are always lying in wait to injure his fame and literary reputation.'[2] Campbell, in 1895, told Ethelwyn Wetherald: 'I fear that between myself and Lampman and Scott there is a barrier of ideals that will render me a lonely man here. I admire their good qualities as men and writers and would like to have a closer sympathy were it possible. But I fear I have fought and lived too long by myself to ever make a very close friend.'[3] From the beginning, and this was a representative, not a unique, situation at the time, Campbell's appointment in the Department of Militia and Defence was a political one. It is clear from his embittered entries in *The Globe* that he came to feel that literary prominence in Canada had more to do with politics and cliques than talent. His final column is a parody of poetry which bears a cruel resemblance to Lampman's, and tongue-in-cheek criticism, which refers to such poetry as 'millet-like in its terse realism.' Lampman made no contribution to the final column.

My own conclusion is that here we have, in microcosm, the symptoms of national fragmentation which are a major concern of these writers in the column as a whole. That Campbell, the most ardent nationalist of the three, was to become within five years an equally enthusiastic advocate of a vaster Britain is another story, but not without significance in the present context. The more nimble-minded and sagacious Lampman remained in the obscurity of the Post Office, but within five years knew 'insomnia' and 'dreadful moods,' while Scott, always more cautious and sanguine, had risen to prominence.

A reading of the bewildering number of eclectic topics in the 'Mermaid Inn' columns, which range from pets, open fireplaces, and a new kind of gold separator, to sea serpents, Wilhelm II's sense of humour, and Trappist monks, could induce an antiquarian or a whimsical interest. My own is emphatically neither, and is best defined by a coincidence at the time of writing this introduction. On 25 September 1976, *The Globe and Mail* revived 'the famous literary column, The Mermaid Inn,' and chose Hugh MacLennan to begin it. MacLennan in a nostalgic mood wrote:

> Lyrics of Earth and Music of Earth – so Lampman of an Ontario where the prime farmland had yet to be covered by the developer's concrete, of a homeland where the paddlewheelers still plied the St John River without anyone dreaming that a time was coming when a concrete dam would keep the salmon out of it. Happy men they seem to have been of the old Mermaid column, at least to the extent that they did not have to worry about politics.

He completely misses the troubled and abrasive nature of a column whose authors were well aware that the political chicaneries of Parliament Hill had contributed to a state of national crisis, and where Lampman expressed his dismay about the vanishing forests and 'the awful destructiveness' of his contemporaries. Lampman, Campbell, and Scott 'swallowed whole Keats' legend about the Mermaid Inn,' continued MacLennan:

> Souls of poets dead and gone,
> What Elysium have ye known,
> Happy fields or mossy cavern,
> Choicer than the Mermaid Tavern?

Anyone who reads the nineties column with the attention it commands can only see Keats's poem as fraught with sinister, unintentional ironies. We must avoid the Elysium or Arcadian fallacy, and the equally fallacious 'modernist' one, which perversely attributes modernism to earlier writers engrossed by problems which continue to perplex our era. Because Lampman, Campbell, and Scott wrote of urbanization, socialism, or the changing position of women does not make them more modern than Carlyle, Ruskin, Morris, or Mill.

The disposal of two more fallacies will clear the ground for a more accurate scrutiny of 'At the Mermaid Inn.' The notion that a considerable time-lag in news of literary and political developments existed between Canada and the rest of the English-speaking world is made untenable by even a cursory reading of the material. If such a lag existed it was a matter of weeks or months and not decades. Tennyson's or Whitman's death, the Shelley centenary, the election of a poet laureate, the morality of Hardy's *Tess*, the barbarity of Kipling's *Barrack-Room Ballads*, Symons's definition of the poet – all are debated with a freshness and intensity which we would hope for in the literary section of the best modern newspapers. Finally, the preoccupation with the affairs of the English-speaking world could only be interpreted as colonial voyeurism by the most myopic of present-day nationalists. Lampman, Campbell, and Scott did not ignore the complexity of the Canadian experience in favour of the sentimental confusions of nationalism, and that in itself is evidence of maturity. But greater evidence lies in the discriminating handling of English and American writers, methods, and institutions, and the judicious selection of what was appropriate to Canadian writers, methods, and institutions.

'At the Mermaid Inn' constitutes a defence of the imaginative life and the values of art in a time which had come to dismiss them as impractical. It is convenient to deal separately with the various issues discussed, while admitting that such an order is artificial in that it does not reflect a continuous interplay which might, for example, lead the writer of an obituary to reflections on national disunity and the peripheral role of the artist in a utilitarian society.

Wilfred Campbell, formerly the Reverend W.W. Campbell and then a layman by choice, plunged into the persistent nineteenth-century debate concerning the authority of the Bible. In so doing he almost wrecked the fragile enterprise floated in part for his sake. Two days after the 27 February 1892 column had appeared, Campbell the international debater received a national reproof from the editor of *The Globe*, speaking no doubt for the majority of his 40,000 readers. He emphatically repudiated Mr Campbell's religious ideas and regretted that *The Globe* should have been used to circulate them. Campbell's rejection of institutional religion, though in conflict with orthodox rigidity, did of course duplicate the attitudes of many intellectuals in North America and England. The grounds for the rejection of, and the possible alternatives to, orthodoxy are clearly reiterated by Campbell in the column. Institutional religion, we are told on three occasions, is conservative, reactionary, or inert. The church has ceased to be an active force in society, is ceremony without ethics, a tool of capitalism, indifferent to the 'destitution, degradation and misery' within the shadow of its spire and the sound of its bell. Its adherents are depicted as narrow, hypocritical, and devoted to a 'sect-prejudice' and 'pharisaism' which perpetuate many moral and aesthetic crimes, actively increasing human distress while simultaneously condemning those who seek to expose them through literature and art as 'abominations of the evil one.' Sectarian theology, moreover, could not survive the findings of Darwin, 'Higher Criticism,' anthropology, geology, and archaeology, and in Campbell's opinion a religion 'bolstered up by ignorance' was but 'poor and tottering' anyway. For, in *The Globe* columns at least, the -isms and -ologies and dreadful clinking hammers did not bring to Campbell the doubts and perplexities of Arnold and Ruskin. What emerged instead was something close to the exaltation of man as in Swinburne, or the transcendentalism of Emerson:

> Let men talk about religions and theologies, but the greatest and best church ever built is walled by nature's horizon and roofed by the great dome of sky, at night or morning, summer or winter, where the liturgies are eternal in runeless books of earth and sky, where the choirs are never desecrate or out of tune, in the endless chancels of wood and meadowcroft, where the preachers are eternal, unconscious influences forever at work. Out in such a temple as this for a man to be irreligious, in the loftiest and holiest sense, is to bespeak him as less than a clod, for even the clod blossoms or girdles itself with green if left to the influences that nature has linked it to. (6 May 1893)

Throughout the nineteenth century the effects of materialization and vulgarization were observable. Like sceptical and honest men elsewhere in England and America, Lampman, Campbell, and Scott in what we now see as an age of crisis protested against trends exacerbated in a country which had not had time to develop. We ought to remember less Lampman's youthful enthusiasm for Roberts's *Orion* and more his opinion by 1892 that Roberts had compromised himself by seeking popularity among uncritical nationalists:

> He is like one who has said to himself that there ought to be a prophet, and he will be that prophet at whatever cost of effort. It seems to me, however, that the times can hardly carry patriotic verse, particularly of a boastful character. Satire would appear to be the species of verse most applicable to the present emergency. (19 November 1892)

Utilitarian political theories and laissez-faire economics, evangelical religion and the equation of prosperity and industrial expansion with happiness provided the recognizable temper of the age. In Canada especially, where these movements were felt by many to be the prerequisites for nationhood, reservations and alternative ideals were not encouraged. Nevertheless, one of the dominant notes here is satirical, if that term includes an antipathy to the attitudes and tendencies of the age, a refusal to compromise because of the pressures of society, an exercise of intelligence and sensibility devoted to closing the breach between the actual and the ideal. Irony and satire are not modes of indifference, but modes of concern.

Had the nineteenth century produced a juster, more equitable, more democratic society? Neither Campbell nor Lampman thought so. Instead they focus attention on a new feudalism based on money, a brutal division between the plutocratic few and the impoverished mob caused by the man who, as Campbell puts it, is 'but a two-legged animal, who preys on his species and believes in the creed that might is right.' The improper distribution of wealth and the motives of an acquisitive society are exposed. Money is sought for the sake of splendour, for 'the power with which it arms,' or from the 'purely brute instinct' of 'watching the pile grow.' Because the demands of trade and industry are not compatible with social sympathy Lampman muses ruefully:

> If, all at once, through some strange moral awakening, men could be got to see the miserable emptiness and vulgarity of this desire for riches, the work of the social and political reformer would be made beautifully straight before him, and all things would adjust themselves to the ideal plan . . . (24 September 1892)

The 'ideal plan' would include massive infusions of socialism, which all these writers endorsed, resulting in a 'paradise of the philosopher and the poor man,' where there are 'no rich men and no poor and the labouring man is King.' Not in England, however, or North America, which is 'too full of practical politicians and railway magnates to be a fit place for any simple and honest man to live in.'

The varied symptoms of corruption lead to the same diagnosis that the age is preoccupied by materialism and utilitarianism. Campbell, like Arnold, pointed to 'hurry and change,' to an inflexible demand for practical knowledge and studies to the detriment of the imaginative, creative, and humane. The age is obsessed with a joyless and 'monstrous puritanical notion' that ensures that 'the mass of mankind were only made to be worked.' Recreation therefore is construed as shocking idleness, and 'to grant a holiday is almost to overturn the world.' The Christmas Eve column for 1892 ends with a poem dedicated to 'The Galley Slaves.' Whether the future will bring an improvement is dubious, for parents moulded by social pressures continue to force their children into 'such paths as appear to be desirable or honourable to them' and are therefore partly responsible for 'a fair proportion of the mental and moral ruin we see about us.'

Progress then is change, but is divorced by Lampman, Campbell, and Scott from moral improvement as they continue their dissection of society by looking at another downtrodden segment, women. The extra legal, moral, and social inequities from which women suffer are unequivocally condemned, and equal rights and opportunities are advocated in the sure knowledge that not only women, but men and society as a whole will benefit:

> Women, no longer weak and dependent, no longer kept in an emotional atmosphere of frivolity and sentimental irresponsibility, but strong, active, and self-reliant as men, will not be subject or exposed to the same temptations, and above all they will not be at the mercy of men. When the moral and intellectual emancipation of women is fully effected many a cloud will be lifted from human life, and no sensible man will believe that the sex will have sacrificed one whit of that grace and beauty which we think to be its chiefest charm; rather there will be added to these a power, a beneficence, a dignity which are only the exception now. (9 April 1892)

It ought to be clear by now that 'At the Mermaid Inn' is important because it reflects many of the issues, conflicts, and general temper of the age. Lack of space prevents me enlarging upon these aspects, and besides, this document could be reinforced by many others – Carlyle's 'Shooting Niagara: and After?', Mill's *Autobiography*, Arnold's *Literature and Dogma*, George's *Progress and Poverty* are some examples. But as a document of a place in time, where is 'At the Mermaid Inn's equal? It is to its special characteristics that I will devote the rest of my attention. Unlike Wordsworth, I am not going to invoke writers of the past because their country needs them. But if Campbell, Lampman, or Scott were indeed living at this hour they would have little trouble following contemporary news and conversation. More likely, they would have a strong sense of déjà vu.

Roy Daniells once made explicit the connection between the land and self-awareness, and stated that it was no accident that Canadian poets of the late nineteenth century were concerned with landscape.[4] Just as the concern with landscape was no accident, so, it seems to me, it was inevitable that the characteristic qualities of the 'landscape' should be conflict coupled with an intense need for resolution. There is no better commentary on post-Confederation poetry, on 'landscape,' than 'At the Mermaid Inn.'

Confederation did not create a nation, declared Campbell, for a quarter of a century later Canada was but 'the scattered and intractable materials of which a nation may be made.' If it were a complex fate to be an American, then the complexity of trying to be a Canadian seemed overwhelming. 'I speak here,' writes Campbell, 'as a Canadian and one who loves his country, but who loves her too well to bury the dangers to her progress, that all true Canadians only see too well, in cowardly evasions for the sake of creating a false hope' (31 December 1892). Campbell's article follows immediately after Scott's, which is written from the point of view of 'an enthusiastic Canadian, one who believes that his country is the brightest and best on earth' and will therefore 'indulge in a little flaunting of the maple leaf.' The poverty of the language here is equal to the poverty of the thought as Scott tritely imagines a future in which present obstacles have been miraculously overcome and when 'we will serve as the example to the world of a people welded by a national spirit and a national love' (31 December 1892). Perhaps Scott's overblown rhetoric was responsible for the vehemence which Campbell expresses: 'If there is one thing I detest, it is a tendency to self-deception and to avoid grim realities.' There is an intricate and tough-minded optimism in Campbell's realization that the conflicts and antagonisms need to be fully expressed. What he most fears as 'the greatest danger to the country lies in trying to smother as inimical what is but the natural expression of this stage of our development.' A national sentiment will be formed by, and will include, what are paradoxically either impediments or characteristics, such as sheer size, regionalism, sectionalism, 'old country feuds of racial, religious, or other origin,' and the subtleties of a relationship to Britain and the United States.

Lampman wrote buoyantly about the conflicting extremes of the Canadian climate, 'of the restless and violent alternatives of heat, and tempest, and rain, of foliage and frost' and its effect upon national character. It was a very different matter when he and his fellow writers pondered the moral, intellectual, and aesthetic climate. In a country hardly out of a 'money-getting and home building stage' the utilitarianism of the nineteenth century was focussed and intensified. The lack of audacity, the puritanism, the prudery and 'frostbite at the roots of the Canadian imagination' of Frye, Bush, E.K. Brown, and Smith receive early expression in Lampman's complaint that 'in a country like this, where people talk so much about progress and prosperity and so forth, the number of those who count artistic and aesthetic development as one of the things to be sought after is so few' (24 June 1893). What could be more unpropitious than an ethos made up of a 'binder-twine' mentality, to adopt Lampman's phrase, in conjunction with Campbell's sense of 'pharasaism' and colonial self-contempt. All create the 'arid poverty of our intellectual and social life' and the belief, as Lampman puts it, that ' the intellectual conditions of our people and the institutions of our public life' are 'destitute of light and charm,' 'barren,' and 'barbarous.' That Canada was not a nation is reflected in the absence of truly national institutions. In two separate columns on a single Saturday, Campbell condemns Canadian universities for failing to be centres 'of the best culture and aspirations of the growing national life.' Part of the reason for that failure lies in the fact that so few of the professors of literature and history 'are truly Canadians in birth, hope, sympathy, and education' (12 March 1892). Likewise, Lampman on two occasions comments upon the 'poor and average-looking room' of the 'so-called national gallery' as symbolic of a contempt for anything not immediately perceived as useful. He censures both the government and the wealthy for their complete lack of interest in 'the beauty, the honour, the real well-being of this country.'

It is hardly surprising, then, that talented Canadians felt obliged to leave, and the evaluation of the meaning of this exodus is one of the persistent concerns of the column. Clearly the sense of Canada as an independent nation was not consistent with 'the folly of ignoring her rising men' and it was a 'disgrace to Canada to say that our young men have to go over to the much-abused neighbouring republic to win recognition in the higher pursuits.' Scott understated what was evidently a critical situation, and his metaphors imply that he felt the exodus to be something approaching treason. He tries to ameliorate the situation when he suggests that Canadian writers are at least appreciated in their own country, a suggestion not endorsed by Campbell and Lampman, or Goldwin Smith and Robert Barr for that matter.[5] It is ironic to note that what Scott has to say occurs during a commentary upon the poetry of Bliss Carman, who had become literary editor of *The New York Independent* in 1890:

> I think it would be impossible to find a more loyal group of men in Canada than her writers. Although from no fault which can at present be remedied our country furnishes for the literary man absolutely no chance of living by his art, the desertions from her ranks of the men of letters have been small indeed, and, where they have occurred, probably the severance was not of the spirit at all. If a man is forced to live by his pen in Canada, or wilfully determines to do so, there is only one refuge for him – journalism – and if what all my journalistic friends tell me is true, even that field is not covered very thickly with clover. So that it happens that all our country can bestow upon her writers is in some cases only a very modest (or, perhaps, a prudish would be the better word) income, in others, no income at all. But it is a source of pleasure to all the writers alike to be appreciated in their own country . . . (24 September 1892)

Yet when he writes of the evident success of Gilbert Parker, Scott is unable to avoid stating that it 'will be a bright day for Canada when men of such ability can find it to their advantage to remain at home.' The betraying phrases remain, however, in 'and exercise their faculties in helping to build up the country in which they were born.' Because of a letter to E.W. Thomson dated 16 September 1891, in which Lampman states that 'I was not going to abandon the soil just yet, but that I had it securely in mind to do so at as early a date as possible,' we can understand that his entries in this particular matter almost constitute a reply to Scott's.[6] Among the prominent Canadians in Britain and the United States who Lampman names are the Honourable Edward Blake, Erastus Wiman, E.W. Thomson, Grant Allen, Gilbert Parker, Dr Schurman, Bliss Carman, and Sara Jeannette Duncan. Then comes the revealing and unequivocal final paragraph:

> it is quite natural that those who seek the widest field for their abilities should wander abroad. Let us find no fault with them on

> that account. They probably bring more honour to their country in the fields which they have chosen than they would if they had remained at home. Here their energies might have withered away in petty and fruitless occupations, and their talent have evaporated in the thin sluggishness of a colonial atmosphere. (4 March 1893)

Lampman and Campbell, then, would have agreed with Scott that Canada did not furnish writers with opportunities to live by their writing. Where they disagreed was in the strength of their conviction that this was a fault which could and must be remedied. Hence the most persistent and crucial concern of 'At the Mermaid Inn' lies in the series of attempts to create an atmosphere in which art and artists could flourish. One characteristic of a country where so few people cared about 'artistic and aesthetic' development was the inordinate tax on books. Both Scott and Lampman complained about the tax and the ill effects it would have upon the educational standards of Canada:

> In this country more than any other we have need of the means of a fine intellectual development for the whole of our people. We look forward, or ought to look forward, to the establishment of a commonwealth freer and nobler than that of any other land. To accomplish this all our people must be educated as no other people are educated, and the best instruments of education must be made as easily obtainable as possible. (11 March 1893)

There was a time, Lampman tells us, when great writers were also active participants in great national efforts, but the antagonism to literary men is reflected in the need to protest that the artist is not a 'monstrosity.' Lampman is especially concerned to make this clear to the 'hard-headed man of the world' and also to make clear that he is referring to the Canadian context in particular: 'There are a very great number of people, especially, I believe, in this country, who regard the word "poet" as simply and completely synonymous with the word "fool" ' (2 April 1892). Later in the column he pleaded against calling the poet a 'singer,' a word which implied that he was a trivial entertainer and shocked him 'with a sudden sense of the absurdity of his position.' Lampman meditates on the unrealized potential of the writer Joseph E. Collins, regarding him as 'an instance of how in a raw and uncultured society like ours a great deal of genuine and original talent may be dissipated and wasted through the pressures of sordid conditions, and the absence of bracing intellectual influences' (19 March 1892). His final comments on this particular matter are bleak, inasmuch as he felt that the Canadian writer's accomplishments, though not what he 'might have done under more favourable circumstances,' provide only ' a grim satisfaction' in face of 'the poverty of opportunities' (27 August 1892).

The recently formed Association of American Authors prompted Campbell to write that a similar organization in Canada might change unfavourable circumstances. His comments are a further indication of other restraints upon the literary imagination:

> We have many writers, and we have no association to bring them together or develop and encourage our literary spirit. The fact that we could not organize on such a large and successful basis as our friends across the line should not discourage us. No class of literary workers in the world today needs so much encouragement as do the Canadians. We have an uphill fight against a narrow spirit of local contempt at the hands of the very class that could help us if it desired to. Therefore Canadian writers would do well to band together on a practical basis of a common fellow feeling. (4 June 1892)

But literary fellow feeling was more often desired then perceived by Campbell, for he felt that 'the grave weakness in our literary conditions is the same as that at the bottom of our national existence.'

This weakness he defines as disunity caused by 'a bundle of cliques, each determined to get what it calls its right and caring little for matters outside of its own interests.' As a consequence literary criticism in Canada was not an objective, informed appraisal of a writer's work but 'mere senseless gush or brutal abuse or mean insinuations.' Some months later, what was almost objective diagnosis became bitterness and loathing in his account of how he had been

> approached at different times by these rings, who through one of their members propose an attitude of 'defence' or of 'offence' against some imaginary enemy of their affected ideas, or against some person like myself, who persistently refuses to enter into a fraternal system of back-scratching among themselves and back-biting of outsiders who refuse to accept their disgusting overtures. Sad to say, this condition of things runs like a dry rot through our system of literary toil and ambition. (4 February 1893)

Scott summed up the matter in more measured terms:

> If your friend knew how most of the literary fame which he envies had been made he would redden to have coveted it. So if his name is left out altogether from the lists of poets which are so commonly ludicrous, and if he is not called the Shelley of Canada, he may perhaps begin to think that there is something in him after all. Perhaps the true test of poetic greatness in our time would be complete neglect, if not contempt. (11 February 1893)

The issue was critical, for Lampman, Campbell, and Scott equated a mature national consciousness with a reliable market for books and a just appreciation of indigenous talent. Therefore one of the causes of the present instability of criticism (and its possible solution) was the obvious lack of a sound Canadian literary journal. Here all three writers agreed and in many articles petitioned for such a journal. Lampman began a broad survey of the magazines and reviewers in Canada. He was lukewarm about *The Week* and polite about *The Globe.* He deplored reviewers for 'the same ridiculous praises decked out in the same fulsome and meaningless phraseology.' What was needed was 'a really good literary magazine, including a department of criticism conducted in a spirit of serious appreciation and uncompromising candour.' Instead, all one met was 'inert neglect' or 'spasmodic and senseless eulogy.' Writers would be stimulated and encouraged by 'an even more searching process of criticism,' and a great deal of dormant talent could be aroused by an 'attractive and stimulating vehicle of publication.' This was the means to an end envisaged as a state of 'intellectual ferment and competition.' Perhaps Lampman's most characteristic persona was, however, the defiant sonneteer who 'broke out into a roar of coarse and offensive laughter' and crushed up his papers into a couple of pellets and, filliping them into my face, strode out of the room.' In the circumstances, the writer has little respect for the public, reviewers, or publishers, and must be content with the judgment of trusted friends or the hope of a more discriminating posterity.

Nevertheless, four new journals came into being during the period of 'At the Mermaid Inn.' The Montreal *Dominion Illustrated Monthly* 'tantalized the patriotic eye with the phantasm of a Canadian magazine,' but was in fact permeated with a 'general air of verdancy and provincialism.' What these writers wanted was a Canadian journal that would reflect Canadian circumstances and cater to particular Canadian needs. Campbell explains the matter in the following way:

> What we want is something that is purely Canadian, and to do this the Canadian editor wants to be a Canadian in his aims and ideals. He does not want to take the American or English standard or style of periodical, with its highly trained and suppressed literature, and force the work of our writers through such a literary sieve to do this as to produce a Canadian journal or periodical which is a puerile imitation of the foreign type. (6 August 1892)

Of the three other journals, *Arcadia*, *The Lake Magazine*, and *The Canadian Magazine*, it was the latter which seemed most likely to supply the desired need. However, as Lampman pointed out, people should not and would not support a journal out of patriotic obligation, and the highest standards must be aimed for:

> People will not buy a third- or fourth-rate article because it is Canadian; and there would be no patriotism in their doing so, as some of our fellow countrymen seem to think. On the contrary it seems to us that a man will best show his patriotism by doing what he can to suppress such things as tend to misrepresent and disgrace his native land. (20 February 1892)

Unfortunately, these journals became little more than Lampman's tantalizing phantasms, for neither *The Lake Magazine* nor *Arcadia* survived beyond 'At the Mermaid Inn.' *Arcadia* failed 'because it is impossible for a journal to succeed in advance of the general culture of the society to which it appeals,' and Scott regretted that 'such a valiant attempt to foster and advance the culture of the country had met with such indifferent treatment.' The reasons for failure are familiar, but nevertheless depressing, and provide a final illustration of how much energy and feeling was consumed in trying to be a writer in Canada.

Now that 'At the Mermaid Inn' is finally available, much more will be written about it, and it will become an indispensable guide to intellectual life of the late nineteenth century in Canada. I have made no attempt to exhaust the rich diversity of the material. My stress has been on the centrality of much of the material to the time and place in which it was written; to trace through themes which seem especially pertinent now. Certainly, as the Literature of Canada series demonstrates, there is a Canadian literature. What is equally important is that

'At the Mermaid Inn' makes it clear that there is a continuum of sensibility and a history of ideas which ought to enable us, in future, to be more specific and confident about the implications of the word Canadian when we speak of Canadian literature.

NOTES

1 PAC, letters from Archibald Lampman to E.W. Thomson, ms Group 29940, I, 16 February 1892
2 Ibid., 6 June 1894
3 Carl F. Klinck, *Wilfred Campbell: A Study in Late Provincial Victorianism* (Toronto 1942) 96
4 'Confederation to the First World War' in *Literary History of Canada* I 215
5 Goldwin Smith, 'Literature in Canada,' *The Canadian Magazine* XIV 1 (November 1899); Robert Barr, *The Week* XI (August-September 1894) 950, 974
6 PAC, letters from Archibald Lampman to E.W. Thomson, ms Group 29940, I, 16 September 1891

Acknowledgements

The text of this book is published by kind permission of *The Globe and Mail*, Toronto, and (with respect to the contributions of Duncan Campbell Scott) Mr John G. Aylen QC, Ottawa. For editorial guidance and support the General Editor and the Introducer offer sincere thanks to Jean C. Jamieson and Jean Wilson of University of Toronto Press. A special debt of gratitude is extended to Patricia Kennedy, Secretary to the Librarian, Massey College, University of Toronto, who transcribed the text from microfilm. This was trying work which she carried out with her customary accuracy and good humour.

EDITORIAL NOTE

Every precaution has been taken to adhere to the original text. Only obvious printing errors have been silently corrected.

At the Mermaid Inn

6 February 1892

Sir Roger: What have we here?

Giles: There is everything under the sun set down with some show of reason; they run atilt at the world, and treat men and manners as familiar as an old hat.

Sir Roger: Think you they protest too much? I like a matter disposed bravely, but –

Giles: Methinks they have a genial tongue. Will you hear them?

Sir Roger: Well, an' it be not too long I'll have some sack, and you read on. (Old Play)

DUNCAN CAMPBELL SCOTT

The year that has just passed has given no remarkable addition to the world of books. But there has been much that is very good. In verse Gilder's *Poems of Two Worlds*, Aldrich's *Sister's Tragedy*, Helen Cone's *Ride to the Lady*, Miss Reese's *Handful of Lavender*, and Riley's *Old-Fashioned Roses* are probably the most notable additions to American published verse. Mr Gilder's work is imbued with the lofty ideal of a true poet. His work is both sincere and human, with a spiritualized regard for nature that makes his verse unique among that of the stronger American poets. The very essence of the human soul in its more spiritual moods is found in his work, which is inspired by the religion of humanity in its greater and broader phases.

It is some time since a boon of short stories has been published worthy of such close and eager attention as *Main Travelled Roads*, by Mr Hamlin Garland. This book has something direct and forcible about it, and proceeds with the touch and point of the truest art: it has something naturally inevitable about it, too, and its tragedy is often the outcome of the old stern laws of life. The contrast between the beauty of nature, ever present and unconquerable, and the sometime hardness and wickedness of the life which we men make for ourselves, comes out with new force. In fact, the only fault to be found with these stories lies in the seeming contradictions of a style which for the description of natural scenery takes a form elevated and poetic and for the dialogue one as coarse as natural man. But possibly Mr Garland had a purpose in this, and we cannot quarrel with him when he has given us a brilliant light on some phases of our mixed and perplexing conditions. He has humour, too, of a caustic kind and in 'Mrs Ripley's Trip' he has achieved a pathetic result by what is in reality a method of geniality or humour. But this book will teach us all something if we read it attentively, and, although not written with a direct purpose, such a tragic picture of human error, carelessness, and selfishness as 'Up the Coulee' brings some earnest warning to every heart. There is plenty of the sunshine of life in this little book, and we commend it to those who would like to feel once more the way young love comforts itself. Mr Garland's book is a distinguished performance.

ARCHIBALD LAMPMAN

Winter for reading and study; summer for loafing and dreaming and getting near to nature; spring and autumn for joyous and active production. The mind does not mount readily to the higher exertions during the severity of our winter season. Most of us gain at that time in fulness and robustness of body, while we lose in intellectual elasticity. We are taken up in eating, digesting, sleeping, and exercising. The whole force of the constitution goes to increasing the warmth of the body, and arming it to endure the prolonged strain put upon it. Only with difficulty do we address ourselves to any original or creative effort. The routine of the hour, the intellectual labours commonly and easily fulfilled, are as much as we find ourselves able to accomplish; yet, undoubtedly, the general rule has its momentary exceptions, and in some hours of these austere winter days and nights we awaken to an unusual intellectual light and happiness. Sitting before the fire in the depth of the January midnight, surrounded by uncertain shadow and penetrating warmth, when the windows glitter in the moonshine against an atmosphere of intense and dazzling frost, and everything is so silent that we almost hear the blood winding in our own veins, have we not often caught ourselves exerting unconsciously an extraordinary swiftness and brightness of intellectual movement? The forms of unseen things present themselves to our imaginations with a vividness and reality of detail rarely at other times attained. Out on a country road, walking in a quiet and silent downfall of snow, when distances are veiled and hidden, and my mind seems wrapped about and softly thrown in upon itself by a smooth and caressing influence, I become immersed in the same depth and intensity of reflection.

But in the main, winter is not the season of great mental activity. Perhaps you point me to the long, quiet winter evenings, and inquire whether these do not lend themselves obediently to the current of intellectual labour. Nay, you are mistaken. If you are like me you will spend most of the long quiet winter evenings with your feet disposed upon an opposite chair, a long-stemmed pipe between your teeth, and some entertaining book of travels placed comfortably against your knee. No, if you have proposed to yourself an intellectual task, calling for high inventive effort, attack it when the long September days grow golden and the first elm leaves fall, or wait in patience till you have heard the shore lark soar and twitter over the first bare hummocks of March.

ARCHIBALD LAMPMAN

Judging from some of the recent acts and utterances of the German Emperor we had been inclined to believe that one of the things that that excellent man most seriously lacked and most seriously needed was the sense of humour. For our comfort and reassurance a writer in *The New York Critic* informs us that Wilhelm II not only possesses the sense of humour, but is a conversational humorist of much power and geniality. He is moreover an enthusiastic admirer of Mark Twain, and is particularly fond of *The Innocents Abroad.*

ARCHIBALD LAMPMAN

In April next Mr W.D. Howells will assume the editorship of *The Cosmopolitan*, and the editor's study in *Harper's Magazine* will be conducted by Mr Charles Dudley Warner. Mr Howells's connection with *The Cosmopolitan* will doubtless lead to the development of more interesting features in that magazine, which seems to us to have been hitherto a rather unattractive sort of publication.

DUNCAN CAMPBELL SCOTT

What is probably the last poem of Victor Hugo which remained unknown to the world has just been published. It was announced at the time when *Les Contemplations* was issued; it was never finished and is published in that form. The title 'Dieu' fixes the profound and sublime subject which Hugo chooses with his usual daring. Mr Swinburne, who of all appreciators is the most appreciative, and who expresses himself as the years go by with more and more adjectival weight, introduces this poem to the English reader in the last number of *The Fortnightly*, or rather he judges it for them and commands their immediate submission. Mr Swinburne has a way of making his reader feel rather ashamed of himself, as if he was the bad boy who did not know his lesson. For instance, he says: 'It is hardly necessary to transcribe any of the parallel passages which no probable reader can be supposed not to know by heart.' Observe that word 'probable' and then imagine the feelings of some poor sciolist who had passed over the very passage without any considerable tremor of the heart, much less the active interest which would lead him to memorize it for the comfort of his weary hours. Then Mr Swinburne has a defiant way of making his comparisons which throws his reader into a state bordering on alarm. The lesser English gods are treated with the respect due them, but he bows the knee to none so adoringly as the great French supreme, who is above either the faults or trivialities of his brother deities. Such furious utterances come well from one who has dwelt so long in the very flames of inspiration; and in viewing as a whole the critical work of this great poet it cannot be gainsaid that he has touched the literature of England at least with an insight and interpretive power which have put the whole race in his debt.

WILFRED CAMPBELL

The class distinction on the continent of America has developed further than we have realized. The concentration of wealth into the control of a few, and the gradually growing poverty of the working classes, is becoming more apparent every day. Here in Canada as in the States the so-called middle class is dying out as the result of the absorption of capital. The liberty and safety of the State has so far mainly depended on the influence of this class. When it goes, then may come the long-prophesied struggle of the rich and poor. For selfish ends of their own men may deny this state of things, but it is heart-rending to go into some of our large cities and see the immense amount of wealth squandered on personal aggrandizement and selfish luxuries and then to note the corresponding amount of destitution, degradation, and misery both within the shadow of the same church spire or within the sound of the same Sabbath bell. Religionists may cry out about the hopelessness of mere humanity as a religion, but it would be better did they put a little more hope into the anguish of this world by putting more of the humanities into their religion.

6 February 1892

WILFRED CAMPBELL

Some notable volumes of short stories have appeared in 1891. Among which the work of James Lane Allen, Miss Wilkins, H.C. Bunner, Octave Thanet, and R.H. Davis are especially strong and subtle.

Mr Allen has a touch in some senses similar to that of Hawthorne, and in 'The White Cowl,' which first appeared in *The Century*, he gives a beautiful but sombre picture of American monastic life. Miss Wilkins, who is regarded now with favour in England, has a fine and subtle insight into New England everyday life, which she, perhaps, attenuates to a perceptibly painful extent in showing its poverty of animation and hopefulness.

Mr Bunner, who is a well-known poet and journalist of a delicate type, has given us examples of his realism and idealism in 'Zadoc Pine.' He sometimes writes with a freer hand than his compeers, but there is a simplicity and naturalness about some of his types that make them realistic and yet good reading. He has a knack of making short and well-balanced sentences, and there is an atmosphere about his work that hints of its being the prose work of a poet, who can charm in a serious as well as in a lighter vein.

Octave Thanet has been for some time a writer for *Scribner's*, and in her short stories shows a freshness of landscape, a masculine vigour, and fineness of touch that mark her out as prominent among the later writers of the South.

Mr Davis, who is a professional journalist, has garnered some of his experiences in that line. He has a strong and nervous grasp, and is akin to Kipling in his observation of society; but perhaps his work should be regarded rather as that of promise than of achievement.

WILFRED CAMPBELL

The Sister's Tragedy shows more of the dramatic element than any of Aldrich's former works – and contains some strong and occasionally remarkable work. *The Ship Master's Tale*, which first appeared in *Harper's*, is startling in its direct and simple mastery of style and conception.

The Ride to the Lady by Miss Cone contains some of the most subtle and delicate verse written by a woman in late years.

Miss Reese's verse shows a kinship with Rossetti's, but she has a genuine lyrical touch that shows much promise.

Mr Riley's work is the antipodes of that of Mr Aldrich, in that it is intensely American and of the time. He is assuredly a poet of the everyday life and of the common people. He has an intense sympathy with childhood, which he celebrates with a pathos and humour that is irresistible. He is probably the most sincere and natural of the younger generation of American singers.

ARCHIBALD LAMPMAN

M. Adolphe Guillot, a magistrate of Paris, has written two histories, one of the morgue, *The Temple of Suicide* as he calls it, the other of the *Prisons and Prisoners of Paris.* The morgue is a low building planted by the edge of the Seine, just behind that other temple, the great Cathedral of Notre Dame, where the sufferer seeks the peace not of death, but of God. There each day on the damp marble slabs, always tenanted, lie the voiceless remains of the saddest and most desolate of Paris, and its history, could it be written by one having the eye of omniscience, would indeed be a narrative of strange and sickening pathos and unimaginable horror.

Scarcely less gloomily interesting would be the history of the old prisons of Paris, the Chatelets and La Force, haunted by the hideous and gigantic spectre of the butcheries of September 1792; Sainte Pelagie, that saw the last tragic hours of Madame Roland; the Temple, where Louis 'Capet,' the prisoner, lay, and the little Dauphin died, the victim of half-revealed brutalities; the Conciergerie with its three towers, one of the picturesque sights of Paris; Fort l'Évêque, the Bicêtre, and the ever memorable Bastille, dead these hundred years with all its villainous memories. But what human soul would dare to penetrate, even if it could, the horrid secrets of these dreadful abodes.

DUNCAN CAMPBELL SCOTT

An Australian poet whose work was lately published in England made a strong stand for the pervasion of local colour in his verse, and has turned the seasons topsy-turvy to let us know how a poet must feel in the Antipodes. After all is said and done it amounts to the same thing; flowers are fair and sweet no matter whether they bloom in August or December, and ice is ice even if it comes in June, or, as Mr O'Hara says:

While June upon the meadow pools
  Was building icy bridges.

In Canada we have a decent, old-fashioned climate, which corresponds in all essential points to that which has bronzed the poets of old England, and our poets can sing of the season in their old round and cannot fail to be understood. Our skies are higher and brighter, the tints of our forests are more varied, our winter comes with greater snows and frosts. Once in a while the critics across the water may look perplexed and ask our poets what they mean by 'timothy,' or some other colloquial term, but in the main we must depend for local colour on whatever there is of real difference in our manner of looking at the old world with its changeful beauty.

13 February 1892

DUNCAN CAMPBELL SCOTT

The thing that attracted our attention and made us stop was the bright light in the window. It was close to the street, so close that the lamp must just have been lighted, else the curtain would have been pulled down. It is no sin to look in at a window; so long as windows are left unblinded and free to the eye the interior is common property. 'Tis much as when a man lifts the veil unconsciously and lets us see what he has behind, deep in his uncontrollable heart. Behind this window we first saw the lamp, standing upon the plain table; then a coloured print from a Christmas number of *The Star* pinned to the wall; then a large rocking chair, with a cretonne cover, picked out with red wool. But the plainest object in the room was a bedstead covered with very white clothes. Upon it lay an old woman; she had a white cap on her head, and a silvery grey shawl around her shoulders. She was leaning back with her eyes closed; a very sweet expression lingered about her mouth, an expression of great serenity and confidence. Almost immediately after we looked, a young girl came into the room; she was about thirteen years old; her dark hair went back straight off her brows, and was braided behind. She carried a china cup, which she set down on the table, then she fixed the old woman's cap and shawl. She opened her eyes, but did not smile; it was not necessary, she had that look upon her face which is better than a smile. The young girl raised the cup to her lips and she drank; then she laid back and closed her eyes as before with the same serene and confident expression. A moment after she was left alone. Instinctively we turned away and were for a long time silent. The new snow was falling softly, almost damply; the evening was mild, with a touch of spring in the air. At last I said, 'We have had a long walk.' 'Yes,' said my companion, 'and we have read a verse from the great bible of human life.'

ARCHIBALD LAMPMAN

There is no limit to the making of fanciful classifications in literature, yet after the manner of men I must needs put forward a little one of my own. Poetry of the imaginative and essentially lyrical sort may, as it seems to me, be divided into three classes: poetry of imaginative inspiration, poetry of impassioned reflection, and poetry of eloquence. The most eloquent of poets was Shakespeare, the most inspired was Shelley, and the most intensely reflective, Rossetti. Shelley's 'Alastor' and Coleridge's 'Ancient Mariner' are perfect examples of the poetry of imaginative inspiration; Rossetti's 'Blessed Damosel' and 'Bride's Prelude' of the poetry of impassioned reflection, and I can think of no finer example of the eloquent in verse than Tennyson's 'Revenge.' The poetry of eloquence lends itself most readily to vocal rendition; that of reflection is the most difficult to interpret to an average audience. Swinburne is also, I think, one of the poets of eloquence. How magnificently readable is 'The Lost Oracle.' Contrast with this the 'Bride's Prelude' of Rossetti, a poem to be held and brooded on, its intense and restrained passion, its subtle and vivid touches only to be thoroughly apprehended upon repeated reading, and not to be successfully interpreted save by a spirit and tongue exceptionally rich in resource and utterly in accord with the bent of the poet.

WILFRED CAMPBELL

It has ever been a pleasure to me since my early childhood to wander alone in the woods on a winter's day. Following a glistening, Polish sleigh road down into some snow-hooded swamp of brown green cedars, where the wind scarcely enters save with a lonesome sigh, as he silts the powdery snow athwart the tented tree tops on the caverned aisles within.

Down under here where the shadowy hare has left his long lope on the snow, over buried logs and around ermine-draped stumps I wander in a semi-dream of frosted and yet warm winter reverie. Now and again a few dried, shrivelled tassels of the cedar fall rustling at my feet. Far overhead among the tree tops there is a sound and motion like the waves on a shore, a subdued sound that scarcely enters here and disturbs the snow-muffled dream of these lonesome, sombre avenues of winter solitude.

Outside sometimes comes the far-away shout of a driver, or the echo of a chopping axe in the distant clearings, but down in these frosty silences, where the trees lean, still and shadowy, and the snows wind like misty grave clothes over autumn's mounds, the great spirit of winter stalks by my side, but I care not for his masked face and icy beard, for to my heart, with the slanting sun rays that blink under the brown-golden, tented branches, from the sloping afternoon, come the soft sighs of melting drops, the balm of winds, the flush and beauty of the far-off spring. God-like is the heart of man which triumphs over cold and rain and sheeted death, and sees beauty in the shrouded snows, the short, lonesome, shrivelled days and long-drawn, iced nights, and the spirit that dwells therein, while under the frost and ruin, under the beard of the wrinkled earth, there comes the pulse and murmur, the music and roseate dream of the eternal, waking world.

ARCHIBALD LAMPMAN

Almost incredible is the influence of mere place in attracting the attention and winning the service of men. Two or three years ago a Berlin bookseller published a work called *Prinz Bismarck's Gesammette Schriften*, a collection of the speeches, essays, etc., of the great chancellor. Orders from booksellers flowed in abundantly. Then came the fall of the Titan. The orders suddenly ceased, and in the succeeding twenty-one months less than a hundred copies were sold. The publishers are now endeavouring in vain to get rid of the plates and the 3000 volumes of the work still on their hands.

DUNCAN CAMPBELL SCOTT

To write a play in blank verse seems to be a lost art. Something alien to the large and generous dealing required for such a task seems to have eaten into our modern life and left it without the great requisites. The task is rarely performed with even a passable success, and the poet who conquers must have, to our humanity, an almost superhuman equipment. Not that the art of playwriting has fallen into the deeps out of sight; far otherwise. Our modern stage is crowded with plays of the last half century which fulfil all the conditions imposed on the playwright and which mirror the complex state of our society with sufficient faithfulness. In truth in the department of the playwright there seems to be actually a renaissance, and, to judge by the discussions of the last two years, something may come of it. The performances of Ibsen's *Hedda Gabler* in London last winter would, I fancy, give hope to any man who had the real interest of the stage at heart. Not that this play need be held up as a model, but when its dissimilarity to the mass of the work which occupies the attention of the public is considered we see what a distance we have come. But, although the playwright may have reason to rejoice at the real advance, the lover of the grand drama must still mourn. Probably one of the most tragic of all failures is the last. The story of Edgar and Athelwold is a likely subject for a drama, but Amelie Rives has succeeded only in showing that here an excellence might have been done. The language of this piece is almost burlesque, and in its freedom and interjectional crudity it would serve to point a comparison. As literature it falls below the level. Elfreda finds Athelwold asleep by the wayside and answers the remonstrances of her woman when she approaches him with 'Would'st thou sour me with this thundering?' This arouses a pretty image in the reader's mind, and the young lady does not disappoint him. By and by she wakes the stranger by kissing him, and then she threatens to bite him if he kisses her. Such 'goings on' may not be entirely unknown to the readers of this authoress, who seems to be never so much at home as in the free description of overwrought passion. We commend the dialogue and general treatment of this subject to anyone who wants to know what to avoid in a similar composition.

ARCHIBALD LAMPMAN

The next best thing to a morning's walk in the woods or along some country lane is a half hour spent in the company of such an excellent book as *A Rambler's Lease*, by Mr Bradford Torrey. Mr Torrey is a poet-naturalist, a botanist, and ornithologist, with a poet's love of nature and a high literary gift, one of the class of writers to which Thoreau and John Burroughs belong. About twelve miles back of Boston are the quiet valleys and wooded hills of Wellesley, a country full of variety and beauty. This is Mr Torrey's haunt. There, intent upon the everyday life of the woods and fields, he watches with a happy and affectionate interest its moods and changes, its multiform activities and intelligences, its little dramas and episodes, and records them in a style full of amusement and sympathy. Like a gentle poet and philosopher as he is, Mr Torrey works into his sketches many wise thoughts, and applies the interesting facts of plant and bird life in many curious ways. In *A Rambler's Lease* there are also frequent touches of a quiet and charming humour, that sort of humour that does not send a man off into an open roar of laughter, but causes him to smile inwardly, kindling his reflections with a softer and more generous fire. Our writer is especially fond of the study of ornithology. His insight into the habits, affections, and eccentricities of birds, and his naïve felicity of phrase in interpreting them make him a bringer of perpetual charmed surprise to anyone who is himself a lover of the wild wood and its gentle inhabitants. He is not one of those bird hunters, ornithologists of the intellect only, men interested in collections and the accumulation of passionless facts, mere scientists who prowl about the country with guns, committing murder on every hand without scruple and without remorse. Mr Torrey is an ornithologist of the heart, who spends many of his hours in the fields and the woods, but never carries a gun, never kills a bird, and knows a great deal more about the inner life and domestic characters of birds than those who do.

ARCHIBALD LAMPMAN

Most human beings have a kindly and amiable weakness for some sort of pet animal. Anybody who has not is surely lacking in humanity. The love of dogs is inherent in a certain robust and active type of man. Most Englishmen are fond of dogs. The cat is hardly so popular, but I have found that all people who have a fine and subtle sense of humour love cats. In fact, if you wish to ascertain whether a man has a really nice sense of humour you can best do so by watching him for a few moments in the society of your household cat. All the movements and attitudes of a sleek and well-matured cat are a study replete with perpetual amusement. At this moment there comes to me from the back yard a medley of sound which indicates that our large white tom-cat Thomas has detected a neighbour's tabby, an animal exceedingly bold and fierce, in the act of penetrating into premises which he regards as his own. Thomas is crouched upon the edge of the shed roof, switching violently a tail at least four inches in diameter, and giving fierce vent to the torrent of his indignant feelings. His is a rich, deep, contralto voice, of great compass, and of an eloquent range of expression. When I first brought Tom to my present place of residence he was subjected to several weeks of very hard fighting. He had not yet learned the secrets of battle, and the enemy had him ever at a disadvantage. Notwithstanding the guardedness of his coming in and going out, no sooner had he passed the threshold than our neighbour's bravo was upon him. A sudden rush, a moment's silence, and then an agonized squall many lots away announced the attack, the desperate fight, and the prompt and ferocious capture. The evidences of our poor pet's sufferings saluted our ears at all hours. But all this was experience for Thomas. Like the allied armies who were so often beaten by Napoleon, he acquired the art of war. The battle shout has now no longer any terrors for him, and his wounds are all in front. Indeed, I regret to say that his ears are beginning to assume the appearance of the tattered battle flags so often noticeable in elderly and experienced tom-cats. I have always had a deep affection for Thomas as for all good cats. He lands upon my shoulders with a spring and coils himself purringly around my neck at meal times, and when I let him in hungry at night he leads me winningly and beckoningly to that kitchen cupboard where he knows that cold potatoes are stored, for Thomas is singularly partial to cold potatoes. No animals display a greater diversity of manner and character than cats. I never knew a cat that was not distinguished from all others of its species by many peculiar tricks of expression and idiosyncrasies of temper.

20 February 1892

WILFRED CAMPBELL

The patriotic idea has come down to us largely as a result of heredity, steadily changing its significance as the national idea progressed with society's development. We are apt to call a man patriotic who claims to love his country and so engraven is superstition on this point that the disclaimer of this virtue is regarded with horror as a sort of political atheist. A most remarkable picture of the practical punishment of this sin in a personality is depicted in Edward Everett Hale's 'Man with a Country,' which all students of, or believers in, patriotism should read.

But in the face of all this, is it not possible that the patriotic idea has so changed with modern progress and the widening of the national idea that it has entirely lost its old significance? The national idea had its foundation in the first crude conception of the family tie, which developed in the matriarchal system before the nation as an institution was ever dreamed of; when the mother-love, the first and last divine essence of all that is greatest and best in humanity, expanded itself, and mirrored itself in the child-love, and filial gratitude which deepened and widened, as in the patriarchal age the family expanded into the tribe and then into the nation, and in the course of time the leading ancestor became the national god. So patriotism and religion sprang like twins from the same source and developed side by side.

It is inspiring to look back on the patriotism illustrated in the great nations of the past, and to note the gradual effect on society. But society and the national idea have been working outward instead of inward, until the cosmopolitan idea has usurped the national to a large extent, so that what was once regarded as a leading virtue and mark of humanity would now be considered as a provincialism and a narrowness of vision. The old nations each had their own gods and religions, which shaped their national ideals. But the conquests of the ages broke down its old barriers, the religions assimilated and, like drops dissolving into one pool, helped to swell the great world religions that grew out of them, and with the change came the larger growth and vision of ambition and sympathy.

The Roman patriotism was great, so was the Carthaginian, as was that of Greece. It was sincere and human in its immolation at the national altar, but it represented a stage when the national ideal and sympathy were limited by its borders. England, more than any other nation of modern times, has developed the national idea, but she has already far outgrown this stage. It was strongest in the days of the wooden walls of Raleigh and when Nelson was a hero, but commerce, emigration, and science have helped to widen and dissolve the national horizon, so that now we look back with a smile as well as a heart-throb at the egotism and nobleness evinced in the pictures of those times. The old idea of loyalty to the sovereign as a person has changed to loyalty to the state as an idea and to us who are children of colonists the idea comes, if at all, in a religious reverence for the soil on which we were born and reared. But in these days of rapid emigration from country to country, where a community is composed of peoples of diverse origin, who have been compelled by the duties of citizenship to forget old heredities of custom, language, and religion, it is impossible to expect a real and natural patriotism to blossom into being. Therefore the idea now becomes largely one of self-interest, with the supposed idea at the centre of the best interests of the community.

Where countries border, having the same language, customs, and almost similar laws, where the commercial interchange is eager to overflow on both sides, where intermarriage and emigration have modified each to the other to a large extent, it is almost impossible to build up a national sentiment in each bearing the slightest resemblance to the so-called patriotism of the past. The antagonism of Rome to Carthage, of England to France and Spain in the days of Elizabeth, would be an impossibility today, say between countries situated as Canada and the United States. The more men travel and read and think the more cosmopolitan they will become. The old national patriotism was a natural outgrowth of the national idea, discriminating, with a prejudice in favour of what was within its borders. The great results of this were an army, a religion, a language, and a literature. These are all necessary to the old-time patriotism. The modern spirit is against all of these. The best element in all nations calls for universal peace. The language is common in many cases, and is growing more so every day. The great religion of humanity as a brotherhood and the ever-widening influence of science are making the human hope as well as the human knowledge universal. The literature of many countries is rapidly becoming the literature of the world. Shakespeare and Goethe have spoken to all Europe as well as America. Emerson and Carlyle, Hawthorne and Poe are classics for the whole English language, and even out of it. Tolstoy is as interesting to the American and English thinker as to the Russian. No country can now claim a great man for more than his birth and residence. This is no sign of the degeneracy of the moral element in humanity, but, on the other hand, is a sign of the greatness of its growth. It won't be long until the national patriotism will be a thing of the past. Like the national religion, and the national egotism, they were great in their day, but they fulfilled in their decay the greatest religion (law) in that they died that the world might live. Onward and outward and upward is the motto of the day, until the brotherhood is come. And if patriotism has lived its life it is only that humanity – mankind – may take the place of the national spirit.

20 February 1892

DUNCAN CAMPBELL SCOTT

While exploring the profundities of *The Prelude* the other day I came upon this passage, which is without a parallel in Wordsworth so far as I remember, for in it there is a description with an evident humorous intent. It succeeds, too, as Wordsworth nearly always does, and this is surprising when we consider how far from his usual ground he was. These words will be found in the seventh book of *The Prelude*, and they are intended to describe a young and fashionable curate:

> There have I seen a comely bachelor,
> Fresh from a toilette of two hours, ascend
> His rostrum, with seraphic glance look up,
> And, in a tone elaborately low
> Beginning, lead his voice through many a maze
> A minuet course; and, winding up his mouth,
> From time to time, into an orifice
> Most delicate, a lurking eyelet, small,
> And only not invisible, again
> Open it out, diffusing thence a smile
> Of rapt irradiation, exquisite.
> Meanwhile the Evangelists, Isaiah, Job,
> Moses, and he who penned, the other day,
> The death of Abel, Shakespeare, and the Bard,
> Whose genius spangled o'er a gloomy theme
> With fancies thick as his inspiring stars,
> And Ossian (doubt not – 'tis the naked truth)
> Summoned from streamy Morven – each and all
> Would, in their turns, lend ornaments and flowers
> To entwine the crook of eloquence that helped
> This pretty Shepherd, pride of all the plains,
> To rule and guide his captivated flock.

The reference to 'he who penned . . . the Death of Abel' is to Solomon Gesner, who was born in Zurich in 1730. His poem was translated into English in 1780.

DUNCAN CAMPBELL SCOTT

Some of our ladies have a Sunday afternoon mission in a neglected quarter of the city, in connection with St Basil's, a fashionable

Episcopal church. Last Sabbath a little girl, evidently dressed in all the finery of the family, took her place for the first time. Her teacher asked her whether she had ever been at Sunday school before. She said, 'Oh, yes, but not here.' Further questioning led to the information that she had only been in town four months. 'And you have not been once to church in this time?' 'No.' 'Why was that?' 'Well, we used to live near St Basil's, but we didn't know it was Protestant. We thought it was Methodist.' This answer may well be left without comment; but there is an unconscious humour in it, and, besides, is there not something more than humour?

ARCHIBALD LAMPMAN

Of all trees the oak is the most British in its character – broad, sturdy, rugged, earth-loving, and permanent. The elm is classic in its generous sweep, Italian in its grace and richness of drapery. The most eery, the most inspiring, the most Celtic of trees is the forest pine, the white pine, as we find it on the northern waste, perhaps the tenant of some lofty ledge, reaching far into heaven, slender, leaning, with a few cloud-like flakes of foliage that seem to have drifted off from its stem and to lie afloat upon the inaccessible air. We hear it murmuring far above us in the quiet wind of morning, and its voice is like the distant sound of many long waves upon a sandy shore. At sunset it stands against the bright and silent west, unchanging, delicate, dark, and with a stillness, as we dream, like the stillness of eternity. The pine is the priest of the forest, leading heavenward the thoughts of men and the flights of birds. Before my door, on the very confines of a growing city, in a little plot yet left of the primeval wood, stands one of the lordly masters, a survivor, I know not by what chance, of axe and fire. At morning, whether the sky be deep with summer or springtime or crystal clear with autumn, or the strands of its foliage be heaped with the January snow, it leads my eye aloft. Far up beyond its silent top my thoughts take jocund flight, bathing themselves like the birds in the radiant ether. In my walks I see it at sunset standing against the rose or gold or the translucent grey, and my thoughts pass off between its branches into regions of exquisite purity and repose.

ARCHIBALD LAMPMAN

The appearance of *The Dominion Illustrated Monthly*, issued for the first time this month, again tantalizes the patriotic eye with the phantasm of a Canadian magazine. There are several remarks which we had felt tempted to make about this publication but which we suppress out of a perhaps misguided tenderness for things Canadian. But there are one or two things that need to be said. In the first place if all the illustrations had been left out the number would have been a good deal improved, and, secondly, we think that surely the editor might have found some things better for his first issue than two or three of the articles and poems contained in it, 'Red and Blue Pencils,' for instance. It is a pity, too, that he could not have avoided the general air of verdancy and provincialism that permeates the whole thing.

Any publisher who undertakes to issue a Canadian magazine at this date must remember that there is a Canadian public, as yet not very large, but rapidly growing, which will inevitably apply to it the very highest and broadest standard of taste and will not be satisfied with anything jejune or provincial. The attempt to publish an illustrated magazine seems to us futile on the face of it. Any illustrated magazine, to succeed, must be placed at once on an even footing with *Harper's* or *Scribner's*. People will not buy a third- or fourth-rate article because it is Canadian; and there would be no patriotism in their doing so, as some of our fellow countrymen seem to think. On the contrary it seems to us that a man will best show his patriotism by doing what he can to suppress such things as tend to misrepresent and disgrace his native land.

We should, however, exceedingly like to see some levelheaded person establish a plain, sensible, unillustrated magazine or review which should honestly represent the fullest intellectual attainment of our country. Surely it is almost certain that such a publication would succeed and both accompany and carry along with it the growing literary force that we see around us.

DUNCAN CAMPBELL SCOTT

Already great interest is being manifested in the centenary of the birth of Shelley. The Shelley society has decided to commemorate the event by a performance of *The Cenci*, and to that end are seeking subscriptions for a fund of £100. The performance will be private. The zeal of the society has in this taken a curious outlet and the result will be observed with interest. The tragedy will, it is thought, be given in May of the present year, but the final arrangements have not been mooted.

27 February 1892

DUNCAN CAMPBELL SCOTT

The letters of Von Moltke to his mother and his brothers, which were published a short time ago by Osgood, McIlvaine & Co., have proved of thorough interest and have in many ways thrown a new and delightful charm about this character so often imagined as one of mere severity and discipline. There was something even romantic about his tastes and his domestic affections. He was tenderly fond of his wife, who, by the way, was an English girl. He had even a sense of humour, and in many places it crops out in these familiar letters. In one of his letters to his sisters he writes: 'My health is wonderful. I often lie unconscious for eight or ten hours – at night; I have no appetite after meals; towards evening such convulsive yawning and stretching, and all day utter sleeplessness, and restlessness in all my body. I only hope you do not suffer so.' This is certainly facetious. In one of the letters from Constantinople he puts into one pithy and apt sentence the character of Turkey and the Turks: 'This is the land of lazy ease, a whole nation in slippers.' Perhaps there is nothing so delightful as to discover the more human qualities of a great man, to find beneath the character which rumour has built up around him the geniality and interest in small things which are the sauce of life; and these are the pleasures in store for the reader of the letters of Count Von Moltke to his family.

27 February 1892

DUNCAN CAMPBELL SCOTT

My dear Francesca: My mind has the full impression of a new book; I have just laid it down, and, in a reader's existence, this is the moment of the fullest, the most perfect delight. The book is finished and he lays it aside. All the excitement, of whatever kind, is past; he has now no such active interest in the characters or arguments or opinions as he had a few moments before. Now he has the scope of the whole work before him, borne in upon him vividly and comprehensively and he is in full possession of the new province he has conquered. Before an hour has passed the change will have commenced, until, like a landscape veiled gradually by the night, he has only the great points of emotion or argument left, like mountains against the sky. I know you, too, would have been delighted with this book, and I choose to prepare you for the pleasure you will have when Aspasia consents to release it and when I send it to you. I have heard you express a curiosity to read some of the criticism of that writer whose name is somehow linked with that of Arnold and Amiel; and now Mr George Saintsbury has given us the essays on English literature of Edmond Scherer, that just and discerning critic, whose work we have before viewed with a potential admiration. Much of this book is taken up with your favourite novelist, George Eliot, and your favourite poets, Matthew Arnold and Wordsworth; and I call the powers of that great public school system, in whose mill you are ground daily, to witness to the taste and moral force of one of the human wheels in its insatiable machine, as denoted by these preferences. To George Eliot M. Scherer assigns a very high place and deservedly so; and although Mr George Saintsbury has written in his pleasant preface that we must not accept the first paper as the final and nicely balanced criticism of the author of *Adam Bede*, I fancy you will dwell with most eagerness upon this very section of the book. It is in the essay on *Daniel Deronda* that M. Scherer pronounces this just and forcible sentence; one which I cannot refrain from copying for you: 'For art lives not by ideas, but by sentiments. I had almost said by sensations; it is instinctive, it is naif, and it is by direct and unconsidered expression that it communicates with reality. Among all the contradictions of which life is made up, there is none more constant than this – that there is no great art without philosophy, and yet there is no more dangerous enemy of art than reflection.'

But to me the most valuable and at the same time the most interesting essay is the one on 'Wordsworth and Modern Poetry.' It contains amongst other appreciative words a tribute to the distinct and individual position held by Matthew Arnold in the literature of his country. He says of him as a poet: 'In every style he has an absolutely personal accent and note of distinction'; as a critic: 'The liveliest, the most delicate, the most elegant of critics, the critic who has given out most ideas, has conferred upon them the most piquant expression, and has most thoroughly shocked the sluggishness of British thought by wholesome audacities.' How apt, how forcible are these words! I have quoted them to prepare you for others equal in power and penetration which succeed one another as this great essay unfolds itself. I must take leave of you; let us again dedicate ourselves to great things; let us again resolve to live with the sweet and beautiful things of earth; let us pass more often into the province of purer thought, of profounder contemplation.

WILFRED CAMPBELL

A writer in *Shakespeariana* refers to the present decadence of Browning societies as an instance of that poet's lack of true greatness. It might be answered that fads are not the true tests of genius. A man's injudicious disciples may be in a sense his worst enemies. As in religion God is more truly felt than He can be described, and theologians are not necessarily the best interpreters of religion, so Browning societies and Shakespearian and Ibsen crazes are not the measures of the several geniuses they claim to represent. That there is much that is worthless and unmeaning in Browning no true lover of literature will deny. On the other hand he possesses a unique greatness of his own that marks him out from all other writers. Such a short drama as *In a Balcony* is an evidence of dramatic greatness of a kind not even found in Shakespeare, and met with nowhere else in any language. Even the immortal William has perhaps been over-estimated as to perfection. Weakness is found in the greatest work. This is an age of sifting the wheat from the chaff, and when this is done no true genius will suffer, though many injudicious admirers may be shocked to find that their idol was not all gold but had its necessary admixture of clay and sand.

ARCHIBALD LAMPMAN

The terrible Russian famine, besides calling forth the helpful enthusiasm of many generous Americans, has brought again before the world's view in the sweetest and noblest light the devoted figure of Count Tolstoy. To anyone who has studied the writings of this wonderful man, the greatest after Shakespeare in his vast and subtle knowledge of the human heart, it seems perfectly natural to hear that he has thrown himself with all the energy of his intensely compassionate nature into the work of healing and relief. An old man, between sixty and seventy years of age, he has gone forth dressed in the peasant's garb, and, as we are told by a newspaper correspondent, 'from morning till night he is on his legs, distributing, administering, organising, as if endowed with youthful vigor and an iron constitution. Hail, rain, snow, intense cold and abominable roads are nothing to him. . . . He is now in the Danskovsky District, moving about from house to house, from village to village, from canton to canton, gathering information about the needs of each family and individual, feeding the hungry, tending the sick, comforting those who have lost their breadwinners, and utterly forgetful of himself.'

There are some people who have spoken harshly of Count Tolstoy, particularly in reference to some of his recent writings, but I fear it is because they do not understand the man, or, more probably, because they do not understand Russia. The articles of Mr E.B. Lanin in the English reviews have thrown an awful light upon that subject.

ARCHIBALD LAMPMAN

It seems impossible for the majority of mankind to realize that every species of affectation is a derogation from dignity. Nothing is more provocative of the sarcastic sense than the spectacle of a character or quality habitually assumed and seriously paraded, and the people who have talent enough to make an affectation pass for reality are so few that one does not meet with more than half a dozen of them in a lifetime. In most cases the fraud is perfectly transparent, and there are always plenty of people about us who are quite clever enough to penetrate it. The assumption of an affectation, therefore, indicates a deficiency in the knowledge of human nature. It indicates also a lack of humanity and real goodness of heart, for the good man desires to bring himself into the nearest and readiest touch with the universal human soul, and this he can only do by the most complete development and revelation of his own individuality. He must be himself most thoroughly before he can enter with real sympathy into the hearts of others.

One of the most offensive affectations is that of roughness and brutality, assumed by some men who wish to acquire a reputation for openness and candour. Another affectation, odd and sometimes unamiable, is that of unkemptness and squalor in personal appearance as a means of creating the impression of mental abstraction and intense devotion to thought. 'I see your price, oh Antisthenes,' said Socrates to the famous Cynic, 'peering through the holes in your cloak.' All these things are the mark of a more or less ludicrous vanity. The man of fine feeling does not desire that the world shall be forever pointing the finger at him; and, so far from cultivating conspicuous peculiarities of outer habit, he endeavours to the utmost of his power to efface those which are naturally his.

27 February 1892

DUNCAN CAMPBELL SCOTT

In his incomparable *Journal* Sir Walter Scott relates two very characteristic anecdotes of Byron. As I do not remember to have read them elsewhere and as they give such a perfect idea of the whimsicality and impulsiveness of the man I retell them here. One evening when Byron and Tom Moore were standing at the window of the former's palazzo in Venice viewing the sunset, Moore was led ('naturally' Sir Walter says) to make some observations on its beauty. Bryon replied, in his usual tone, 'On! come, d---n me, Tom, don't be poetical.'

Upon another occasion and in the same place, as two Englishmen passed beneath the balcony in a gondola and cast a careless glance at Byron and Moore, Byron, crossing his arms and half stooping over the balcony, said, 'Ah! d---n ye, if ye had known what two fellows you were staring at, you would have taken a longer look at us.'

ARCHIBALD LAMPMAN

How utterly destitute of all light and charm are the intellectual conditions of our people and the institutions of our public life! How barren! How barbarous! It is true that this is a new and struggling country, but one would think that the simplest impulse of patriotism, if it existed at all in our governing bodies, would suffice to provoke some attempt at remedy.

Today I spent a little while in what is called the National Art Gallery at Ottawa. Here, scattered about the walls of a poor and average-looking room, are two or three paintings by distinguished old-country artists, half a dozen fair specimens of our native product, and a considerable number of nondescript articles hardly to be considered or named. Of what use is such a collection in its present condition? What pleasure can it afford to anyone? What educational stimulus?

If our public men had any interest in the beauty, the honour, the real well-being of this country they could as well as not provide that a hundred thousand dollars or double that amount be annually set apart by the government for the purpose of buying good pictures. A few fine foreign paintings might be added to the collection every year, and a fair sum might be expended in the purchase of Canadian work of the highest merit. In this way our native art would receive both culture and reward. The best models would be provided for its study and the benefit conferred upon it of encouragement and support would be incalculable in its effect. One would think that no sacrifice would be deemed too great, which might tend to relieve in any respect the arid poverty of our social and intellectual life.

WILFRED CAMPBELL

One of the most interesting of studies for those who have the leisure is that of mythology. Many persons associate this branch of study with old Greek gods and goddesses. But by far the most interesting branch is that pertaining to the north European nations. The name mythology is very deceiving, as it suggests something the opposite of reality, and therefore of little interest to the practical world of today. Of course it is a favourite study with poets, but others also can gain much benefit from what it reveals, for it reveals much. The fact is, mythology is more nearly connected with our present life than we have realized, and studied in connection with ancient customs and beliefs will explain away in a simple manner many strange superstitions and customs that extend even to the present. In no age has the world needed more common sense and real simple fact than it needs today. The mind to do battle in this age needs to be well balanced and practical, and the only way to attain this is by good scientific training in facts founded on solid reason. But we want something more to really understand and to be able to judge the present; we want to know the past as it really was. A man who still holds on to a superstitious or false notion of things pertaining to the past is not really competent to build up the present so as to aid the future.

The Irish peasant who will tell you that there are no fairies in this country but that there are in Ireland is no more befogged than the man who accepts as a natural phenomena now what he regarded to be a miracle having taken place 2000 or 3000 years ago. The Irishman is freed from his superstition as far as this country is concerned but is still bound to it by the influence of his late environment. So the man who claims as a miracle of old time what he recognizes now as a natural occurrence is the creation of a false conception of the past. With the Irishman so soon as he comes to look at the old as he sees the present, so soon will he be freed from his false conception. For this reason mythology is of great value to the casual student. It is really the history of the infant world, when the mind of mankind was the mind of the child or savage. It may not be generally known that much of the so-called history of the past is pure mythology. Much of the earlier part of the Old Testament, such as the stories of the Garden of Eden, the flood, the serpent, the story of Jonah, have all been proved to belong to the class of literature called mythic. The story of the cross itself is one of the most remarkable myths in the history of humanity connected with the old phallic worship of some of our most remote ancestors. What more remarkable instance of myth which was long mistaken for actual history than the now well-proved myth of William Tell, who never existed at all in real history. Probably the greatest stumbling-block to real knowledge of the past is the false religious prejudice which is hampering modern society to a large extent in countries like Canada; but even this is rapidly passing away in the more cultured localities. It is a poor and tottering religion that has to be bolstered up by ignorance. Mythology is a beautiful and instructive study, and to beginners I would recommend no better book than *Myths and Myth-Makers* by John Fiske, the celebrated Harvard professor, who is one of the strongest and ablest thinkers of the day. This book is to be found in every first-class city or town public library. I will have more to say on this subject later on.

5 March 1892

ARCHIBALD LAMPMAN

A very singular book is Mr Barry Pain's *In a Canadian Canoe.* Mr Pain is a brand-new English humorist, or rather wit, for he is certainly not a humorist in the true sense of the term. The full title of the book is *In a Canadian Canoe: The Nine Muses Minus One, and Other Stories.* It is one of the White Friars library of wit and humour, edited by Mr W.H. Davenport Adams. The first article, 'In a Canadian Canoe,' is a sort of dreamy irrelevant series of allusions to the author's experiences on the Thames in a Canadian canoe, mixed up with a lot of other ludicrously out of the way and equally irrelevant matter. 'The Nine Muses Minus One' is more forced, and its fantastic alternations of pathos and burlesque do not attract the imagination. 'The Celestial Grocery' is an enormously clever bit of work, and even more whimsical and fantastic than the rest. 'Bill' and 'The Girl and the Beetle' are the best things in the book, and there are phrases and incongruities of idea scattered about these sketches which throw one every now and then into an agony of laughter. But Mr Pain has an extraordinary and disheartening fancy for interweaving his mirth with psychological subtleties, and driving all the wit and frolic out of a sketch by ending it up with some dreadful and unexpected stroke of pathos. In Mr Pain one discerns traces of Stevenson, traces of Stockton, traces of Mark Twain, and this mixture is brewed up with a liberal allowance of an odd and eccentric faculty of his own. His book is ingenious, brilliant, witty, and the reader is occasionally prostrated with paroxysms of laughter, but nevertheless one wearies of it; it lacks the warm human sense, the true touch of humour; it leaves no flavour of lingering pleasure and sweetness upon the intellectual palate. So far has pessimism darkened the spirit of our time that even the humorist cannot bear to leave us in the enjoyment of his drollery, but must poison the last taste of it with some morbid sting.

DUNCAN CAMPBELL SCOTT

It was a curious and uncomfortable experience of the Duc de Lévis when he presented himself at Abbotsford without his letters of introduction. He, the representative of the oldest family in France, lay under the suspicion of being an impostor, and I fancy that the real tact and kindness under such trying circumstances of that great-hearted Walter Scott had more to do with the extravagant dedication to him of the duke's book than any mere admiration for his qualities as a writer. This is only a fancy of mine, however. There is something about the idea of a duke astray in the world without his credentials that is grotesque to say the least for it. The human mind revolts from the position; would there not be some mark of distinction, some authoritative grace of carriage, some delicate and unmistakable aroma which would mark him no matter where he had left his 'papers'? In vain the sentiments demand this in the name of society. The sentiments may go on demanding. The duke exists by reason of his documents. Armed with these he limps into the salon on his one sound leg, his weak soul wavering in his distorted body, dangling his blasé sentiments before a delighted and captivated crowd. Without these he is the bagman in masquerade, a fellow of the baser sort who would trick society with his audacities. But let us do the duke justice. He may have lost the vouchers for his aristocracy, but he may be a man and a gentleman; he may have charmed us with his wit, with the breath of his sympathies, with the humanity of his candour; we may have exclaimed time and again as we remembered his fine manner and exquisite thoughtfulness, 'What a splendid fellow!' And then one dull day we find out he was a duke. Our feminine relations would say, 'I told you so,' but would not the wisest of us say, 'What matter, it was the man we met and not the duke'?

DUNCAN CAMPBELL SCOTT

I have every reason to remember the pleasant hours I passed last summer reading *The Chevalier of Pensieri Vani* by H.B. Fuller. The days were dull and almost cold; the sea kept plunging under a mist; but this disastrous weather was made bearable by this charming and spirited book. Whoever wants a book to hand to his friend with the words, 'this is good, fanciful and humorous and finely done too,' should ask his bookseller to send for a copy. There is something of the whimsicality of Sterne in the work, and the writer has that quality called the 'light touch.' In the story of 'How the Chevalier Gained His Title' there is a fine description of the Chevalier's organ-playing, which is the best thing of the kind I have seen. The Chevalier was a great organ player and a ready *improvisatore*. I am writing from memory, I have not the book before me, and the titles of most of the sketches elude me in the way peculiar to titles and other things, but the general impression of a really delightful book is strong in my mind, and, even if I cannot sketch all Mr Fuller's characters and call them by name, this is a work I may fairly leave to the readers I would like to gain for him.

ARCHIBALD LAMPMAN

A good deal of interest has been taken in Mr Arnold Haultain's suggestion in *The Week* that some Canadian publisher should issue a memorial volume of contributions by Canadian authors in honour of the Shelley anniversary. It is to be doubted whether there is a sufficient number of Canadian writers who would be naturally impelled to produce enough writing of a high standard of excellence to form the volume proposed. Of course we should expect to find in the essays and poems composing such a memorial volume the expression of a sort of religious enthusiasm for the object, and most of the writing would have to be done by the professed Shelley devotees.

There will always be a class of minds – and I confess myself to be one of them – who do not find themselves drawn to Shelley in the intensest degree. As I read over and meditate on those wonderful poems I find myself often a little repelled by the absence of something, which for lack of a nearer term I would call 'the human.' Shelley appears to us not as a normal being of this world, but as a spirit, strange, radiant, and inspired, whose joy had in it the glow of an unearthly light, and its gloom a shadow fantastic and without the bound of mortal conception. The world and its life floated before him not as the substance of reality, but a glorious and awful vision, full of seductive vistas, peaks strangely lighted, and gulfs of profound and terrible darkness. We miss in him that earthly human heartiness and neighbourly warmth of touch which render the great passages of Shakespeare so imperishably beloved to all tender hearts of men, the quality that glows in Keats's and Wordsworth's best, and lends the sweetest charm to the greater poets of our own age.

Nevertheless, even those who are not specially worshippers of Shelley would, no doubt, have something interesting to say in regard to him, and we have several writers who are avowedly of this poet's cult. Professor Roberts would certainly have something strong to say of the poet whom he is said to look to as a master. Mr Bliss Carman, who should have been mentioned in Mr Haultain's brief list of Canadian writers, has already written a beautiful and original poem, which might form a chief ornament of any memorial volume. The late Mr Cameron of Kingston also wrote an admirable poem on Shelley.

DUNCAN CAMPBELL SCOTT

The February *Fortnightly* opens with a poem by James Thomson, author of 'The City of Dreadful Night.' It is intensely gloomy. The author seems to speak to us from his grave. The manner of the verse is the same as in the poem the title of which I have quoted above, the lines reminding us here and there of Rossetti. To Canadians the most interesting paper in the number is that of Francis Adams on 'Some Australian Men of Mark.' Mr Adams is an uncompromising writer. He has dealt with the social conditions of his country with no desire to make them out better than they are, and now the public men receive similar attentions. He commences by saying that the athletes of Australia are the only men known by name to the 'general run' of Englishmen. I suppose this may also be said of Canada. But there is, or appears to be, a bitterness in Mr Adams's tone which Canadians, and perhaps Australians, will not feel when confronted by this fact. If it is a desirable thing to have forced our existence upon the attention of the mother country, it is no contemptible thing to have done it with our men of muscle. But we have to some slight extent done it by our men of brains and that we are continuing to do it by our men of action and by their trade and transportation schemes is a fact incontestable. That we will continue to do so, as the years go by, in an increased measure, is also indisputable, but this is not the end and purpose of our national life; the ultimate object of this is to build a nation, strong, great, and enduring. If, when this is accomplished, we or our posterity discover that Canada, her public men and her institutions are known and admired in London, Bombay, Yokohama, Melbourne, and New York, we will not be surprised, and we will be careless of a fame we never desired for its own sake.

LETTER FROM W.W. CAMPBELL

To the Editor of *The Globe*:

Sir: As I notice, by a short but decided editorial in your Monday's issue, that a statement of mine in the article on Mythology had offended the religious feelings of some of your readers, I feel it my duty to myself to explain that in the sentence speaking of the story of the cross as mythical, I had not the slightest allusion to the history of early Christianity or the death of Christ. What I meant was the story or history of the cross as a symbol of religious worship, as found in ancient nature religions, such as the Mayan, Babylonian, Egyptian, Aztec, and other ancient religious systems in connection with their mythic origins as deduced by Max Muller and other distinguished authorities. I can readily understand, on re-reading the statement, how readers unacquainted with mythological study might, 'owing to the common use of a similar term,' take my reference to mean the mythological origin of the history of Christianity. But I repeat again such was not my meaning at all. I would say further, that I had not the slightest idea of an attack on Christianity, my idea being merely a short introduction of the study of mythology to any readers who cared to take up the subject. The article in question was written hurriedly, and in a time of much work and care, and was necessarily compressed to fit the department it was to fill. I am heartily sorry that my remarks unintentionally placed you in a false light before your readers. I might also add that no person has more reverence for the sacred and hallowed in the universe than I have, and I am sure my principal writings, which are in verse, will prove that I believe with Tennyson:

12 March 1892

Let knowledge grow from more to more,
But more of reverence in us dwell.

I would ask that if you have occasion in the future to refer to me, would you kindly drop the 'Rev.,' and oblige, as I have voluntarily renounced that title, not from any disrespect to my former calling, but from the simple wish to be regarded as a layman.

Ottawa, 3 March

12 March 1892

ARCHIBALD LAMPMAN

The Wakabees of the Arabian Nedjed, who are to the general body of Islam what the Puritans were to the Church of England, maintain that, next to blaspheming the name of God, smoking and drinking 'the shameful,' as they define tobacco and wine, are the two deadly and unpardonable sins. To me the most touching passage in Francis Palgrave's story of his journey through central Arabia is that in which he describes how in the Wakabee City of Bereidek he and his companion, Barakat-es-Shamee, the Syrian, being overcome by the sinful desire of tobacco, made their way out through a neglected fissure in the city wall, and, creeping down into a tall field of Indian corn, indulged themselves for a blissful hour in silent and surreptitious fumigation. We notice that the Wakabee is not confined to central Arabia but is getting quite common in almost every land; wherever we go we meet the Wakabee, who stares and makes faces at our pipe, plainly indicating by his manner and expression that he regards us as a beast. I always make it a point to agree with the Wakabee. Assuming an expression full of hypocrisy I admit that tobacco is a deleterious weed. I admit that it injures the digestion, that it weakens the will power, that it causes a man to waste valuable time that might be more meritoriously employed in boxing or doing hurt to his fellow creatures, and that it is a lamentable waste of money ($5 or $6 a year, perhaps, if he is a moderate smoker of plain tobacco). All this I admit, and when he is gone, I adjust myself comfortably and fill another pipe. If a man talks about tobacco he will find himself forever rehearsing its praise and blame, in violent strophe and antistrophe, just as Charles Lamb did; but on the whole I think that the smoker of moderate – perhaps I should say very moderate – tobacco finds the injury not so great after all as the benefit. What does the Wakabee say, I wonder, to the spectacle of the immortal Alfred Tennyson sitting for hours with a long clay pipe between his teeth, puffing the smoke 'straight out from the lips,' and patiently evolving, let us say, 'The Charge of the Light Brigade.' I find tobacco very conducive to prolonged meditation. It allays the disturbance that the mind is in, owing to the competition of too many subjects of thought. Out of the condition almost approaching reverie, which it produces, the subject which is actually most momentous gradually emerges; and at the end of a little time we find ourselves pursuing some single line of steady and effective thought. This result, as it seems to me, is not wholly due to the influence of tobacco as a stimulant, but is largely caused by the sort of gentle occupation that the act of smoking affords – an occupation not pronounced enough to draw the mind's attention, yet sufficiently an occupation to keep the nerves at rest. The practice of knitting with those women who have attained such skill in the art that they are wholly unconscious of the movement of the fingers and progress of the work has the same effect of allaying the nervous and distracting energies of the body, and composing the mind to thought. I have sometimes obtained a similar result from fishing – especially on a tepid and motionless summer day and in waters, where, as I subsequently ascertained, there were hardly any fish.

WILFRED CAMPBELL

We hear a great deal said about the (so-called) influence of our universities, of which we have many, in the different provinces. Now I do not want to say anything derogatory to these institutions, but I would like to put a question if it be not too pertinent. What are these colleges doing on behalf of the national life? To be direct, what are they doing for the national literature? Have they ever in the slightest way shown that they recognize such a growth in the land? My simple statement is they have not. It is a disgrace to Canada to say that our young men have to go over to the 'much-abused neighbouring republic' to win recognition in the higher pursuits, while our universities are utterly callous in the matter. To say the least there is something radically wrong. We will never have a true nationality while this miserable condition of things lasts. And those who desire to build up Canada's future as an independent nation may see too late the folly of ignoring her rising men, while our universities are being stocked with old country professors and tutors who can have no real interest in or knowledge of our nationality and literature. This kind of thing has gone on too long. The older Canadians may think the younger men are fools, but the result must be that in a shorter time than most dream we either must take the position in our own land that is due to us, or else we will go where we can at least get fair play and a chance to develop.

ARCHIBALD LAMPMAN

You can always tell a gentleman by the manner in which he addresses his servant. If a man is not a gentleman he will either address him as if he were the dirt under his feet or he will treat him with a coarse familiarity equally offensive. So deeply are we affected by the democratic spirit that to the thoughtful and sensitive mind of our time and country the very relation of master and servant seems unjust and unnatural, and consequently in the most delicate type of character you will find this relation characterized by a hesitating and almost shamefaced courtesy.

WILFRED CAMPBELL

Now and again we meet a self-opinionated being who condemns all fiction as trash and beneath the notice of the choice elect. This being is generally found to be engrossed in some particular occupation or study which gives him no time for personal expansion. His condition is very similar to that of the young girl, as described by her mother, when asked did Angelina Maria get time to read. 'No, she don't, Angelina Maria's a good girl, she don't waste no time on sich things, she's too took-up with her studies.' There is also an extremely narrow class in religion which condemns all novels as 'abominations of the evil one.' This class, in its sect prejudice, is unanswerable to any law but its own egotistic ignorance. But to the first, the 'too took-up with their studies' class, we would say that it may be possible for a man to fill himself up to the brim with histories and biographies, as a cistern is filled with rain water, and yet for him to be only a narrow, attenuated soul after all, utterly devoid of any knowledge of or sympathy with the great world of humanity about him.

The man who claims to know, understand, and love history and yet condemns Scott, Bulwer, Thackeray, Dickens, Hawthorne, Eliot,

Kingsley, Cooper, Lever, etc., as light reading or silly fiction or evil abomination is either a fool or a hypocrite, and no language is too strong to express contempt for him or his kind. We have, sad to say, too much of this class in Canada today, where literary culture and a broad human knowledge is terribly needed to soften and annul the bigotry and narrowness we see around us.

WILFRED CAMPBELL

In another place I have referred to the lack of interest in the national literature in our universities and colleges. Now, all intellectual men will admit that this is a grave condition of things, to say the least. We all know that the ideal university ought to be the centre of the best culture and aspirations of the growing national life, and it is to them that we look for the coming thought and inspiration that is to make or mar the future. It is true of all great foreign seats of learning. How about Canada? I would like to ask some of our most ardent patriots – some of those who are so sure of our 'certain glorious future' – do they know how many professors of literature and history there are in our many colleges who are deeply imbued with the national spirit; who are truly Canadians in birth, hope, sympathy, and education? If we have not been merely playing at nation building this is a grave and all important question, and will go far towards solving the much bemoaned question – the Canadian contempt and lack of feeling for a Canadian literature and nationality. The younger Canadians who have been born on Canadian soil will be put off no longer with indifference or contempt. Even the most ardent believer in the unity of the empire must admit that we are no longer mere colonists. Canada for the Canadians must be the first thing now, or else we must reluctantly admit that we have no country at all; and God help the young Canadian who has to bitterly admit that without any fault of his own he is 'a man without a country.'

ARCHIBALD LAMPMAN

In this age of instantaneous and universal communication literary reputations spring up and spread with bewildering rapidity. Just now comes to us the fame of Maurice Maeterlinck, a very young Belgian poet, who was suddenly and enthusiastically hailed a short time ago by the literary press of Paris as 'The Belgian Shakespeare.' One of his short plays has just been translated and brought out in a London theatre, but it appears with only indifferent success. This young writer is the author of a volume of poems, described to be rather absurdly imitative of Walt Whitman, a tragedy, and two short plays. The latter are said to be the chief evidences of his genius, and the power of the author consists in a knack of giving startling reality to tragic situations by touches of extreme simplicity and naturalness.

DUNCAN CAMPBELL SCOTT

Amongst the many good gifts for which we have to thank the enterprising publishing house of Roberts Bros, Boston, we must count the edition of the novels by George Meredith. In this sentence I have written myself an enthusiast, and if in the one I am now writing I could emphasize the statement I would do so. And yet, I trust I admire with temperance and prudence and have not been rendered uncritical and undiscerning by the great and supreme excellencies of my favourite. I can see his faults; but some of them I won't admit, out of human perversity, I suppose, and from a desire to show a bold front to those who want it to frighten the hosts of readers who would be delighted by his genius and benefited by his wisdom. It must be said, I think, that this author is prejudged with a hasty and unjust finding. Our peculiar method of reading, which is to read everything that we can lay our hands on written about a book, and leave the book itself alone, has operated disastrously for George Meredith's fame. At present he exists in the minds of many persons solely by reason of the confusion of thought which arises when they think of Owen Meredith; they never can remember which one wrote *Lucile.* Now, this is unfortunate, because George Meredith is a living force, a genius of incomparable power and energy; and the author of *Lucile* is a sentimental poet of limited range. It is unnecessary to press the antithesis further; it would be an injustice to both writers. But these are mere generalities; the purpose of this writing is to deal with only one of George Meredith's novels, not in every sense the greatest, but in some respects at least the equal of any fiction he has ever given us. I have chosen *Harry Richmond*, or as the full title goes *The Adventures of Harry Richmond*, for this first review because, although it is not the first in order of publication, it is one which will, I think, attract most readers. By it admirers may be won for *Sandra Belloni* and *Diana of the Crossways*, who would have been repelled by *Evan Harrington* or *The Egoist. Harry Richmond* is more than any other book of Meredith's full of stir, robust force, and genial human interest. It is so rapid, so full of charm, so crowded with life, so brim full of a humour that it is by turns pathetic and beneficently satirical, and it is done with such command, such virile force, and completeness. The very opening chapter has an authority which demands attention; from this picture we cannot escape; the strokes are cut too trenchantly; the image of old Squire Beltham struck off in these first pages follows us to the end of the book. Awakened at night by the visit of his hated son-in-law, he calls out to his steward, 'Hand me my breeches; I can't think out of my breeches.' It is the same old man who lashes this same son-in-law in the inn at the watering place with a tongue too honest to be nice about his words and a heart too impetuous to soften them. Squire Beltham is a success, and where shall we point to the failure? To have created Roy Richmond would have been possible for George Meredith alone of all novelists; and, not only has he done this, but he has created Dorothy Beltham and Janet Ilchester; the host of his minor characters exist with the distinctness of one's own acquaintances, but his great men and women are one's personal friends. I need not say his boys are one's personal friends. If George Meredith is supreme in anything it is in this. Let anyone who wants to live over again his boyish days read the first fifteen chapters of *Harry Richmond*; when he has finished them he will have regained his youth and will have read one of the raciest narratives in the language. Captain Welsh comes in by the way, and Heriot and Julia, and Harry's friend Temple; and the effect is so lively, the whole relation moves with such a rush and play of fancy. Surely here at least George Meredith is the ideal writer. And very often afterwards is he the ideal writer; far more often than one would suppose to hear those wise ones talk who allow the occasional vagaries of a man of genius to overtop his ever-present excellencies. But have I gained a reader anywhere for *Harry Richmond*? That is what I set out to do. If I have succeeded in making only one reader my time will not have been lost, and I will only consider that I have discharged a little of the debt of pleasure and profit I owe this splendid novel.

19 March 1892

DUNCAN CAMPBELL SCOTT

One service more is one more beauty. (Hugo)

I would write a sermon on this text.

Here the external acts of life communicate with the subtle and divine mind; the link so delicate, so secret, becomes for a moment visible. Into terms of spirit we translate the motions of reality or service, and are aware of the complex reaction of the soul upon itself. The promptings to kindness result in a greater humanity, to abstinence in a more sublime self-control. And who shall measure the effect, or set a bound to the force of the objective value of service? The washing the disciples' feet, the acts of tenderness and mercy start at once a thousand roots of peace and promise in the heart. But these present virtues we communicate with the millennium; we are part of that circle of goodness and beauty which shall widen out into eternity. By this service we are linked to the past, and its throes are triumphant in us. So between the two abysses we stand conservators of the past, pioneers of the future. But we are most of all pioneers, the function of our service is one for progress, for advance; by these acts of humanity and usefulness we increase the store of the beauty and goodness of the race. No individual excellence was ever lost; today we are protected by the valour of one of our ancestors, who stood in the breach of the wall and would not let the enemy pass. And will we not by our present self-control make the task of life easier for someone who is to come after us. Beauty is not a term of form alone, it is the secret and ever-present essence of the spirit of absolute truth, of supreme goodness, so that each service, each stroke of kindness, each expression of geniality is one more beauty.

ARCHIBALD LAMPMAN

Hitherto English literature in Canada has been cultivated by so scanty a population, scattered at great distances over so vast a country, that it has not been a matter of any great public interest whether our native writers produced good work or bad. Consequently anything like an efficient critical press has been out of the question. Certainly those occasional writers in the daily papers, who greet every new production of whatever merit or demerit with the same ridiculous praises decked out in the same fulsome and meaningless phraseology, have the least claim possible to be considered critics. Of late years we have had to depend solely upon *The Week*, and it may be observed here that, considering the difficulties with which the publisher of that journal has been obliged to contend, it is surprising that he has been able to supply its pages with so much really excellent matter. It will probably be a generation or so before the study of literature will become a matter of daily interest and solicitude to so large a body of our people that it will be necessary to adjust the claim of each new publication according to a rigorous scale; but even now much benefit might be done to our growing literary movement by the establishment on a solid financial basis of a really good literary magazine, including a department of criticism conducted in a spirit of serious appreciation and uncompromising candour. There could be no sounder stimulus to the young talent of Canada than the knowledge that its work would be seriously examined and honestly ranked by competent authority, instead of meeting either with the inert neglect or the spasmodic and senseless eulogy which are its lot today. But in the meantime, in the absence of any such acknowledged authority within our own country, let each one of us be the more careful to exercise the severest self-criticism. Let the young writer not fall into the mistake of imagining that, because he appears to be a little better than his more deplorable neighbours, his work is therefore satisfactory. Let him remember that he must 'scorn delights and live laborious days,' that he must apply himself to intense study, to unremitting observation, to perpetual practice, if he would win fame that is worth the having. There is only one standard for all the world. Let us ascertain what that is, and direct our labours solely with reference to it. Nothing less will do.

DUNCAN CAMPBELL SCOTT

Yes; he borrowed the book. I had rather it were put that way than to have it said I lent it to him. He was a professional book borrower and so I have only myself to thank for it. I knew it by his pose and by the peculiar, innocent wheedling of his tone of voice. It was years ago, but I remember it all as if it were day before yesterday. He was leaning against the bookshelves with his hat and gloves in his hand. I knew he was going and I felt glad; but the admission of this feeling was my ruin. I suppose by the subtle spirit that is in these fellows he must have known that his moment had arrived, for he said, 'Oh, by the way, I'd just like to take this Boccaccio, I won't keep it long.' 'Oh certainly,' I said, 'take it with you.' My heart quaked as I heard the words, but he went off very speedily, trying to stuff the book into his pocket although it was much too large. I never saw it again. Many times I asked for it but the devil always put a good excuse into his mouth. Very often he met me on the street and said: 'By the way I have a Boccaccio of yours; haven't I?' Twice he wrote me a note about it. One of these notes was characteristic. He said that last night (it was years ago) he had just put that Boccaccio of mine aside to bring it over when the fire department turned up at his house and insisted on laying the hose; they broke a window and deluged the place with water and his natural indignation at their conduct, for there was no fire anywhere in his house, his family being in the country and he having meals at the club, made him forget all about the book. He moved several times and each time further away, and at last he left the city altogether and took my Boccaccio with him.

Strange! I have just taken up the evening paper. I see that wretched fellow has been sent to Baghdad to enquire into the state of the coffee trade in Turkey and Arabia. Good-bye, Boccaccio.

Stranger still! The postman has just left a parcel, and it was my long-lost copy of Boccaccio. But how changed, how altered with the flux of time. Three of the plates have disappeared; a child has drawn a house on the red cover with a blue pencil; his wife must have got hold of the book, for she is a very pious person, and many of the leaves are gone, or has he saved these and taken them to Baghdad with him? The book is a wreck. I wish I could forget what it once was. Is it any consolation to be told, under these circumstances, that I will be the first person to get a sack of real Mocha direct from Arabia via the CPR? Is it likely that a man who could not send back my book will remember me in Arabia, especially when he has returned the Boccaccio and has nothing left to remember me by?

ARCHIBALD LAMPMAN

Many Canadians were deeply affected by the news recently received of the death of Mr Joseph Edmund Collins at New York. *The New York Critic* referred to him as a man 'of strong individuality and considerable ability.' As a journalistic statement, cold and brief, this was accurate enough. Mr Collins was a man whose personality will always be vividly remembered by everyone who was brought into contact with him, and I think that his ability might be regarded as potentially more than considerable. He was an instance of how in a raw and uncultured society like ours a great deal of genuine original talent may be dissipated and wasted through the pressure of sordid conditions, and the absence of bracing, intellectual influences. In Mr Collins there was a genuine streak of genius. He had an exceedingly rare faculty of appreciation as regards the true and the good in literature, and especially in poetry. He was one of the only two or three good readers of verse whom I have ever met with. His genuine delight in fine literary work and his boundless enthusiasm for it were a source of refreshment and help to all who were much in his company. The fact that Mr Collins never attained real excellence in his own efforts of the pen was no doubt owing to the circumstances of his early life, the utter want of proper education and discipline, his long journalistic experience which was deadly to the literary gift, the society into which he was thrown, and the perpetual struggle he was obliged to maintain for self-support. All these causes have no doubt been the ruin of many another goodly talent in Canada.

There are two or three – perhaps more – young writers, whose names are now well known in the Dominion, who remember Collins with an especial feeling of tenderness, gratitude, and almost of reverence. To his helpful enthusiasm, his kindly praise, his eager excitement, they owe the courage and self-confidence which enabled them to take the first daring step in the difficult and unpromising path of literature. Collins was almost the literary father of some of the young men who are now winning fame among us. There are only a few people who know what Joseph Edmund Collins has done in this way for our literature, and perhaps all that he has done will never be known. The few who were his nearest friends – and one of the nearest was myself – will always tenderly remember his passionate constancy of friendship, his prodigal generosity, his contagious humour, his gift of story-telling, and all the strange whims of his emphatic personality.

26 March 1892

DUNCAN CAMPBELL SCOTT

'You know I sometimes write myself,' the young fellow said.

'Indeed,' said I, 'I am interested.'

'Sometimes I seem possessed by a familiar spirit, a sort of demon, and the consequence is – I write.'

'Quite natural,' said my friend Simon Peter, in his most caustic tone; he hates a literary man of any kind. I tried to soften his asperity. 'I believe that is a common experience; all the greatest poets have certified to it,' the youth blustered. 'I wish you had something here you could read us now,' I continued. I saw Simon Peter take his pipe out of his mouth; I knew he was glaring at me. But if he will smoke in my rooms why should I not have some revenge on him? 'Well, you see I have something,' said the young fellow, fingering at his pocket. 'Well let us have it,' I said, looking straight at Simon Peter. That worthy had taken out his cigar case; he knows of all things I abhor cigar smoke. But the young fellow had got into his pocket and unfolded his paper, clearing his throat, which had become choked with Simon Peter's vile incense. He read these words:

Like a demon sits the cloud,
Alight upon the shoulder of the world,
And tempts her with the promise of renown,
To be the greatest planet of the lot,
If she will have him let his lightnings loose,
And tear the haze from off the dreamy wood
And blast the promise of the fertile year.
But the old world smiles on.
I know you, gentle sir, you are the Fiend,
Begone! for I am well content, being small,
To have a trusty heart; we will go on,
I and my children, doing some good, be sure,
And being contented in our homely way;
And you may flash about from star to star,
Hobble your thunder in the fields of Mars,
Maybe sometime you will be tired, and come
To turn a mill within the gorge of Time;
You will be happier then, but, until then,
Good-bye!

It was difficult for me to say anything, and I knew there was no use expecting Simon Peter to say a word, so there was an awkward silence. Then I asked whether he liked writing blank verse. I thought this was the easiest way out of it, and the conversation did drift away from the peril. Simon Peter was so grateful that he stopped smoking his cigar. There is something human about that man. When the youth went away Simon Peter shook hands with him. I asked him why. 'You put him in a beastly false position,' he said, with some harshness, 'and I was sorry for him.' I thought this was paying me off with a vengeance.

ARCHIBALD LAMPMAN

One at least of the frequenters of the Mermaid Inn desires to congratulate Mr George Martin on his excellent poem 'To My Canary Bird,' in the March number of *The Dominion Illustrated Monthly.* Mr Martin when he is at his best, as in these stanzas, shows himself to be a very good craftsman in verse. His lines are full of feeling, tender, and impulsive, and the workmanship of the entire poem is remarkable for skill of construction and charm of phrase. Mr Martin has evidently learned his art from Keats, whose note we catch in very many of the lines. I find the following stanza exceedingly pleasant to the ear and the fancy:

There is no touch of winter in thy song,
  No wall of winds, my yellow-coated friend;
All beauties of the spring to thee belong,
  All blooming charms, and all the scents that lend
A drowsy gladness to the summer hours;
  Again I hear swift rivulets descend
The mountain slopes, like children loosed from school;
  Again I see the lily on the pool,
And hear the whispered loves of leaves and flowers.

If I may judge from such former work of Mr Martin as I have seen, he is one of those poets whose gift, like wine and tobacco pipes, to use Lowell's comparison, improves with age. The older he grows the better work he does. His is surely a happy destiny who can occupy and amuse a fresh and vigorous old age with the composition of such eloquent and workmanlike verses as these.

WILFRED CAMPBELL

A great deal has been written as to the comparative merits of the greater novelists and novels of this century. And invariably, the first place has been given to such writers as Scott, Thackeray, Eliot, and Dickens. It is very hard to make a complete list of the greater writers of fiction in the English language. Many would be inclined to include

Bulwer and others. There is no doubt that much work of a strong and remarkable character has been done by such writers as Reade, Collins, Trollope, etc. I would be tempted to place Kingsley above them all, and close in rank with the first mentioned, while such men as Hardy, Blackmore, and Norris, form a later and strongly distinctive school, more akin to the better American fiction writers of today. George Meredith stands by himself as a strange personality, remaining from the older school, and yet not of them. It may not be generally known that one or even two of the greatest works of fiction of modern days came from a New England mind, that of Nathaniel Hawthorne. Probably the two greatest novels of this or any other country are the *Scarlet Letter*, by Hawthorne, and *Silas Marner*, by George Eliot. Both are simple in construction and unaffected in manner, but both, and especially the former, deal with subjects of so great a character and in such a way as to make them the most remarkable dramas of human life, in prose or poetry, since Shakespeare.

ARCHIBALD LAMPMAN

Now in the first breaking of spring, when mind and body take rest after the prolonged struggle with tempest and frost, and the fair promise of the fruitful year is before us, there comes upon the natural human soul of the poor man the longing to possess land, to have the lordship of some little plot of fertile earth, where he may plant and tend and know the triumph of harvest. Next to the care and education of children, I think that the freshest and happiest occupation is the planting and rearing of an orchard. In our climate the difficulties with which the orcharder has to contend and the skill and intelligence which are required of him perhaps render this pursuit all the more exhilarating. What can be more interesting to anyone who loves the soil and all that grows upon it, than by careful and persistent experiment to discover what trees and fruitbearing plants can be utilized, and how best they can be utilized, to give to his land that bountiful and fruit-laden aspect which is so closely associated with the idea of home and the homestead. The most noticeable defect in the farmland scenery of middle and eastern Ontario is the lack of orchards. The wild scenery of the forest is beautiful, and not less lovely in another way are the fields of our forefathers, mellowed by long years and the patient and affectionate usage of men. But these bare and almost desolate farms, where there is neither the wild beauty of the wilderness nor the genial loveliness of old possession, beat down the imagination, and their melancholy influence must tend to harden and depress the generation of young people growing up among them. Let every man, unless he be indeed in that degree of poverty that compels him to devote himself to bread-making alone, do something for his children and his country by planting trees, and especially fruit trees. When he has done this he will have accomplished things which his thought has probably not patience to follow out. He will have contributed to the growth of patriotism in a succeeding generation; he will have established a moral and intellectual influence, which shall enter into the lives of many hundreds of his descendants.

2 April 1892

ARCHIBALD LAMPMAN

A great many people have the idea that a poet, or, indeed, any kind of literary artist, must be a sort of monstrosity, a person whose dress, language, and habits are quite out of the line of their ordinary experience. They expect to find him a being wrapped in fiery abstractions, of frenzied glance and disordered locks, forever impelled by the most gorgeous sentiments, and getting off impassioned remarks, full of unintelligible profundity. And how astonished they are to find the poet so wonderfully like other sensible men, the chief difference being that he is possessed in a much higher degree of that quality which they least looked for, namely, common sense; for the faculty of genius is nothing more than clear, plain common sense, carried to a high degree and kindled with imagination. The poet differs from the ordinary man of affairs in that he applies the quality of common sense to all the relations and activities of life; the man of affairs merely applies it in a limited way to things as they are related to certain accepted ideas, which he has been taught to regard as the sum of existence. The hardheaded man of the world always distrusts the poet as a dreamer or unpractical person. It is a curious thing to reflect that the very reverse is the fact. The businessman, for instance, who with ingenuity and labour accumulates a fortune, spends his whole life in the pursuit of a dream, which in the end is the most empty and futile imaginable; a dream which to the unsparing eye of the poet is not only despicable for its narrowness but possesses in a gigantic degree all the elements of the ludicrous. The poet attaches himself to no dream. He endeavours to see life simply as it is, and to estimate everything at its true value in relation to the universal and the infinite. But the man of affairs still calls the poet a dreamer. There are also a very great number of people, especially, I believe, in this country, who regard the word 'poet' as simply and completely synonymous with the word 'fool.' They expect to find in the poet a very erratic person, with weak eyes, a flabby complexion, an effeminate drawl, and an alarming tendency to be affected to tears on slight provocation. What is their astonishment when he proves to be the wisest, the manliest, the most self-contained, and sometimes even the austerest and apparently most unimpassionable of all men. Let us instance a few of the great names: Aeschylus, Sophocles, Dante, Shakespeare, Milton, Goethe, Wordsworth, Tennyson. Are there in the annals of statecraft or business or philanthropy any goodlier or wholesomer figures of men than these?

DUNCAN CAMPBELL SCOTT

We may now look forward to numberless papers and reviews on Shelley and subjects connected with his life and works. The first of these in the article in the current number of *Harper's* by Guido Biagi, entitled 'The Last Days of Percy Bysshe Shelley.' The author is chief of the Laurentian Library of Florence. The paper is exceedingly interesting and contains much new matter collected by Signor Biagi. It is to be hoped that the Shelley centenary may bring forth some new matter dealing with his life and work, but it is extremely doubtful whether research could discover any unknown particulars in connection with a subject so well and so lovingly studied. But we should certainly look for some new editions of his works – there is room for them – and one in three or four small volumes, with good-sized print, would be the most acceptable. The tercentenary of Tasso's death, which will be celebrated in 1895, is likely to be made of considerable literary interest, from the fact that a new, a heretofore unknown manuscript, by the author of 'Jerusalem Delivered,' has been discovered in Italy, and will be published during the year above mentioned. The manuscript deals with a journey made by the poet to Egypt and Palestine, and also contains several new sonnets.

2 April 1892

DUNCAN CAMPBELL SCOTT

Mr Hardy's new novel [*Tess of the D'Urbervilles*] is a splendid performance. It has all his old picturesqueness and his personal singularity, but it springs from a deeper, a more human motive than much of the work which has preceded it. There is less of that theatric disposition of scene and incident which has not been uncommon in Mr Hardy's work, and, although it is full of distinctive happenings which could not have been arranged by any other hand, they fall naturally and inevitably. The book is replete with descriptions of external nature which catch the strangest, the most bizarre efforts with exquisite truthfulness. Anything weird or obscure in a landscape Mr Hardy reproduces with perfect impression and his new book is even more striking in this particular. I remember in *The Return of the Native* some descriptions that will hold with these later ones, but it is only in his books that this special treatment of landscape is found. But he has nowhere equalled the tragic pathos of this story, which is almost too heavy for the heart to bear and which is yet so true to the conditions of life. It is only upon reflection that the true insight of the tale comes out. Mr Hardy has left us to work out the lesson for ourselves, like the artist that he is, and has only interfered with the complete impersonality of his work in the subtitle [*A Pure Woman*], in which he seems to have felt the need of emphasizing the main feature of his heroine's character. It is upon reflection that one derives the true value from the book, and in the end we cry out once more against the code of morals which visits destruction upon one sex and allows the other to go free for the same crime. We may blame Angel Clare for not being stronger than the society in which he was reared, but to me the most heartrending thing in the whole book is to feel how slight the veil was which separated him from his happiness and Tess from her fate, and how any one of many possibilities might have rent it asunder and left them heart to heart as they should have been. But in life it is just these infinitesimal things which will not happen and to avoid such catastrophes we would need a prophetic power of insight and a god-like power of criticism.

ARCHIBALD LAMPMAN

The investigations of a certain Vienna professor into the language of monkeys constitute one of the latest curiosities in the way of scientific research. This professor affirms that monkeys have a quite intelligible language, and it appears that he has already made considerable progress in the study of it. He holds long conversations with some of the apes in the zoological gardens at London, and whenever he appears these apes call to him, it is said, with the greatest impatience and show manifest pleasure in his society. The professor is now on the point of setting out for Africa in order to prosecute his studies among the native simian tribes. Let us hope that he will be cautious in interviewing some of them. An interchange of sentiments with an impulsive and able-bodied gorilla, for instance, would call for a degree of delicate diplomatic skill not at the disposal of every man.

DUNCAN CAMPBELL SCOTT

The item of most interest in this month's literary news is that Mr Swinburne has a tragedy in press, which will be ready before long. It is called 'The Sisters,' and is written on a Northumbrian subject. Mr Swinburne has been silent now for some little time, and his new tragedy will be received with general interest. Mr David Nutt has commenced the publication of a series of Tudor translations, the initial number of which is to be Florio's Montaigne in three volumes. Mr Nutt will also publish three dramas by W.E. Henley and Robert Louis Stevenson.

9 April 1892

ARCHIBALD LAMPMAN

Of the many inspiring phenomena that make this teeming age wonderful and noteworthy, the most hopeful and the most significant is the change which is so rapidly taking place in the social position of women. The sentimentalist of the old school looks askance, and pictures to himself with disgust and dread the 'masculine' woman of the future. The rest of us need have no fear. Most of the frivolity, the vice, the sordid brutality that have characterized too much of human society in the past have been due to the condition of comparative social inferiority in which women have been forced to live. Give them perfect independence, place them upon an exactly even footing with men in all the activities and responsibilities of life, and a result for good will be attained which it is almost beyond the power of the imagination to picture. In the first place the effect upon the institution of marriage will be in the highest degree wholesome and beautiful. The degrading necessity for marriage, which is one of the wretchedest curses of society as we see it, will be removed. The woman will marry from choice, and the intellectual and moral training derived from her improved condition will enable her to choose rightly. The man will no longer choose a wife; it will be the woman who will choose her husband. Who can follow out in all their many branches the beneficent results of this one gain alone. The high standard of excellence which the woman will certainly look to in making her choice cannot but ensure the elimination or repression of a great part of the fool and the brute that is in men. Then as to those vices and dreadful degradations which many of us pass over in ashamed silence when we speak of the conditions of life, what will the effect be upon them? Assuredly it will be great. Women, no longer weak and dependent, no longer kept in an emotional atmosphere of frivolity and sentimental irresponsibility, but strong, active, and self-reliant as men, will not be subject or exposed to the same temptations, and above all they will not be at the mercy of men. When the moral and intellectual emancipation of women is fully effected many a cloud will be lifted from human life, and no sensible man will believe that the sex will have sacrificed one whit of that grace and beauty which we think to be its chiefest charm; rather there will be added to these a power, a beneficence, a dignity which are only the exception now.

DUNCAN CAMPBELL SCOTT

The affair of Dollard on the Ottawa has been one of the most popular stories of New France. Many poems and more than one novel have been founded on it. But our latest historian has refused to allow us to believe in the heroic purpose of the expedition. Dr Kingsford conceives the facts to be as follows:

> Dollard, who had left France under a cloud, desirous of regaining his character by some dashing act of gallantry, enticed sixteen young men to join in an expedition against the Iroquois. The intention appears to have been to surprise some of the bands of the marauding Mohawks and to exterminate them, and so give confidence and security to the settlement and remove the feeling of terror which was paralysing it; at the same time inflict a lesson on the Iroquois, so that they on their side would feel it was insecure for them to approach Montreal with hostile intent. De Maisonneuve reluctantly

> consented to the expedition. The party either fell into an ambush or unexpectedly became engaged with over-powering numbers. The fight must have been desperate and determined, for all of them were killed or made prisoners.

He concludes that 'the expedition had doubtless a defined end, and one considered practicable of attainment, and was so accepted by De Maisonneuve; he could never have foreseen so unfortunate a result.' It is interesting to note that the Jesuit Relations locate the encounter at Chaudière, in fact at Ottawa, although the Long Sault rapid at or near Carillon has long been popularly fixed as the scene of this desperate encounter. It would certainly seem that the Relations, written in 1660, shortly after the event, would be the best authority for a detail of this kind. Dollier de Casson did not arrive in Canada until 1666, and by that time the affair must have commenced to take on 'the strained and lofty accents of romance.' But even at the time of writing the Relations the whole occurrence must have been shrouded in mystery. But the story in its romantic form has come to live with us, and it is well. There is probably as much foundation for it as there is for the majority of the romances of history, and these are amongst the dearest possessions of the race. Nothing can dim the gallantry or overcloud the valour of the fight between these sixteen young men and their Mohawk antagonists. If they had no fort to shelter them, but only a breastwork hastily thrown up, their defence becomes still more heroic. It requires no labour of the imagination to conjure up the scene on their leaving Lachine for that wilderness of the Ottawa. They made their progress to death through a lovely landscape which then must have been more romantic than it is now; the Lake of Two Mountains with its sheeny distances, its pale and shallow lights, its shores covered with rising forests and dappled with immense shadows. I can never pass Carillon and see the Long Sault tossing its white foam without a thought of Dollard and his heroes.

WILFRED CAMPBELL

One of the strongest and most remarkable personalities of this century has just passed away at Camden, New Jersey. By the death of Walt Whitman, America loses her most distinctively national poet, in the sense that he was the voice of the greater part of the people. Not one of the great New England school, not even Emerson or Lowell, with all their natural and untrammelled vigour, voiced, as did Whitman, the American life and sentiment. Emerson was universal in his largeness of intellect, but in his local characteristics was essentially New England. Lowell, the laureate of the civil war and of the republic at its best in Lincoln, voiced the aspirations of the more cultured few with regard to the republic. Longfellow was essentially the laureate of the home and of the higher sentiments of a large class who are now already passing away. But if we want to find a poet, and a great one, who was as truly the singer of the great, crude, material, and yet aspiring republic, as Dante mirrored the Italy of the middle ages, we must go to Whitman. Much of his verse has been rightly called grotesque and even brutal in its barbarous egotism; but in this he was essentially the voice of the larger part of the common American people of the last quarter century. His very grossness of expression and untrammelled search for individual freedom show him to be the point at which the greater, cruder, and unformed part of the republic had found its poetical consciousness. If we were to have dreamed a poet for the era of the republic just gone, Whitman is the sort of individuality that might have been prophesied. His very simple and unaffected egoism, his intense enjoyment of life, and his ever-abiding interest in the country and nation as a whole, has no parallel in any other American poet. His was a largeness of heart and sympathy that was in keeping with the great institutions and the marvellously gigantic natural scenery of the republic. There is much in Whitman that jars on and repels the sensitive mind and cultured artistic sense, and a large part of his verse would hardly be admitted by many within the canons of recognized poetry. But this is nothing more than should be expected of the natural poet, who is the poetical voice of that strange, heterogenous, and magnificent but grotesque and inconsistent humanity which went to make up the larger part of the great American republic during the last thirty years. Of course even now the nation is outgrowing the Whitman era, and a larger culture and a new conservatism is coming in that Whitman could not have dreamed of nor have understood. But when history looks back to the golden age of the greatest republic of modern times she will note two titanic figures stand out as the blossom of the development of the age, the statesman Abraham Lincoln and the poet Walt Whitman. Both are grotesque and rude as was the age, but both must be judged not by any social standard of human culture, but both being judged by natural standards of a large and robust humanity, which, leaving the old world trammels behind, found a new development and blossom of characteristics, both will be found unique in the history of the world – Lincoln, the flower of the best ideals of the new republic; Whitman, the voice of its unmentionable reality of thought and existence.

DUNCAN CAMPBELL SCOTT

A late critic of Mr William Morris's last book of poems occupied two full pages of *The Athenaeum* in a dissertation on the inexactness of the nomenclature of the poets generally and the probable effect that the spread of scientific knowledge would have on the value of the impressions intended by the use of certain definite words. His whole argument was hung on the line in the poem, 'The Folk Mote by the River,' 'Woke up the swallows under the thatch,' the point being that it was martins Mr Morris meant and not swallows. The critic avers that the line as it stands may now give us a vivid picture of 'the snowy throats gleaming and throbbing through the little doorways of their nests,' but that it will be less so to a reader equipped with a more exact vocabulary. This may be so, but the time which will elapse before that day makes the discussion profitless. As a picture of the early morning, the lines from Mr Morris were very beautiful and impressive, but the impression from the line quoted will not be such as the critic supposes. Surely it refers merely to the sudden stir and twitter of the swallows (I use the inexact word) in their nests disturbed by the 'clattering latch.' In the first line of the next couplet we learn that it was too dark for the men to see their scythes. 'It was dark in the porch, but our scythes we felt.' So that the impression of the snowy throats of the swallows has to be forced into the line at first quoted. But it serves the purpose of a very subtle discussion, and Mr Morris's book, although it plays a prominent part in the first columns, is gradually lost sight of until the writer finds himself dealing with the decay of the epic.

ARCHIBALD LAMPMAN

It is the nature of men never to be satisfied. We complain of the length and severity of our winters; of the shortness of the summer months, those periods of enchantment that rush upon us with leaf and flower and vanish like a tumultuous dream; of the restless and violent alternations of heat, and tempest, and rain, of foliage and frost. How seldom we reflect upon the real and solid advantages we derive from these very circumstances. Does not the return of the year, the sudden and golden dawn of our summers, come to us with an energy of exhilaration quite unknown to the people of southern latitudes? In those gorgeous countries of the tropics, for which it is our nature often to yearn, with all their teeming glory of life and colour, there is a voluptuous monotony, enervating alike to body and mind. With us the coming of spring is the signal for a physical and intellectual revolution and revival, a new birth of buoyant and unconquerable energy rendering us capable of undreamed-of labours and immense undertakings. Our summer heats are keen and wholesome, and neither depress nor enervate. Autumn with its refreshment of splendid colours and its tonic days comes before we have lost anything of the vital impetus, and carries us on with renewed energy into the depth of that trying season which is our severest test. Yet even through the winter months, bitter but bracing, labour is a moral necessity, and we continue to prosecute it with strenuous energy, if not with actual joy. In Canada with the snows and frozen months of Stockholm or St Petersburg we combine the long days, the blue sky, and the splendid sunshine of the north of Italy. There has never been any other nation on earth so situated, and we cannot but suppose that our people will in the future develop an unusual buoyancy and novel energy of character.

WILFRED CAMPBELL

The comfort and enjoyment that many men find in their pipes is afforded to me by an open fire. A coal grate is cheerful and attractive, but for really delightful reverie give to me the crackle and blaze of a wood fire, especially one of maple or beech. A not over-large room with bookshelves lined with volumes, enough curtains of a dark, rich shade to add suggestion of warmth, two or three easy chairs, and an open grate or fire-place to light all with its glamour of heat and radiancy, is to me the ideal of the earthly paradise of the man of thought and aspiration.

I have often thought that my remote ancestors must have been sun or fire worshippers, for in the genial seasons of the year, when the lord of day is at his meridian, I find it almost impossible to stay indoors, but choose rather the sunny slopes and the golden ray-kissed shades of the leafy-tented woods; but when nature withdraws her warmth and shrinks into lifeless sleep, and in the frost-nipped seasons of long, iced nights and short, dull days, I need the companionship and inspiration afforded by a wood fire. Nothing seems to me more unbearable than the semi-modern manner of heating houses and rooms by a concealed heat. As a literary workman, my fancies are dulled and my faculties repressed by such a room. The crackle and glow, or even the smoulder of embers on the hearth, stir and inspire an imagination as nothing else can within doors.

There is something very marvellous and mysterious in this influence of light and heat. As a boy I always enjoyed the campfires we built in the great woods or on the shingly beach of some lone lake shore, when the stars came out and peered down on the windy darkness and swallowed up the sparks and flames from the crackling logs and dry branches we had heaped up; while the local warmth and radiance added a contrast to the outside vastness and mystery of darkness and void.

The fire-place as a social centre must be an institution of great antiquity, and must have owed its origin to the chance discovery of some of our remote cave-dwelling ancestors, who found the convenience of the smoke draught in the roof, and who, when they began to make artificial dwellings, at first rudely, and afterwards more accurately, copied the idea, until after long use and improvement we have the modern mantel and hearth of today.

Much of the glamour of the old-time Christmas season of the past, so beautifully described by the genius of Washington Irving, Dickens, and other writers, is closely associated with the old-time, large, open fire-places in the inns, hotels, and private mansions, which are now largely a thing of the past.

This, sad to say, is an age of hurry and change, but, if the family circle is to be preserved, the home comfort and sacredness to remain, I would advise all persons of even moderate means to have one room in the house – that in which the family usually congregates – ventilated and heated by one of those old-time fire-places. We hear a wide grumble as to waste of fuel and the extra trouble, but if home wives and mothers only knew that such a spot of rest and comfort in every home, with its unique attractions, can do much to enlarge the humanity and create a fellow and social feeling in the misanthropic mind, no home in the land would be without its cosy, warmly-curtained rooms, its genial bookshelves, and its open fire.

16 April 1892

ARCHIBALD LAMPMAN AND DUNCAN CAMPBELL SCOTT

At the first flush it might seem necessary to apologize for what may be considered an act of temerity in venturing to write a notice of the Academy exhibition just closed. If there is any department of criticism that needs special knowledge it is that of the plastic arts, and if our idea in the following sketch had been to point out what was excellent in technique it would have been necessary to accompany our words with a protest. But such was not the idea. It seemed that no task would be more congenial than to set down the impressions which some of the pictures had left upon the minds of two persons whose art is different but whose surroundings and mode of life are the same. And this is what we have tried to do. The position of the painter in a country like our own is one of peculiar difficulty. His art depends more than any other on the culture, the experience of the past, and, in a land like Canada, where we have practically no great pictures available and no eminent resident artist, the young painter finds himself without the means of overcoming the technical difficulties of his profession. To do so he must go abroad; he must seek in the ateliers and in the galleries of Europe for the practical insight which he could never obtain at home. That our exhibitions from year to year show a marked advance in technical skill is due in the main to the fact that our artists often by their own energy and self-denial have sought for knowledge at the source. This has raised the general excellence of the work, and has also had an effect for good upon those native geniuses whose art has often developed an astonishing vigour and individuality under unfavourable conditions. With this last idea in mind one naturally thinks of the pictures of Mr Homer Watson. Here is an artist who owes less perhaps to influences from without than any of his fellow workmen. But how fine his native manner is, how instinct with energy! He has so thoroughly mastered a certain kind of landscape under definite conditions of atmosphere that he reproduces it without a trace of uncertainty. He speaks from his canvas with something of that authority which is the unfailing indication of genius. In two of the pictures in the present exhibition, which are very characteristic, he reproduces the landscape under the presence of those cool, half-stormy days when the fields are darkened by great shadows and swept by splendid gleams, and he conveys a delightful impression of the reality. How different is the work of Mr Brownell, whose pictures are characterized by an exquisite skill governing a pure, natural taste. His 'Low Tide, N.E.' is perhaps the most satisfactory bit of work in the collection. The delicate clouds part fleecily below the blue, the sandy shore runs into lines of quiet grey, the rocks are yellowish brown, and the sea creeps in with fragile foam from a palish-green distance. The impression is exquisite. His technical perfection is again convincing in 'The Step Child,' where the figure has tone pensiveness and the surroundings absolute verisimilitude. Mr Brymmer, another painter who has had the advantage of the schools, produces work in which there is always charm as well as careful sincerity and truth of observation. His 'Wreath of Flowers' in the National Gallery is one of the pleasantest pictures which our art has produced, and if none of Mr Brymner's work in the present collection equals this there are nevertheless three of his contributions which are of very high merit. Conspicuous among them is 'In the County of Cork, Ireland,' a painting to which the observer will return again and again with increasing pleasure. Mr Brymner has treated us to one of the few local and specially national scenes in the gallery, that of 'Champ de Mars, Montreal, Winter'; and his smaller canvas, 'Near Killarney, Ireland,' contains a felicitous impression of a cloudy sky and crowded clumps of low trees and bushes. It may be remarked here that Mr Brymner and Mr Watson, our two most characteristic landscapists in oils, each possess excellences which, if the power presiding over genius would let them exchange at least in part, would render their work in a still higher degree satisfactory. It would appear that Mr Watson might spare some of his vigour and wealth of movement to Mr Brymner, and that Mr Brymner might transfer to Mr Watson some of his care and prudence. Unfortunately such loans are impossible or else we would have two perfect painters.

It has seemed to us that, in this exhibition at least, our landscape artists have been most successful, and this statement leads naturally to the mention of Mr Reid's large canvas, 'The Foreclosure of the Mortgage.' This picture, with all its points of excellence and notwithstanding the interest which naturally accompanies a serious and important attempt, hardly succeeds in realizing the painter's motive. The figures in the left foreground – the woman bowed and prostrated by grief and the child at her side looking on with wondering eyes – are done with truth and pathos, and if the painter had exhibited in his completed picture an equal vigour of expression and attitude the result would have been decidedly more impressive. As it is the rest of the figures are detached and fail to produce a satisfactory unity of effect. In bringing into his picture the weakness and misery of the sickroom, the artist has, we think, by overshooting the mark, signally missed the opportunity offered him to represent simply and typically one of the commonest and most significant tragedies of our everyday life. If he had placed before us the figure of a strong man in the full possession of health and strength, beaten down at last in the long struggle with financial difficulties, he would have realized a situation, less painfully pathetic, perhaps, but infinitely more tragic and more imposing.

Mr Harris's medium-sized canvas in a somewhat similar vein, which he calls 'Going Wrong,' is perhaps more successful, although it will not strongly impress those who are familiar with Mr Harris's finest work. With 'Cradled in the Net' Mr Carl Ahrens makes his first appearance in the Academy. He is to be welcomed and congratulated at the same time. The quiet dreaminess of that sun-flooded corner of the room, where the little child lies in the hammock so sound asleep, leaves us with a perfect sensation of repose and contentment. Miss Bell's 'Twilight Reverie' aims at a remarkable effect, and, although not particularly attractive, may be considered one of the most prominent pictures in the gallery. To return to the landscapes again, Mr Woodcock's 'Cabbage Garden' strikes one immediately by its subtle scheme of colour and by its craftsmanship, and, although somewhat affected, it shines by comparison with his other pieces, which appear mannered and conventional. Mr Raphael, too, has several landscapes which are interesting but unmarked by any individual qualities. Of the portraits, Mr E. Wyly Grier's 'Portrait of a Physician' appears to be the best, although it would have been greatly improved by a warmer background; the present blank wall looks like poverty of invention and leaves the figure unprotected. Mr Patteson's two portraits and Mr Forster's 'Portrait of My Mother' are good pieces of work. The latter we would rank next to Mr Grier's, if not with it. Miss Tully's portrait of Mr Kivas Tully is also noticeable. It fell to the lot of Mary Hester Reid to make a complete success with her 'Roses and Still Life,' which is quite indescribably delightful. Here and there about the walls were groups of flowers excellently painted, but this picture was the richest and most natural of them all. The small canvas of Mr A. Watson, 'A Kitchen Corner in a Humble House,' if faulty from the painter's point of view, nevertheless deserves special mention for a certain pleasant touch of nature which we find to be rare.

Turning to the water colours, the conspicuous figure is once more Mr L.R. O'Brien – conspicuous more by reason of the excellence than the number of his pictures. 'Grand Falls on the St John River' and 'The Mill Pond at Blair' are, we think, his best exhibits. In the former the beautiful painting of the snow-white, misty cataract with the light upon it is a delicious surprise. Mr O'Brien's style and method are so well known that any extended observations of his work seem uncalled for. Mr Manly displays a vigorous touch and much truth of observation. 'A Street in Point Lévis' is a very picturesque representation of a sloping street with ancient-looking houses, and 'Leafy June A-Summering Comes' is an accurate delineation of a natural bit of river scenery by one who evidently loves the fields. One of the pleasantest pictures of the collection is 'Sunshine and Shadow,' by Mr Fowler, who again displays his characteristic decision of colour and strenuous vigour of touch. Mr Bell-Smith appears to have been in Paris and to have filched some of the mannerisms of the French watercolourists. His success is rather doubtful although the 'Street Scene near Notre Dame' is certainly worthy of careful attention. His 'Rocky Mountain Canyon' is decidedly good, although the handling of such subjects by our artists in general is usually an opportunity for complete failure. The Rocky Mountain scenes to which we are being constantly treated are impressive and amateurist, of this we consider most of Mr Matthews's present exhibits to be noticeable examples. His 'Pleasant It was When Woods were Green' is somewhat more satisfactory. Mr Charles Moss has two very pleasant bits of colour inconspicuous in size, but of real distinction. A clever bit of local antiquarian interest is Mr Watt's 'Old Mill at Lachine,' a little picture, pleasant in tone and very truthful; and Mr Colin Scott's 'South Harpswell, Maine,' has some exceedingly attractive features.

In looking over these walls covered with interesting and promising pictures, a melancholy and frequent thought returns to us that the perverse fates continue to bestow riches on those who neither know how to use them for the benefit of the community, nor have the taste to acquire, by a noble employment of them, a rational satisfaction for themselves. We amuse ourselves by making a short list of the smaller paintings, which even if we were only moderately well-off we should assuredly make haste to buy. Most of all we covet: Mr Watson's 'Evening on the Thames,' Mr Brownell's 'Low Tide, N.E.,' Mr Brymner's

'Near Killarney, Ireland,' Mr O'Brien's 'Grand Falls on the St John River,' Mrs Reid's 'Roses and Still Life,' Mr Woodcock's 'Cabbage Garden,' Mr Fowler's 'Sunshine and Shadow,' and Mr Manly's 'Leafy June A-Summering Comes.'

23 April 1892

WILFRED CAMPBELL

There is no doubt but that much of the charlatanism of today is due to a corresponding weakness in the great mass of humanity which is willing to be imposed upon. One of the most glaring instances of this is to be found in the many attempts to publish comprehensive volumes of verse and periodicals devoted entirely to literary people. Two or three striking instances of this have come to the notice of the present writer, who has been pestered on this score. Cincinnati and Chicago seem to be the chief homes of such philanthropic situations for the immortalizing of 'inglorious' if not mute literature.

The whole trouble is that man has a craze for notoriety, and some people have a madness to see themselves in print even if they have to pay for it. The Homer of Michigan or the Sappho of Texas gets his or her divine utterance embalmed in covers, with a myriad of sisters and brothers (immortals?) for the small sum of ten dollars, and price of subscription additional. Such a condition of things is but natural in a large population where there must necessarily be a great literary impetus, without restraint of self-imposed standards, and we may afford to pass this phenomenon with a curious smile. But there is a graver condition of things, when really admirable and aspiring writers are willing to give their work for nothing to the first periodical or journal that is ready to impose upon them. Many of our writers here in Canada would do wisely if they forbore to print until their work was worth paying for. Young writers especially make the grave mistake of rushing into print without due consideration, hence we have college papers, and any amount of unbaked work in other journals as well which seem unable or unwilling to pay for proper material. It may be hard to check this sort of thing, but as long as it continues it will be injurious to the development of good literature. It seems a shame that a periodical or journal which pretends to uphold a high standard of literary work in a community should accept most, if not all, of its best work without payment. In this case both editor and contributor are lowering the status of the profession which it should be their first duty to uphold. The result is the endless amount of twaddle and inane matter that goes to fill up the journals of this class. We may forgive the college paper, as merely amateur, but there is no excuse for journals and contributors who claim to be grown up. I wish all young and sincere Canadian writers would make a compact with themselves not to give any work to a journal whose editor does not think that matter worthy of even nominal payment. By doing this they might for a while deprive themselves of the doubtful pleasure of seeing their work in print, but in the long run they would be conferring on themselves and contemporary journalism and literature a lasting benefit.

DUNCAN CAMPBELL SCOTT

The last poems of Phillip Bourke Marston have been collected by his friend Louise Chandler Moulton. They may add no additional lustre to a name already famous, but they will prove to have the qualities which have made Marston's work such a definite quantity in literature. With him one was always sure of certain things: of sombre beauty, of weighty and tragic lines drenched with sorrow. No writer has so completely translated his life into his verse. That life was shut in by suffering as by a wall; and although we are told he was cheerful and resigned, yet when he lets his heart out the cry is one of passionate pain. In his way of looking at things and in his style of expression he was influenced largely by Rossetti and his sonnets are identical in method. Some of the latter are equal to anything in *The House of Life* but his range was more restricted and his hand less firm. I must confess the sense of misfortune which anyone must feel when he finds a thing admittedly good which he cannot enjoy. I cannot delight in Marston's sonnets, and most of his verse I have to pass by with a feeling of regret. But he had an individual note which does appeal to me, and which I find his true admirers lay too little stress upon. His garden fancies, those poems to flowers and about them, are very fresh and lovely. Flowers must have appealed to him strongly. There is no object in nature that seems to have such a living, personal charm as a flower; its scent seems to be a language; if it has no perfume it still looks as if it would speak. These poems of his are full of fancies which the odour of the blossoms must have brought him. When the flowers are talking about the wind and where he sleeps at night, the lily says, 'In branches of great trees he rests'; the rose, 'Not so; they are too full of nests.' Such sweet, childlike ideas are found abundantly in the poems to which I refer, and to me they are very touching and very beautiful.

ARCHIBALD LAMPMAN

No writer in the region simply of poetry or fiction has ever been greeted by the reviewers with a stranger variety of championship and assault than the venerable old Scald just dead at Camden. Even in the case of Browning the contrast between praise and blame has not been so vehement and sharp. We all know with what burning enthusiasm a good many Americans and a few Europeans talk about Whitman, and some of the old reviews, both in America and England, so loud-mouthed in mockery and abuse, are not yet forgotten. Even yet what dissenters there are! I suppose that Mr Theodore Watts, the companion of Ruskin and Rossetti, might be chosen as the representative of that subtle, poetic culture which is the product of centuries of literary and artistic activity in an historic land; and this is the way in which in a recent number of *The Athenaeum*, he speaks of Walt Whitman, to whom he most irreverently alludes as 'Jack Bunaby of Parnassus': 'That Whitman had the temperament of the poetical thinker no one, I suppose, would deny. Whenever he writes about death, and in one or two lyrics about Lincoln, he is fine – sometimes he is almost sublime; and it is by no means sure that if he could have been compelled to give his attention not merely to English metres, but to English grammar and English common sense, he might not have left something notable behind him.' He professes to be unable to find out what Whitman's message to humanity is, and avers that 'it is easy to disguise puzzle-headedness the moment that you pass away from prose statement.' 'As to his amazing indecency,' he adds, 'that may be forgiven. It has done no harm. It is merely the attempt of a journalist to play "the tan-faced man" – to play "the noble savage" – by fouling with excrement the doorstep of civilisation. In England, to be sure, he would have been promptly run in.' *The Saturday Review* also in an article written in the well-known manner of that very smart and decidedly offensive weekly, grants to Whitman a measure of genuine and enduring poetic power, but dismisses all his political, social, and moral ideas as too infantile to be worthy of any serious notice whatever. In truth it may be said that personality enters into the quality of Whitman's work more prominently than in the case of any other writer. It is his personality that so keenly attracts and repels, and there will always be a class of gentle and delicate minds to whom, however willing they may be to recognize the frequent beauties and grandeurs in Whitman's work, his brawny egotism and raw aggressive force will be instinctively repulsed. The old world will acknowledge his power in theory and at a distance, but it will approach him with a shrug or a shudder.

WILFRED CAMPBELL

Probably few Canadians are familiar with Emerson as a poet. Like Whitman and Browning, he wrote a great deal of stuff that is worthless, but now and again produced something remarkable for its originality and power. I have no patience with those who would do homage to him as a poet. He is nothing but a rhyming philosopher, who often lost himself to no effect in long-winded doggerels. It was as a prose writer that Emerson was in his own way a master. But here and there in his doggerels he struck chords of beauty in his thought that are unique and irresistible. Emerson had certainly high and reverential thoughts with regard to nature, and possessed a keen insight into all her forms and phases, but he lacked two important essentials – power of expression in any kind of form, and a knowledge of human life. He had a large vision with regard to history and the philosophy of history, but was but a child as to the life about him. Perhaps the most beautiful thoughts expressed in his verse are found in the following lines:

The hand that rounded Peter's dome,
And groined the aisles of Christian Rome,
Wrought in a sad sincerity;
Himself from God he could not free;
He builded better than he knew;
The conscious stone to beauty grew.

But here the beauty lies entirely in the thought. The expression, as in all his verse, is crude and the rhyme and metre often abominable. I can easily understand Emerson's appreciation of Whitman, despite his disregard of the canons of verse. They had much in common, but Whitman's crudity was the defect of a true poet with no sense of the necessity of form, while that of Emerson was the result of an attempt to put into rhyme thoughts, that he could and did express much more fitly and satisfactorily in prose.

30 April 1892

WILFRED CAMPBELL

One of the most promising among our portrait painters is Mr W.A. Sherwood of Toronto, whose fine picture of Dr Scadding stands high in the scale of Canadian portraiture. While Mr Sherwood's work on exhibition this year does not quite do justice to his best effort, it shows a power which if properly controlled and developed would give him high standing. What many of our young artists need is a close study of realism, without becoming slaves to mere technique. Mr Sherwood has a bold and a rapid touch and a genuine enthusiasm for his art, which shows promise; and he is, we also understand, a hard worker, which is necessary to the accomplishment of the best works.

WILFRED CAMPBELL

The May number of *The Cosmopolitan*, which has just appeared, is the first number under the joint editorship of Mr Howells and the proprietor, Mr J. Brisben Walker. In securing such a distinguished name to an already strong editorial staff Mr Walker has achieved a triumph worthy of his best ambition and has placed his magazine on a sure footing for popular favour in the foremost ranks of the giant monthlies of the continent. The initial number under the new regime is unusually strong and includes such names as Lowell, Stedman, Hale, James, Stockton, Fawcett, Jewett, Hay, Howells himself, and a number of other established and promising littérateurs. The world of today owes much of its refining influence and higher enjoyment to the high-class magazine, so we congratulate Mr Walker and wish *The Cosmopolitan* all the success it deserves.

30 April 1892

ARCHIBALD LAMPMAN

If the fates ever furnish me with the means of building a house, and give me the liberty of placing it where I will, I shall certainly set it either on a lofty hill, or, if I am not thoroughly suited in that respect, in a very deep valley. Men who dwell upon the hills should be cool-blooded and large-minded. The outlook over a vast stretch of country is magical in its effect upon the mind, and if we make it the habitual circumstance of our lives it cannot fail to exercise a permanent influence over the character. He who looks abroad from the hills is reminded at every hour of the day of the largeness and beauty of life, of the variousness of human labours, of the inexhaustible freshness and loveliness of this earth. His vision passes to the utmost visible limit and projects itself into the immensity beyond. The infinity of space and time, the multitude of worlds, the strangeness of human destiny, the smallness and insignificance of the unit which is himself, are always present to his thought. One can hardly conceive how he should be a mean man, or harbour thoughts otherwise than calm and spacious. The dwellers in valleys also are more fortunate, I think, than those who have built upon the plain. The upward sweep of the enclosing hills, especially if they be plumed and ruffled with forest, leads the mind out of itself, and conducts it to regions of morning, freshness, and beauty.

DUNCAN CAMPBELL SCOTT

I happened to pick up a copy of Gottschalk's *Notes of a Pianist* the other day. It is a jumble of all sorts of remarks about the places he visited and the incidents of his concert tours. Some of his references to Canadian towns are interesting. Writing in 1862 he says of Ottawa: 'They are building a House of Parliament here which, considering the narrowness of the town and the number of deputies which it is required to accommodate, give it the appearance of Robinson Crusoe's canoe.' He makes great fun of the French spoken by the Canadians in Montreal and Quebec, and the names of the people he finds very amusing – 'Mr Cauchon was the Minister of the Interior for some years.' Then he makes fun of him for his pronunciation. In Quebec he finds that everything 'reflects the sacristy.' But he everywhere abuses the French Canadians. He calls them with scant courtesy 'ugly and apathetic.' He spells Caughnawaga 'Coylmawaggher,' which is certainly a very extraordinary attempt. He played in Toronto on 18 July 1862, but he does not say anything about the town; he says merely that his concert was under the patronage of Major-General Napier and that he met some officers he had known in Paris.

WILFRED CAMPBELL

Nothing more truly American has ever been written than the strong and original collection of *Pike County Ballads*, by John Hay, editor with J.G. Nicolay of the famous *Life of Lincoln.* These remarkable poems were first written for *The New York Tribune*, and republished in book form in 1871. While these verses show something akin to those of Bret Harte, they have about them an originality all their own which makes them unique in American literature. The ballad 'Jim Bludso,' the most characteristic, is an epic of Mississippi steamboat life, told in strong and pathetic language, with a quaint humour and a practical theology evolved from the rude western environment, and truly human in its freshness and boldness of conception. The quaint originality of statement in this western epic, is shown in such lines as:

Wall, no! I can't tell whar he lives
Because he don't live, you see;
Leastways, he got out of the habit
Of livin' like you and me.

Or,

A keerless man in his talk was Jim,
And an awkward hand in a row,
But he never flunked and he never lied –
I reckon he never knowed how.

Then the lines relate how the steamer, the *Prairie Belle*, who wouldn't be passed though she was the oldest craft on the line:

Came tearing along that night,
With a nigger squat on her safety valve.

What could be finer than the description of the fire that broke out, and

Burnt a hole in the night.

Then is told of how the heroic Bludso, after holding 'her nozzle agin the bank,' till 'the last galoot' was 'ashore,' went up alone in the smoke of the *Prairie Belle*. Then comes the summing up in the simple and childlike theology of the last stanza:

He weren't no saint – but at judgment
I'd run my chance with Jim,
'Longside of some pious gentlemen
That wouldn't shake hands with him,
He seen his duty, a dead sure thing,

And went for it thar and then;
And Christ ain't agoing to be too hard
On a man that died for men.

In a similar vein is 'Little Breeches,' with its quaint humanity; and that remarkably terse relation of a fight for a 'whiskey skin,' called the 'Mystery of Gilgal.' Those who have not already perused these irresistibly charming ballads can obtain them in a small edition of Routledge's *Companion Poets.*

DUNCAN CAMPBELL SCOTT

The late Lord Lytton seemed to have inherited the fatality which haunted his father when he wrote *King Arthur.* He seemed predestined to write verse that, practically at least, is a failure. His long novel in verse, 'Glenaveril,' was in every way a lamentable performance, so tedious that it has even failed to find a place in the list of his works. 'Lucile' now forms the interior of many gaudily-bound gift books, and it may be read by the gentle young ladies who receive it on the anniversaries and holidays of the year, but I have genuine misgivings even upon that last point. I fancy even they turn with a sense of relief to the freer atmosphere of Mr E.P. Roe and 'The Duchess.' Yes, these books are immensely dull and have no touch of poetry from cover to cover. It is hardly possible to consider seriously the work of a man who could write this stanza:

Whate'er the gain by these from love expected,
Whether its acquisition be in pelf
Or pleasure, it is wholly unconnected
With love itself.

Yes, that is true, very true; but then what a bore it is to have it said that way. Anyone could have said it as well, and no one would in consequence feel like calling him a poet. But Mr Blunt asks us to put 'Owen Meredith' among the immortals. This, of course, prevents us from putting Mr Blunt among the critics, and leaves us with a feeling of bewilderment as to just what to do with him. It is possible that a poet never existed who could not charm one ear with his rhyme. This is probably a provision of considerate Nature, who does not care to leave any of her children uncomforted, and who recognized the ultimate of human misery in the man who would write verses and have no single admirer.

30 April 1892

ARCHIBALD LAMPMAN

The art of reading is one which is left for the most part to take care of itself. Many people go to a teacher to learn music, but very few ever think of having themselves taught how to read, ie, how to read with precision and effect. The art of elocution might be made to afford almost as much pleasure and inspiration as that of music if it were as honestly cultivated and as widely practised. The systems of professional elocution taught in the reading schools and practised on our public platforms seem to be applied only to a very narrow range in literature. We all know the sort of thing we may expect from the elocutionist who advertises a public reading. It must be something affording opportunity for a vehement display of voice and plenty of vigorous gesticulation – something dramatic – more often something melodramatic. I wonder if anyone ever heard the 'Ode to a Grecian Urn' or 'The Blessed Damosel' from the lips of a professional elocutionist. The greatest part of which is strongest and most beautiful in our literature remains untouched by this art as an art. There is no reason why it should be so, except that its masters are themselves deficient in the deepest and truest culture, or that they are not content to undertake the slow and somewhat ungrateful task of reforming the taste of the thoughtless multitude. However this may be, there is room for a splendid new departure in the art of elocution, and there would be a high reward of ultimate fame, if not of fortune, for the man who should successfully undertake to fill it. It seems to me not by any means impossible that great bodies of people from the general masses might in time be drawn together for the purpose of listening to the deepest and subtlest products of thought and imagination, if only these were rendered by persons possessing at the same time a high literary faculty of appreciation and the necessary technical training. What a benefit, too, to the body of the people would be the establishment of a system of elocutionary training based upon delicate and comprehensive literary taste. We meet with very few people who are able really to read. Not one person in twenty is able to read plain prose, and not one in a thousand – I had almost made it more – to read verse. Yet a great many people have in them the natural capacity to do both. All that they need is culture, encouragement, and the proper vocal training. Surely there can hardly be a greater delight than to listen to some magical story or poem rendered by a sweet and sonorous voice, perfectly governed and informed by the spirit of what is read. Every household should have its reader and every school its competent reading master. In our higher public schools, I understand, reading is practically untaught, and the result is made awfully apparent in the coarse accent and barbarous pronunciation which torture us daily from our pulpits and platforms. It would no doubt be unreasonable to expect that these schools should furnish any very exquisite or elaborate culture in elocution; but they should at least make a certain sound and practical exercise in reading under a trained master a part of their course in order that their scholars might go forth able to enunciate correctly and convey something of the sense and feeling of any ordinary passage of literary English.

WILFRED CAMPBELL

We ought to be very careful how we praise Canadian work, merely because it is Canadian, but we have a man in Canada of whom we are all justly proud, and whose genius is unique in its peculiar originality. I mean Mr Bengough of *Grip*. His work as a caricaturist is considered by many to be superior in its simple suggestiveness to any other of the kind in the world. Certainly his work compares favourably with the elaborate work of the American and German schools of cartoonists. He always hits the nail on the head, and while unmerciful on fraud of any kind is never brutal. But, famous as he is, it is not as a caricaturist that I would now speak of Mr Bengough, but as a literary man. In a late number of *Grip* I noticed a strong and simply beautiful poem in memory of Mackenzie that has touched me very much; a poem that in conception and style is worthy of the personality it depicts. There is a stately simplicity about such lines as:

> No God-like gifts were his;
> His Scottish tongue could speak unvarnished truth;
> Better than great, he stood for what was right,
> Just plain Mackenzie – nobly commonplace.
>
> He was a Christian of that old-time sort –
> Unfashionable now and growing rare –
> Who knew no sacred barr'd from secular,
> But worshipped God by doing honest work.

Such lines as these need no recommendation other than their own merit.

7 May 1892

WILFRED CAMPBELL

On my humble bookshelves a place has ever been set apart as sacred to volumes of wit and humour. I cannot exactly understand the nature of a man who is impervious to the influences of this essential department of literature. Like Shakespeare's man who did not appreciate music, he would seem to me a sort of moral monstrosity, lacking one of the qualities that go to constitute an all round personality. He may be a heavyweight, to use a sporting expression, in the affairs of life, but he is among his fellows but bread without leaven, sandwich without the mustard, wine without the sparkle; and, no matter what may be his ideas or qualities as a worker, such a man is sure in the end to be a failure. I think we ought to be very charitable towards many bigots and other persons of narrow and extreme tendencies, who have attempted rabid and impractical changes in society. History may regard them as fanatics and even as brutal persecutors, but it seems to me the poor fellows meant well, but, lacking the necessary balance, they failed in the essential quality, a sense of humour. Men and women of an intensely zealous nature, who are wrapped up in their own ideas of bettering the world, are perfectly incapable of looking at the ridiculous side of anything. On the other hand, the great reformers of all ages have been intensely susceptible to humour, and appreciated it to the fullest extent. Hence all of the greatest humorists have been closely identified with the world's progress. Many brutalities have been ridiculed out of society that graver influences would not have removed. So humour and satire have their essential place and work to do. In the education of the young this should always be kept in mind. The sense of shame and of the ridiculous are closely allied in character, and have much to do with moulding the finer feelings and yet in keeping the normal balance. It is a pity that some of the most famous wit and satire of the past is so allied to indecency of thought and expression that it is unreadable, and disgusts and repels rather than pleases and instructs, and nothing shows the gradual elevation of modern society more than our disgust for this sort of thing in the old writers. The remarkable genius of Rabelais and of his apparent follower Swift cannot recompense the coarseness of thought and expression they have left behind them. The same must be said of the humour of Fielding and Smollett, and of the rhymed satires of Pope and Dryden. At the best, we can say that the age was coarse, and that they mirrored its grossness. It is with a sense of relief that we turn to our modern humour and satire, and at once we are struck by the kindly humour of Irving and Dickens, and the worldly-wise but kindly satire of Thackeray. And the world will never in a sense tire of such creations as the Connecticut schoolmaster in Ichabod Crane, the cockney immortal Sam Weller, or of the genial worldly wisdom of the somewhat blasé but almost lovable (society man) Major Pendennis. To come down to humorists pure and simple, Canada and the United States have produced three of the most famous of this century – Sam Slick (Haliburton), Artemus Ward (Browne), and Mark Twain (Clemens). Of the three the Canadian Haliburton was undoubtedly the founder of this school of American humorous writers, and in his Sam Slick immortalized the sharp, shrewd Connecticut Yankee, who, from being a vendor of impotent clocks and wooden nutmegs, rose to be an ambassador, and still remaining the same remarkable and interesting personage. The followers of Haliburton were legion, but Browne in his Artemus Ward, the travelling showman of the era of the war, with his moral waxworks and civilized wild beasts, rivalled and surpassed Haliburton. Both Haliburton and Browne became noted in England as well as America. The present king of humour, Mark Twain (Samuel L. Clemens), is one of the most remarkable personalities of the American Republic, and his famous *Innocents Abroad*, which all have read or ought to read, and his *Tom Sawyer* and [*A Connecticut*] *Yankee at King Arthur's Court* are books that mark an epoch in the upward grade of the humorous literature of the age.

ARCHIBALD LAMPMAN

This year the French will celebrate the centenary anniversary of the composition of the 'Marseillaise,' a song which did more for the armies of France in the last days of the old revolution than all the genius of their generals; and though it did not avail to save the decrepit wreck of their power at Woerth or Sedan, nevertheless when the next war shall arise its thunder will be terrible upon the Rhine. Modern France is the France of the revolution, and the very soul of the revolution pulses in the 'Marseillaise,' a spirit wild, daring, and titanic. It is the most tremendous call to battle that ever sprang to the lips of man. Its note is inspired, fierce, aggressive. But like the military fervour that gave it birth its passion is too high to be maintained. It represents the charge, the first splendid fury of the attack; it does not fit so well the hour of uncertainty, of dogged defence, still less of miserable defeat. 'The Watch on the Rhine' is a much better 'working' battle song. It represents the feeling of a nation of serious, home-loving people, who in the hour of solemn necessity go forth not to conquer or even to win glory but simply to defend their fatherland. It is strong, sonorous, somewhat sad, a spirit and a cry that will stand, and not give back. The Germans have a great many very fine battle songs, most of them the product of the War of the Liberation. Through all of them there runs a peculiar vein of tragic sadness. In the midst of their romantic heroism they never lose sight of the awfulness of the battlefield and the piteousness of the soldier's death. They are tenderer, more human, more deeply tragical than the French songs.

DUNCAN CAMPBELL SCOTT

A review of Lord Tennyson's *Foresters*, in a recent issue of *The Athenaeum*, after stating the eagerness with which the production of that play will be awaited in England, goes on to make some rather startling observations on the relative importance of verdicts of playgoers in England and America. He concedes without an argument that the superiority is 'with the Americans in regard to the acceptance of drama as a literary form. An American first night audience is almost as intelligent and almost as artistic as a Parisian one, while the intelligence and culture of England are poorly represented on such occasions in London.' There was no urgent call for the writer to say this, and the statement must have proceeded from reflection, and must have had some personal experience of both audiences as a foundation, otherwise it would have been hazardous. It would be hardly prudent to found such an assertion upon the success of the new play in New York, for there are special reasons why it should attract and interest an American audience. In fact, the production of the play is almost an international episode, as the part of Maid Marian was at first intended for Miss Mary Anderson, and was afterwards altered for Miss Ada Rehan. Even if the writer is not qualified to speak with final authority of the position of the American audience he is certainly at home in his criticisms of the English one, and he gives a very clear and unhesitating opinion as to its culture and acuteness. 'It is only in the cheaper parts of the house that intelligence and attention are still awarded to the play.' I find that sentence genuinely gratifying, and it is what one would naturally expect; it is probably just as true of the American audience if the skits of the caricaturists have any foundation in fact. It must necessarily follow that the class of the population who have the most active interest in life, and whose outlook is not limited by any sacred social code, will bring to the consideration of any work of art a livelier perception and a more nimble intelligence. It is inevitable that the people whose life and whose experience is of the earth and the rough facts of life will most readily see the truth and beauty of those types by which the artist has endeavoured to reproduce the essence of events and emotions which have been and will be to them matters of daily occurrence. It is in their case more a matter of sympathy than of culture. Our own audiences would have an equal appreciation if they had a chance to exercise their native taste. But unfortunately the 'stage' is non-existent in Canada, and it will be some decades yet before we add that final flower of culture to our national civilization.

ARCHIBALD LAMPMAN

Certainly custom is a more thorough inculcator of patience than all the precepts of the stoics. I have often wondered as I sat in church on a quiet murmurous summer morning, longing for the end of some pathetically futile sermon, and battling with the sea of sleep that threatened every moment to overwhelm me, why it is that so many sensible people in so many thousands of churches persist in placidly subjecting themselves to a torture which they would not endure for a moment in any other sort of building. I do not see why it should be established as a kind of eleventh commandment that every good Christian soul must submit to be plagued with a sermon, good or bad, at least once a Sunday. In the Presbyterian, Methodist, and other bodies, where the ceremonial of religious service is so slight, I suppose that the sermon is unavoidable and the only resource for those who follow these branches of the common faith is to insist on it that their clergy be selected only from those who have the gift of eloquence. In the Roman and Anglican bodies, however, the case is different and they ought to do away with the incompetent preacher. The clergy should be divided into two distinct classes, the parish priests and the itinerant preaching priests. We know to our discomfort that many – one might say most – of those clergymen who are most useful and most beloved as parish workers and private spiritual comforters are hopelessly incapable of exerting any powerful influence from the pulpit. These men should be restricted to the work for which they are fitted, and in which their interest is most centred. Those priests who are found after thorough probation to be gifted with the power of moving speech should be set apart and formed into an unbeneficed body of preachers, whose duty it should be to go about among all the parishes in rotation delivering genuine and effective sermons. In this way the working parish priest would not be withdrawn from the occupations nearest to his heart by the necessity of composing toilsome and unendurable discourses, and the naturally-gifted preacher would be enabled by undisturbed study and meditation to develop to its utmost the bountiful power that is in him. Church men might not have sermons every Sunday, but when they did have them they would be of that magical and inspiriting kind that would more than compensate them for an occasional silence.

14 May 1892

DUNCAN CAMPBELL SCOTT

It is not often that the consideration of tariffs and their accompanying problems troubles a literary man, but they unfortunately force themselves upon his attention occasionally in a rather disagreeable way. When he finds that he has to pay his retail dealer thirty-five cents on the shilling for every book he imports, the retail dealer and the whole system of tariffs and profits are liable to a searching criticism, expressed in rude and figurative language. But the trade suffers as well, although the wrathy purchaser is hardly likely to think of the trade. Just now the English book trade is feeling the effect of the McKinley tariff, which levied upon English books a duty of twenty-five per cent and admitted free of duty all books printed in foreign languages. The result of this provision has been that the flow of French and German books to the United States has naturally advanced the sale of American books to those countries. In Canada we have to pay too much for our books; to a person of limited means the collection of a library is a slow and irritating work. There are so many things he wants which are just beyond his reach, and he has no second-hand bookstores to visit where he could once in a while land a copy of some longed-for book 'as good as new.'

14 May 1892

WILFRED CAMPBELL

Mr Thomas Hardy is conceded by the best authorities to be the leading writer of fiction, with one exception, in England today. Some of Mr Hardy's most characteristic works have first appeared as serials in the great American monthlies. *The Return of the Native*, one of his strongest achievements, came out first in *Harper's Magazine*, as have his later *Wessex Folk* [sic], and *Two on a Tower* first saw the light in *The Atlantic Monthly*. His most popular work when in book form is undoubtedly *Far from the Madding Crowd*, a strong and tragic pastoral of English life. But it remains for Mr Hardy's latest book, *Tess*, to give him a prominence still more commanding than he has hitherto attained. This book has attracted unusual attention in literary circles on both sides of the Atlantic, and is regarded by the great English and American critical authorities to be one of the most remarkable works of fiction of the day. In these high quarters the book has been treated with the respect and consideration it has deserved, both because of its subject and treatment. But certain petty critics of less fame but more captiousness have attempted to pronounce it immoral and as unfit to be read because of its evil tendency. In answer I would say that a critic in *The New York Independent*, a famous religious and literary journal, says in a long review of the book that any person who goes to this book to satisfy a morbid craving for the improper will be sadly disappointed. The book is a dramatic picture of one of the most tragic subjects to be dealt with in our humanity, a subject that society cannot afford with impunity to ignore, the sacred relationship of man to woman, and the inevitable tragedy that is so closely connected with it under certain conditions. He who in a spirit of pharisaism would denounce such a book as immoral in its tendency would not only be going against the judgment of the greatest literary tribunals of our time, but would also be guilty of false witness of the most contemptible kind. No man of normal moral calibre could get evil in such a work. The whole story is intensely sad, and pathetic in its intensity. All that Mr Hardy approaches is treated with the sincerity and dignity characteristic of his work. And no man with any claims to true literary insight would dare to insinuate otherwise. One of the purest literary minds was that of Nathaniel Hawthorne, the famous New England writer. Of equal nobleness of character was George Eliot, the most remarkable literary woman of modern times. No one I am sure would impugn the motives and ideals of the immortal Sir Walter Scott, and yet the most widely recognized of the greatest works of these three famous and standard writers were *The Scarlet Letter*, *Adam Bede*, and *The Heart of Midlothian*. Mr Gladstone, who is as orthodox in morals and religion as any famous man of these times, says that these three books just mentioned are the three greatest books of fiction in the language, and yet these have for their subjects the same though in slightly different phases as that dealt with by Mr Hardy.

These books are great in their beauty and pathos, and of this class is in its degree *Tess, the History of a Pure Woman* [sic], by Thomas Hardy. To the evil all things are evil, but true men and women, who admit practically as well as by mere lip confession that there is a dark side as well as a light side to our humanity, are growing to realize more and more the importance of studying our inner natures, and so arriving at the real secret springs of the imperfections that the world long ago acknowledged to exist in our being. The highest morality is not to be found in ignoring the sacred and most important relationships of humanity, but by a brave study of the situation as it is, not as some of us might wish to imagine it to be; and such a study, terrible in its realism, is that which Mr Hardy has placed before us.

ARCHIBALD LAMPMAN

April and May are the months of wood flowers; June the season of blossoming in the inner recesses of the forest; August the time of perfume and colour in meadow and field. He who journeys homeward from the woods on one of these quiet, murmurous April evenings, when the light still lingers in the clear, greenish west, bears with him a handful of the tenderest and most delicate of all our flowers. Here are the hepatica, white, violet-blue or tenderest pink, plucked with the last year's rusted leaves; the adder-tongue, drawn cool out of the moist earth, with purple-spotted leaf blades and white, slender root stem, curling joyously back its yellow petals under the noonday sun; the little striped blossom of the frail spring beauty; the dicentia or squirrel corn, with its pink-stemmed wreaths of tremulous creamy drops, springing from the midst of an abundance of delicate and intricate leafage; most exquisite of all, the bloodroot's clear waxen bloom, set between its half-opened irregular grey leaves. He will have also perhaps a bud or two, just beginning to open, of the splendid white-winged trillium, or some of the blue cohosh, that mystic-looking plant with its strange and dusky but very beautiful blossoms. By the way, I should think that this last plant would be an inexhaustible treasure to the decorative artist. I know of no plant in bloom which has so peculiar and mysterious a hue and shape. When June comes we shall get the rare and beautiful lady's slippers out of the deep wet woods, and many another surprising blossom far hidden and seldom sought; but for the present let us be content with the brave little first-comers, the happy denizens of the less secluded wilderness. These, as with the race of poets, are indeed the fairest and freshest of all.

DUNCAN CAMPBELL SCOTT

My dear Alexis: I am glad you have written to me for advice; not that I like to give it, and not that I think it will be of any particular value to you when given, but it shows that I am still occasionally in your thoughts, and of all the pleasant things in the world the most pleasant is to be remembered by one's friends. I fancy that you have really decided the question for yourself; in fact I think you did so before you wrote to me. You ask me whether you should publish the poem entitled, 'After-thoughts,' which has just been accepted by the editor of the -------- *Magazine*, with a nom de plume or with the name given you by your godfather and godmother at your baptism. I answer emphatically, with the latter. I know you consider your name unfortunate, but, although it is sometimes the only grudge a man has against his parents, I think it the wisest provision in the world that our names are chosen for us while we are in a state of unconsciousness. Sometimes an unfortunate name will get into a family and go sliding down the generations like an hereditary disease, making life hideous. 'Peasley' is in itself an inoffensive name, but when the name 'Green' happens to be in the same family and one boy in each generation is called 'Green Peasley' it becomes a question whether the trouble should not be stopped by act of Parliament. Yet if we had the terrible responsibility of choosing our own names all our honest 'Johns' would be 'Algernons' and our 'Marys' would have I know not what sentimental cognomens hunted out of the romances. Your name may in some sort be a slight torture to you as you see it tacked below your poem, but any other that you select would grow to be quite unbearable to you, and you would long for that decent, useful name with which you endorse notes and furnish other unlimited kindnesses to your friends. Yes, put it down in full, 'Alexis Johnson Greenhill,' and if you are really a genius posterity will find something strangely poetical in it and 'Greenhill' will fill their ears with a distinctive pleasure, just as ours are filled by 'Keats' and 'Shelley.' My pleasure runs before the fact, and by anticipation I have a thrill from seeing it upon the chaste cover of that popular monthly.

ARCHIBALD LAMPMAN

Certainly the world of English letters – if any kind of journalism may be included in that term – has never seen a more singular or more noticeable figure than that of Mr W.T. Stead, formerly of the *Pall Mall Gazette*, now editor and inventor of *The Review of Reviews.* For some years past we have heard a great deal about Mr Stead and his indefatigable activities in many curious quarters. His character sketches in *The Review of Reviews* are a feature of strong interest to the readers of that useful journal; the judicious reader, however, finds himself always under the necessity of toning down the colours and making allowances for the sallies of a too roseate imagination, remembering – always remembering – that the writer is a journalist of the journalists, bent upon making his article entrancingly interesting and full of picturesque hits. These sketches are a thoroughly modern product, and their chief interest arises from the somewhat reportorial qualities which Mr Stead is able to give to them, owing to his extraordinarily wide and intimate personal acquaintance with both men and affairs. He appears to have chatted with everybody from Mr Gladstone down to the rudest striker on the street, and to have been mixed up in every political or social movement of the time. He gives the impression of an interesting and curious mixture of journalistic intelligence, quixotic enthusiasm, and amiable egotism – with just a slight touch of the charlatan; and in this age, brought up and developed in the atmosphere which has always surrounded him, a touch of the charlatan is perhaps scarcely avoidable.

21 May 1892

DUNCAN CAMPBELL SCOTT

Reading again that admirable 'Letter to a Young Gentleman Who Proposed to Embrace the Career of Art,' to which course I was impelled by the prominence given it in a late review of Mr Stevenson's collection of essays and papers, I found myself at variance with the plain cynicism which pervades it. No conclusions could be more sound, no advice more weighty than are contained in many of the lines of this 'letter.' But surely it is a whimsical comparison to liken the artist to the follower of a profession not in the code and to borrow, with an alteration of sex, a title applied in France to women who live by pleasure, calling the artist a 'Son of Joy.' This is unforgivable; the difference in quality of the pleasure should have made it impossible. If Mr Stevenson had followed out the natural development of his subject from the point when he announces that the artist 'works entirely upon honor,' where he bears such plain witness to the fact that in art the worker is subject to an imperative and austere law, he would hardly have landed in such a desert of cynicism. The whole 'letter' is written to a young man who has to decide deliberately upon a profession, and from this point of view the stress laid upon the material conditions may be just enough. Under the imposition of breadwinning the artist may be compelled to strain every nerve to please, but the result of such a desire alone will be disaster. With success the artist should have no haggling. If it comes it should come as an accident of his career; and equally so if it passes. He is compelled by his own spirit to create, and whether he pleases or no he must create. He must follow that inner, secret law of his personality which may lead him away further and further from the sympathy of his contemporaries or which may place him as their friend and benefactor; but with the fulfilment of which he has absolutely nothing to do. No matter what the result, his reward comes from within. It is this abandonment to the ideal which, as Mr Stevenson remarks, 'makes his life noble.' And this nobility, this elevation, which Mr Stevenson so loyally recognizes, should have secured for his craft a more fitting designation than 'Sons of Joy.'

WILFRED CAMPBELL

Some recent writers in certain Canadian journals, speaking of Canadian literature and the subscription book system, direct Canadian literary men to follow the example of Sara Jeannette Duncan and Grant Allen, and write books that will command a large sale abroad. These writers seem to forget that the most promising Canadian writers are poets, and that poetry is not in any age of the world a marketable article. Miss Duncan wrote a very clever book of the kind that has a ready sale, but such a book brings no enduring fame. Poetry of the class produced by

Will Carleton is a paying product, but the best order of verse is the least marketable. Longfellow, probably, in his day, the most popular of high-class poets, made but a pittance from the sale of his poems. This is an established fact to all critics who know anything about literature. But the above-mentioned would-be critics, who are so ready with their lordly advice to Canadian literary folk, should take a little of their own advice and show us how it is to be done. I have no doubt, from the self-confident and lordly tone of some of these critics, that the American periodical and journalistic world would be sensibly flattered at their acquisition. The only difficulty in the way is, should they so condescend, what, in the meantime, would become of Canadian literature? Would it not grow altogether irrepressible without these critical turkey cocks who hitherto have ruffled their august feathers, fanned their tails, and quelled the literary brood into self-contempt by the disdain of their thunders?

ARCHIBALD LAMPMAN

In an article entitled 'William' in the April number of *The Contemporary Review*, a writer, who does not give his name, handles the present German emperor in a manner extremely offensive to Mr Poultney Bigelow, who, in the May number of the same review, proceeds to paint the great Bismarck with the same kind of a brush. To anyone who has a heart for human destinies, the present European situation, charged as it is with forces which may explode at any moment in incalculable horror and ruin, cannot fail to be intensely interesting; and a good deal of this interest would in any case centre in the German Emperor, as the man upon whose shoulders the largest human responsibilities rest. This interest which naturally attaches to his position is very greatly increased in the case of Wilhelm II, who is certainly, if not a great, at least a very noticeable man. We have two very different pictures of this personage presented to us from time to time. The anonymous writer in *The Contemporary Review* paints us a man vain, restless, selfish, indifferent to the feelings of others, with a mania for notoriety and a hunger for perpetual activity – activity barren and purposeless, a kind of moral disease, at once uncomfortable, costly, and dangerous. Mr Bigelow, on the other hand, while enumerating the blunders and failures of the great Chancellor, the titanic old dragoon now sitting and growling at Friedrichsruhe, points us to the gallant, generous, popular young Emperor, who has already corrected half the follies and salved the bitter wounds which were largely the policy of the former tyrant. Mr Stead, that versatile and ingenious journalist, in a recent number of *The Review of Reviews*, institutes several curious comparisons. He finds Wilhelm II to be like Lord Randolph Churchill in his versatility, originality, and love of the unexpected; like the great Napoleon in his restless and devouring activity and his astonishing capacity for mastering details; and like General Gordon in his consciousness of a special mission from the Almighty, 'Our Ancient Ally,' as he calls him, addressing the Brandenburgers. At any rate Wilhelm, whatever his shortcomings may be, is a striking and picturesque figure, and to anyone who loves the study of human nature it will be exceedingly interesting to watch the development of his destinies.

WILFRED CAMPBELL

One of the great charms that nature possesses is her power to soothe. Running or wind-stirred waters always have a quieting influence on my nerves. No matter how tired and jaded I may be the sound of a running brook or the lapping of waves on a shore soon calms my pulses and gives me renewed vigour. My home is on the outskirts of the city on the banks of a beautiful river, and on a hot, dusty day it is like a cooling draught to escape from the jar and noise and hurry out to this quiet spot, where limpid waters and green of fields and woods soothe the eye and ear and renew the soul within.

Flowers and music have a similar effect. A dreamy sonata or a rhythmical waltz, when the melody is far and elusive, carries me out of myself to suggestions of leafy haunts and drowsy summer sounds, and is as effective a nerve tonic as I require.

A couple of years ago I was in New York City in the June heat as they have it there. The day was intensely sultry, the sun beat down, and the air was close. I was tired out with overpress of business and the jar and hurry of the city oppressed me with its confusing sounds. At last I got on to a 25th street horse car. The passengers, like myself, looked tired and worn with care and the close, stifling heat, when a man got on at one of the avenue crossings carrying a large bunch of lilac bloom that filled the car with its odour. That man seemed to me like a visitant from a kinder world. In an instant the car seemed as cool and restful as a country lane. The noisy streets, the roar of the overhead trains, the moving crowds became dim and distant and my mind was borne out to visions of quiet villages, peaceful hillside farms and dewy woods, [and] the singing birds, loving hearts, and running brooks seemed to possess my dreams. When I got off at 9th avenue I felt as rested and fresh as if I had come from a cool morning walk over the farm fields rather than from a hot journeying of crowded thoroughfares, and my heart revived with an exultation which was marvellous.

ARCHIBALD LAMPMAN

Literary activity in Canada does not increase very rapidly, but it does increase, and the growth is made manifest to us every now and then by the appearance of some new writer or some new journal. This month it is *Arcadia*, a bi-weekly journal of music, art, and literature, which comes to us from Montreal, and it seems to me that *Arcadia* makes a very good bid for the popular support in its appearance to begin with. The print, paper, and general aspect of its pages prepossess the eye. In its literary department I perceive a disposition to deal roughly, rather too roughly, with that sort of amiable gush and nonsense which is making literature in this country somewhat ridiculous. *Arcadia* evidently designs to be an anti-humbug paper. But in counteracting humbug it should beware of going too far in the opposite direction. Perhaps that will be its danger. It should avoid *The Saturday Review* kind of thing. Its article on Whitman was hardly just or appreciative. Surely this country is able by this time to support a good literary journal, and *Arcadia* strikes a new note and, in the main, a wholesome one.

28 May 1892

WILFRED CAMPBELL

A most delightful volume of verse is James Whitcomb Riley's *Old-Fashioned Roses*. In these days, when there is so much artificial verse-making, it is refreshing to come across such a collection of human- and nature-blossoms. Mr Riley has a quaintness and pathos all his own, and also an earnestness of spirit that makes his verse a part of his personality. He has a true insight into child life, and to him people and meadows and flowers and bees are all brethren, only of a different variety. The wind and the sun and the barefooted boys are his boon companions. The following lines we quote at random from the book:

The orchard lands of long ago!
O drowsy winds, awake, and blow
The snowy blossoms back to me,
And all the buds that used to be!
Blow back along the grassy ways
Of truant feet, and lift the haze
Of happy summer from the trees;
Blow back the melody that slips
In lazy laughter from the lips
That marvel much if any kiss
Is sweeter than the apple's is.

Or of the 'South Wind and the Sun.'

Arm in arm they went together
Over heights of morning haze –
Over slanting slopes of lawn.

This is an excellent poem all through, and so is 'The Beetle,' wherein he tells us how

O'er slumbrous blooms,
  On floods of musk,
The beetle booms a-down the glooms
  And bumps along the dusk.

Among the dialect pieces we miss 'The Absence of Little Wesley,' one of his most beautiful human touches, which appeared in *The Century*; but we greet with renewed pleasure 'Knee Deep in June' and 'Nothin' to Say,' and the popular 'Little Orphan Annie,' and 'The Frost on the Pumpkin.' In 'Knee Deep in June' Mr Riley's experience must be Canadian, when he sings in Hoosier style of the fraudulent character of the spring months:

March ain't never nothin' new!
Aprile's altogether too
Brash for me; and May – I jes'
'Bominate its promises;

But when June comes – clear my throat
With wild honey! Rench my hair
In the dew!
June wants me, and I'm to spare!
Spread them shadders anywhere,
I'll git down and waller there,
And obleeged to you at that.

Mr Riley has a true philosophy of life running like a brook all through his verses, a philosophy of the best and most durable kind, not found so much in books as in the morning sun and the summer fields, it is a wisdom of the toiling and suffering, yet joyous many. In one place he truly says:

I've allus noticed grate success
Is mixed with troubles more or less;
And it's the man who does the best
That gits more kicks than all the rest.

There is a quaint, good-humoured carelessness of fate running through this thought, that takes the bitter sting out of its only too evident truth. Among the sonnets, all fine, and some very beautiful, we would prefer the tender one called 'When She Comes Home.' America has produced many talented men and women, and not a few souls of real genius who have a revelation from nature and humanity, but, among her singers who have drunk at the pure springs, Mr Riley is one of the most sincere and natural. His voice is not for America alone; wherever the genius of the English language is felt, and his work is read, he will be acknowledged by the hearts and intellects of the few as well as the many to be a new and distinctive note in our literature.

DUNCAN CAMPBELL SCOTT

It has often been said that obscurity can go no further than it has done in the poems of George Meredith; that there is to be seen the perfect flower of the style which in attempting to express thought or emotion ends by hiding the intention as thoroughly as silence. This seems to be a hard saying, and I would not like to agree with it hastily, but there is excellent ground for the charge. It would be impossible for anyone to read *Modern Love* for the first time and understand it, or for the second time. But there is a possibility of understanding it, and I think it is well worth trying to compass. It is hard to speak this way of poetry, which should be of all things perfectly simple and straightforward; but in the case of *Modern Love* it is quite impossible to say anything else. At the outset Mr Meredith might be charged with having chosen an inartistic form for the physical drama which he had to present. The divisions of the poem are sometimes dramatic as if written by one of the characters, and sometimes critical as if written by an observer. This is misleading at first and results in intensifying the obscurity. When this is conquered or even partially so, one is apt to be carried away by an insight which is present in everything Mr Meredith writes and often by poetic beauty of a striking kind. There is development in the sequence of poems, and, although the steps are not always evident, and although the purpose of certain of the poems does not appeal with irresistible force, the story is told and told with remarkable fullness and power. In the short compass of eight hundred lines the emotions and thoughts of two people during a certain crisis in their lives are stated or hinted at. The gaps in the development and the strange phrases in the lines leave the greatest scope for ingenuity in interpretation, and it is a wonder that some admirer such as Mr Gallienni has not given us a running commentary on the poem. To enjoy it thoroughly one needs to have a subtle mind and acute perceptions. I have no room to quote many of the curious observations that are scattered through the poems, but here are a few:

O, have a care of natures that are mute!
They punish you in acts. Their steps are brief.
Imagination is the charioteer
That, in default of better, drives the hogs.

The forty-seventh section is a rarely lovely piece of work, charged with meaning and full of pathos, and the lines that close the fiftieth section will serve as an example of how felicitous Mr Meredith's expression may sometimes be:

In tragic hints here see what evermore
  Moves down as yonder midnight ocean's force
  Thundering like ramping hosts of warrior horse,
To throw that faint, thin line upon the shore.

'The Sage Enamoured and the Honest Lady' is less difficult, although it would probably prove quite as unattractive to a reader looking for a pastime. But, while these poems are not upon the surface attractive, they are capable of giving a rare pleasure, and are full of unique and profitable philosophy. As I said before, they are often beautiful, and, although they cannot be said to represent the greatness of Mr Meredith's genius which is supreme in his novels, yet they are not unworthy of it.

ARCHIBALD LAMPMAN

Now if any of our wealthy men wished to do their country a patriotic service, I do not think that they could find a better way of putting their wish into effect than by starting a magazine. A country only reaches full national consciousness when it has developed a literature. Our literature is yet to make, and the literary impulse in the present age, especially in America, appears to seek its first outlet in the magazine. It is very difficult for young Canadians to gain access to the great magazines of the United States. There are only four or five of them, and these can publish only a very limited quantity of matter each month. We may be sure that a nation of 65,000,000 will produce writers enough to supply this without any assistance from the neighbouring nation of 5,000,000. Such English literature as we already have in Canada shows an extraordinarily large proportion of verse. This is simply due to the fact that the literary impulse amongst us has not yet received any general stimulus. In any country where so wide literary activity exists, those few persons whom the imaginative impulse possesses so strongly that they must write will naturally write in verse. It seems to be the primitive germinal method of expression. When the intellect of a nation first becomes conscious of the beauty and mystery of the life around it, that consciousness has in it a religious quality which utters itself most fitly in poetry. This fact is not as discernible now as it was in ruder days, but it still holds good in a certain degree. The various forms of prose literature, fiction, criticism, etc., are an aftergrowth, appearing with the rapid propagation of the creative impulse. There can be no doubt that a great deal of talent for every kind of writing lies dormant in the youth of Canada simply for the want of some attractive and stimulating vehicle of publication. We can have no literature of any consequence where there is no interested public, no publishing facilities, no journals or magazines, to whose pages it is a matter of profit and pride to win admission. But when these are found we shall have plenty of literature, I believe the best on the continent.

However, many things will be changed by that time, and it is hard to predict what will happen. Much could be done now to draw out the naturally abundant talent of our people by the establishment and endowment of a great and attractive magazine. Swarms of writers would appear, and the intellectual ferment and competition aroused, together with the growth of an ever more searching process of criticism, would bring the best to the front and urge them to the attainment of an excellence which would otherwise be completely beyond their power. I know that our country is yet hardly out of its pioneer stage. It is necessarily engaged in money-getting and homebuilding as yet, and we cannot expect much attention to art or literature. These must come with a generation of money already got and houses already founded, a generation of people having time to read and riches wherewith to buy. Yet, I think we are approaching near to the turning point, to a season of awakening creative consciousness in which such an experiment as the establishing of a powerful magazine might perform for us the midwife's task and place us in possession of a new-born literature. A year or so ago half a dozen San Francisco millionaires subscribed $20,000 each and started a magazine called *The Californian.* It was established for the purpose of bringing out the literary talent of the Pacific coast, and those who have seen numbers of this publication will probably agree with me that it is not very much of a magazine after all. If half a dozen of our wealthy men would put together the same sum I believe we could soon place upon the market an infinitely better one.

ARCHIBALD LAMPMAN

Sleep

Behold! I lay in prison like St Paul,
　　Chained to two guards that both were grim and stout,
All day they sat by me and held me thrall;
　　The one was named Regret, the other Doubt.
And through the twilight of that hopeless close
　　There came an angel shining suddenly
That took me by the hand, and, as I rose,
　　The chains grew soft and slipped away from me.
The doors gave back and swung without a sound,
　　Like petals of some magic flower unfurled.
I followed, treading o'er enchanted ground,

Into another and a kindlier world.
The master of that black and bolted keep
Thou knowest is Life; the angel's name is Sleep.
(*Harper's Magazine*)

4 June 1892

DUNCAN CAMPBELL SCOTT

Put forth thy leaf, thou lofty plane,
East wind and frost are safely gone;
With zephyr mild and balmy rain
The summer comes serenely on;
Earth, air, and sun and skies combine
To promise all that's kind and fair:
But thou, O human heart of mine,
Be still, contain thyself, and bear.

December days were brief and chill,
The winds of March were wild and drear,
And, nearing and receding still,
Spring never would, we thought, be here.
The leaves that burst, the suns that shine,
Had, not the less, their certain date:
And thou, O human heart of mine,
Be still, refrain thyself, and wait.

I know of no more apt quotation for the present season than the poem of Arthur Hugh Clough printed above, 'Nearing and receding still, /Spring never would, we thought, be here.' This has been our condition for the last six weeks, enjoying one day of perfect weather and then three of the north wind and bleak rains. But our leaves and suns have had their certain date, and we are now in the possession of summer, having had no genuine spring. The poem is a beautiful example of Clough at his best, with his power of comforting the spirit and his lofty thought. Such poems are very rare, and this one is amongst the highest achievements of lyrical poetry, where both the form and the thought are noble and exalted, and the art is so concealed that the poem seems frigid in its freedom from rhetoric, its absolute plainness. But it succeeds absolutely, and its power of comforting and sustaining the spirit is very great. This is the final test of the highest poetry; it may not be picturesque or vivid with images, but it brings peace.

WILFRED CAMPBELL

The Association of American Authors just formed on the eighteenth of this month has for its leading officers Thomas Wentworth Higginson, president; Julia Ward Howe, first vice-president; Moncure D. Conway, second vice-president; Maurice Thompson, third vice-president, and the Board of Management will include W.D. Howells, and Charles Dudley Warner. All the leading writers of the country have enrolled as members, and the association promises to be a great success. The main object of the society is to co-operate with publishers in putting American literature on a better footing. Could not such an association be formed in Canada? We have many writers, and we have no association to bring them together, or develop and encourage our literary spirit. The fact that we could not organize on such a large and successful basis as our friends across the line should not discourage us. No class of literary workers in the world today needs so much encouragement as do the Canadians. We have an uphill fight against a narrow spirit of local contempt at the hands of the very class that could help us if it desired to. Therefore Canadian writers would do well to band together on a practical basis of a common fellow feeling. And such an association, if at all feasible, might be of great benefit as a stimulus to the whole country. The artists have their gatherings, and why should not the literary folk do likewise?

ARCHIBALD LAMPMAN

My friend the sonneteer has been at it again. He knows in what abhorrence I hold those persons – so exasperatingly numerous in our time – who profane and misapply the sonnet, and he takes a sort of inhuman delight in torturing me with sonnets of his own composition on all sorts of flippant and improper subjects. He came into my room the other day with two papers in his hand. I knew at once what that peculiar grin of malevolent satisfaction meant. 'I am going to treat you to a couple of sonnets,' he said. 'I am sure they will give you pleasure,' and drawing a chair to the table he carefully spread out the first of the papers before him and began to read as follows:

4 June 1892

Falling Asleep

Slowly my thoughts lost hold on consciousness
Like waves that urge but cannot reach the shore.
Once and again I wakened, and once more
The wind sighed in, and with a lingering stress
Brushed the loose blinds. Out of some far recess
There came a groping as of steps; a door
Creaked; mice are scuffling underneath the floor.
And then, when all the house stood motionless,
Something dropped sharply overhead. A deep,
Dead silence followed. Only half aware
I sat and strove to waken, and fell flat.
A moment after, step by step, a cat
Came plumping softly down the attic stair;
And then I turned, and then I fell asleep.

'Well,' I said, 'that doesn't seem to be so bad – in a certain sense, from a certain point of view – rather true to life, quite picturesque in fact – but could you not have arranged to cast your impression in some more suitable form a little less ridiculously inapplicable to the smallness and homeliness of your subject?' 'No I couldn't,' answered my friend, fixing me with a defiant glare. 'The best way to impress your subject on the reader is to cast it in a totally unsuitable form. It's the contrast that does it, you know,' and he took up the other paper, and read the following utterly atrocious and impudent production:

Reality

I stand at noon upon the heated flags
At the bleached crossing of two streets, and dream,
With brain scarce conscious, now the hurrying stream
Of noonday passengers is done. Two hags
Stand at an open doorway piled with bags
And jabber hideously. Just at their feet
A small, half-naked child screams in the street.
A blind man yonder, a mere hunch of rags,
Keeps the scant shadow of the eaves, and scowls,
Counting his coppers. Through the open glare
Thunders an empty waggon, from whose trail
A lean dog shoots into the startled square,

Wildly revolves and soothes his hapless tail,
Piercing the noon with intermittent howls.

'Certainly you have outdone yourself this time,' I cried. 'You have violated every law of moral dignity and literary decency. I prefer not to hear any more of your so-called sonnets.' My friend instead of answering me broke out into a roar of coarse and offensive laughter. He crushed up his papers into a couple of pellets, and, filliping them into my face, strode rudely out of the room. The poor fellow has talent if he would only apply it in a serious and sensible way.

WILFRED CAMPBELL

A story of most exquisite touch is Barrie's *Little Minister.* There is a genuine realism running through much of the tale, and yet when you have laid the book down it is with the impression that Blackmore might have written just such a romance had his environment been a Highland Scotch instead of an English one. There is a marked resemblance in the work of the two writers, which is especially shown in the character of the heroine, who is the most unreal, and yet the most fascinating character in the book. Her strange elfin beauty, the mystery surrounding her, her marvellous escapades, which end all right, and, above all, her coming with a suggestiveness of aristocratic influences and looser social culture into the narrow environment of a small village, with its deep-rooted religious and other prejudices, at once suggest a similar manner of working in Blackmore. The realism of the book is to be found in many characteristics of the little minister and his struggle to be true to his people and his old connections, with the realistic background of the people themselves, who by their very worship of his character and position threatened to come in the way of his happiness. Mr Barrie uses a heroic action which is too melodramatic to be real on the part of the minister to overcome their prejudices, and so makes the story end happily. Of course this is as it should be in story books, and it is this that makes *The Little Minister* more of a romance than a realistic picture. But we cannot help feeling that if the drunken hero, who is the scapegoat as it is, should have been allowed to have killed the girl or have frightened her to death as he nearly did, and which we fully expected to be the dénouement, that Mr Barrie's story, while certainly painful, would have been more in keeping with the irony of fate. He just failed of making *The Little Minister* a picture of sad and pathetic beauty. As it is, the story is a strange mixture of quaint realism, and daring and fascinating romance.

DUNCAN CAMPBELL SCOTT

The sequel to *Kidnapped*, which Mr Stevenson is now writing, will likely appear before the close of 1892. It will be called *David Balfour.* Mr Stevenson is also writing a *History of Samoa*, which he is sure to make interesting. Leaving the question of history aside, there will be room for picturesque writing. The chapter describing the hurricane of March 1889 has already appeared in *The National Observer.*

11 June 1892

WILFRED CAMPBELL

There are two kinds of poetry that may develop in a country, one born of the soil, and yet dependent on universal sympathy for its audience; the other largely of local growth, and the result of the various vicissitudes of national development. They may both be great in their way, but the latter is the most certain to acquire a quick sympathy. It is patriotic, cast in a large and heroic mould, and a necessary part of the pulse-beat of the day. Such a school was the great New England one of the era prior to and following the civil war. It was human and popular, and the writers were necessarily strong men, with large human instincts and enthusiasms. But it might be said that the time made them as much as they helped to make the time, and that much of their largeness of mould and high ethical vision was due to the high pitch of the national spirit at the time they wrote. Then again, their work contained much sentiment that was merely local and passing, but of no effect now when the community is not pitched to appreciate it. They had a note that was impossible in a less heroic day, but it carried them beyond the natural which endures, and so rendered their work necessarily ephemeral. Much of the work of Whittier, Longfellow, and Lowell is of this class, and, as literature of immediate interest, perished with the passing of the time and events that gave it being. When we go back to the works of these poets to find poems of enduring beauty on subjects that might be treated about, and have been treated about, in all ages of our literature, we find that what they have left is small indeed. If we look for complete poems that will rank with the old English masterpieces we have to be chary in our choice. Longfellow has many tender and heroic tales in verse, and his [*Song of*] *Hiawatha*, while not original in construction, is almost an epic, but it has not that haunting beauty of expression to be found in the best work of many of the great poets. It is diffuse and full of mannerisms, and grows tiresome after much repeating. The opening and closing lines of *Evangeline* are fine, but the poem as a whole also is diffuse, and lacks solidity even in the nature descriptions, for which there was great scope given. It is a decided failure as a great poem, if not as a story, and much of the charm lies in the pathos of the incident embodied. Many of his shorter pieces are by far his best. A noted reader for a famous New England publishing house told me that he always considered Longfellow did his best work in *Voices of the Night*, his first small published volume, and I think he was right, though for pure beauty and simplicity, in my opinion, 'The Wreck of the Hesperus' is his finest bit of work. This poem, while not by any means his most ambitious attempt, is such as a poet might accomplish in any age, even of less heroic pitch than that in which he wrote. To Whittier and Lowell this test is even more applicable than to Longfellow. Freedom was the great inspiration that gave the keynote to both, and yet poems like 'Snowbound,' 'In School Days,' and 'Maud Muller' are the gems that one leaves to posterity, while the other will endure in such poems of deep insight as 'Extreme Unction,' and nature descriptions as found in 'The Dandelion,' and in 'Indian Summer.' The former class of verse, which I mentioned at the beginning of this article, is that produced in an unheroic age, such as ours is today in Canada, when the ethical pulse is even below the normal, certainly not above it, and when to be a true poet one must be a born singer, without the aid of any unusually strenuous environment to inspire the song. This class of singers run no great chance of being overrated in their generation. They may leave no lofty epics or funeral paens to mark the historical eras, but their note, if true, is liable to be deep and lasting. They are interpreters rather than chroniclers, and their message from humanity or nature, or from both, if they are great enough, is sincere and direct. There is a shallow idea that the length of a poem is the test of a poet's greatness. But, on the contrary, most of the greater poets have written at the most half a dozen poems, and most of them less than a hundred lines, that have given them their claims to immortality. The greatest epics in all languages are but, as someone said of Milton's *Paradise Lost*, rare oases of beauty in a desert of verbiage. Like in all other cults, there is no end of writing and of the making of books, and happy is the man who has produced one poem that can be classed with those of even a century's endurance.

DUNCAN CAMPBELL SCOTT

I have been once more looking over a book which a friend had sent me from Scotland, and which in all respects is one of the most curious I ever opened. It is not entertaining and is quite unintelligible, but very often it is unconsciously humorous, and sometimes it is touching. In fact, I am not sure whether it is not always more touching than anything else, and whether the whole contents of the book do not twitch one's heartstrings, and make one feel guilty of having laughed when the sentence has proved irresistible. But perhaps my impressions are influenced by the history of its production, which is certainly sad enough. It was written by an old man in one of the towns of Scotland, who makes his living by teaching when he can get anyone to teach. He lives high up in one of the tallest buildings in the place, a situation from which he can see the four quarters of the heavens. Here he stays all the year round, for he is a cripple and deformed, surrounded with heaps of old books and pamphlets, and abandoned to great thoughts and lofty ideas. Passionately fond of music, he solaces himself with a small barrel organ, which plays selections from the great masters, and when he is weary with study he is borne through the domain of faery as he turns the crank of this wonder-box. The knowledge of these facts is what has made his little book seem to me sad, for although he seems to have had the desire for expression very highly developed very few have had less of the faculty.

> And little ones a-gathering lilies will hear flutter o' angel wing.
> And that will be religion for every star.
> And, surely, they will not die for knowing not, anent
> The pig iron and antimony in Aldebaran,
> Will they now?

He coins words or transfers them bodily from forgotten languages, and mixes the whole mass of his ideas with them.

> Blastoderne, that's to evolve its neurosis and psychosis,
> Lies asleep in atom venerable

Awaiting psychogenetic avatar!
But, the while, shall poet be stayed
From dragging matter by the heels behind
Chariot triumphant of thought?

He has a perfect faith in the 'plan of things': 'yea, blasphemy of belladonna is redeemed with euphemy o' lemontine.' The absoluteness of mind is ever his theme. Listen to him:

Your microbe now will only need a day
To make fifteen millions, and kill a king,
While smile o' lily sleeps in her swathe o' green.
Matter is septic, mind antiseptic;
Reason staggers at thought o' dead mind.

Here the materialist has no chance whatever. The crippled Scotch tutor, almost starving in his garret, has perfect faith in the triumph of the soul, and although he cannot express his thought in any but the most uncouth terms, still it is to him a living spring of pure and crystal inspiration, making green the desert of the earth. I can imagine him reading these things to himself as he holds his book close to the sunset pane to save candles, with the tears in his eyes as he sees all the beauty and nobleness of his ideas transfigured by the light of his mind, as those clouds far over the sea are crimsoned by the light of the sun. And not in vain are your tears, not in vain your lofty ideals and your pure faith. Somehow in the development of nature, through no fault of your own, your proud and inquisitive soul became possessed of your twisted and wracked body, and amid circumstances that seem fit for such a deformity you live alone in poverty, often beaten by anguish, but never overcome, often pinched by hunger, but never discontented. But it will not always be so. You who have succeeded amidst such discouragements in keeping alive a perfect trust will take the next step in your destiny with your soul well knit. 'Tis but a little shift and you will have done with this world; you will have taken the irremediable path and journeyed beyond your hall. But it will be well with you; you will have forgotten the sordidness of this planet, and your contemporaries in immortality will wonder at the largeness of your accent, the sweep of your vision.

18 June 1892

ARCHIBALD LAMPMAN

The happiest man is he who has cultivated to the utmost the sense of beauty. The man who is able at all times to find perfect and prolonged satisfaction in the contemplation of a tree, a field, a flower, or a 'spear of grass,' can never be bored save by his fellow creatures. For him life is full of variety; every moment comes to him laden with some unique enjoyment, every hour is crowded with a multitude of fleeting but exquisite impressions. If health and a reasonable destiny attend him he cannot be otherwise than happy; pessimism for him is impossible. The beautiful is everywhere about us. As a matter of fact, there is nothing fashioned by nature herself that is not beautiful, either in itself or in its relation to its surroundings. You do not need to go to the Rocky Mountains or the Yosemite Valley in order to find the beautiful; it is in the next field; it is at your feet. Wherever there is earth and any live or growing thing not perverted by the hand of man, there is a study in beauty that one cannot exhaust. The capacity for the enjoyment of natural beauty is rare in its perfection. He whose first impulse on projecting an excursion into the country is to carry with him a gun or fishing rod has certainly not attained it. To the real lover of nature the gun and the fishing rod are an encumbrance. Even the scientist – great as is the enjoyment to be derived from the mere acquisition of knowledge – does not experience the illimitable delight that falls to the lot of the pure loafer who has accustomed his eye to the perception of every beauty. To such a man as John Burroughs or Bradford Torrey life cannot offer any greater good than they have; and this serene source of satisfaction is in a greater or less degree within the reach of every man, if he will but accustom himself to the intelligent use of his senses.

WILFRED CAMPBELL

The other day I read in one of our papers that many leading western miners are at present visiting the Canadian gold mines at Marmora, attracted by the successful working of the Crawford gold separator, which has rendered these hitherto unworkable mines payable concerns, and that Mr Erastus Wiman controls the North American working of this machine. Now, I happen to know the particulars of Mr Crawford's career, having been brought up in the same vicinity. It is not many years ago that Mr Crawford was a poor boy on a small farm on the shores of Colpoy's Bay, an inlet of Georgian Bay. Without any more learning than the common education of a country school, and not too much of that, he had to depend altogether upon his remarkable native genius, which struggled with all odds and through many viscissitudes and reverses. As a boy he was a born inventor, and early turned his attention to solving the problem of perpetual motion, as many a genius has done before him. His first practical effort was the invention of a flour-bolter, which was a decided success and attracted some attention, but for some reason was a financial failure. But Mr Crawford was not to be daunted. He next turned his attention to a cotton seed separator, for which he got $50,000 for the American right alone. Then he tried his genius at a long-sought-for but vainly desired machine, one that would decrease the price of separating gold ore so as to make many mines workable that otherwise would be valueless. I am not well enough informed on the subject to state the exact revolution Mr Crawford has worked by his wonderful invention, but sufficient to state that he has rendered many mines, all over the world, rich in resources hard to be got at comparatively easy to work. He owns more patents in different countries of the world than any other man. He has enriched himself, but has done it by his own genius, which has been of the greatest benefit to others. I understand that a great company of Englishmen and Americans have the sole control of Mr Crawford's wonderful invention and are engaged in reopening all the mines in many countries that so far have proved valueless.

DUNCAN CAMPBELL SCOTT

Death and the Young Girl

Within the chamber where the young girl lay,
The early light lapsed through the unconscious air,
No sound of all the sounds of life was there,
Only the quiet of death. The breaking day
Brought back the familiar forms in softer grey;
The covered table, and the plain, worn chair;
The low-draped couch before the window, where
The mute blue gentian drooped and pined away.

So still – it seemed as if kind death had said:
Before they find you, for a little while

Have rest, here where no rest might be;
Have comfort for pained hands and weary head.
Look up, beloved, see the angels smile!
See the fair threshold of eternity.

ARCHIBALD LAMPMAN

The literature of the day in America, as far as fiction, poetry, and criticism are concerned, is concentrated in the magazines. These publications are attracting to them most of our literary and artistic effort. All classes of literary people complain that it is only writing for the magazines that pays. The magazines, therefore, must be exercising a very strong formative influence on contemporary American literature. This influence, I think, we see in the growing disposition of American writers to confine themselves to brief efforts, short stories, short poems, and the like, and to aim at artistic perfection rather than free, spontaneous expression. The influence of the magazine in this and some other respects is, I think, decidedly harmful. They are avowedly published for the benefit of the average educated reader and the average educated reader does not desire anything very original, unless, indeed, it has the good fortune to retouch in a peculiar way some common chord of feeling. The magazines therefore do not look for original work, but for work of a high order of excellence in veins which editors understand to be popular with the mass of the better reading public. The man, then, who undertakes to supply the magazines must begin by sacrificing originality, and he must cultivate a certain sort of thing. That sort of thing he will soon learn by reading the magazines. For a nation of 65,000,000 the number of really original writers in the United States is extraordinarily small, and, though this result is owing to various causes, it seems to me that the magazines have a good deal to do with it. The man who desires to develop an original literary gift had better beware of writing 'for' the magazines. Let him sell his work to the magazines after he has written it, if he can; but let him never set to work beforehand with the purpose of writing something for a magazine. If he once make a custom of doing that he is done for.

25 June 1892

ARCHIBALD LAMPMAN

It is not the brilliancy, the versatility, the fecundity, or the ingenuity of a poet that makes him 'great'; it is the plane upon which his imagination moves, the height from which he looks down, the magnitude of his ideas. This largeness of vision is often accompanied by extreme simplicity in the literary faculty, and it is on this account mainly that the really great poet is often partly obscured from public recognition by the greater brilliancy and fertility of some of his contemporaries. We are too apt to measure the greatness of a writer by the degree to which he astonishes us or interests us, rather than by the actual spiritual benefit and enlargement of ideas which he confers. There was a time when Dryden was considered a greater poet than Milton. Dryden was a writer of great intellectual power, great literary activity, and an admirable range of accomplishment; but we know now that that obscure old man, who did not write so very much in all his life, and who but for his obscurity and his blindness might never have written our grand epic at all, was so far greater than the renowned Dryden by the grandeur and breadth of his imagination that the latter sinks altogether into a lower rank in the record of literature. So, too, in more recent times. Lord Byron, with his dash and daring and his immense cleverness and gift of verse, overclouded all the reputations of his age, but I think that we are now nearly all of us agreed that three at least of his contemporaries dwell upon an intellectual level far loftier and purer than his, and were, therefore, essentially greater poets than he.

In our own time I think we allow ourselves to be a little too much dazzled by the supreme literary gift and magnificent versification of Tennyson, and the insight, vigour, and extraordinary versatility of Browning. We are apt almost to pass by a poet who in this last age occupies the clearest and noblest plane of all. I mean Matthew Arnold. Arnold is not so triumphantly the poet as Tennyson, nor is he so various or so clever as Browning, but he looks from a grander height than either, his imagination has its natural abode in a diviner atmosphere. The whole range of life, time, and eternity, the mysteries and beauties of existence and its deepest spiritual problems are continually present to his mind. In his genius is that rare combination of philosophy and the poetic impulse in the highest degree, which has given us our few solitary poets. The only test by which we can measure the greatness of a verse writer is the quality of the effect which he produces upon the mind of the reader. He who has been reading Browning till his head spins with the multitude of subtleties and splendid tours de force, or he who is even weary, if such a thing may be, of the rounded perfections of Tennyson, betakes himself to Matthew Arnold, and then he seems to have reached the hills. With a mind blown clear as by the free wind of heaven he surveys the extent of life. He passes through an atmosphere where only the noblest emotions, life, beauty, and thought, possess him. He becomes gentle and majestic as the mind of the master who commands him.

I believe that the time will come when Matthew Arnold will be accounted the greatest poet of his generation, and one of the three or four noblest that England has produced.

DUNCAN CAMPBELL SCOTT

Now that the artists are making preparations for an exhibition at Chicago in 1893, the thought naturally arises that in some way the literary men should be represented also. Here the latter are distinctly at a disadvantage. If in Canada we had a large native literature to draw upon, our books might be placed on sale during the time of the exhibition; but this is not the case, and even if it were so it might not have the desired effect. It has occurred to me that one of our enterprising publishers should arrange with some person of known taste and judgment to collect a representative mass of Canadian literature, and publish it as a Canadian memorial volume. This could be placed on sale in the proper section of the exhibition, and I have no doubt but that the publisher would be substantially rewarded for his trouble and outlay. The volume need not be a large one, two hundred pages would cover the ground, and this space would compass a collection in which Canada could feel a genuine pride.

[ANONYMOUS]

I have always believed that nature poetry was not limited to mere description of external nature, but that it extended to all natural phenomena, and that the really great nature poet would desire to get back to primeval man when he was closely united with nature, and scarcely beginning to dream of conquering her elements. Among the great elements of nature that have had a strong fascination for me is the element of fire. It seems to me that of all the elements it is by far the most remarkable and the nearest to man in its personality, if it could be said to have a personality. How man first became aware of its use, and the gradual stages through which he came to have it in such wide use, and yet in such comparatively supreme subjection, has always been a matter of deep interest to me. Fire has appeared to me to be a strange demon, whose very nature is essentially cruel, and yet perfectly natural and necessary to the existence of the universe. The following is an attempt to personify fire in its relationship to man:

Fire

In the night I sit beside you,
Dream the dreams that glow inside you,
As you sparkle ever higher;
While your flame-whip goads and lashes
The red back logs into ashes
On their rackling, hissing pyre.
Clinging, kissing, like a leman,
Writhing, twisting, like a demon;
How I love and dread you, Fire!
What a strange, uncanny spirit
From some far past you inherit,
Some weird, unappeased desire
Like some unavenged devil,
Leaping, lurid, red in evil,
That the ages cannot tire;
Clinging, kissing, like a leman,
Writhing, twisting, like a demon,
Strange, weird, red, unholy Fire!

How and whence was thy beginning?
From what liberty of sinning?
From what genie's licensed hire?
From what dread power that possessed you
Did the men of earth first wrest you,
Causing unavenged ire?
From what liberty of sinning?
From what weird and strange beginning
Wrested, chained, and bound thee, Fire?

25 June 1892

There within their iron prison
Did they hold you, shrunk and wisen,
Coiled your red tongue like a wire;
Curbed in iron teeth your malice,
Till as in the golden chalice
Leaps the wine in ruddy spire;
So with glowing madness gleaming,
From your trance of evil dreaming,
Leaped you forth in hatred, Fire.

Leaped you forth an evil gladness
Shining through your demon madness,
Lusts that rudest hates inspire;
Growing, growing, ever younger,
With an unappeased hunger,
With an appetite so dire,
Went you forth, a thing of horror,
Desolater, hell-restorer,
Scourging earth and heaven, Fire!

Imp-like, laughing, far-sky-shining,
Like ten million serpents twining,
Ruddy, ray-like, ever higher;
Imp-like, climbing, ever-building
Over earth one flame-house, gilding
Land and heaven with red desire.
Cities fell in lurid thunder,
Souls that lived were mute with wonder,
Earth and man were conquered, Fire.

All wide earth was one red clamor,
Moan of bell and stroke of hammer,
Shriek of souls ere they expire;
Glare of town and forest flaming,
Sights of horror past tongue's naming,
Even death would not require;
Till at last men starved and bound thee,
Built an iron cage around thee,
Sleepy, snake-like, once more, Fire.

And they think they hold thee prisoned,
But whene'er I see thy wisened
Look of serpent-like desire,
Then I know that thou art dreaming
Over in a sleepy seeming
All the madness of thine ire;
Then I know that thou art longing,
With a hate to hell belonging,
For thy freedom, Demon-Fire.

Yet I love to sit beside you,
Dream the dreams that glow inside you
As you leap up ever higher,
While your flame-whip goads and lashes,
The red back logs into ashes
On their crackling, hissing pyre;
Clinging, kissing, like a leman,
Writhing, twisting, like a demon,
Strange, weird, red, unholy Fire.

DUNCAN CAMPBELL SCOTT

A critic should have the most amiable disposition of his time; he should possess the gentler qualities of humanity developed more sweetly and evenly than his contemporaries. With a breadth of sympathy and keenness of vision that will embrace the horizon and notice an irregularity in the petals of a flower, he should have a taste less individual and more catholic than any one of his readers. He should be able to mingle praise and blame in such exact proportions that the true value of the work which he criticizes will at once become apparent. As Lauder says: 'It is only thus a fair estimate can be made, and it is only by such fair estimate that a writer can be exalted to his proper station. If you toss the scale too high it descends again rapidly below its equipoise; what it contains drops out, and people catch at it, scatter it and lose it.' If he is the owner of some crotchet which he endeavours to force upon the notice of the world, and which he cries, using the shoulders of the man nearest him to perch upon, the world finds out speedily that his own limits do not give him the elevation, and that his voice has no authority. If he is violent and sounds a rattle when anything dangerous or formidable approaches, he may for a time have the credit of being a faithful watchman over the moral treasure chest of society, but the next generation usually finds that he was keeping it from its inheritance. The effect of violence in criticism is to discredit a man's utterance. We do not allow a lunatic to claim inspiration by reason of the foam on his lips.

The watchword of the critic should be 'Freedom of Mind.' As Amiel says: 'The reward of the critic is to feel himself freer than his neighbour,' and although this implies a knowledge of his superiority to his surroundings, this knowledge brings with it no triumph. The reward is esoteric, and is the mere consciousness of truth within. It has no note of personal victory, the desire for which is after all the most dangerous passion in the human bosom.

2 July 1892

WILFRED CAMPBELL

It may be an easy thing to look back over the long range of our poetical literature and pick out a favourite here and there, but when it comes to a decision as to supreme greatness there ensues a wide difference of opinion. From Chaucer and Spenser down to Browning, Tennyson, Arnold, and Swinburne stretch a great host of names that stand for work that will not easily perish. Though not deemed great in his own age, Shakespeare, in this age, is by common consent acknowledged to be the king of English poets, the one supreme mind whose genius has glorified the language to which it belongs. If this general opinion concerning Shakespeare be true, might it not be well to ask ourselves what are the special qualities that lift him to this supreme place in literature? The common answer would be that it is his great dramatic power that makes him supremely great. But we might again ask, in what does this dramatic power consist? And the answer to this question would be that it is made up of many qualities, each of which would endow a lesser genius. In other words he must have contained in himself all the essential qualities that go to make a great poet, such as unparalleled insight into human life, both as regards his own time and also in past history, so as to render human any history he touched. Then he must have had a remarkable fecundity to have produced all he did, and his range is so wide as to embrace all types of humanity met with in any age. In all of these lie his supreme greatness, not to speak of a wonderful gift of expression. Many poets have a deep insight into nature or into a certain type or class of humanity, but in Shakespeare we find a universality, if I might use such a word, that is found in no other writer. When we try to apply this test to the other great English poets the decision as to supreme greatness becomes difficult. All genius, whether it be that of a Wordsworth or a Byron, calls for our homage, and to deny the one or the other does not harm the greatness we ignore; we but clip the wings of our own humanity to that extent. I would dare to say that for genuine greatness as a poet Coleridge comes next to Shakespeare in the language but there would be many who would prefer some other singer. There are those who elevate Wordsworth to this position, but to do so would be to revolutionize all literature and to strip poetry of her lyrical and dramatical qualities and make mere philosophy usurp the divinity of song. In short it were to strip Shakespeare himself of his supreme greatness. The great glory of poetry in all ages is not mere thought; it is creation which leads to inspiration. In this Homer will always be greater than Plato and Shakespeare than Bacon. A man may be a great thinker and not be a great poet. Philosophy is worked out, song is inspired. Philosophy deals with problems, song with ideals. Philosophy deals with history, song with men; and where the one agonizes to seek for what it calls the truth the other contents itself with the beauty that is ever present and always enjoys what the other ever desires in vain. Philosophy lays bare where poetry clothes; and herein is where poetry is in the highest sense spiritual. A man may clothe in delicate language some philosophical thought and yet not be a great poet. The poet is first and last a creator. He does not need to moralize; his creation speaks for itself. The greatest English poets have been in their highest moments of this order. A certain class of poets, such as Matthew Arnold and Emerson, have, with a philosophical tendency, idealized history, they have attempted to poetize the philosophy of history, but great as they are as thinkers they have failed as poets in the highest sense. They recognize man as a unit in history, but knew nothing of him as a living soul; at least not in the dramatic sense, as Shakespeare did.

ARCHIBALD LAMPMAN

There is nothing more exasperating to the free lover of this earth than the spectacle of a placard stuck up in front of a plain pasture field or bit of inviting woodland, bearing some such legend as this: 'No trespassing on this property!' Now, to the scientist, the artist, and the poet, this earth belongs to no man in particular; everything that he treads upon is his for the moment, and wherever the ground is not encumbered with the actual flesh and impedimenta of the owner he proposes to go at will. To the owner of forest and field, I would say that if he find any poor soul illegally using his property for an hour of innocent research or quiet reflection, and be moved to institute against him the rigours of the law, let him first ascertain what manner of man the offender is, and if he belong to any of the classes mentioned above, let him be careful to leave him alone, for it may chance that he has made more out of that land for the benefit of mankind than the owner or all his descendants will ever do. Moreover, if he is of the true stock he is incorrigible, anyway, and will go where he will no matter what you do.

ARCHIBALD LAMPMAN

Now is the season of the splendour of the fields. The gardens are heavy with the breath of the syringa and the meadows with the perfume of clover. Everywhere the hayfields are floated over with the stars of marguerite and buttercup; we find the bladder-campion and blue-eyed grass in the meadows, and in the deep pine woods the twin flowers intense with perfume and the fair little honey-scented sanilacina. Now it is that in the long afternoons we dream of some place of wind and flowers.

Full of sweet trees and colour of glad grass, and find it if we can, for we know now with the fullest intensity of sympathy that we are of one birth with everything about us, brethren to the trees and kin to the very grass that now, even at noon in the shadowy places, flings the dew about our feet.

DUNCAN CAMPBELL SCOTT

The reviewers of Mr Rudyard Kipling's *Ballads and Barrack-Room Ballads* [sic] have made mention of their astonishing force and freedom, but I have nowhere discovered the statement that they are pleasant reading. I think I have a genuine appreciation for Mr Kipling's best work, whether in prose or verse, but the failing of both are similar, and for my own part I could have wished them different. Mr Kipling is a genius, and one of a very positive quality. It is impossible to mistake his distinctive touch; after having read one of his tales the virile and incisive power and the direct forethought stroke are recognizable in everything he writes. But with all this genius there is mixed a coarseness like the coarseness of a man who despises nature, something sceptical and rude and sinister, something vulgar, born of the unlicensed passions. The glory in the description of what is merely effete in society may have arisen from the surroundings of his early life, but the note is too constant to be passed over in silence. The power with which he describes human suffering and human bloodshed and the ease with which he addresses himself to the task are equally remarkable. In half a dozen of his best tales and in a very few of his ballads these qualities are entirely absent, but when it comes to a question of deciding upon the main mass of his work these characteristics are too strong to be glossed over. And the final question with reference to Mr Kipling's work, as well as every other man's, is, does it give pleasure? This question everyone will answer for himself, and I must say that the qualities which I have mentioned above as almost ever present are to me intensely disturbing and disagreeable. There is hardly a ballad in this new book which has not some violent barbarity of expression, some rude thrust that unsettles the mind. It is no palliation to say that the strokes are forcible and often tragically powerful; it is no consolation to a man who has been thrashed to think that the beating was well and deftly done. It is too unnerving to meet in a ballad which, although admittedly free, does not always sink to the level of my quotation, that a certain warrior behaved in this fashion:

> He crucified noble, he sacrificed mean,
> He filled old ladies with kerosene.

It is, I say, unnerving to meet with such things, for they are neither humorous nor powerful, and they rather degrade than otherwise. I might multiply examples, but another will be sufficient:

> I had nailed his ears to my capstan-head, and ripped them off with a saw,
> And soused them in the bilgewater, and served them to him raw;
> I had stripped his hide for my hammock-side, and tasselled his beard i' the mesh,
> And spitted his crew on the live bamboo that grows through the gangrened flesh.

It is useless to ask whether this is fitting in its place; the question is, is it pleasant reading? Certain of the barrack-room ballads have a humorous quality, notably the one 'Tommy,' and, in common with their companions, they have a swing and a bounding rhythm that is as free and forcible as the wind. I can only regret, for my own part, that the wind which bears Mr Kipling's message had not passed over more fragrant hollows and hills and had come less often laden with the scent of blood and fire.

ARCHIBALD LAMPMAN

It is a noticeable fact that the greatest poets, those few who are eminent above all others for dignity and majesty of tone, have been men of affairs before they were poets, and that those men who have been poets only have belonged, however illustrious, to the second class. Aeschylus was a soldier and an active patriot before he was a poet. The speech that came naturally to his tongue was not the mere utterance of the brilliant playwright. Active participation in great national efforts and the experience of battle and victory were necessary to awaken and confirm in the poet of Agamemnon that mood and note of rugged, sustained sublimity. The mind of Dante, trained in the great cares of statecraft, studying and experiencing the vicissitudes of an active and dangerous time, became capable of the *Divina Commedia.* Our own Milton could never have written *Paradise Lost* had he not first been the friend and assistant of Cromwell and concerned in the mighty cares and the proud cause of the Commonwealth. The mood of soul that he learned in those full years of thought and labour and intense experience is the mood of *Paradise Lost* – grand, ingenuous, austere. If the youth of Byron could have been bred in the hardening atmosphere of great affairs instead of being given over to foppery and dissipation, if the Greek revolution had called him earlier, or if he had lived longer and passed through periods of strenuous deeds and important purposes, he might have given to England a poet more splendidly fruitful, if not so mighty of tongue as Milton.

9 July 1892

DUNCAN CAMPBELL SCOTT

I read in *Arcadia* the other day that Thomas Cooper the Chartist, as he loved to call himself, had been granted a pension by the English government. I read this with unmixed gratification. Thomas Cooper is usually referred to as the author of the 'Purgatory of Suicides,' but this poem will hardly give him the fame he deserves. It was the life he lived, a life full of fightings, imprisonment, and trouble of all kinds that is his real claim to remembrance, and his most interesting book is his own account of his life: *The Life of Thomas Cooper, Written by Himself.* It is a thoroughly entertaining book, written in a simple style full of energy. Anyone might profitably spend the few hours required to read it in following the struggles of this intrepid old man, who would never give in if he thought he was right, no matter what hardship he had to undergo in consequence. He was at one time of his life an enthusiastic musician, and before the 'Chartist' times he spent his energies in organizing the choral societies in Lincoln, England. But his zeal raised up enemies against him, and after making the society a success he was forced to resign. He was also forced out of the Wesleyan Church by one or two men who have their types in every religious community. It was shortly before this time that my late father knew him, and I have before me now four letters addressed by him to my father, with reference to the work in which they were then engaged. One of the most entertaining portions of his *Life* is that describing his efforts in finding a publisher for the 'Purgatory of Suicides.' He had the usual experience of persons seeking a market for verse. He was refused by all the publishers with whom he most desired to deal. At last Douglas Jerrold found him a publisher, and his book reached the public. I think he had a success which gratified him, and the connections he formed with famous men gave him huge pleasure. He dedicated the poem to Mr Carlyle, and the philosopher wrote him a letter which no one else could have written. He found in the poem traces of genius, 'a dark Titanic energy struggling there, for which we hope there will be clearer daylight by-and-by.' But he advises that Mr Cooper write his next work in prose. 'We have too horrible a practical chaos round us; out of which every man is called by the birth of him to make a bit of cosmos; that seems to me the real poem for a man, especially at present. I always grudge to all any portion of a man's musical talent (which is the real intellect, the real vitality or life of him) expended on making mere words rhyme. These things I say to all my poetic friends, for I am in real earnest about them; but get almost nobody to believe me thitherto.' Carlyle afterwards assisted Cooper in many ways, and the latter says: 'Twice he put a five-pound note into my hand when I was in difficulties, and told me with a look of grave humour that if I could never pay him again he would not hang me.'

If Mr Cooper lives until the 20th of March next he will be eighty-eight years of age, and I hope he will live for many years yet to enjoy his pension.

WILFRED CAMPBELL

Among the chief glories of the natural scenery of a country are its forests and trees, and among the countries of the world Canada may be said to be supreme in this respect. But of all her native trees the maple, the fitting emblem she has chosen, is by far the most beautiful and most suited to the high, dry atmosphere of her climate. In our city and village streets the maple is unique in beauty because of the sunny splendour of its foliage, as if the sunlight not only fell on it, but pervaded and lighted it up, till the whole tree seems aglow with warmth. But to see the maple in all its native splendour you want to seek the virgin woods of northwestern Ontario, which, I am sorry to say, are yearly growing less and less with the development of the country. Here its rugged and massive trunk, its spreading, skyward branches and gold-green foliage make it the supreme monarch of the Canadian forest. We have many beautiful trees, but none in the Canadian forest can compare with the maple.

WILFRED CAMPBELL

The river winds down from the dim country ways, creeping and sliding over pebbly shallows that glint and sparkle in the sun, then glides, turbid and deep, round steep curves where elms lean and mirror in its inky depths. Now and again a kingfisher swoops down from a decayed branch and skims the water with his purplish wings. Far out where the river winds in a thin haze, in sunlight and shadow, lie the country lands, undulating in hill and hollow, with level meadow lands, dotted with trees and sleepy cattle, who lazily gaze, or stand meditatively chewing their cuds and whisking their tails under the trees in the fence corners. A road like a brown riband winds over one of the hills from the eastern horizon, and crosses the river by means of a dilapidated wooden bridge. Now and then the stillness of the sleepy summer afternoon is disturbed by a stray wagon that rumbles over the bridge and up the eastern hill, raising a cloud of dust as it disappears.

Near the bridge there is a small, dilapidated frame house by the roadside. Two lilac bushes fringe the fence in front, and a thin, care-worn woman moves within, now and again coming to the door with an anxious look on her sallow face. A sickly dog lies in the dirt in front, and thumps his tail in the dust as he leers contemplatively at an old hen and a brood of active chickens in a coop near. The sky grows closer and near the earth with a sultry expression. There is a low, far-off rumble of thunder in the eastern horizon. The sky grows closer and blacker. Great clouds roll up over the farm lands. The cows have ceased to low and the birds to twitter, and nature has grown intensely still. Soon a patter of large drops is felt, that comes faster and faster, the dog has crawled under a corner of the house, the chickens can be heard twittering in the coop under the old hen's wings, and the rain descends with a roar and rush on the fields, river and roof-tops, till the roads run in rivulets and the hollows turn into pools, while a fine mist shuts out the distant landscape of farms, woodland, and horizon.

After a while a voice is heard singing snatches of a maudlin song, coming round the bend of the hill beyond the bridge, and the figure of a drunken man reels round the bend, staggering from side to side as he approaches the bridge. His clothes are drenched and muddy and his hat is jammed over his eyes. He reels for a moment and, losing his balance, completely tumbles into a muddy pool. With a muttered exclamation he staggers to his feet, looks for a moment with a sort of indignant reproach at the spot where he had fallen, and then zigzags slowly and methodically over the bridge, braiding his way till he comes to the dilapidated house, where the sad-faced woman who is waiting opens the door and ushers him in from the storm. The day declines, the rain is harder and comes with a steady pour, till night gradually lets its misty curtains down in murky folds about the wet, lonely, and bedraggled world.

ARCHIBALD LAMPMAN

It is a common saying of the ordinary Englishman that in America we have no singing birds. It is true that we have no singer possessing the fire and compass of the nightingale or the skylark, ie, I believe we have not, for I have never listened to either of the latter birds myself, but I am inclined to think, from what we read on the subject, that not even in England have they as great a variety of dainty and appealing voices as are to be met with on any summer day in our Canadian fields – the song sparrow, and the robin, and the blue bird that come before the wind-flower and the lilium – the vesper sparrow, tenderest and most lyric of singers, whose song seems most touching and most in season as his name implies, when we hear it from the dusky, scarce distinguishable fields at evening; the bobolink, who is the merry love-making, gay-coated cavalier of our breezy meadows, forever joyous and alert, thinking that his life is intended for nothing but the old-fashioned troubadour business of strumming the guitar and singing rondeaus and villanelles to one's lady love; the white-throat sparrow, the piper of that strange, clear, long-drawn, meditative note that comes to us from the swamp or clearing, and embodies the very mood of him who whiles away a long May day in idle stroll and meditation; the grave thrushes, the veery, with his revolving, metallic note, having something in it like the sound of shot running round and round in a gun barrel, a note suggestive of midsummer quiet and heat; the hermit, according to Burroughs the finest of our songsters, whose distant, lingering music, heard in the forest depths or from the untilled mountainside, is the very voice of the spirit of solitude, laden with the memories of forgotten flowers, and fading away into a silence and shadow as remote and spectral as they; the wood thrush, not so common with us, and the brown thrush, a singer of great energy and variety; the catbird, the vivacious mimic and eccentric songster; the pewee, with its peculiar infantine, appealing note; the great highholder or higho, whose jolly, flute-like laughter rings far away out of the woodside or the rough field; the drawling pipe and silvern sputter of the meadowlark; and many another of the warblers, flycatchers, vireos, and the rest, too numerous to recount. All these voices from April to August, and later, are a perpetual delight to the ear, and just as each man will have his favourite poet or his favourite story-teller, so each will have his favourite songster of the wood or field. I myself have almost concluded that I find most pleasure in the song of the little vesper sparrow. There is an abandon, a fitting tenderness, a lyrical gush in the utterances of this exquisite little bird that causes him to grow upon the heart of the hearer. The ear seeks his song at morning and eventide, and if it is missing we feel the loss of something that tempers our thoughts with a gentle and humane emotion.

16 July 1892

WILFRED CAMPBELL

Now in the midsummer heats, when the roar and discord of cities become unbearable, and hard thought and reading are almost an impossibility, the spirit of life, if it calls at all, beckons to us with illusive finger from the far-off hill countries or breezy shores. Under the open sky is the suitable place for summer existence whenever it can drop for a space the fetters of toil. The country ways and shady lanes, the clover-scented meadows melodious with song of birds, and drowsy tinkle or gurgle of brooks, under the grasses, where the bumble-bee soars with a dreamy hum, or the greedy dragon-fly skims the lazy air – all call us with their drowsy suggestions and somnolent sounds. Happy is the man who can throw off his age and responsibility with his office clothes and city cares, and hie him to the shores of some rushing river or some pebbly lake, and dream or ruminate as best may please him, and let the winds of heaven and the glad sunlight drench him, body and soul, and blow out all the sickly fancies from heart and brain. The far summer hazes, the far summer sounds, that quiet tired nerves and revive jaded energies, are better than all the elixirs discovered by man. But many of us are not contented to study and drink in nature's draughts and nature's voices alone; we need a companion from the world, and we often choose a book as one the least liable to bore us, as it can be taken up and laid down at leisure. We want something that will charm and soothe, rather than worry and excite. It is a difficult thing to recommend books to readers nowadays, the taste for the new sensational is so strong, and I, for one, prefer the old-time books to the new. For delightful and self-forgetting charm give me Washington Irving, especially his legend of the Hudson River and his *Tales of the Alhambra.* Another charming writer who was of his day and had something akin to Irving in his genius was Donald G. Mitchell, who, by-the-bye, still lives. His pen name is Ike Marvell, and his earlier essays had a charm all their own. Another delightful American writer is John Burroughs, whose works many have read. For those who love nature and nature's studies Burroughs is a never-dying friend. He is a hunter of the woods and fields and the companion of birds and trees. A delightful out-door writer of today, who is a poet, is Maurice Thompson. He is much akin to Burroughs, but adds the additional charm of song to his great love of the common mother. But most of us are not contented with nature alone, in either field or sky or book. We may turn our backs on dull care, but we cannot forget our human brother, and even in our books he is of enduring interest; so the story, the drama of today, be it realistic or romantic, must claim our attention. Here I would ask those of this spirit if they have read the remarkable tales of Björnstjerne, the great Norse writer of today. Any young and thoughtful reader who has not done so will find a freshness and charm, a strength and simplicity not found in any other writer. He mirrors Norway, her mountains and deep fjords, her strong, rugged, and intellectual people, who are so much akin to us, and yet so much grander in their desire for supreme attainment. Björnstjerne's stories read like beautiful poems, They have an epic quality and a dramatic strength that is unique. *Arne* is a very beautiful tale, and like all the rest of his work is in contradistinction to all other European works, close to nature, human, hopeful, and inspiring. It is fitting reading for young men and young women. Where there is pathos it is the pathos of reality. A beautiful, a strong, a human writer is the great poet and novelist of the north, and the reader will find his work in keeping with the outdoor life, as in his pages he will find the strength of the hills, the beauty of the skies and waters, and the freshness and hope of the morning.

DUNCAN CAMPBELL SCOTT

My dear Francesca: I am glad you have resolved to keep a journal. The word sounds more portentous than 'diary,' and is a sign that you are in earnest. I suppose everyone sooner or later makes up his or her mind to keep either one or the other; the sense of it being a duty takes hold upon one very strongly, and may be a survival from the time when it was certainly a social duty, if not a moral one; and then the feeling that we all have that our lives are slipping away and leaving no visible trace urges us to write day by day the things we have been thinking and doing. We feel a sort of consternation when we reflect that we cannot tell where we were this time two years ago, or what we thought at the time of the Northwest Rebellion, and we take refuge in the pages of our everyday book, and hope to escape the imputation that we have not lived. Many of us never find time to complete the good intention that blossomed in our youth, and go down without a chronicle of our deeds or misdeeds, and the excuse that so many of us make, 'want of time,' is really the death of many another pleasant occupation. That you have time and the will to undertake the writing of a journal, or 'Gurnal,' as Sir Walter used to spell it, is really [of] a piece with your general good fortune, and you must succeed or bear the blame of having failed when every wind and tide were with you. There must be something pleasant about the occupation you have resolved upon, for truly it is an occupation, and I hope you will never allow it to descend to anything less. At present we expect posterity to get an idea of our age from the novels we write, and from our newspapers, but I do not imagine the image will be a faithful one. Our novels have hardly any true pictures of social life, and our papers have none; to judge from the one we are merely thinking machines, with our eyes fixed, like the monks of Athos, upon the centre of our beings, and our daily journals give the idea more and more strongly that the contemplation by each man of his neighbour's vice is the chiefest of our pleasures. So you have just as good a chance to make a lively picture of manners and customs as had Pepys or Cellini, and the manners and customs will be of as much interest to the succeeding age. And so you have a chance for fame, and your effort will be of the most disinterested kind, for no one except myself and a few others will have any idea of your labours, and you can never reach any tangible reward unless it be that all the while you will be enjoying the laugh, as it were, upon your own age. I need not advise you as to the sort of thing to write; you have read Pepys, Benvenuto Cellini, Walpole, and Sir Walter so you will easily see that everything, no matter how personal, may have an interest if it is set down properly. You need not even omit to tell us that on Tuesday last you made twenty pots of strawberry jam, and you might even preserve the recipe in order that coming generations may test the quality of your confection.

ARCHIBALD LAMPMAN

The greatest difficulty that a man meets with in life is generally that which faces him at the very outset: the question of deciding upon an occupation. It means the wasting or the saving of a life. A life spent in an occupation out of harmony with one's natural bent can never be quite happy or genuinely faithful even in the most fortunate circumstances; while a life of congenial labour, unsubjected to any exceeding pressure, is really the supreme happiness. Each man has been gifted by nature with some special inclination, more or less marked, which points him to his life pursuit. Unhappily this original and individual bent is very often not sufficiently urgent, not imperious enough in its call, to induce the young man to throw himself confidently upon it, trusting to its genuineness. He yields to the dictation, or persuasion, or example of others, or else blindly enters upon the first offered field of activity without considering whether it corresponds in any degree with that irrepressible vision in his own soul. It is well for a man not to be idle, and to lay hold of any honourable pursuit rather than be so; but he should never allow himself to consider any occupation permanent but the one that is naturally his. He should never rest for a moment till he has found and claimed his appointed place. Each life is a force intended by nature to be exerted upon some particular line. If it is set to work on any other its usefulness is dissipated, often totally annulled. Such a life is in abeyance, and its possessor may be truly said not to have lived. A great responsibility in this matter rests upon parents, who frequently have it in their power to educate and make clear the way for their children's special talents. We know how often they are blind enough to do the very reverse, not only neglecting to render any assistance to this natural inclination, but even endeavouring to guide or force the minds of their children into such paths as appear desirable or honourable to them. Such parents are responsible for a fair proportion of the mental or moral ruin we see about us.

23 July 1892

DUNCAN CAMPBELL SCOTT

The explanation in the Scandinavian mythology of how the art of poetry arose is so curious and so interesting that I have abbreviated it from Anderson's translation of *Bruge's Talk.* It began with a war between the gods and a people called the Vans. They agreed to hold a meeting to fix terms of peace, and they settled their dispute in this way: both went to a jar and spit into it. As they were unwilling to let this mark of peace perish, they shaped it into a man, who was so wise that he could answer any question put to him. Once when this man came to the home of the dwarfs two of them killed him, and let his blood run into two jars and a kettle; then they mixed honey with the blood, and made a mead, and whoever drinks of it becomes a scald and a sage. After this exploit the dwarfs drowned a giant by the name of

Gilling, and when they told his wife she began to cry. One of them plotted her death, as he was tired of her bawling, and his brother let a millstone drop on her head. This proceeding of the dwarfs enraged Suttung, the son of Gilling, and he took the dwarfs out to sea and left them on a rocky island, which was flooded at high tide. To get away they promised Suttung the precious mead. He accepted it and hid it away, putting his daughter to guard it. The Asas became possessed of the mead in the following manner: Odin set out from home, and came to a place where nine thralls were mowing hay. He offered to whet their scythes, and did it so well that they asked if the whetstone was for sale. He answered that he who would buy it must pay a fair price. But as each one wanted it Odin threw it into the air, and in the scramble each thrall brought his scythe upon the other's neck and cut his head off. When the giant who owned the thralls complained to Odin that he did not know where to get other workmen Odin said he would do the work of the nine men if the giant would get him a drink of Suttung's mead. The giant promised to try to get it for him, and Odin did the work of nine men for the summer. But when they went to Suttung he refused to give them any mead. Then Odin proposed to the giant that they should get the mead by some trick. So Odin produced an auger, and the giant commenced to bore a hole through the rock where the mead was hidden. When the hole was bored Odin changed himself into a serpent and crept into the hole. He made friends with Suttung's daughter, and she promised him three draughts of the mead. He emptied the ten jars and the kettle with these three draughts. Then he took on the form of an eagle and flew away, and Suttung also changed himself to an eagle, and flew after him. When the Asas saw Odin coming they put their jars out in the yard, and when Odin reached them he spewed up the mead. But Suttung had so nearly caught him that he dropped some of the mead. As no care was taken of this it became the share of poetasters. But Odin gave the mead to the Asas and to those men who are able to make verses.

ARCHIBALD LAMPMAN

Along with the increased abundance of every other kind of popular literature the present day has become very prolific in children's stories and all kinds of writing intended for the benefit and amusement of children. A great deal of it is wonderfully excellent of its kind, although, as in most other things, there is room for many new departures.

I have been reading with satisfaction a new story for boys written by a Canadian, Mr James Macdonald Oxley, in many respects an interesting and instructive book. One of the good things that can be done for children is to provide them with interesting and wholesome stories, in which much practical information in regard to this earth and the things that move and grow upon it is incorporated. In 'Fergus McTavish' Mr Oxley has given a lively sketch of the working of the Hudson's Bay Company, its organization and personnel, together with many instructive pictures of the wild country, with which it has to do. All this information is conveyed to the mind of the young reader through the medium of a pleasant and vivacious narrative. The narrative may be forgotten, but the lad's mind will be clearer and fuller than it was before. Mr Oxley's story is in some degree a lesson on the bringing up of boys, and, though I do not agree with some of the precepts delivered by the elder McTavish to his son, there is plenty of wisdom in this feature of the book. It seems to me that this kind of work might be carried much further, and with excellent artistic as well as moral and educational effect. A great deal of the higher class of knowledge, scientific results, and the serious thought of the day in simple forms might be infused into the minds of children of fourteen or fifteen years of age by means of beautiful and attractive stories.

WILFRED CAMPBELL

Miss Molly Elliot Seawell has returned to the attack on the literary inferiority of women, in a letter to *The New York Critic*, in answer to Mr Higginson, who had valiantly taken up the cudgels for the other side. Some time ago Miss Seawell wrote a strong article in *The Critic*, in which she put forward the theory 'that in the nobler part of human nature – the emotions and the affections – women are superior to men. In the inferior part of human nature – the mere intellect – men are superior to women.' To the first part there was no answer, but the second part raised a very storm of literary indignation, especially from the gentler sex, though there were a few champions. The intellectual result of the storm was a lack of denial by proof of Miss Seawell's statement, that no woman has accomplished immortal literary work, that is, work that has lasted down the ages. That there has been no female Homer or Shakespeare is perfectly true, and in the main Miss Seawell is right in her brave assertion. The only question that arises is concerning George Eliot. Mrs Browning and George Sand can easily be passed by when compared with the giant, masculine literary intellects of the ages, but when we come to George Eliot I am doubtful. The mind that produced *Silas Marner* got as near to the Shakespearian level as any this side his day. The only way I can explain George Eliot satisfactorily to myself is to deny for her the truly feminine qualities, in short, to say she does not represent the normal woman at her best, but that her great intellectual genius is due to an abnormal masculinity in her nature. Many persons in looking at her portrait have noticed this. The features suggest those of a Savanarola. But is this conclusion perfectly fair to either George Eliot or her sex? Perhaps Mr Higginson is partly right, and woman's intellect has only begun to develop. We do not know what the future may bring forth in this direction. We have many remarkable women today in literature, but when we come to look at the great range of all literature Miss Seawell is right; the immortals are of the sterner sex. This is, without doubt, an important question, and while we would be moved to agree with Miss Seawell's conclusion, yet, to use Sir Roger's impartial dictum, 'When it comes down to a hearty discussion, much might be said on both sides,' and, as the present weather is too hot, we would rather not fall foul of any of the gentler sex in an argument of this kind.

WILFRED CAMPBELL

In connection with the above it is interesting to note the list of strong female writers that America has produced during the last two or three decades. Such names as Helen Hunt Jackson, in verse and prose, and Edith M. Thomas, Helen Gray Cone, and many others in verse, and half a score of strong prose writers, such as C.H. Craddock, Miss Wilkins, Octave Thanet, Rebecca H. Davis, Mary Hallock Foote, show that if women cannot obtain supreme excellence in literature they can, at least, reach comparatively lofty heights in contemporary writing, and that the woman of today is closely pushing man in this direction.

ARCHIBALD LAMPMAN

I find the following statement in a literary journal: 'A series of papers in which eminent novelists will tell how they came to write their most popular book has been arranged for by the editors of *The Idler*, Mr Jerome's new magazine.' Papers are to be contributed by Mr Clark Russell, Mr Besant, Mr Bret Harte, Mr Kipling, Mr Barrie, and others. If there is something rather disgusting in the hunger of the public of our day for an undignified familiarity with the habits and craft secrets of distinguished persons there is something much more disgusting in the readiness of distinguished persons to gratify it. People are beginning to complain, and not without truth, of a decadence in literary art. It would be strange indeed if literary art did not decline under the influence of a state of things such as is indicated by the quotation made above. It is only in solitude and seclusion from public curiosity that the fruit of a man's genius can be fully and wholesomely developed. Praise, indeed, and recognition of a serious kind, are very useful to him; but the coarse contact with the popular touch, which is getting to be the demand of the day, cannot be otherwise than utterly destructive of that silent and patient concentration which is the secret of the great in art. It is as if the writer's personality were dispersed among the multitude, and only by a feverish and violent effort is he able to gather his forces together for an important undertaking. This is no doubt the reason why our younger writers, while they produce so much, never succeed in giving to any one work the large and generous stamp of immortality.

30 July 1892

DUNCAN CAMPBELL SCOTT

From Amiel's Journal – (Six O' clock)

Once more the day is drawing to its close.
The heat of afternoon has vanished quite,
And all the mountains lose their tender light,
Save Mont Blanc, rising flushed with perfect rose.
Alas! the restless hours, without repose,
How they oppress the soul with sudden night.
In vain we cry, 'Oh, time, suspend thy flight'!
In vain! for as we cry the moment goes.
What days to keep? The glad days? Yea, we will.
The lost days, too; the first memory retrieves,
The last are but remorse and mockery.

30 July 1892

(Eleven O' clock)

A gust of wind; a few clouds in the sky;
The nightingale is silent, but it leaves
The cricket and the river singing still.

WILFRED CAMPBELL

Matthew Arnold, who is Wordsworth's most famous admirer, and without doubt the best judge of his finest work, considers the poem called 'Michael' to be his greatest poem. Therefore as a brief study of the poet's worth (for poet I concede him to be, though not of the highest order) I would like to direct attention for a space to this particular poem. I would begin by denying that it is a poem at all in the true sense of the word. If poetry is mere thought or sentiment, no matter how expressed, then many of the essays and sermons, not to speak of short stories, prevalent today are poems. But we know this is not so. Then on what grounds can this poem be called great or even passably beautiful, according to the poetical canons? Can any of Wordsworth's admirers state such grounds so as to satisfy the average mind? The tale, for such it is, has a certain pathos, naturally pertaining to the subject. But so far from being a poem, the story might just as well have been written in prose, in fact it is written in prose, as far as the language used is concerned, which is simple, commonplace prose, marked out in blank verse metre, but not any more beautifully expressed than such tales of life as we commonly meet with in the magazines of today. Many of these tales, for beautiful and fitting simplicity of diction, far surpass this so-called poetical tale of Wordsworth's. To prove my statement, I will quote at random:

> Upon the forest-side in Grassmere vale there dwelt a shepherd, Michael was his name, an old man, stout of heart and strong of limb. His bodily frame had been from youth to age of an unusual strength; his mind was keen, intense and frugal, apt for all affairs, and in his shepherd's calling he was prompt and watchful, more than ordinary men.

Now, this is nothing more than ordinary prose, and of the most commonplace character, and the whole tale is of this order of language. As I have already stated, there is a certain pathos in the story, but no more than is found, as I have stated, in many strong and original short stories of today. We feel sorry for the old shepherd who is left alone in his old age to mourn his erring son, but there is a touch of the patriarchs of the Old Testament, as seen through modern religious ideals, that suggests a borrowed pathos, if unconsciously so. The idea of David weeping for Absalom, or, more in keeping, the patriarchal fatherhood of Abraham, comes to mind. The current characteristic of the whole poem is that of the orthodox idea; it is a story told by a religious moralizer. I admit there is humanity and pathos in the story, but it owes this largely to, as I have said, its imitation of the Old Testament type. Mr Richard Harding Davis, a young prose writer of today, had a short time ago a strong and pathetic tale in *The Century Magazine*, called 'The Ninety and Nine.' It had the same pathos, and yet, like Wordsworth's tale, it is a modern edition of the prodigal son. No one denies the strength and beauty of Mr Davis's short tale, but he would be mad to call it a poem. Now, I contend that 'Michael' is no more a poem in the real sense than 'The Ninety and Nine.' In both, it is the pathos inherent in the story, it is the human incident that appeals to us. But to call 'Michael' a great poem is another thing. There is diffuseness, there is moralizing, there is a certain touch of nature, the tale is even picturesque, if it were not so long-winded and commonplace in its detail, but there are not six lines of poetry in it.

On the whole, I fail to see Wordsworth's greatness as a poet. I would like one of his intense admirers to quote from his works enough instances of really great verse to prove their admiration. Wordsworth was thoughtful, I grant, but it was largely the thoughtfulness of a prosaic order. He was even poetical at times, when he was not carried away by a commonplace moralizing, which he expressed in blank verse or crude rhymes. He had in a gentle, innocent, but childish manner, an interest in life and man's destiny, but his mind was not original enough to lead him beyond the commonest orthodoxy of his day, and he was too much wrapped up in himself and his own little world of shepherds and lambs and commonplace gardeners to feel the pulse-beat of the great humanity outside. We hear stories of his intense interest in the French Revolution, and we see some of it in his works, but he never really was a part of it, as was Shelley, who, with all his faults, was a born poet. Wordsworth was a good, innocent soul, no doubt, but it can be seen he was rather selfish, and too self-centred to be great, in the best sense. He much resembled many good, old-time clergymen, whose lives were good, in a sense, because they had no great tendencies to practical evil, but who have bored us by longwinded sermons. His disciples see in him greatness, hidden meanings, and lofty heights he would never have dreamed of. His descriptions of nature are mere catalogues, mingled with all sorts of digressions as to his own experiences. Now and then he strikes a good thought or expression but such instances are like rare oases in a desert of tiresome verbiage. In short, you can find hundreds of young minor poets of today who show more real practical power of expression than he ever had. The mass of his work, if written now by an unknown man, would not be tolerated, even by his most ardent admirers. I admit that much of his thought is often sincere and pure, but mere sincerity and purity of thought do not give a patent greatness in any age. He is childish in his sympathies, almost senile in his descriptions. He lacks the most ordinary taste in his choice of subjects, and is about as advanced in his ideas as the ordinary parish rector of his day. He is just the kindly, simple, placid old man (for who could ever think of Wordsworth as being young?) who wandered about, leaving the everyday cares to his wife and sister, and weaving his tiresome doggerels and inane platitudes in the quiet English lake country. Considering the peaceful life he led, his evident desire to express himself and his charming environment, it is to marvel that now and again he uttered a thought that might stir the mind and touch the heart, but it is a strong argument against his having high poetical gifts, that in such favourable surroundings he wrote so much utter trash as to form and thought. When we look on the scores of geniuses who have had to struggle with infirmities, both moral and physical, and had to bear privations and intense misery away in busy haunts of men, far from peaceful nature; men like Hood and Burns and Poe, who yet managed to give us even single gems of song, which can be called song, it seems to me that it is passing strange that such a man as Wordsworth should be placed among the first poets in the English language. To say that his supreme greatness consists in the height from which he looks on life, is to insult all the other poets who have written. No one poet can claim such a plane as his own. No poet was a true poet who did not get on to a high plane. But a mock spirituality in poetry as in religion is not a sign of greatness. Sermonizing is not necessarily evidence of a great mind, but very often proceeds from a small, distorted, and self-complacent environment, that would shrivel up the whole of this great universe of humanity and nature with its marvellous and weird beauty, its terrible tragedy and pathos, into the narrow horizon of a country sheep-fold.

ARCHIBALD LAMPMAN

In Robert Louis Stevenson's last book, *The Wrecker*, we find ourselves possessed by the shifting, various, omnipresent spirit of our own age. We flit about the world as if it were a thing measurable by a few strides. We are in the South Seas, then in Paris, in San Francisco, in Edinburgh, in the midst of the Pacific, in Austria, in Devonshire, in Barbison. We meet with strange varieties of scene, and strange varieties of men and manners; and all this gliding panorama is made real to us with a deliberate clearness and sureness of touch that might be the envy of the avowed realist. If we look for any particular quality in literature we are very likely to find it where it is least professed. I think that Mr Stevenson is a much more genuine realist than most of those who are commonly named as master of the realistic school. He never describes a scene which he has not beheld, and his characters, striking and singular as they are, are manifestly in every case founded upon the careful study of actual models. Then there is a keenness of insight and accuracy of understanding evidenced in that picturesque and clinging phraseology of his, so instinct with Scotch strength and Scotch imperturbability, that afford us a perfect guarantee of artistic truth. One can read Stevenson with comfort; we are seldom harassed by the sense of an inadequacy of the result as compared with the design. He never undertakes what he cannot do, and he always brings to his work that rare and priceless faculty of artistic judgment which enables him to know what is too much or what is too little, or, in other words, precisely what and how many strokes should go to the picture.

The same observation may be made, however, about Mr Stevenson's books, that applies to all the best fiction writing of our time. It is good art, but not good drama. It is very clear, strong, subtle, picturesque, but it has not the fine breath of life. The art of conveying the reader into an actual moving world of delightfully animated people appears to have died with George Eliot, and even with her was on the decline. In *The Wrecker*, notwithstanding its rapidly-changing scene and its diversity of actors, every movement is studied, every speech is deliberately thought out, and the reader knows it. In this book there is, perhaps, less spontaneity than in some of Mr Stevenson's former works, *Kidnapped*, for instance, in which some very life-like passages occur.

Mr Stevenson is very fond of the study of characters, common enough, as every humane person knows, in which the mixture of good and evil is strongly and strangely marked. His sea captain Nares and his little disreputable San Francisco lawyer seem to me quite true and successful portraitures, and the capacity the writer shows for understanding human nature in this way inclines one to form a favourable estimate of his own qualities of heart. The figure of Pinkerton – almost the principal one in the book – is that of the buoyant, indefatigable, unconquerable, and forever inventive American man of speculation – a delightful figure, although I think the naïvety is just a trifle exaggerated. The story of the wretched lawyer Bellairs is one of the truest and most tragical things in all Mr Stevenson's literature.

Mr Stevenson has not yet discarded his diabolical taste for bloodshed. In this case it is no less than the murder of a whole ship's crew, a slaughter so sickeningly horrible that one cannot help feeling that the abrupt termination of the story and the absence of any further tragic consequence are a dramatic defect. With all his manifest delight in the ever-varying human spectacle, there is certain want of gentleness and contagious humanity. He is too fond of an artistic triumph, and does not always sufficiently consider the actual import of the thing portrayed with reference to the laws governing human motive and action. It seems to me that the narrative of the *Flying Scud* is not altogether good work from an ethical point of view.

6 August 1892

DUNCAN CAMPBELL SCOTT

I had the misfortune to first read *Diana of the Crossways* in that mangled edition of the Seaside Library, and as a stroke of retributive justice it seems as if the book would never assume its proper form in my head; so I warn all prospective readers of this novel of George Meredith away from the slough into which I fell when I attempted to steal my enjoyment. For he who reads from a pirated edition is very like the small boy who crawls head first under the circus tent and purchases with his only five-cent piece his glass of pink lemonade. His constant trepidation gives his beverage a too acrid tang, and the jokes of the clown come to him partially blunted. There is nothing like the safety of the main entrance and the first row of spectators, where the authorities will smile on one, even if it requires a year of self-denial to save the requisite half dollar. And in my own experience I was even more like the small boy in coming in for only half the entertainment, for he who reads *Diana of the Crossways* in the aforesaid edition will find half his pleasure stolen. The end is altogether lopped off, and a halt is made just at the very point where an advance is imperative, and where Mr Meredith does stride on to a truly characteristic ending with a justification of his Diana and her flights. Any ending other than the union with Redworth is an impossibility, and it is worth a whole warehouse of 'modern' novels, that closing picture of the two women hand in hand after such a reign of uncertainties. Did anyone else ever begin a novel in such a genuinely perverse mood? A sixteen-page dissertation in grotesque style on 'diaries and diarists,' with criticisms aside upon the art of the novelist ending with the sentence: 'Wherewith let us to our story, the froth being out of the bottle.' Those who are not of the limited audience which Mr Meredith asserts himself satisfied with will at once to the contents of the bottle and let the froth go. But it would be better for them if they handled the corkscrew and took their potation with the usual preliminaries. That the brew is of Meredith's finest there can be no doubt, and although for my own part there are at least two other books which I find swimming above *Diana of the Crossways* in my constructed firmament of his works, yet it has a peculiar lustre which makes the lack of magnitude almost imperceptible. I have a curious feeling that the characters in *Diana* are dissociated from any landscape, that they move without a background, as it were; but then they are strangely human; they walk the earth if ever characters did, and my feeling may be a fancy after all. It is the power of delineating character not only in its external manifestations but in its secret recesses that makes Mr Meredith supreme among English novelists. He knows his individuals through and through, and he makes them felt by the reader in a way that we can never hope to know our fellows in the flesh. This quality, in which he is supreme, makes his work peculiarly valuable, and we can forgive him seventy times seven the vagaries of his genius when he has enriched our knowledge and resources. I could not call Diana Warwick his finest woman, because I would have to forget Sandra Belloni, Cecilia Halkett, and many another, not to think of Emma Dunstane. These two women revolve around one another and form the real centre of interest in the book. In no work of Meredith's is the interest so undivided, so constant in its attendance upon the central figure and her fate. But the minor characters are all as sharply drawn as ever – Sir Lukin, Arthur Rhodes, Mrs Watkin, Mr Sullivan Smith, and the rest. Percy Dacier and Tom Redworth are conspicuous examples of Mr Meredith's power over his own sex; but Diana fills the canvas. As he says of her himself: 'Not always the same; not impeccable; not an ignorant innocent nor a guileless; good under good leading; devoted to the death in a grave crisis; often wrestling with her terrestrial nature nobly; and a growing soul.' The book abounds in those strokes of sheer insight which force the blood through the veins of these creatures of the imagination and make them palpitatingly alive. Let me quote one which flashes upon the characters of Diana and Redworth. It was the evening before their marriage, and Diana had discovered by her clearer vision the lofty manliness in Redworth, which, I may remark, the reader has all along been conscious of.

> Penitence and admiration sprang the impulse. It had to be this or a burst of weeping. She put a kiss upon his arm. She had omitted to think that she was dealing with a lover, a man of smothered fire, who would be electrically alive to the act through a coat-sleeve. Redworth had his impulse. He kept it under; she felt the big breath he drew in. The impulse of each had wedded – in expression and repression – her sensibility told her of the stronger.

ARCHIBALD LAMPMAN

When Keats said, 'Beauty is truth; truth beauty; that is all ye know and all ye need to know,' he might have added, if he had been writing prose, that goodness is another synonym for both truth and beauty. The love of beauty is the love of truth and goodness. By the love of beauty I do not mean the artistic instinct, of which it is only a branch. Art is not necessarily true or good. Perfectly genuine art may be neither beautiful nor true nor good. Art is a non-moral thing, and may be good or bad, according to the nature of him who uses it. The man of fine and noble instincts is all the finer and nobler for being an artist, but the man whose instincts are originally weak and base becomes all the weaker and baser in the atmosphere of art. It is not thus at all with the sense of beauty. This can only be of truth and goodness. Art may disturb, but beauty can only bring rest. Beauty expands the soul and raises it to quiet heights. Everything that is mean or cruel or impure shrinks from the sense of beauty as a disease shrinks from the mountain air. Beauty is the essence of harmony. The moment the soul is shaken by any unworthy passion, any distress or bitter remorse, the sense of beauty is undone. Only with those who live nobly can the spirit of beauty dwell secure. So absolutely true is it that 'beauty is truth' that this is the perfect justification of many things in art that are condemned by the rigid realist. That art, which is the accurate transcription of nature, since it is true, is beautiful, but there is also the art of creation which is not contrary to nature, but parallel with it. The painter may paint us a flower different from any flower that exists upon earth, and yet he may paint it under so clear an impulse of creation that it may be actually as beautiful and true a thing, and as fully entitled to existence, as anything we have seen with our eyes. He has made no unreal thing. He has simply been active under the influence of the same eternal spirit that moulded and constructed the universe. A great poem may be built up of images utterly unreal, and yet its beauty and imaginative fitness may be so convincing that we feel that nature herself might have fashioned it in some such manner had she not followed another vein. The poem, therefore, is artistically true. The novelist may paint us a character such as we never actually met with, nor believe to be anywhere existent in life, and yet it may be so life-like, so in touch with the warm human impulses within us, that it becomes real to our imaginations, as genuine a human being as any whom we cannot hear or see in the flesh. Such a character, no matter what the extreme realists may say, is true. There is scientific truth, and there is also artistic truth, and the latter is of almost as much value in the economy of intellect as the former.

WILFRED CAMPBELL

I have just had the pleasure of perusing a copy of *The Lake Magazine*, the new Canadian periodical published in Toronto. If the name and personality of the editor has to do with the success of a magazine, then *The Lake Magazine* ought to be a success. Mr Mowat, so well known as 'Moses Oates,' is the editor-in-chief, and his long and successful career as a journalist augurs well for the good quality of the magazine. The articles by Mr Hopkins and others on imperial federation, Mr Blake, and the political situation in the States, give the magazine some of the heavier qualities of a review, perhaps too much so for the success of a popular periodical. Mr Haultain and Mr Charlesworth have each something to say about literature and art, and both say it well. There are two good poems by Miss Pauline Johnson and Mr Tassie. 'My Friend Mark' is rather a good sketch, but on the whole the fiction, which should be the strength, is the weakest part of the number. Here lies the great obstacle which Mr Mowat has to overcome to make his magazine a success. It is the old weakness pertaining to all our Canadian periodicals – the utter failure to produce interesting and original fiction. There are two mistakes made by Canadian editors in this respect – they either avoid the creative literature altogether, contenting themselves with essay and critique, with a weak or commonplace bit of verse sandwiched in, or else they make the equally bad mistake of trying to ape the American standard in both fiction and verse. It is ridiculous for our magazines to try and equal or copy the outside magazines, and the effort is the great cause of failure. What we want is something that is purely Canadian, and to do this the Canadian editor wants to be a Canadian in his aims and ideals. He does not want to take the American or English standard or style of periodical, with its highly trained and suppressed literature, and force the work of our writers through such a literary sieve to do this as to produce a Canadian journal or periodical which is a puerile imitation of the foreign type. An instance of this weakness is the strange method all our periodicals have of advertising for short stories, and boiling the idea asked for down not only as to subject but even as to space and style. The result is that the work is truck work done for the money. Our editors ought to remember that if they want to find any work produced by Canadian genius they ought to try and procure work that has already been written as a work of love, and that in the budding stage of a country's literature the best writers are not liable to curtail their work. Then, again, the best work is not that of history and adventure; what we need is more of the really imaginative, of a virile nature, in our fiction. Some of the best work we will produce just now in the near future will be considered too unfinished for the eastern American market; but even Hamlin Garland is conquering the east by his vigorous imagination and human realism. Our editors will do well to study this matter, for it applies to our verse as well as to our prose. Meanwhile, we wish *The Lake Magazine* many years of at least paying continuance and an ever-growing constituency.

13 August 1892

WILFRED CAMPBELL

The frequenters at the Mermaid Inn, desiring an outing, decided to seek the cool and nerve-bracing breezes of the Valley of the Gatineau. This river, which flows from the north on the Quebec side, is the largest affluent of the Ottawa, and, in stateliness of sweep and grandeur of scenery, is a rival of the larger river. The Gatineau is about three hundred miles long and, strange to state, its source is in close neighbourhood to that of the Ottawa, the land between making almost an immense island. The Gatineau is geologically one of the oldest of streams, and runs with sullen stateliness or angry surge along an immense valley or gorge, winding in and out down through the spurs of the Laurentian hills. The scenery along the banks, seen from the gliding train, grows more lonely in its grandeur as the titanic solitude through which it flows is entered. Deciding to take a flying trip with one of the farthest hamlets as our destination, we left the CPR station at Ottawa at 5:15 on Saturday afternoon, on the single train that runs daily over the Gatineau Valley Railway. The run to our destination occupied two hours, but at least half the time was spent in stoppages at the intermediate stations for purposes of local traffic. The first stoppage after leaving Ottawa was at Hull, on the Quebec bank, where we branched off on to the Gatineau Valley Railway, and where the man who smokes the pipe of peace at the Mermaid Inn got on board. After a rapid run of some miles we at last struck the valley of the famous stream, and not as it peacefully enters the Ottawa did it appear, gliding imperceptibly between green banks and gleaming villages, but dark, sullen, and tortuous, its black tides shot swiftly between great, frowning shoulders of primitive rock, which rose in hill after hill, steep and overhanging, crowned with virgin forests, and threw their desolate shadows on its sombre tides. There came over the soul an indescribable sense of the eternal wintry desolation that seemed a part of the wild and angry stream that for ages has swept through these inhospitable defiles of the lonely hills.

At the Cascades, where there are some beautiful rapids and falls, we met a picnic party from Ottawa who were making ready to embark in their homeward-bound train. They seemed to have overrun the quaint little hamlet, with its white houses and gleaming spires. At another place, Kirk's Ferry, we could have crossed the river and have visited a famous cave some miles back in the mountains. There was a large number of passengers on the train when we left Ottawa, prominent among whom was the Roman Catholic archbishop, who, with his fine, portly person, dark, swarthy visage, and the peculiar tuft or plume on his large, soft-brimmed hat, looked very much like a happy, old-time cavalier. But when we reached our destination there remained but our own party of five and another party, who were bound for the same place and whose presence filled our minds with sad forebodings as to the sufficiency of accommodation. After the swaying train had swept with a long, shrill and resounding raucous scream round a sharp curve, filling the cool and gloomy air with far-off echoes, we gradually slowed up at a little station-house of a Swiss style of architecture. Headed by our chaplain, who 'kenned the country,' we did not wait for importunate porters and jostling 'busses, for there were none, but, dropping from the rear of the car, we raced for the house of entertainment. Mine host of the inn was of the longed-for type as to outward appearance, but he evidently was distressed by superfluous custom, for he did not greet us with the effusive heartiness that our hungry stomachs desired, but surveyed us with a passing contempt, as of a fisherman who had an overplus of fish on the bank and is careless as to how many he will carry home in his basket.

Our chaplain, with commendable courage, ignored the evident unconcern, walked forward and said: 'How do you do, Mr ——— ———, I stayed here once before, but I suppose you don't remember me.' 'No, I don't,' blurted out the king of the situation, and, turning his back, he unceremoniously retreated to his bar, which, from all appearances, was a favoured resort of his. This was decidedly discouraging, but, with still hopeful hearts and aching stomachs, some of us entered the house and proceeded to await patiently the serving of the evening meal, while others promenaded outside. The hamlet was composed of one store and a meeting-house, and the hotel was a modest little structure, situated in a beautiful spot on the banks of the Gatineau. Across the road from the house, beneath a steep bank overgrown with foliage, the stream swept past, dark and still, and bearing on its sullen breast many logs that, forever, morning, noon, and night, float down from their ancient solitudes to play an important, if a passive, part in the great business and bustle of the outside world. On the opposite bank of the river rise the wild, rugged, fir-clad hills, overshadowing the locality with their sombre desolation. Here, at night, the stars come out and the mists creep down, filling the sombre silence fold on fold, wrapping the stately hills and the sullen river, the scanty patches of oat fields and the clustering, tiny hamlet in a luminous gloom, where, under and between all, the never-resting river, like a haunted soul, bearing its burden of saw logs and tumultuous song, runs without cessation to the outer world. After over an hour of anxious waiting on our part, and scarcely apologetic grumblings on the part of our host, the most adventurous of us invaded the dining room in a body, and the meal began. We had certainly no reason to complain of the fare, with which the table was crowded from end to end. It is true the boiled pork was over-fat, the butter was slightly rancid, but for the rest there was abundance of what the locality afforded. We were a jolly and hungry party, and from the chaplain, who occupied the head of the table, to a small boy, who was mostly stomach and who seemed bound by some gruesome oath to put himself outside of as many of the viands as possible, all seemed to appreciate the digestibles, when suddenly, like an uncalled-for skeleton at the feast, the most original and independent of hosts appeared and delivered himself of the following remarkable statement: 'Say, if you folks has had enough, you'd better get out, as there's some more as wants yer places.' There was a second's silence at this most unexpected command, and even the hungry boy paused in the process of a quick swallow, with his mouth open. 'Of course,' continued this most inhospitable of hosts, 'I don't want any of yez to leave if ye ain't satisfied, but if yer satisfied yer had better get out.' At this there was a long and ironic laugh, but a number seemed suddenly to realize that they were 'satisfied,' and the table was soon empty. That night when we retired to bed this strange host did his best to make some of us sleep three in a bed, but we prevailed on him to reduce us to two in a double-bedded room, and with the window and door open we managed to exist.

Next day we communed with nature in that glorious region. We crossed the ferry, bribing the infant shock-headed and barelegged charon who ran the concern with our spare coppers, and having piled our coats in a safe place struck out over a shaded wood road, filled with the delightful reverie and glamour of an August morning. We climbed many hills in this shaded, winding old wood road, revelling in rich, luscious raspberries by the wayside, and filling the sun-drenched, hazy August air with our shouts and laughter. The birds sang with indescribable sweetness, and every now and again we heard, sweeter than all, the far-off haunting song of the hermit thrush from some illusive solitude. Near at hand the rat-tat of the woodpecker vied with the shrill cadence of the high-bred locust, who seemed to voice the heat that filled the summer world. After leaving the woods, there burst on our view a wide vista of farm land and valley cradled in magnificent hills that stretched off and out to the ends of the world. Crossing this bit of country land we climbed the ragged sides of a small mountain of probably 1000 feet in height, and got a splendid view of the surrounding country. North, south, east, and west lay the great region of the Laurentide hills, with the Valley of the Gatineau winding in between. Here and there we could see a lake, or the glimpse of a lake, out between the hills, or a gleaming curve of the river as it widened into view. After devouring this magnificent view, and as many blueberries as we could pick, we named this majestic peak by the sacred name of the Mermaid Mountain, and building a small cairn of stones on the loftiest summit we descended, leaping like goats in glad exhilaration.

That night two of us were left to the tender mercies of our peculiar host, the rest having gone farther to perhaps 'fare worse.' One of us desired to make up for the day's fatigue with a glass of Brading's stout before retiring, and having procured that special brand of seductive intoxicant had retired to a sitting room to enjoy it quietly, when suddenly the door opened and in walked an aged servitor of mine host. 'Say,' he said, 'I want that glass, so you'd better hurry up.' It goes without saying that the guest 'hurried up.'

We two lonely ones retired with at least the consolation that we should have a bed apiece in our double room, but the latest of us had hardly lain himself away comfortably for the night, with the light blown out and the window open, when the door opened and our unconquerable host appeared with a lamp in his hand. He looked at us both meditatively for a moment, and then said, 'Ye'll both have to sleep together. I want one of them beds.' As there was probably no denying this strange statement, the writer of this chronicle suggested that his companion come into his bed; and it is needless to write that the transfer was soon made, the astute host of the inn carrying the bed clothes and the light off with him.

The next morning we were up bright and early, and were soon whirring on our return trip, leaving behind us our strange host, with his most eccentric, but persuasive manner of managing his guests, and with him the strong, bracing airs, the lonely hills, and the grand, majestic breast of the upper Gatineau, with its silent, stately tides and wintry solitudes.

DUNCAN CAMPBELL SCOTT

For such of the readers of this column as might not otherwise meet with it, I insert here Mr Swinburne's fine sonnet on the centenary of Shelley, printed in *The Athenaeum* of 30 July:

Now, a hundred years agone among us came
Down from some diviner sphere of purer flame,
  Clothed in flesh to suffer, maimed of wings to soar,
One whom hate once hailed as now love hails by name;
  Chosen of love as chosen of hatred. Now no more
  Ear of man may hear, or heart of man deplore.
Aught of dissonance or doubt that mars the strain,
  Raised at last of love, where love sat mute of yore.

Fame is less than love, and love is more than gain,
  When the sweetest souls and strongest, fallen in fight,
  Slain and stricken as it seemed, in base men's sight,
Rise and lighten on the graves of foemen slain,
  Clothed about with love of all men, as with light,
  Suns that set not, stars that know not day from night.

20 August 1892

ARCHIBALD LAMPMAN

Mr W.D. Howells is reported to have said: 'Whenever I have given way to the so-called inspiration of the moment, and have worked with reckless enthusiasm, I have always found the next day that my work was rubbish and all lost.' I imagine that Mr Howells, when he said that, was speaking with a somewhat exaggerated force. If he meant the statement to be taken literally, I think he was in error. Every writer who does much work and has been writing for many years accomplishes a certain part of everything he undertakes under the influence of no special imaginative excitement – almost in a routine sort of way; but there are many points in a work of fiction, if it be a dramatic work at all, which are all the better for being carried by storm, so to speak, and the greatest writers have no doubt sketched out momentous situations in their novels under impulse of great excitement. If Mr Howells had allowed some of those runaway adventures of his pen to be incorporated in his stories, whatever he might have thought of them himself the world would probably have decided that they were far better than anything he has actually printed. An author, especially if he be gifted or cursed with a strong critical faculty, is often not a fair judge of his own work. In the pale light of the reaction which always follows an outburst of mental excitement, the result assumes an unnatural colour, and the author underestimates the force or beauty of what he has done. When the imagination is carried away by enthusiasm and thoroughly rejoices in the work it is doing the result must be good.

DUNCAN CAMPBELL SCOTT

The Siege of Lucknow, by the Hon. Lady Inglis, is an interesting and absorbing chronicle of one of the most exciting occurrences of the Indian mutiny. Although this is not the first diary of the siege which has been published, it has the first claim to recognition, not only on account of the illustrious name which the author bears, but because of its intrinsic merit as a faithful and graphic narration of this gallant defence. The popular idea of the siege will always be involved with the fiction of the Scotch lassie who heard 'The Campbell's are Comin'' played by the bagpipes of the relief, under Generals Outram and Havelock, and it is interesting to read an authentic account of that first relief without any heightening of the facts. Mrs Inglis's style is admirably simple and unaffected, and she has been enabled to make use of the notes of Colonel Birch, who was her husband's aide-de-camp during the time of the siege. We therefore have two accounts: one from inside the walls of the building, where so many women and children were confined, and where the active life of the garrison was only a matter of report, and the other from the very thick of the fight. We have a detailed description of the holding at bay of 15,000 rebels by 1800 regulars and loyal natives, who had to defend the residency and eight hundred women and children. This they did for eighty-seven days. The garrison was commanded during this period by Brigadier Inglis of the 32nd, who joined the regiment in 1832, when it was stationed at Quebec.

As an example of Lady Inglis's style, I quote from her notes on the 25th of September: 'At 6 p.m. tremendous cheering was heard, and it was known our relief had reached us. I was standing outside our door when Ellicock rushed in for John's [Brigadier Inglis's] sword; he had not worn it since Chinhut, and a few minutes afterward he came to us, accompanied by a short, quiet-looking, grey-haired man, whom I knew at once was Gen. Havelock.' Colonel Birch gives the following account of the arrival of the relief:

> It was indeed a gallant feat of arms by which Generals Havelock and Outram and their small force threw themselves into our entrenchments. They were outnumbered 100 to 1, and had to make their way through narrow streets and dense parts of the city. Indeed so dense were the suburbs that they completely swallowed up the force, preventing our seeing them. The first sign of their approach was the evident panic amongst the citizens. Crowds streamed out of the city in headlong flight. Horsemen rode to the banks of the river, and, cutting the tight martingales of their horses, plunged into the stream. The enthusiasm of the garrison was tremendous and only equalled by that of our relievers. HMS 78th Highlanders and the 14th Sikhs raced up to our gate, which was earthed up, and which we did not dare to open, as the enemy kept up their fire till the last moment. Generals Outram and Havelock came in at an embrasure which had been pretty well knocked about. Gen. Havelock was buttoned up to the chin in a blue coat. We, of the old garrison, had long deserted red and blue, and, with flannel shirts, white clothing, dyed dust-color and soiled with gunpowder, we looked more like buccaneers than officers of the British army.

WILFRED CAMPBELL

A century ago there was born into English life a soul of remarkable and lofty genius, whose song added a new and subtle essence to the quality of English poetry. In Shelley we have, without doubt, the greatest lyric poet in the language. All true poets, while they may have affinities, must prove their right of place in the literary constellation by showing a peculiar original quality of thought and expression which is theirs alone, and which can be found in no other writer. This is the patent of genius which distinguishes the great and original mind from the child of the schools, from the mere imitator. To be great is to have all the qualities that are called god-like, supreme among which are emancipation from the petty thraldom of life so as to be able, from earliest childhood, to contemplate the wonder and greatness of the universe, and to realize in and through all the realms of humanity and nature, in the good and evil, in the hope and despair, in ocean and land and the misty stars of Heaven, a weird, haunting beauty that is forever present in it all, and yet behind it, where dwells the invisible. To be this is to be a poet. He is of the world and yet he is apart from it. He sees faces and dreams dreams that none others know of. He may often seem to be lawless and erratic, with the voice of a god in the body of a satyr, but he can never be less than great. A man who is born with a soul of this nature, though he may be shunned or even execrated by his own age, is sure to be vindicated by history in the end. There is a divine essence running all through our humanity that loves and feeds on greatness; it is a quality of history that periodically revolts against bigotry and tyranny; that sifts the wheat of the ages from the chaff and straw, and places eternal genius on its pedestal in the sight of men. This quality, that is, the power to appreciate genius, is stronger than race or creed or environments. In the exquisite genius of Shelley we have a wonderful example of the peculiar originality that is the true mark of greatness. It might be said of him that he is a paler, more ethereal Shakespeare. But in Shakespeare we have a sun, while Shelley is a white star of the first magnitude. It may be said of Shelley that he is too ethereal, and did not get close enough to the earth. This may be so, but what was his weakness was also his greatest strength. He seems to me to be a poet of the stars and dew, and whatever adverse critics may say they can never dethrone from the kingship of true English (lyrical) poetry the genius who wrote the 'Lines to an Indian Air' and 'The Ode to a Skylark.' Or who has surpassed in English such exquisite and ethereal description of the night as:

Yon orbed maiden,
In white fire laden,
Whom mortals call the moon;
Glides, glimmering o'er
My fleece-like floor,
By the midnight breezes strewn.

ARCHIBALD LAMPMAN

The management of the Chicago Exhibition made a mistake, it seems to me, in offering a prize for the best collection of stuffed birds. The result will be a wholesale destruction of these beautiful and innocent creatures that every true naturalist and lover of nature must deplore.

ARCHIBALD LAMPMAN

Mr W.T. Stead has also made a mistake in promoting the publication of a version of the Bible in the common language of the day. What reasonable object he can hope to gain by this it would be hard to say. As regards force, melody, and dignity of diction the proposed version is sure to be a failure, and no improvement in perspicacity can possibly be attained, inasmuch as the old version of King James unites almost in the ideal degree the different rare qualities necessary to convey the true force of the original to a religious imagination. The men of the sixteenth century knew how to translate the Bible, because they believed it in a sense which is not intelligible even to the devout people of our day, and because they were saturated with its spirit. A translation by a modern newspaper man would be about the same as a translation of Homer by Will Carleton or Martin Farquhar Tupper. It would be enough to make heaven and earth crumble together before the eyes of the true, old-fashioned man of letters.

27 August 1892

WILFRED CAMPBELL

Probably the strongest and most individual of New England's women writers of today is Miss Mary E. Wilkins, whose *New England Nun and Other Short Stories* has been so successful in England as well as in America. Miss Wilkins's stories can hardly be called stories in the true sense of the word. They are merely short, concisely told episodes in a number of New England lives among the work-a-day people. The rural village is her environment, and the pathetic side of woman life, chiefly that of the single old women or attenuated girls who drift into old maidenhood, and who are a leading characteristic of New England life, is brought out in these homely pictures. There is very little of what might be called dramatic action in these sketches, but the charm lies in the pathos that enfolds the characters who are placed before you. It might be said that these sketches are monotonous in their similarity, but any person who has lived in rural New England will see that this is owing to the environment, which is dreary in the extreme and envelops the woman's life in a sameness of sentiment and occupation. When Miss Wilkins lays stress on the life of the women in her sketches, we must remember she is a woman herself, and more likely to sympathize with that side of the picture, but outside of this fact it is apparent to the outside observer at once that the New England women of this class are superior to the men in intellect and general character. One strong reason for this is the natural intelligence of the past generations, and the lonely life led by the women of the present generation, who still hold on to the superior part as a sort of golden age, while the men for the most part have gone west or south, or died off or degenerated. When Miss Wilkins speaks of a New England nun she brings out this fact of the lonely, contemplative life of the many elderly maidens, who gather rose leaves, live in refined loneliness, and look back to the ante-bellum past; and the outside world would be surprised at the amount of sentiment that is hidden away in some of these old, quiet lives. Many of these women have themselves plucked up courage, and have gone west or south as schoolteachers, and have borne with them to the more rude localities of the busy world some of that culture and refinement that is a part of their existence. A few have by a miraculous accident been married, but for the most part this is out of the question. The young men all went west or south after the war or during the California gold fever, and most of them took to themselves life partners among strangers, and forgot the more refined and more high-strung, if less beautiful, maidens who for the most part put them in the shade at the academies and debating schools of their eastern home. Here and there is found a man who went neither west nor south, or did both and came home, a failure, and married one of these pensive maidens, who all the rest of her life tried to respect him. But to the New England female mind the young man who went west and never came back, save for a short time as a western senator or judge, is the ideal of the successful hero. The other class, who stayed or came back to live a second-best kind of existence, generally chew tobacco and drink cider and New England rum, and develop a coarseness of exterior that is extremely painful to the women, who are remarkably dainty in their household matters. Miss Wilkins has given us many instances of this pathetic type, but she has failed to give us one that is perhaps the most pathetic of all – a picture of the home life where the woman tries her best to respect and live happily with the sort of man I have described. The New England man of this sort is generally more of a man, in the accepted sense, than the woman is a woman, but he necessarily is more of an animal; and when a man who loves tobacco and rum and cider and obscene stories, and is decidedly lazy to boot, is allied to a prim, active woman, who dotes on Ruskin and paints and is a lover of flowers and poetry, and yet polishes her house from end to end to chase the flies out – when, as we have said, this class of man and woman are tied together for life we have a sort of dog and cat mixture that is more pathetic in its dramatic possibilities of the finer sort than any Miss Wilkins has described. And yet this picture I have suggested is common enough in New England life to make it one of its most pathetic characteristics.

ARCHIBALD LAMPMAN

There is a sensible article in the July number of *The Contemporary Review*, entitled 'Are We Really So Bad?' It is about 'the girl of the period,' and is in some sort a refutation of the dismal things said by Lady Jeune and Madame Adams in *The North American Review*. I cannot understand the objection that many women have to the growth of wider tastes, more robust activities, and freer manners among their own sex. It is absolutely necessary that this change should take place if the race is to reach its noblest and fullest development, and if, as in our time, the new state of things leads to some extravagances and unseemliness, that is simply the effect of a natural reaction from the condition of stunted growth and 'intolerable ennui' which were the boast of the past.

We say that women are unfitted for such and such occupations, forgetting that their unfitness is due simply to the fact that the rudimentary capacity for those occupations, which certainly is in them, is immature through never having been allowed exercise. Women are quite fitted for all the intellectual occupations undertaken by men, and for many of the physical. In some of the intellectual ones they decidedly excel. When the coming generations of women shall have been admitted to full freedom of movement and to the practise of every human activity, and shall have perfectly adapted themselves to the changed conditions, our children's children shall know a type of women of which we can only dream – natural queens among men, to whom they shall look up, as the Goths of old did to their Abruna women, superhumanly beautiful, superhumanly wise.

27 August 1892

DUNCAN CAMPBELL SCOTT

It was that time during the month of August when the September magazines commence to come in. It was a typical August day; the drowsiness of the heat, showering down from a grey, hazy sky, and the dull, sultry horizon could have been produced by no other month. A cicada threw his long stinging crescendo from a butternut tree. But, although it was August, I was reading a September magazine, and as there was nothing in it to keep me awake I gradually fell asleep, hardly conscious that I was going, for the cicada kept hunting me through the first descents of slumber until I was beyond reach of his note in its deepest caverns and recesses. Suddenly I became conscious that it was Sunday. I was intensely aware of the fact, although I was perplexed by smelling soapsuds, and before long I saw a very small Chinaman hanging out clothes on a line. I was walking along the street all the time and observed many other things, but the Chinaman and the clothes line, with the effect that an amateur photographer obtains when he takes two pictures on one plate, were always sliding in front of everything else. By and by I stopped in front of a store where a man was selling pith helmets, and I asked him what was the day of the week. He replied, 'We call it Monday.' I suppose he noticed my surprised air, because he added quickly: 'You know we're all mixed up in the time now.' 'Would you think it too much trouble to explain?' I asked. 'It's no trouble at all,' he answered, 'but I can't explain, nobody can; our scientific people have stopped discussing whether Mars is inhabited and all that sort of thing and are trying to discover the ratio of advance, as they call it.' 'What is the "ratio of advance"; what do you mean by it?' I asked. 'I don't mean anything by it; that's the difficulty; but, as you're a stranger, I will tell you all that anybody knows about it. We call today Monday, but last year it was Wednesday, and the year before it was Friday, and this year is really 1968, but we call it 1997 – ' 'Well,' I said, 'that must be very confusing.' 'It is,' he replied, 'when you think of it, but the best way is not to think of it.' 'But how can you help thinking of it? When you have to date your correspondence you must know what year it is.' 'Well,' he replied, 'we get that from the newspapers, in fact that is the only way to get it, and now the scientists are trying to find out how the newspapers know.' I asked him how it came about that the world had got so far ahead of itself, as it were. 'Well,' he said, 'the magazines were to blame. They commenced to issue their numbers in the preceding month, and very soon they got two months ahead, and that's the way the difficulty commenced. I believe myself it would have been all right if the newspapers hadn't taken it up. But they did. They began to anticipate, and then there was no end to it. Why, some of the radical journals are away into the twenty-first century, and there is no stopping them now. Some of the wise men try to make out that the whole trouble originated from the desire of mankind to peer into the future, and, failing that, they tried to cheat themselves by anticipating time.' 'Do you believe that?' I asked. He did not give me a direct answer, but he asked me if I would like to buy a pith helmet; it would keep my head cool. I was just on the point of telling him he needed it for that purpose more than I did when I heard the cicada quieting down after an immense crescendo.

ARCHIBALD LAMPMAN

Those who do accomplish anything in literature in this country have, at any rate, the grim satisfaction of knowing that if it is not what they might have done under more favourable circumstances, it is at least the product of sheer natural talent. The Canadian littérateur must depend solely upon himself and nature. He is almost without the exhilaration of lively and frequent literary intercourse – that force and variety of stimulus which counts for so much in the fructification of ideas. The human mind is like a plant, it blossoms in order to be fertilized, and to bear seed must come into actual contact with the mental dispersion of others. Of this natural assistance, the Canadian writer gets the least possible, and, if out of the poverty of his opportunities he accomplishes something, let him not be blamed for being, perhaps, a little boastful and inclined to rate himself at a little more than his actual worth.

Our only remedies for this want are an occasional visit to the American literary centres, or to London if we are fortunate enough to have the means of getting there, and the friendly help of books, especially those memoirs which distinguished people in the older countries have left behind them for the entertainment and encouragement of those that come after. For the rest we shall have to do our best to create by degrees what we so much feel the need of now, by drawing towards one another as much as possible and bridging the long distances that separate us by friendly and helpful correspondence.

3 September 1892

DUNCAN CAMPBELL SCOTT

At the Congress of Experimental Psychology an interesting paper was read by Dr Berillon, dealing with the uses to which hypnotism might be put in educating and improving the moral nature of children. The doctor's experience has been large in this department of experimental psychology, for he has personally attended to the education of 250 children. He found it possible to give, in some cases, a check and in others a perfect cure to habits of stealing, idleness, cowardice, and impudence. The paper naturally caused discussion, and although the doctor found opposition to his theory that it was useful to aid the transformation of the moral nature of children by physical methods, yet the consensus of opinion seemed to show that hypnotism might be advantageously used to these ends. Mr F.W.H. Myres mentioned that Mr Wingfield had found no difficulty in persuading a Cambridge undergraduate to give up his bad habits, to 'sport his door' every morning and get a very creditable degree. Here is a new method of action for weary and discouraged parents, who are in despair over their recalcitrant offspring: take them to the nearest hypnotizer, or, better than that, learn how to use the 'influence' themselves. All that would have to be done in the latter case would be to transfix the unruly John Henry who persists in stealing the neighbours' pears, and suggest to him that he hates pears and that climbing over orchard fences is a thing to be despised. He would awake after a few applications of this influence to refuse pears even at dessert, and this would leave his parents the full enjoyment of the fruit basket and reduce the family expenses. Even in a well-regulated family this influence might result in producing anything but model members of society; but what would be the result if the parent was himself vicious, and turned his child, who loved to go to Sunday school and was by nature the model boy of the ward, into something a good deal worse than himself? It is to consider too whimsically to consider so; but the possibility of hypnotic influence being used from evil as well as good motives must be recognized. In fact at this very congress an instance was cited by Professor Liegeois of this vicious application of the force, where a lady in Algeria was supposed to have killed her husband and children, acting on the suggestion of a man who had fallen in love with her. The plea of hypnotic influence or suggestion may in the future be a favourite one with criminals, but a jury would have to be specially constituted before such a defence would receive much consideration.

WILFRED CAMPBELL

There can be nothing more life-inspiring than to read the well-written biography of a great man. To live over again in fancy his deeds, his aspirations, and even his faults is to give one a larger idea of man and his destiny.

Much has been said about the influence of example on others, and there is a plain truth underlying this idea, sadly as it has been abused. We have been taught in many quarters that man should live good so as to be an example to others. With many biographers such a simile as this is the chief motive, and they are right in a sense, but also gravely wrong. They are right in saying that example is a stimulative to better life. But they fail in not discriminating between examples and examples. All the strength in this position is got from quoting the lives of great men, not men who have consciously striven to be known as good, but whose lives were great and hence good. True greatness must always precede true goodness. And the best biography, or in fact the moral one, to speak plainly, is the realistic biography, which gives a man's life as he really lived it, or as near as it can be got at for the purpose to be attained. It is not necessary to gloat over a man's weaknesses and follies in order to avoid them ourselves, but at the same time a man's life, if it is worthy of being studied, must have some greatness in it, and our true experience is that in all great natures there is what some call an alloy. The true value of the biography as a stimulus lies in the greatness which inspires us, but another work the biography does is to convey a knowledge of human life, so that it is necessary for us to know the good and ill, the strength and weakness, and in their natural relations, or else we will fall into the error of hero worship and cultivate a false idea of life, and become, in a sense, saint worshippers. The old and foolish idea of padding up a good life till the goodness was nauseating, and of exaggerating a bad life, after the manner of the hero and the villain in the show, may have been convenient to the teacher in enforcing his lesson, but it had its evil effects all the same, and has largely resulted in turning the sympathy completely over to the other side, the villain becoming the most interesting character. We have a startling example of this in one of the masterpieces of literature – Milton's *Paradise Lost*– where, whether unconsciously or not, the great poet makes the majestic fallen angel the great central figure of the play, and the reader becomes impressed with the idea of his greatness as the most interesting personage in the poem. In truth, take Satan out of *Paradise Lost* and the poem is a mere shell. The great power and interest here lies in the human qualities ascribed to the fallen one, as a rebel against authority, but we are also impressed with a certain sympathy for the soul that grew sick of the ever-monotonousness of the Miltonic heaven. Satan here is nothing more or less than a great human military leader. And there is no doubt that Milton had Cromwell in mind when he was writing his majestic epic. In this sense, *Paradise Lost* is one of our most remarkable biographies, and as such it has had an unconscious influence on more minds than ever suspected it, even to the extent of a theological reform. As a biography it is akin to those of Plutarch, which while largely imaginative were truer than is common to the real greatness of human life in its relation of good and evil in the human heart. Many of Shakespeare's plays and many of the characters in the greater novelists partake of this character and are of the highest value as biographies of human character. The mingling of the good and evil in character is becoming more evident all the time, where the old idea was an almost childish and most unnatural distinction into purely good and purely evil. But the reader's common sense outgrew this stage, until we have reached this age of realism when we like to take men as they are. We have found out that even men like Washington used occasional bad language, and that the story of the cherry tree, with its accompanying moral, is an imagination, but none the less do we respect the first great president of the great republic. We may not worship him, but we have more sympathy with him for having, as a biographical figure, stepped down a peg lower, and become a little more like ourselves. I do not think, even with much of the evil around us, that the world has not gained a little at any rate, and that it has gained a good deal by desiring to know the truth as it is. For this reason the realistic biography is of the greatest importance.

ARCHIBALD LAMPMAN

It is at this season that the streams – those streams that loiter slowly through low-lying meadows – put on their utmost beauty. Bordered by trees and exposed in little reaches to the sun, the golden heats and full shadows of August lie upon them. The bittersweet hangs from the close branches of the alder and ripens its berries. Innumerable water weeds and mosses float and sway in the sluggish stream, and the swift spiders upon its surface flit hither and thither, throwing their spotted shadows upon the bottom. The loosestrife, knotted with ruby bloom, curves down its willowy stems to meet the water. Masses of blossoming plants line its edges; goldenrod in miniature slender groves arching into gold, purple boneset or trumpet weed, in whose soft and woolly heads the bees love to trample and burrow; tall stems of chelone or turtlehead, with their white spout-like blossoms; tangled drifts of white-starred bed straw; jewelweed in delicate profusion of translucent stems and rich-tinted, sensitive bloom; cloudy spots of white snakeroot; tufts of closed gentian, whose long violet corollas that never open the bumblebees spread asunder with their feet, thrust themselves into them, and almost disappear; these, with patches of yarrow, many shades and sizes of aster, delicate blossoms of arrowhead that seem made of snowflakes that may melt as you look at them, and an occasional bed of purple pickerelweed springing from the shallow edge of the water, almost cover and conceal the little stream with their wild vigour of growth and mingled splendour of colour. It is in the midst of some such scene as this, in a late August afternoon, when the sun rests hot upon the harvested fields, and the woods are deep with mellow glooms, and the elms cast long shadows, that the season seems to present herself to us like a divine personality in all the gracious joy of her prime and the calm confidence of perfect achievement.

ARCHIBALD LAMPMAN

Since Mr Aldrich left *The Atlantic Monthly* his verse has appeared more frequently than of old in the magazines, a circumstance which has added much to the interest of the magazines for lovers of poetry. Mr Aldrich's fame as a poet has been one which has grown slowly, and his gift, though indeed very genuine, will probably never command wide popular applause. He is one of those literary poets of a high order, like the late Lord Houghton or Coventry Patmore, whose work will live because it gives an exquisite, if not very passionate, pleasure to a certain order of minds whose tastes and inclinations are guided by the pure love of beauty. Mr Aldrich has in a pre-eminent degree that gift of beautiful phrase-making which has been enough in itself to make some delightful, if not actually great, poets. The mass of the public, however, is somewhat indifferent to delicate artistic power and beauty of form and phrase, and is likely to be better pleased with Mr James Whitcomb

Riley, another writer of the second generation who has come prominently into notice, and bids fair to absorb the common affection of the people. Mr Riley stands almost at the opposite pole from Mr Aldrich. With him the desideratum is not a motif which promises artistic success, but one which touches some homely, popular chord. To this love for the homely, the popular, the emotional, he adds a certain nimble wit and whimsical cleverness which are delicious to all, and render his poems especially irresistible to his own people, whose mood they thoroughly represent. With Mr Aldrich and Mr Riley at the head, American poetry is perhaps not quite so dismally on the decline as many people just now imagine.

10 September 1892

DUNCAN CAMPBELL SCOTT

The Life and Times of Sir George Grey, KCB is the record of a most useful and eventful life, a life devoted to his country's service in the colonies. Although we missed having the distinguished subject of these volumes as our own governor-general, the record of his labours and successes in other less civilized quarters of the empire will be read with interest by Canadians. He was promised the promotion from New Zealand to Canada, but he went back to his duty at the former field in 1861, giving up his chances for the larger honour. He entered upon his career in 1836, when he went out to explore northwestern Australia in the employ of the Colonial Office and the Royal Geographical Society. Immediately after this service he was appointed Resident at King George's Sound. From 1841 to 1844 he administered the affairs of south Australia, and brought order out of chaos, saving the colony from threatened ruin. From south Australia he was transferred to New Zealand, and in two months he had closed the war with which the colony was oppressed and restored quietness. During the eight years of his rule New Zealand progressed with the greatest rapidity. He was then sent to the Cape, and one of his exploits while there will give a better idea of the self-reliance and boldness of the man than pages of criticism. Cape Town was a coaling station, and he took the responsibility of ordering to Calcutta the ships with soldiers for China. He also sent all the troops under his own command, and these reinforcements reached

Sir Colin Campbell in time for the relief of Lucknow and the saving of India. His boldness was overlooked, and he even received the thanks he so richly deserved, for he probably knew as well as anyone the risk he was running, which, if the exploit had not ended successfully and to the satisfaction of everyone, would have cost him his official head. In several other instances, however, he was not so fortunate, and he had to deal with superiors in office who were not slow to show their dislike. Lord Carnarvon considered him a 'dangerous man,' and the Duke of Buckingham discharged him in a way that 'would not have been courteous if dispensing with the services of a temporary clerk in a merchant's office.' It would have been interesting to have had such a man as governor-general of Canada, to have had all his activity and experience working for our interests. Sir George is yet alive at the hearty age of eighty-one years, and is, according to Mr Murray, 'the only person in New Zealand to whom everybody took off his hat.' His biographer says:

> He might have added with equal truth 'The only man who took off his hat to everybody.' It was an amusing sight to watch the gravity and courtesy with which the 'great pro-consul' returned the salutations of even tiny children of six and seven years old. Little shy boys pulling off their hats to him in a shame-faced way always saw him in return bare his venerable locks with the same gesture with which he would have responded to the greeting of an archbishop.

ARCHIBALD LAMPMAN

The quarrel between realism and romanticism is about as empty a one as that over the iota in the Nicene Creed. Between realists and romanticists, provided they be men of genius, there is very little difference that any but the professional critic can see. The aim of both is artistic truth, and the difference of method fades out of sight before the larger meanings and grander motives of their work. If a writer's work have the charm of beauty, the convincing power of sincerity, the kindling fire of enthusiasm, or if it propels the mind along mightier avenues of thought, opens wider breadths of vision, or plants in the heart the seeds of a juster and tender humanity, what matter whether his method be that of one or the other? Perhaps in the truest sense we should say that every writer of real gift is a realist. If he has surrounded his picture of life with a scenery different from that which we know, he has made his figures act in it with the force and freedom of essential truth; he has conferred upon them by the power of his imagination the right to exist, the right to charm, convince, or influence us, like beings singled out from the actual world about us. Perhaps by the strange setting he has only brought them into grander relief, made their just influence more penetrating and their genuine charm more complete.

To the full-minded, humane reader, unacquainted with the schools, all that is necessary in a writer of fiction is force of imagination and a sympathetic knowledge of the human heart. When he recalls *Rob Roy* or *Old Mortality*, and a host of immortal figures, odd or beautiful or heroic, spring to his memory, bringing with them a radiant, indefinable pleasure, it does not matter to him that an occasional realistic critic snaps about the shadow skirts of Walter Scott. Dickens and Thackeray and Charles Reade are enchanted worlds, filled with delightful people, quite as real to him as his next door neighbour, and probably more companionable. The only regret he has in regard to them is that he has read them all, searched their enchained countries through and through, made friends with everybody, and there is nothing more to discover. When a writer has made his book electric with the representations of creatures that move before our imaginations under the influence of forces and thoughts and passions almost as vividly realized as those of actual life, why should we snarl at him as a romanticist because he has not filled page upon page with minutiae of circumstance and motive, merely for the sake of displaying his power of observation, and without any regard to the relative importance of things? When I read *Middlemarch* or *Daniel Deronda*, and consider the majesty of the intellect that planned those two books, the insight, the imaginative grasp, and the fervid and compassionate wisdom that possess them, and make them in every sentence a revelation and a stimulus, it seems a miserable impertinence to find fault even with the least detail of form or execution.

He who has read *Roderick Hudson*, *The American*, or *The Portrait of a Lady*, if he be a follower of the romantic school, may complain of the somewhat unimaginative hardness of the details, which Henry James piles up in such pitiless quantity about his characters, of the lack of easy transition in the movement of whatever action takes place, of the too finely drawn subtlety of many of the character sketches that make us feel as if we were moving over a floor covered with delicate pottery in a dimly-lighted room, picking our way nervously for fear of rude contact with any of those exquisite things; he may complain of the general irrelevancy of the narratives themselves as regards the deep meanings of life, and that they are scarcely more than psychological treatises, rendered attractive to less laborious readers by being cast in a dramatic form; so may he complain, and yet after he has finished one of those heavily-weighted books, the characters portrayed in it will be chiselled into his memory as by thousands of strokes, so that they will remain to him after the contents of books that perhaps pleased him better are forgotten. They were real characters, and their section of life cut out and conscientiously recorded was intensely interesting. What matter by what method the effect was obtained? The result is the same. We bear with us the companionship of lives that did not exist, but are as real to us as those that did.

DUNCAN CAMPBELL SCOTT

Mr Arthur Symons, in his article on Mr Henley's poetry, in the August *Fortnightly*, has given us incidentally a definition or description of what a poet's life should be, with what sort of variety and entertainment it should be filled. It is a pronouncement of what a certain 'cult' means when it thinks of poetry and the poetic temperament.

> A villa and books never made a poet; they do but tend to the building up of the respectable virtues; and for the respectable virtues poetry has but the slightest use. To roam in the sun and air with vagabonds, to haunt the strange corners of cities, to know all the useless and improper and amusing people, who are alone very much worth knowing; to live as well as to observe life; or to be shut up in hospital, drawn out of the rapid current of life into sordid and exasperating inaction; to wait for a time in the anteroom of death; it is such things as these that make for poetry.

It is certainly true that experience must be the basis for all art work, and that the poet must write from a fullness of knowledge. But no special set of circumstances will develop or render more complete the expression of a man's genius. There is no value to the poetic temperament in knowing the obscure and vicious side of life; it can hardly make a man's work of greater value to write knowingly about vagrant and wayward things. This definition of the kind of experience required for poetic utterance really marks a decadence in literature. There can be nothing pure in such an ideal, and to follow it would mean a passage into limbo with the rest of the forgotten things. The human mind willingly lets die the disagreeable and the hurtful, and any work of art that attempts to perpetuate them has within itself the seeds of its own mortality.

17 September 1892

DUNCAN CAMPBELL SCOTT

I have been reading with much pleasure and no little profit the volume of Mr Wetherell's selections from the poems of Wordsworth. The book is an immense advance from the days of the old 'Red Book series,' which we can all so vividly remember, and to judge of its usefulness I have only to recall that it was between the humble covers of one of that very series that I first became acquainted with a single poem of Wordsworth, 'Fidelity.' I can remember distinctly the great attraction this single poem had for me, and I can form some idea of the force for good which such a carefully edited volume of Wordsworth's selections must inevitably have. The book is decently printed and well bound considering its low price, which of course is a requisite in a book intended for the use of the schools; the illustrations are not bad, and, as they discreetly represent only familiar haunts of the poet and a very tolerable cut of his face, they are acceptable. It was a rare piece of taste that kept the illustrations of special poems out and spared us all the unnamable horrors of a delineation of 'The Highland Reaper.' The biographical sketch and the essays are admirable and serious, and the notes are not absolutely superfluous, as is so often the case with notes. The selection of special criticisms on individual poems is also a good idea and should serve to stimulate reading. Of course we must not forget that this volume is a textbook and that notes and counter notes are the real reasons for its being, otherwise we might feel that the author of the preface might have spared us his notes on the essays with their insistence on what he desires the student to find in them. When he asks us to believe that Mr Roberts 'shows us clearly that Matthew Arnold's estimate of Wordsworth's genius is misleading and demands correction,' there are not a few of us who will refuse to assent. It would have been wiser for Mr Wetherell to have allowed Mr Roberts's thoughtful essay to stand for itself; its context cannot be strengthened by the assertion that it is an absolutely safe guide to the true position of Wordsworth in the poetic firmament. But even if it were impossible for the Wordsworthian to agree with Mr Roberts, there is so much of sound, healthy criticism in his remarks that this minor point, for it is really a minor point, may be very well left for the controversialists. We have one more thing for which to thank Mr Roberts. His own genius is essentially un-Wordsworthian, and it is pleasant to find him able and willing to give us such a wholesome dissertation on the great poet. The closing words of his essay convey the true value and power of the poet's work:

> The distinctive excellence of Wordsworth's poetry is something so high, so ennobling, so renovating to the spirit that it can be regarded as nothing short of a calamity for one to acquire a preconception which will seal him against its influence. One so sealed is deaf to the voice which, more than any other in modern song, conveys the secret of repose. To be shut out from hearing Wordsworth's message is to lose the surest guide we have to those regions of luminous calm which this breathless age so needs for its soul's health.

To me it seems an evident contradiction to write so, and then to make the subject of the criticism equal with Byron and Shelley. For this 'luminous calm,' this 'repose,' which we need for our soul's health, is surely for us among the very greatest of all powers, the one to which we turn as the centre of all things when the spirit is at rest and contented. But the agreement or disagreement with this view will be settled by personal characteristics. It is to be hoped that for every student this little book will be a prelude to the reading of Wordsworth's poetry; there is always too great an insistence upon the tediousness of much of the poet's work; this has come to be a sort of cant in criticism. He who will pass from the selections to *The Prelude* and the longer works will find ample compensation for the lapses into dullness of which we hear so much. We should thank Mr Houston for his just remark upon the memorization of poetry, which, he says, is 'invaluable for life.' This is very true, and no one can properly judge the comforting power of poetry until it becomes a thing of the memory, to be called up when the heart is troubled or distressed.

WILFRED CAMPBELL

The last of the great group of American poets has passed to his long home after having lived to a ripe old age, and in the death of Whittier

New England loses her most characteristic poet. Holmes, who is the only one of the old writers now living, while just as famous a personality in his own way, will be less regarded as a poet than as a humorist, though 'The Chambered Nautilus' is a poem of exquisite beauty. Whittier was essentially the poet of a cause, and he so identified himself with the abolition movement that many have failed to see the real beauty of several of his other poems. 'Maud Muller' is a poem of enduring quality in its human interest and pathos, and 'In School Days' is also very touching. Whittier has also done some exquisite nature work, and has written some strong ballads, such as 'The Witch of Wenham,' but to my mind his most enduring poem is 'Snow-Bound,' which is the great New England pastoral. Like Longfellow and Lowell, Whittier lived in a heroic age, that of the great Civil War, and so gained a widespread fame, that might have been more slowly achieved in more prosaic times. That he was great as a man none will deny. His heart was large and tender; and the most religious of the poets of his day, he was also intensely human, so that even his hymns, notably his 'Centennial Hymn,' are great in their way. While restless and progressive as a reformer, Whittier's mind was gentle and almost child-like in its faith in the great Ruler of the universe. No dark problems seem to have ruffled the serene tides of his soul, no hideous doubts appeared to confront him, but his was a large and simple creed, that gave little room for doubt and speculation. Then we must remember that he lived in an age that was advancing to easier achievements than are possible now, and that he was reared in a healthy rural environment, prolific with hope for the individual, and hence the universe, and strong in those nerve-giving qualities that brace the spirit to great deeds. In those days there was plenty of room for all, men on this continent were not so crowded. The tides of immigration and of human freedom had not reached the points where the ebb sets in. In the days of Whittier's prime the era of personal independence and self-assertion was at its best. When we look back to the widespread popularity of the leading singers of his school, we find that the age was sympathetic to their song, which was largely sentiment, pure and yet only ephemeral in its existence. While their song was large and human, it was largely the stretching out of the hands of liberty and the heart-strings of hope in a world where there was plenty of room. Now and then we catch a gleam of the deeper sounding with the plummets into the human ocean, where life is always the same, no matter what the age or its wants. After all, it seems to me that the real greatness of the New England school lay in its largeness of personality, so that they made great anything they laid hands on, and their age never failed to take them seriously. Even if poets like Whittier cannot be classed with the greater singers of the earth, they have built for themselves such a pinnacle of nobleness of effort and aspiration, such a large human love and sympathy, that they never can be less than great. And all true souls cannot but be thankful that such souls have dwelt on earth. Even if we, with clearer if less hopeful sight, see afterwards that the evil was not crushed, in the real sense, but only hurled to the ground to rise in another, perhaps more hideous, form, yet the voice that is large and strong against evil is never lost on this earth. The beautiful souls that teach us of beauty in life and thought, they are the voices of morning at noonday and evening. Whatever be our standards, whatever our hopes, they will ever be to suffering, weak, and maimed humanity as the angel voices of earth.

ARCHIBALD LAMPMAN

Sonnet writing is fascinating exercise. Every man who writes verse at all must write a sonnet. The form has been abundantly cultivated in America. Our magazines and journals are full of sonnets, many of them revealing an excellent gift of versification and true thought and feeling; yet America has not produced any poet who has been a really eminent sonnet writer, and she has produced very few sonnets of a very high order, perhaps none of the highest. It may be that the unsettled social atmosphere of this continent is not fitted to develop that particular union of austere dignity and lyric fervour which makes the fine sonnet writer. The sweetest sonnets and the most beautiful in all the American collections are undoubtedly Longfellow's. His 'Nature,' 'Sound of the Sea,' 'Milton,' 'Tides,' and 'Chimes' are very lovely little poems and only need a little strengthening, a slight access of ruggedness, to make them sonnets of the highest order. The cleverest sonnets we have are those of Mr Edgar Fawcett. They are the cleverest, the strongest, the most ingenious, and the least touching. Like all Mr Fawcett's work, they are the product of a powerful artistic genius, devoted to a sort of subtle imitation of passion and equipped with an unusual faculty of invention. Some of them are splendid as bits of versification – 'Sleep,' for instance – others are simply horrible, the more so for being able, and not one of them has the accent of real tenderness or moves with the freedom of the noblest beauty. Edgar Allan Poe came nearest to writing the grand sonnet of this continent in 'Silence.' Bryant nearly succeeded in 'October,' and so did Lowell in some of his sonnets addressed to persons, in which he seems to have been moved by a specially lofty and musical spirit. Mr Aldrich has written some exceedingly able and grandly sounding sonnets, but he has generally erred, as Americans are so apt to do, on the side of cleverness. Many of his pieces are marred by a line or two of much too evident effort at fine writing. He has not often the patient ear and majestic self-restraint of the true sonneteer. Sydney Lanier injured the character of his sonnets not only as sonnets but even as poems by weaving them full of careful subtleties of phrase and meaning and weighting them too heavily with intricate imagery; for the sonnet – most particularly among all kinds of poetry – should be simple. Mr Gilder, who also came very near the ideal American sonnet in 'The Life-Mask of Abraham Lincoln,' has written a number of other beautiful ones – 'The River' and 'The Holy Land,' especially. His sonnet on the sonnet, which is much extolled, seems to me rather a spasmodic little production, a sort of task momentarily imposed, and done by tour de force, but very cleverly. Some of James Whitcomb Riley's sonnets are exquisite in their almost impish cleverness and their dainty and whimsical beauty. For with him the sonnet has put off her fair and majestic robes of wisdom and has donned not exactly the cap and bells, but certainly some sort of gay and rather impudent apparel. The sonnets of Emma Lazarus are the finest of those written by American women. One or two of them – 'Success,' for instance, and 'The Venus of the Louvre' – are strong, and bite keenly into the memory. A certain looseness, however – the flagging of a line here and there – prevents them from ranking with the very best work of their kind. Our own poet, Chas. G.D. Roberts, has written at least one sonnet of a high order, 'Reckoning,' and several others of marked and individual excellence. Among the poems of Mrs Moulton, Helen Gray Cone, Mrs Jackson, Clinton Scollard, Charles H. Luders, Bayard Taylor, and R.H. Stoddard are scattered sonnets of considerable beauty, but not often with the genuine sonnet ring.

24 September 1892

DUNCAN CAMPBELL SCOTT

In its issue of the 19th September last *The Week* devoted one of its editorial paragraphs to a comment upon the general obscurity of the younger verse writers of Canada, and a special request for light upon a poem of Mr Bliss Carman. The writer is so frank in setting forth the generous disposition which he brings to the subject, and so candid in his admission that the fault or misfortune is his own, that he disarms criticism. For my own part, I have no desire to criticize or find fault with the paragraph itself, for there is much in it which can only give pleasure to a Canadian writer, even if he finds himself weighted with the charge of obscurity. 'In common with other loyal Canadians, we have felt and still feel a legitimate pride in the success with which so many of our gifted young men and women have courted the muse during the last few years.' This sentence is almost compensation enough for any stripes that come after, for there is nothing so gratifying to a writer of whatever standing as to know himself admired by his fellow countrymen. I think it would be impossible to find a more loyal group of men in Canada than her writers. Although from no fault which can at present be remedied our country furnishes for the literary man absolutely no chance of living by his art, the desertions from her ranks of the men of letters have been small indeed, and, where they have occurred, probably the severance was not of the spirit at all. If a man is forced to live by his pen in Canada, or wilfully determines to do so, there is only one refuge for him – journalism – and if all my journalistic friends tell me is true, even that field is not covered very thickly with clover. So that it happens that all our country can bestow upon her writers is in some cases only a very modest (or, perhaps, a prudish would be the better word) income, in others, no income at all. But it is a source of pleasure to all the writers alike to be appreciated in their own country; and when we have advanced a step further, and when it is possible to have a criticism, genial but not flattering, just but not envious, the lot of a Canadian literary man will begin to be not undesirable. I have no intention of presenting a commentary upon Mr Carman's poem, for, with the majority of the readers of *The Week*, I am unfortunate not to have had the opportunity of reading it, and what that journal now owes to Mr Carman and its readers is to publish his poem in full. It was hardly what would have been expected, from the chivalrous tone of the paragraph, to find it ending with two verses only of a poem of nine, which, from the extract, must contain some story, lyrically hinted at, after Mr Carman's manner. It was, I am sure, unintentionally unfair to give only an excerpt from a poem which should be judged in its entirety. I am tempted to answer the question as to the italicized words, which I have no doubt have been many times ere this explained. It will hardly satisfy the questioner to be told that they do not mean anything in the sense of conveying a definite idea, like the words, 'the bird is a thrush,' and that from this point of view they were not intended to mean anything. But poetry is an art by which impressions are conveyed as well as ideas, and this translation into words of the cadence and pause of the thrush's song must be judged successful or unsuccessful, as it conveys an impression of the song itself. This must be decided by each individual reader, but no one can be expected to form any definite opinion without the possession of the whole poem; at present what he is requested to do is similar to the task imposed if a definite meaning were asked for a shred torn from one of Corot's landscapes, which in its proper place led the eye from a foreground of hazy sunlight into the deeps of a forest, with only vestiges of light dappling the amber pools.

WILFRED CAMPBELL

The New York Critic has the following note in connection with the death of G.W. Curtis:

> *The Athenaeum* is the leading literary journal of England – the leading literary journal of the English-speaking world. The United States is an English-speaking country containing some 65,000,000 inhabitants, whose authors' names are known and their books read in England as well as in America. Yet when one of the best-known men of letters in America, our most distinguished orator, the political editor of our most influential weekly newspaper, the writer of an editorial department in an old-established magazine widely read not only here but in England, and the leader in the movement for civil service reform in the United States Government offices – when this eminent American passes away, still in the active discharge of all his duties, *The Athenaeum* finds only this to say of him: 'Dr. Curtis, the editor for 34 years of *Harper's Magazine* and a high authority on

educational questions, died on Wednesday last at New York, in his 69th year.'

George William Curtis was never known as 'Dr.' Curtis; he was never the editor of *Harper's Magazine*; and while he held the (almost honorary) post of chancellor of the University of the State of New York and was well informed on matters pertaining to education, he was not generally known as 'a high authority on educational questions.' It is as if *The Critic* should note the death of Mr Morley (may it be long before it has occasion to do so) in some such wise as this: 'Mr Morley, literary editor of *The Pall Mall Gazette* and a high authority on the subject of copyright (or church history, or French poetry, or what not,) died' etc.

This fact is strangely significant in its bearing on current English literary periodicals and their attitude towards American and even colonial literature. The leading English literary journals are *The Athenaeum*, *The Academy*, *The Spectator*, and *The Literary World*, all published in London, and the common characteristic of these journals is their intense stupidity as to American literature. It would be wrong to call it wilful neglect. Stupidity is the best word that meets the case. The fact is there is no place in the world more insulated and provincial than literary London. The literary people there are at what is considered vulgarly to be the centre of intellectual thought, but such is not the case nowadays. As Mr Howells pointed out a short time ago in *Harper's*, the American literary centres have lost their one-time greatness, and much of the best and promising work is done by writers far removed from such centres. And so it is in London. There was a day when we might have looked up with awe to these thunderers, who made or unmade a writer by a paragraph. But the true genius today lives his own life and works out his own ideals, careless as to the opinions of such dethroned gods. When we realize that each of these journals is surrounded by a small clique of ambitious and often disappointed literary men and women, who know nothing of the great development of literature as it really is, we cannot wonder that these journals are not worthy the notice of a sincere worker. These circles have their prejudices and vain likings, and are often influenced by the dislike or likings of a rival journal. Then all these hangers-on have their rising literary friends, whom they have to foist on the public. So that no one can place any real value on a critique he may see in these papers. All the same it is a shame that this condition of things should exist, a condition which is rapidly spreading to America, so that very little literary work goes on its face value; hence the literary man needs to be a politician in a sense, and try and get in with these cliques, which are the vermin of our literature. They are made up of small men who build up false reputations for themselves and friends by occupying the literary journals. Under the existing circumstances it is no wonder that a growing contempt is rising in respect to the so-called literary centres and literary journals. If the young writer, who is dazed by finding himself patted condescendingly on the back by one of these journals, only knew who the real writer was, and his real standing, his self-exultation would soon evaporate. Until we have a humble desire to know the real growth of true literature at our so-called literary centres, we may expect many of our much over-estimated critical periodicals to be the immense frauds that they are at present.

ARCHIBALD LAMPMAN

It is a fact which we all know, that the commonest pursuit among men is the pursuit of wealth – the accumulation of riches – either for the sake of the splendour which it enables them to assume or the power with which it arms them, or, in the lowest case of all, for the mere sake of watching the pile grow – a purely brute instinct. This importance attached to the possession of wealth is due to a species of madness or mental blindness which is endemic in no particular country, but has been a universal pestilence affecting every age and every climate. People of almost all religions assert this life to be but a period of sojourn, a period of probation in which we shall prepare the soul for the better use of an after existence, and yet most of them employ it in a pursuit from which the least possible good can accrue to the soul – from which indeed the result can be no good at all, but only degradation. Those who spend their lives in the acquisition of knowledge, in the cultivation of art or of any intelligent industry for its own sake, in prosecution of political or social reform, not to speak of the more intimate works of benevolence, these are indeed increasing and deepening and expanding the capacities of the soul and rendering it a fitter inhabitant of a purer world. But what shall we say of the men who have merely accumulated vast wealth and concentrated it under the roofs of glittering palaces – and that in the presence of all the hungering despair and misery which we know to be the lot of thousands to every one of these? All this vanishes like smoke at the touch of death, and they carry nothing with them, if it be true that there is a life beyond the grave, but the hardened, distorted, and attenuated soul. There is only one excuse for a life of money-making – an excuse which has just saved some of our wealthy neighbours of the United States from the reprobation under which they must fall with every really wise man – and that is that it furnishes the power to do good. Even this is an echo of the old plea that the end justifies the means.

If, all at once, through some strange moral awakening, men could be got to see the miserable emptiness and vulgarity of this desire for riches, the work of the social and political reformer would be made beautifully straight before him, and all things would adjust themselves to the ideal plan; for, as we have been told many times, and most truly, 'gold is the root of all evil,' and the real enemy of mankind is that emissary of satan who says with the Cyclops in Euripides: 'Wealth, my little man, is the wise man's god; all other things are mere boasts and refinements of words.'

1 October 1892

DUNCAN CAMPBELL SCOTT

The readers of *Harper's Magazine* who have for so many years been accustomed to turn to the 'Easy Chair,' sure of half an hour's enjoyment, will miss that humour and good sense which have made the name of George William Curtis a household word. He had many another claim to the world's attention and respect, and he was in his own country as active a politician as he was a writer, but to the thousands scattered over the world his literary work will be his title of remembrance. He was born in 1824. His father was a businessman and intended his son to follow in the same path, but he had hardly been in business a year before he took up farming. In 1842 he joined the community at Brook Farm, and resided there for four years, making the acquaintance of all the enthusiasts who formed that extraordinary group – Margaret Fuller Ripley, Hawthorne, Emerson, Parker, Alcott, and Thoreau. Afterward he resided at Concord, and cemented many of the friendships he had made at the Brook Farm with Emerson, Thoreau, and Hawthorne in particular. In 1846 he went to Europe and travelled for four years.

After his return he joined the editorial staff of *The Tribune*, and in 1852 was the editor of *Putnam's Monthly Magazine*, to which he contributed 'Prue and I.' When the magazine changed hands he became a partner in the new concern, and when the firm suspended payment he sank his whole private fortune and worked with all his energy to save the good name of the firm, which he was at last successful in doing. His first connection with Harper Brothers was in 1852, when he wrote for *The Monthly*, and in the following year he assumed control of the 'Easy Chair.' Upon the establishment of *The Week* [sic] in 1857 he became its leading editor, and held the position until the time of his death. He was thus closely identified with the success of three important periodicals. Although he will never take rank as one of the foremost literary men of America, with those friends of his youth, Thoreau and Hawthorne, yet his books will be read for their charming style and unaffected geniality. For years thousands of people looked to him for a weekly and monthly return of pleasure, and one may safely say that they were never disappointed. His death will leave a gap which it will be hard to fill, and as yet no announcement of the continuance of the 'Easy Chair' has been made. To many it will never be the same, no matter how brilliant a successor may discourse from the seat they will always remember George William Curtis.

ARCHIBALD LAMPMAN

Some little discussion having arisen in regard to one of Mr Bliss Carman's poems, it is not inopportune to say something in regard to Mr Carman in general. The number of people who have the time or inclination to interest themselves in young contemporary writers is always very limited, and of the few who care to do so in this country, still fewer, I fancy, have any notion of the immense promise – nay, more than promise, the immense accomplishment – there is in Mr Carman's work. Mr Carman has published very little of his work, probably because he is confronted by the same obstacle that stands in the way of every new writer of obstinate originality – the impenetrable stupidity, that invariable shortsightedness of publishers. Those few personal friends of Mr Carman, however, who have been specially favoured with an opportunity to judge his work, know that there is hardly any limit to the expectation that may be had of their friend's future. With great imaginative power and a most uncommon gift of musical versification, he has discovered and taken up a quite new poetic standpoint. His poems are suffused with a new and peculiar and most beautiful imaginative spirit, a spirit which is that of our own northern land, developed in the atmosphere of the Norse, with tinges of Indian legend. Many people will complain of his obscurity, and he is often – very often – obscure, because he does not aim at conveying clearly-cut images and ideas, but prefers, in obedience to a powerful impulse of his own mind, to steep his reader's imagination in splendid moods through the agency of magnificent metrical effects and a vast and mysterious imagery. Whether obscure or not, for the true lover of poetry there is one presence that covers a multitude of faults – the presence of beauty. We cavil in vain at a man's work if it is beautiful, and Mr Carman's work is exquisitely beautiful.

WILFRED CAMPBELL

I am told that the poetry of Mr T.B. Aldrich sells better just now than that of any other living American poet, with the exception of that of Jas. Whitcomb Riley, and that it is increasing in popularity. Mr Riley's work has such a popular quality that it cannot help but be marketable, but the work of Mr Aldrich is noted for its artistic delicacy and strength of fancy, qualities that without unusual power attached should restrict a poet's constituency to a cultured few. Mr Aldrich, who is slightly over fifty, can now be conceded to be the most prominent of living American poets who have produced a large volume of high class work. Of course, we still have Dr Holmes, the oldest and most distinguished all-round littérateur, but it is as a humorist that Dr Holmes will live longest. Then, Mr Stedman, the distinguished critic, has denied himself too much the exercise of his undoubtedly high poetical powers in order to identify himself as he has done with his monumental works in criticism. In Richard Henry Stoddard, America has a lyrist of whom any country might be proud, but he has grown old in the toils of journalism. But Aldrich, since he has severed his editorial connections, has tuned his lyre anew with much ambitious effort to achieve loftier work. Aldrich is essentially an artist, and on this side will take high rank, but he is too much the artist, I am afraid, to be a great popular poet to the people, who require a stronger heart-touch than his artistic repression will allow. He has attempted such a wide range of work that it would be a hard matter to give a proper idea of his powers by adequate quotation, but there is no doubt that he is at his best in exquisitely delicate cameos. He has no burden of song for the righting of wrongs, as

Whittier had. He has no spiritual sombreness of sentiment such as made Longfellow a household friend. He has not the clarion note, the manly, human didacticism that fired Lowell; but perhaps in the long run he may prove to have the most enduring qualities of them all. He has certainly proved himself to possess the strongest artistic powers of any American poet who has ever written, and perhaps, after Tennyson, than any of this century in the English language. Certainly, none show to a better extent the Greek-like polish and repression of the artist. But it is as a thinker and as a poet of the heart that Aldrich falls short in all-round greatness, or else he would have outshone Tennyson. He appears to have so many moods, or else such a general lack of mood, that it is hard to get at his feeling, outside of his art. That he loves nature no one can doubt from his exquisite suggestion of Herrick, whom he resembles on one of his lighter sides, but he loves the well-kept lawns and parks and the cultured haunts of the old world too well to ever be a genuine American nature poet. As a thinker, where his marked repression allows us to see it, he might be called the most worldly of all the greater American singers. His philosophy is ever governed by his art, and is almost heartless in its want of bias. His whole work has a general lack of that pathos found in poets who have probed deep down into life. But Mr Aldrich's verse structures are not human houses wherein men and women dwell, and suffer and enjoy, like to those of Burns, Hood, and Wordsworth. Nor are they demon caves of a weird imagination, such as were conjured up by Coleridge and Poe (not that he does not possess the qualities requisite to such production, for some of his earlier work had a kinship to the former school, while such a remarkably strong poem as 'The Shipmaster's Tale,' in a recent *Harper's*, shows a strong affinity to the latter). But for the most part his verses are airy turrets carved with exquisite skill from gems. Within are dreamy boudoirs of the artist's imagination, where he may sit on cushioned divans and flawless bric-à-brac, and dream eastern dreams toned down by a western artistic repression, wherein the weird and fanciful are strung together on a cynic fatalism that pervades the whole. This is Aldrich, pure and simple. That he has written poems depicting great deeds, as in 'Judith,' or the soul struggle, as in 'Friar Jerome's Beautiful Book,' we must admit, and that they are poems of a high order, especially the latter, no one can deny; but in both it is the artist who is supreme, and somehow we miss the man who feels, despite the exquisite art and stately verse. There is all through felt the lack of an uplifting thought, nor is there a touch of the really lofty imagination that exalts though it may not touch. All through it is the master artist, who dazzles by deft and often stately phrases, or quaint and sometimes exquisite fancies. But the true poet, apart from the artist, who stands forever on the threshold of the unknowable and reports to his fellows the majesty of life, is not to be found, for the most part, in these magic pages. I do not say he is not found, for art, even in verse, has its revelation of life beauty, but where it is here found, it is for the most part whispered in under-breath interludes rather than sung. His exquisite sonnet, 'Sleep,' is a good sample of his best work, and is by some regarded as his masterpiece. The fancy here is almost transcendent in its delicacy of expression, but the thought involved touches no high chord in the reader. As already stated, the master-artist is there, but that is all. For the uplifting quality, the divine gift of revealing the unseen, and the beauty of thought in its relations to the universe, we must go to another school. We are glad to see the ever-growing popularity of this master in artistic and exquisite verse; but Mr Aldrich must know himself that, much as his work may be admired and read, as certainly it deserves to be for the artistic genius shown therein, he has given himself over to too much artistic repression ever to be beloved as a poet.

ARCHIBALD LAMPMAN

It is satisfactory to note a considerable recent increase in our literary activity, as indicated by the rise of new periodicals and the improvement of old ones. In *Arcadia* we have a journal vigorously edited, filled with a great quantity of interesting matter, some valuable original contributions, and of an exceedingly attractive appearance. It has also kept completely clear of that tendency to over-bubbling nonsense, which has been the besetting sin of Montreal literary periodicals heretofore. *The Lake* promises well as a magazine. We have hardly seen enough of it yet to judge, but there is no reason why an unillustrated magazine, wisely edited, and backed by a little money, should not succeed in this country, sufficiently well, at any rate, to maintain its place and standard. *The Week* has much improved in the last year or two, and its editorial department in particular has become a very important addition to our means of guidance in the practical questions of the day. A weekly journalistic expression of opinion characterized by undoubted sincerity and impartiality is a rare and valuable thing. *The Dominion Illustrated*, if it would drop the illustrating and the articles on football and such things and go in for literature, would also have a good prospect of success. It enjoys the advantage of seniority, and needs only to enter upon the right path. Let us not neglect to mention that great journal whereof this, 'The Mermaid Inn,' is a humble part, and to praise the largeness of that enterprise which has scattered weekly broadcast over the Dominion so vast a quantity of useful information, and various and interesting matter of all sorts, literary and otherwise.

8 October 1892

ARCHIBALD LAMPMAN

The legend that Keats's death was caused by certain malignant criticisms in *The Blackwood's Magazine* [sic] and *The Quarterly Review* appears now to be altogether exploded. Anyone who has read the letters of Keats is brought to the extreme point nearest to conviction that the story is absurd. No one ever expressed more thoroughly manly views in regard to verse criticism in the public press than Keats, and his words have in all cases the unexcited and sedate tone of perfect sincerity. That Byron should have believed and put it on record is not surprising. Byron was not a particularly honest man, not a particularly generous one, nor a particularly decent one. He was not unwilling to credit his brother poet – whose earlier work he himself had abused in a manner hardly less brutal than that of the writer in *Blackwood's Magazine* – with a weakness of which he deemed himself in his god-like superiority incapable, and, moreover, the supposed fatal injury done to Keats furnished him with material for a very clever stanza in *Don Juan*, a thing in itself quite irresistible. It is, however, strange that Shelley, who knew Keats well enough, one would suppose, to be thoroughly acquainted with his disposition and even with his attitude in regard to this very matter, should have so confidently accepted the tale, and given it the tragical prominence that he did in 'Adonais.' This is the one fact yet remaining which tempts us to suspect that there may have been a shade more truth in the old story than recent writers are willing to allow.

8 October 1892

DUNCAN CAMPBELL SCOTT

With its wide margins, its heavy soft paper, and large print, Mr William Morris's *Poems by the Way* is a delightful book to read – delightful as well from the many beautiful things it contains (Robert Brothers, 3 Somerset Street, Boston). Some of the poems are old favourites, such as the song from 'The Life and Death of Jason,' but most of them are new. Mr Morris has even given us two or three socialistic poems, full of hope for the future and denunciation of the present. In one, 'The Day is Coming,' he writes:

For then laugh not but listen
  To this strange tale of mine
All folk that are in England
  Shall be better lodged than swine

Then a man shall work and bethink him,
  And rejoice in the deeds of his hand,
Nor yet come home in the even
  Too faint and weary to stand.

And what wealth then shall be left us
  When none shall gather gold
To buy his friend in the market,
  And pinch and pine the sold?

Nay, what save the lovely city,
  And the little house on the hill,
And the wastes and the woodland beauty
  And the happy fields we till?

But the three or four poems which deal with these subjects have not the freedom or the exquisite ease of his best work. It is in such poems as 'Mother and Son,' 'The Half of Life Gone,' 'The Folk-Mote by the River,' where there is scope for those clear pictures of landscape, with their gem-like tints, and for that knowledge of the human heart, that we find Morris at his best. Over such subjects he throws a glamour, a penetrating simplicity, the sadness of the remembrance of lost things.

High up and light are the clouds,
  And though the swallows flit

So high o'er the sunlit earth,
They are well a part of it:
And so, though high over them
Are the wings of the wandering heroe,
In measureless depths above him
Doth the fair sky quiver and burn;
The dear sun floods the land
As the morning falls toward noon,
And a little wind is awake
In the best of the latter June.
They are busy winning the hay,
And the life and picture they make,
If I were once as I was
I should deem it made for my sake;
For here, if one need not work,
Is a place for happy rest,
While one's thought wends over the world,
North, south and east and west.

The book abounds in pictures of life and nature, drawn with that firmness of outline and coloured with that vividness and depth which are characteristic of Morris as a poet. We can nowhere else find such pictures, so ample, so full of air and light, and so tender:

All things I saw at a glance:
The quickening fire tongues leapt
Through the crackling heap of sticks,
And the sweet smoke up from it crept,
And close to the very hearth
The low sun flooded the floor,
And the cat and the kittens played
In the sun by the open door.

That is from 'Mother and Son,' and as an example of his treatment of an early morning landscape I would quote this from 'The Folk-Mote by the River':

Then into the mowing grass we went
Ere the very last of the night was spent.

Young was the moon, and he was gone,
So we whet our scythes by the stars alone.

But or ever the long blades felt the hay,
Afar in the east the dawn was grey.

Or ever we struck our earliest stroke,
The thrush in the hawthorn bush awoke.

While yet the bloom of the swathe was dim,
The blackbird's bill had answered him.

Ere half of the road to the river was shorn
The sunbeams smote the twisted thorn.

WILFRED CAMPBELL

Last week I spoke of the qualities of the poetical work of Mr T.B. Aldrich, the distinguished American poet, and now I will give some quotations from his poems. In the [title] poem to *Cloth of Gold*, one of his volumes of verse, Mr Aldrich gives us a hint of his artistic ideals in verse-building when he says:

You ask us if by rule or no
  Our many-colored songs are wrought
  Upon the cunning loom of thought,
We weave our fancies so and so.

The busy shuttle comes and goes
  Across the rhymes, and deftly weaves
  A tissue out of autumn leaves,
With here a thistle, there a rose.

With art and patience this is made
  The poet's perfect Cloth of Gold;
  When woven so, nor moth nor mould
Nor time can make its colors fade.

A strong individual piece in his best vein is 'Destiny':

Three roses, wan as moonlight and weighted down
Each with its loveliness as with a crown,
Drooped in a florist's window in a town.

The first a lover bought. It lay at rest,
Like flower on flower that night, on beauty's breast.

The second rose, as virginal and fair,
Shrunk in the tangles of a harlot's hair.

The third, a widow, with new grief made wild,
Shut in the icy palm of her dead child.

One of the most remarkable of his weird pieces is 'Identity':

Somewhere in desolate, wind-swept space –
  In twilight land, in no-man's land –
Two hurrying shapes met face to face,
  And bade each other stand.
'And who are you?' cried one agape,
  Shuddering in the gloaming light.
'I know not,' said the second shape,
  'I only died last night!'

'On an Itaglio Head of Minerva' and 'In an Atelier' are too long to quote, and so is 'The Flight of the Goddess,' where he describes how:

A man should live in a garret aloof
  And have few friends and go poorly clad,
With an old hat stopping a chink in the roof
  To keep the Goddess constant and glad.

Wretched enough was I sometimes,
  Pinched and harassed with vain desires;
But thicker than clover sprung the rhymes
  As I dwelt like a sparrow among the spires.
Midnight filled my slumbers with song.
  Music haunted my dreams by day;
Now I listen and wait and long,
  But the Delphian airs have died away.

I wonder and wonder how it befell;
  Suddenly I had friends in crowds;
I bade the housetops a long farewell,
  'Good-bye,' I cried, 'to the stars and clouds!'

And the woman I loved was now my bride.
And the house I wanted was now my own;
I turned to the Goddess satisfied,
But the Goddess had somehow flown.

Flown, and I fear she will never return;
I am much too sleek and happy for her.
Whose lovers must hunger and waste and burn.
Ere the beautiful heathen heart will stir.

In 'Judith,' a long and ambitious poem in blank verse, there is some magnificent description. As in the flight of Judith and her maid from the camp of Ashur after the slaying of Holofernes:

They fled like wraiths
Through the hushed midnight into the black woods,
Where, from gnarled roots and ancient, palsied trees,
Dread shapes upstarting, clutched at them; and once
A nameless bird in branches overhead
Screeched, and the blood grew cold about their hearts.

Among many fine sonnets is the one called 'Sleep,' which many critics have considered his masterpiece. It is certainly among his best work. I have not attempted by these short quotations to give an idea of the artistic beauty of Mr Aldrich's work, but hope that I may have succeeded in introducing his exquisite genius to some of those Canadians who have not had the good fortune to be already acquainted with the entrancing work of this master artist in the domain of poetry:

When to soft sleep we give ourselves away,
And in a dream, as in a fairy bark,
Drift on and on through the enchanted dark
To purple daybreak, little thought we pay
To that sweet-bitter world we know by day.
We are clean quit of it as is a lark
So high in heaven no human eye may mark
The thin, swift pinion cleaving through the grey.
Till we awake ill-fate can do no ill,
The resting heart shall not take up again
The heavy load that yet must make it bleed;
For this brief space the loud world's voice is still,

No faintest echo of it brings us pain.
How will it be when we shall sleep indeed?

ARCHIBALD LAMPMAN

The number of poems which have been translated from other languages into English with just effect is remarkably small – smaller even than need be, notwithstanding the great difficulty of transferring from one language to another the inner spirit of a fine poem. This is due of course to the fact that the work of translation has been left in most cases by the creative poets to writers of inferior power – people who had not sufficient aesthetic grasp and metrical gift for the task. Those who are unable to read originals, and even those who are, must be eternally grateful to Browning for his 'Prometheus,' to Shelley for the 'Cyclops' of Euripides, that delicious piece of English; to Dryden for the *Aeneid*, a noble rendering despite many faults; to old Chapman, whose Homer still towers heavily over so many a more ambitious attempt; to Edward Fitzgerald for the *Rubaiyat*, to Rossetti for his one translation from Villon, and to Swinburne for some others; to Emma Lazarus and James Thomson for several genuine translations from Heine, particularly those of the former, who, by a subtle affinity of genius and perhaps of race, seems to have taken upon her tongue to an unusual degree the distinctive tone and accent of her original. Dante is said to be very ably translated by Charles Elliot Norton; and even the old translation of Carey must convey to us something more than the bare tissue of the Italian. We owe Coleridge a good deal for the Wallenstein. Goethe has been translated, but surely not adequately, and nearly all the rest of the vast field remains unturned save in the clumsiest and most unsightly manner. To have at our command real translations of all the noblest poems of other tongues so that we might be able to enter somewhat into the inner spirit of them without undertaking the impossible toil of mastering seven or eight different languages would be an advantage which the wise at least would repay with the truest kind of fame to those mightier ones in their succeeding generations who should be self-sacrificing enough to confer it. If each genuine poet would reproduce even one of these masterpieces it would not be very long before we should have a tolerably complete series.

15 October 1892

DUNCAN CAMPBELL SCOTT

My Dear Francesca: You will ere this have heard of the death of Tennyson. I know how profoundly this will affect you, with what a sense of loss, and the regret that follows when we know that a great force has finally ceased. We have that feeling of satisfaction, too, at the rounding and due fulfilment of a perfect career, and, as a reaper who finishes his work, we have seen him at sundown collecting the last gleanings and going joyfully home, 'carrying his sheaves with him.' And what a glorious harvest his has been! From the commencement how individual was his utterance, how perfectly clear and sincere. Although in those first poems you can detect sometimes faint echoes of Keats and Milton, yet his accent was emphatically his own. He may have caught from Wordsworth that desire for simplicity in narrative which we find completed in 'Dora' or 'The Gardener's Daughter,' but how different is the actual result from the simplicity of his predecessor! He was the fountainhead of nearly all the main streams of poetic expression in his own age. In him we find the germs of the school in which Morris and Rossetti were the leaders. Matthew Arnold could not escape his influence, nor Coventry Patmore, nor anyone who has written verse since the year 1832, when *The Lady of Shalott*, *Oenone*, and *The Palace of Art* first saw the light. In fact no poet has ever influenced the style and aims of his contemporaries to such an extent. And his influence was all for good. In the mere technique of his art he set a standard which raised the level of the verse of his time and which made every writer strive for a similar perfection. If it was Keats's object to 'load every rift of his subject with ore,' it was Tennyson's to make every line ring like pure gold; and, if absolute success were not impossible for mortals, it might be said absolutely that he had succeeded. And his generation came panting after him, lured on by that style which seemed so easily perfect, by that diction which seemed so simply pure. But both were his own, and, although he has had imitators, he has had no approach of a rival. He had a way of transfiguring the common incidents and occupations of everyday life, making them melt and glow, as it were, in the heat of his imagination. I would recall to your mind those lines in *Enoch Arden* where he tells of Enoch's visits to the hall with the Friday's fish:

For in truth
Enoch's white horse, and Enoch's ocean spoil
In ocean-smelling orier, and his face,
Rough-reddened with a thousand winter gales,
Not only to the market cross were known,
But in the leafy lanes behind the down,
Far as the portal-warding lion-whelp,
And peacock-yew tree of the lonely hall,
Whose Friday's fare was Enoch's ministering.

That is a fair example of his incomparable art. Its greatest achievement is *In Memoriam*. To have carried a poem in a stanza which has all the elements of monotony inherent in itself to such a splendid and amazing perfection, so full of variety both in material and execution, abounding in such infinite charm of description and melody and music, is a sufficient reason upon which to base his claim for immortality. This one poem is also evidence of what labour he was willing to give to his art. It is only the man who has himself written verse who can appreciate the work which went to the making of those lines which seem the perfection of natural ease. And this consummate art was in the service of a lofty and beautiful idea. The desire for and belief in the ultimate good in human destiny, and the wish for a larger faith and a more hopeful creed, these were the subjects of which he naturally wrote. And with what an effect we know, for there is hardly a public speaker either in the pulpit or on the platform who does not enforce and vivify his argument for liberality of thought or for belief in the ultimate good of human pain and defeat by quotations from Tennyson.

This year 1892 will take its place with those other dates, 1616, 1674, 1850, in the memory of mankind as marking the close of a genius in the direct line of Shakespeare, Milton, and Wordsworth, and, in common with yourself and that multitude of souls who have been elevated and carried away by his spirit, I would drop a blossom of remembrance upon the grave of Alfred Tennyson.

ARCHIBALD LAMPMAN

One would give some of his happiest hours to know what were the thoughts of Alfred Tennyson as he lay through that last night silent, the autumn moonlight all across his bed, the wind whistling in his manor oaks, and his left hand, that blameless hand, resting upon the open pages of *Cymbeline.* Surely no man's death was ever more beautiful; the master poet of his race and age, gentle, 'noble and sincere,' passing to sleep in the very fulness of his fame, with all the pride and love of England at his feet! When Tennyson was laid in Westminster Abbey by the side of Browning the two greatest and most beloved Englishmen of their time were laid close together. Browning was the more robust nature. His grasp of life was more various, more eager, more abundantly fruitful. But Tennyson was the nobler mind and the more picturesque and dignified figure. All the art and intellect of his country and all its generous spirit have attached themselves to him as they have to no other man since Dryden.

About the circumstances and details of Tennyson's life we know little. In his case, as in the case of Browning and Matthew Arnold, a noble reticence has always been maintained, which is rare and admirable in an age when a ravenous curiosity and hunger for petty notoriety override the sense of dignity even in those from whom we expect better. But this at least we know, that the name of the dead laureate has always been associated with the fairest and loftiest impressions; that he was one of those who never did or 'uttered anything base'; that his life was that of a poet-philosopher, wise and dignified, a life eminently human in the distinctive meaning of the word, the life of one who realized to the point of practice the beauty, sacredness, and deep meaning of this earthly existence. His only fault, we are told, was a tendency at times to be moody, abstracted, and unsocial.

Notwithstanding that the world has read Tennyson for more than sixty years, his rank among English poets is not yet surely settled; it may, however, be taken for granted that he is among the half dozen greatest. It is a trite observation in criticism that he is the poetic successor and inheritor of Keats and Wordsworth in an almost equal degree. While he has not the exquisite and unapproachable spontaneity in beautiful creation that Keats possessed, nor that strange simplicity of touch which in Wordsworth was so powerfully penetrating, yet he has a kingly and triumphant mastery of versification, a march and sweep of numbers, a perfection and variety of phrase and cadence, in which through the study and practice of a long life he has far exceeded his masters. In *The Lady of Shalott* he fathered the pre-Raphaelite school. His *Oenone* is one of the most beautiful poems in the language – of its kind the most beautiful; and the *In Memoriam* the wisest and the loftiest. In blank verse he does not compare favourably with Milton or

Keats or Wordsworth, or even with Shelley, a fact of which he was, no doubt, conscious, inasmuch as he gave so modest a form to his stories of Arthur, calling them idylls rather than anything more pretentious, yet in these very tales there is a quality of dignity and beauty and sweet human sympathy that will be more than sufficient to render them immortal. It were useless to go over the long list of lyrics and meditative pieces which are belovedly familiar to every English ear, and which assuredly can only perish with the language.

WILFRED CAMPBELL

By the death of Tennyson England loses the greatest and undoubtedly the last of her great line of truly national poets. He was the ideal laureate, not only of the court but of the nation. No other English singer has sung as he has England's heroic deeds by land and sea. The ballad of the 'Revenge,' probably the most heroic ballad ever written, may never be equalled in any literature. And such poems as 'The Charge of the Light Brigade' and the magnificent 'Ode on the Death of Wellington' are alone in the language for strength and beauty. As the court singer he has also done better work than might have been expected. His lines to the Queen [in] *In Memoriam* are full of depth of feeling and stately beauty, and could not be improved upon. All through he is essentially the great English singer. He cannot be called the laureate of the empire, nor is he a great world-singer but by right of his large genius. In this field it may be finally found that Browning is the greater. But whatever judgment the future may bring as to his lasting qualities, Tennyson's place as the greatest English poet of the nineteenth century, and as one of the greatest of any other century, is well established. It is almost certain that he is the last of the great English poets, and this fact adds to the greatness of his loss to the English people. And in his death we feel a sense of the gradual passing away of that great kingdom which has ruled for so long the modern world. There may be the great empire of the future with its singers, or perchance a republic, for all we know, but with Tennyson dies the last of the grand old Saxon bards whose hearts were England's and for England alone. All of the greater bulk of his work, from *The Idylls of the King* down, is on English themes, and imbued with the old English spirit. And no one will ever be able to disassociate the name of Tennyson from that of the historical greatness of his native land. Like Chaucer and Spenser, he seems a part of the soil, and his memory will ever be connected with her

Castle walls
And snowy summits old in story.

Even in the early unrest of his young manhood, which we find in *Locksley Hall*, his nature was in close sympathy, though unconsciously, with the great aristocratic nationality of which he was one of the noblest developments. Then the easy success of his work, and its sudden great popularity strangled in its infancy the demon of unrest that would never at its worst have made him the republican that Shelley was. With all the majestic splendour of his lofty lyrical faculty, which would in itself have given him a high place in the world's literature, the close association of his best work with all that is best in the life of England will, I think, ever remain his most distinguishing characteristic. Browning is decidedly un-English, and is a poet for all the world, and Swinburne has identified his genius less with the history of his people than with its language. Matthew Arnold has been, and is, the poet of the higher thought, not so much of modern England as of all English-speaking peoples of the last part of this century and of the immediate future. These three, Browning, Arnold, and Swinburne, have much to do with the great republic of letters the world over, the first two for thought, and the last in his capacity as a great political artist. But this is not, truly speaking, so of Tennyson, though in his prime, as a literary artist, probably no one man ever influenced his contemporaries as he did. But widely now as he may be read and appreciated, and for all his great gifts, he will never be the close friend to thinking and poetical minds that Arnold or Browning will be. His splendid genius has covered more ground than any other contemporary poet except Browning. But so much of it is so artistically well done that it palls by its very fineness of finish, and it is so like one of his cultured English parks that we long for a ruggedness that is more of nature. He has touched on so many subjects that it has been said that to read him well is to acquire a liberal education. But for all its greatness his verse is not the poetry of the mature man of today, but leads up to it. I mean as far as the inspiring thought is concerned. *In Memoriam* is a poem of remarkable beauty, and is perhaps as great a mirror as we have of the modern soul in its relationship to final hope and aspiration, and in this sense it is his greatest poem. But in a certain way we of the latter end of this century have outgrown this stage of 'the Infant crying in the night,' though we will never outgrow the artistic beauty of style in which it is expressed.

We, that is many of us, have accustomed our eyes to the gloom as it is, and begin already to see beauties and vastness of glory in the darkness that our fathers but lately dreaded. This must be, I believe, the keynote of the poet of the future. In creating a new religious attitude we have made a new world with its ideals, and our poets must, as ever, be our truest religious leaders or else fall into disuse.

It can be said of Tennyson that he was great as a national poet, great as a lyrical artist, perhaps the most exquisite song writer in the language, and almost great as a dramatic writer. This is where he failed, and in this he failed all through. He had the great artistic qualities, but with too little grasp of human life outside of history and society so-called. Noble, polished, stately, serene, his splendid genius might be likened to a lofty table-land high up on the slopes of Parnassus, far above the little peaks and foothills, and yet not so high as to reach those ethereal peaks many of whose rugged and uneven slopes stretch far below him.

ARCHIBALD LAMPMAN

An Autumn Landscape

No wind there is that either pipes or moans;
The fields are cold and still; the sky
Is covered with a blue-grey sheet
Of motionless cloud; and at my feet
The river, curling softly by,
Whispers and dimples round its quiet grey stones.

Along the chill green slope that dips and heaves
The road runs rough and silent, lined
With plum trees, misty and blue-grey,
And poplars pallid as the day,
In masses spectral, undefined,
Pale greenish stems half hid in dry grey leaves.

And on beside the river's sober edge
A long fresh field lies black. Beyond,
Low thickets grey and reddish stand,
Stroked white with birch; and near at hand,
Over a little steel-smooth pond,
Hang multitudes of thin and withering sedge.

22 October 1892

Across a waste and solitary rise
  A ploughman urges his dull team,
    A stooped grey figure with prone brow
    That plunges bending to the plough
  With strong, uneven steps. The stream
Rings and re-echoes with his furious cries.

Sometimes the lowing of a cow, long-drawn,
  Comes from far off; and crows in strings
    Pass on the upper silence.
    A flock of small grey goldfinches,
  Flown down with silvery twitterings,
Rustle among the birch cones and are gone.

This day the season seems like one that heeds
  With fixed ear and lifted hand
    All moods that yet are known on earth,
    All motions that have faintest birth,
  If haply she may understand
The utmost inward sense of all her deeds.

(*Harper's Magazine*, October 1892)

22 October 1892

DUNCAN CAMPBELL SCOTT

Canada has lost one of her most talented artists by the death of Paul Peel. He was cut off before he had commenced to realize his powers, just at the time when the technical difficulties of his art were conquered, and when he might expect to use to advantage the control and experience he had gained. I am not able to give a sketch of his life or works; that must be furnished by those who knew him; but it would be amiss if in this column no reference were made to one who gave himself up to his chosen art, and who died before his life work was finished. I am not aware that any of his work dealt with Canadian subjects; those pictures of his which I have seen seemed to show French ideals, and were painted from French subjects. His work always had a charm of its own, and the reproduction by the Autotype Company of his 'After the Bath,' where two little children warm themselves before an open fire, is very tender and charming, and the original picture must have these qualities in a still higher degree.

WILFRED CAMPBELL

I notice that Mrs Cotes (Sara J. Duncan) has an article on 'The East' in the present number of *The Popular Science Monthly.* This fact reminds us that Canada has many very able writers among her women. Prominent in a long list are the well-known names of Miss Machar, Mrs Harrison, Miss Wetherald, and Miss Pauline Johnson, the Indian poetess. All of these women are able writers of fiction, as well as poets. Miss Wetherald, who is one of the youngest, has also a reputation as a journalist and has written many a strong editorial. She has been for some time associate editor of Mrs Cameron's clever paper, *Wives and Daughters*, and is often a contributor to American periodicals and journals. But it is as a poet that I think Miss Wetherald has not done justice to herself, and it is hard to say what she might not have accomplished had she but wooed her muse a little more faithfully. As it is, she has produced the finest sonnets ever written by a Canadian woman, and stands in the front rank of Canadian sonnet writers. It is a pity that such a woman as Miss Wetherald, with her strong practical sensibilities and literary powers, has given herself over to the drudgery of journalism. It is all very well to say that women cannot write verse. Some of the strongest verse of today in America is written by women, and we hope that Miss Wetherald has not entirely deserted her muse. Miss Machar's spiritual lyre is so well known to Canadians that she needs no introduction to the readers of the Mermaid Inn. Mrs Harrison is also well known to us all in prose and verse. Miss Johnson is becoming known in England, where, I understand, Mr Theodore Watts has espoused her cause. She has written some strong and original work, which should deserve our notice outside of any interest her personality as an Indian may create. Those who would know more of her evident genius, I would direct to the fine, if rather enthusiastic, article on Miss Johnson's verse in the September number of *The Lake Magazine*, by Mr H.W. Charlesworth, of *The Toronto World*, who is himself one of our rising littérateurs.

22 October 1892

ARCHIBALD LAMPMAN

Patriotism with us is not an instinctive but a moral quality. We cannot be patriotic as the Englishman is patriotic. Born and bred in an old and famous land covered with the monuments and remnants of a romantic history, a land still ringing with names that were illustrious centuries ago, surrounded by all the epoch-making stir of a great race, the Englishman, indeed, were not at the level of humanity if he had not patriotism. Rather than that all this should suffer hostile touch or be affected by any breath of shame, he springs to arms by an impulse as natural and irrepressible as the indignation that would fire him at seeing a child or a woman beaten and abused. With us it is very different. We have no magnificent race history behind us, nor visible memorials of its beauty and splendour; we have not even a homogeneous people; we are, indeed, only the scattered and intractable materials of which a nation may be made. We cannot have, therefore, any impulse of patriotism. Our patriotism is founded upon duty and the sense of honour. But it is none the less real, and in those who possess it will do duty as unflinchingly in the hour of danger as that other patriotism of the blood whereof we have spoken. Even among our neighbours of the United States, with the inspiriting memory of some heroic national experiences behind them, the old-fashioned fiery and affectionate love of native land is not fully developed, as the exaggerated gasconading exhibition of it in their public press distinctly shows. The ordinary American only loves and clings to his country as long as he can make money out of it. He is ready to nationalize himself anywhere where the dollars are. Nevertheless, there is a great deal more patriotism of the instinctive sort in the United States than in Canada, and most naturally so – their power, independence, and considerable historic background giving them that spiritual as well as material advantage over us. No one can go into some of the American cities and study the inscriptions – those many tender and solemn inscriptions – on the monuments to their dead of the Civil War without a thrilled consciousness that these are the records of mighty events, and that he is listening to the impassioned voice of a people. We shall not know what national consciousness and patriotism are until something like that happens to us. If it ever comes to a question with each one of us of either sneaking off into a corner and playing the coward or else going forth sternly for pride and honour's sake, if not for love, to risk our blood for this land's unity or independence, then in a little while we shall learn what patriotism is. The brave among us shall make it possible for our descendants to be patriotic in the true sense, and not till then.

DUNCAN CAMPBELL SCOTT

We can all remember a book in which an American behaved with some audacity, and with plenty of that humour and good sense, coupled with self-reliance, which the world has come to recognize as the characteristic of a type of the neighbouring republic. I refer to Christopher Newman in Mr Henry James's novel *The American.* Nicholas Tarvin, the westerner who occupies so large a portion of the canvas in *The Nahulakah*, is cast in the same mould; he proceeds with his impossible tasks with an assumption of the same humour and self-reliance. But one cannot consider them as anything but an assumption; behind all his valorous deeds and presence of mind one seems to see a really threadbare character. Christopher Newman was a gentleman, and even in the most trying situations he never becomes absurd. This is, of course, an evidence of Mr James's wonderful power. But Tarvin is created not from the life, but from that idea of it which certain American playwrights bring so prominently before their audiences. From first to last there is no touch of the gentleman about him, and he remains to the end as vulgar as he promises to be at the beginning. The book is frankly one given over to antithesis, and we have the rawest and rankest western life forced into the most dreamy and ancient eastern civilization; we even have a little native prince reciting a poem of William Blake's:

> Tiger, tiger, burning bright
> In the forests of the night;

and the fortunes of a western town, in which it is impossible to take any interest, depending upon the success of Tarvin's more than quixotic enterprise. If it is fair to separate the work of the joint authors, one must confess that those portions which bear the imprint of Mr Kipling's genius are successful, and brilliantly so; the ride to the 'Cow's Mouth,' the descriptions of the prince's wedding fete, and many another passage in the book, are as vivid and picturesque as possible. It is curious to notice here and there tricks of the novelist's art which are certainly out of date, and which have a grotesque appearance in a modern novel; witness Tarvin's ridiculous address to his horse before he commences his journey to the 'Cow's Mouth,' which adds yet another stroke of the unsubstantial to that most visionary figure.

29 October 1892

ARCHIBALD LAMPMAN

No man is more sincere than the poet; yet no man is more given to expressing under different circumstances the most opposite sentiments. Let none quarrel with the poet for this variableness of mood; in fact it is his chiefest charm; it is that which brings him into the most tender and intimate relation with the general soul of humanity. The listener, as he is touched in turn by so many rapid and equally passionate alternations of hope and sorrow, anger or despair, perceives that he is in contact with one who knows the most secret impulses of his heart, and whose spirit, through quickness of sympathy, is in the closest friendliness with his own. I have a friend – a lyric poet – whose mind is, as a general rule, more stolid and less violent in its changes of colour than is the case with many of his kind; yet he has just furnished me with a very pretty example of this fine fickleness of thought. It had been an unfortunate day for my friend. Unpleasant sensations had followed closely one upon another. He had been worried by some small monetary difficulty, a thing that to another man would have been a very trifle, but to him was like the breaking of the Bank of England. He had been in contact with businessmen, men who deal in money, and their cold brutality and callousness of heart had affected his spirit with a kind of gloomy horror. When night came he was sad and weary, and enveloped in a cloud of portentous darkness. Yet it was not long before the old and ever-active remedy began to insinuate itself and work among his distracted thoughts. As by some happy accident, a touch of song kindled his reflections with a sudden illumination, and after meditating a little while he composed with little effort a sonnet which he has called the 'Cup of Life,' and here I give it just as he read it to me a few days later:

One after one the high emotions fade,
Life's wheeling measure empties and refills
Year after year. We seek no more the hills
That lured our youth divine and unafraid,
But, swarming on some common highway, made
Beaten and smooth, plod onward with blind feet,
And only where the crowded crossways meet
We halt and question, anxious and dismayed.

Yet can we not escape it. Some we know
Have angered and grown mad, some scornfully laughed,
Yet surely to each lip – to mine, to thine –
Comes with strange scent and acrid, poisonous glow
The cup of life – that dull Circean draught –
That taints us all, and turns the half to swine!

The following morning seemed to usher in a complete change of destiny for the poet. As he passed the threshold, the sunshine greeted him with an unusual heartiness of warmth, and the great elm before his door, whose vast level fleece and pendent draperies seemed afloat upon the air, invited his eyes coolly and alluringly into its shadowy recesses. The birds sang in their gayest and happiest humour. A few paces on a friend met him with good news. When the long day's toil was over, still under the influence of the morning's first joyous impressions, he made his way into the fields, and as he returned homeward after an hour of easy accord with nature, at peace with all mankind, the following verses formed themselves naturally and almost unconsciously in his mind. I give them exactly as he set them upon paper at the moment of his return:

I love the warm bare earth and all
    That works and dreams thereon;
I love the seasons yet to fall;
    I love the moments gone.

The valleys with the sheaved grain,
    The river smiling bright,
The merry wind, the rustling rain,
    The vastness of the night.

I love the morning's flame, the steep
    Where down the vapour clings;
I love the clouds that float and sleep,
    And every bird that sings.

I love the masted pines that soar
    Above the mountain villas;
I love the silent wood whose floor
    Is spread with golden lilies.

I love the heaven's azure span,
  The grass beneath my feet;
I love the face of every man
  Whose thought is swift and sweet.

I let the merry world go by,
  And like an idle breath
Its phantoms and its echoes fly;
  I have no dread of death.

I hear the jar of right and wrong;
  Yet both are things that seem;
Each hour is but a fluted song,
  And life a lofty dream!

Assuredly one may say that these verses are light, and inconsiderable in texture, and ethically of little value; yet I give them as the happy and sincere expression of a wonderful change of mood and of all the relations of the poet's mind. Under what different aspects indeed did this life present itself to the poet when he composed these two diverse poems, yet they are both equally sincere.

DUNCAN CAMPBELL SCOTT

A lyric to be perfectly successful should not need any special interpretation. It should not be so involved with personal feeling that it would need a commentary upon the event or upon the special mood which called it forth. All the great lyrics which have been preserved by the common decree of the people have some expression of general experience which renders them capable of proof, as it were, by any human soul. Thus it has often happened that a writer who toiled to win fame by some creation of great length, filled with imagination, accomplished his object by some fragment wherein he gave voice to some common experience of the race. There are too many of the lyrics in Mr W.E. Henley's new book of which it can be said that they require a special interpretation; that they are not self-evident. Although the mass of the work leaves an impression of extreme cleverness, the effect is not one either of pleasure or profit. Mr Henley seems to have looked at everything which he attempts to portray with the eye of a painter, and a painter of the impressionist school. The poem dedicated to Mr Whistler is an attempt to reproduce the effect of one of the painter's harmonies. But it is far from being a success. The choice of words and imagery gives no effect of beauty, which must be the basis for every work of art, however small in dimension. And this principle of beauty would be present in the scene which inspired the picture or the poem, no matter to what thoughts the associations which accompany the scene might give rise. Now these associations are specially the material of poetry; painting cannot reproduce them and it is fatuous for poetry to attempt to give by the choice of special words the exact value of tone and colour in painting. The beauty of a scene is ever present, and although it may influence the mind in many different ways the effect can never be immoral, no matter how terrible the associations may be. And in such work as the third of the 'London Voluntaries' the feeling of beauty is entirely absent, and we have the sense of actual immorality forced upon the material picture. The wind 'comes sullen and obscene, in a cloud unclean of excremental humours,' and every natural appearance wears a sort of lewdness, an abject awfulness of shape and purpose. There is present neither the element of beauty nor the element of human interest, but the landscape exists by itself and for itself in this unreal and grotesque masque as if it had a separate, conscious, and rather immoral personality. An example of the legitimate treatment of a weird and terrible landscape is Browning's 'Childe Roland to the Dark Tower Came,' where we have a human interest informing the whole poem, accompanied by a sense of strange wild beauty. In his actual choice of word and phrase Mr Henley has been undoubtedly influenced by Rudyard Kipling, and, although in some instances the result of this insolent realism of expression is fine, in the majority of cases the striving after an effect is too apparent. Mr Henley's philosophy is not deep. When he leaves life he but leaves 'books and women and talk and drink and art,' and he goes into the ways of death stoically with a sense of relief and release.

5 November 1892

[ANONYMOUS]

I was surprised the other day to come upon a passage which convinced me that we Canadians as a people had passed into literature, in at least one instance, as a rough and a rude nation. The reader of Sir R.F. Burton's *Ultima Thule* will find in his section devoted to society in Iceland these words: 'Yet the Icelander, franklin or pauper, has none of the roughness or rudeness which we remark in the manners of the Canadians and of the Lowland Scotch.' Sir R.F. Burton was a wide traveller, and at the time he wrote these words (1875) he had visited nearly every country on the face of the globe, and, as he was an acute and careful observer, one must take some notice of his remark. It must have some foundation in fact. We have always considered Iceland and the Icelanders as out of all comparison with other nations, and here we find a noted traveller telling us very plainly that we are behind them in courtesy and fine manners. I hope we have improved since the time when Burton formed his opinion of us, and if it were possible for him to visit again the 'glimpse of the moon' he might find it possible to say that we were a little softer, a little more civilized. There is some doubt in my mind of the fairness of travellers generally to the countries and peoples they visit; it is so hard to be exactly just, and still more difficult to arrive at the absolute truth or to strike an average, when considering the characteristics of a people. It is impossible to do that fairly until you become thoroughly familiar with their home life and habits. To view a country from the hotel window or even from the smoking room of a club or to judge finally of the people by the specimens one meets on a railway train are all hazardous and untrustworthy. All the atrabilious people may have taken a melancholy holiday and be travelling on the same train, or the clubroom may be haunted by the local 'crank,' or the meals at the hotel may not be what one would care to praise. But a people should hardly be judged by these casual impressions; the home life should be the test, and in Canada we are developing a standard of home life which is different from either the English or American, and which may in the end be better and more enjoyable than either. I am bound to say that amongst our rural population there is a good deal of surliness and heaviness of mind. I do not think it is by any means general, but it is certainly present, and it may be passing away. But its presence is not to be wondered at; we must remember the hardships which the settlement of this country brought on those who determined to live here, hardships that will never have to be gone through again and of which our Manitoba settlers can know nothing. And among the worst of them was the isolation, the absence of society, in its wider sense; this, with the severity of the climate, was sufficient to breed distemper and moroseness, to say nothing of rudeness and roughness. But, as I said before, I hope we have improved. We can never be a little-hearted, careless people, but there is no reason why we should not be kind-hearted and considerate.

WILFRED CAMPBELL

It has been claimed by many critics that a man cannot be a truly great writer unless he pictures what is hopeful in humanity and passes over what is dark and tends to despondency and despair. We hear so often of what is called the healthy imagination, which is essential to and is found in all the greater writers. All the literary works from those of Shakespeare and Milton to Browning have been scoured for extracts carrying out this theory. But I would just here like to note that the very opposite is true, and that, strange to say, all that is strongest and most lasting in literature depicts not the bright and joyous side of life, but rather what is gloomy, despairing, and tragic. For all the theories of the critics of today, the poets who have endlessly sung life is happy because I am happy have been of the weaker and more ephemeral class. The work of a great poet, like that of any other great man, is not to hypnotize the world into a false or fancied dream of security and selfish indifference, but rather to show life as it is in all its reality – but as a god would show it. The great man is he who truly knows life but still sees the divine back of the most hideous manifestations of its existence. Were the season always springtime and the day always morning, we all would be lotus-eaters. But it is the struggles and the longings, the memories and the might-have-beens that make us great. This wonder and awe of the greatness of life in its sombre aspects is impressed on us by the greatest writers of all ages.

Beginning with Homer, called the greatest epic poet of any age, we find him depicting almost wholly endless battle, which, with all its good side, is perhaps the most awful spectacle humanity can dwell upon. Battle and deceit, rapine and despair is what he gives us. The downfall and destruction of a great people, the Trojans, is his chief theme. Virgil, the noble Roman who followed him, is certainly greater in his epic, which is largely influenced by the *Iliad*, than when he described piping shepherds and fleecy flocks. Dante, the next great poet, has dedicated his whole magnificent genius to the description of hell. Milton, the literary descendant of the Greek, the Roman, and the Florentine, and the greatest English poet after Shakespeare, made the fall of man and the attendant evils the subject of his great epic, which has rendered him immortal. Shakespeare has four or five masterpieces among his marvellous dramas, and what are the subjects of the greatest? We will name them: *Macbeth*, *Lear*, *Hamlet*, *Othello*, *Julius Caesar*, *Richard the Third*, *Romeo and Juliet*. I have named seven, which include all of his greatest works. Now what are the bare subjects of these dramas? The hideous murder of a king, and the attendant horror and punishment of the murderers. The despair and death of a despised old king ruined by his own children. Madness, death, graves, and spooks are the stock in trade of *Hamlet*, and so on through all of these remarkable productions. The dark, the hideous, the tragic side of life is shown in these plays, if they have ever been depicted in literature. Surely if any poet ever lived in the weird, the awful, and the despairing in humanity that man was Shakespeare. And yet we hear so much about the healthiness of the minds of the greatest poets. All that is great in literature will always be connected with the tragedy of human sin and human despair as long as the humanity we are walks this earth. In this lies the greatness of genius. And true genius must always be sad, because it sees the true state of things so acutely. 'The man who went down into hell,' it was said of the great Florentine as he walked the streets, and so it will be unto the end – greatness must suffer.

ARCHIBALD LAMPMAN

It is a great question whether literature can be taught; that is, taught in schools. It seems to me that every man must learn his literature for himself, and that all that ought to be done for him to that end is to teach him to read – to read in English, French, Latin, Greek, or whatever one will. After that if he have an inclination towards any particular literature, he will follow it of himself in the most natural and fruitful manner. If he have no instinct for literature it is waste time to endeavour to force it upon him. In our Canadian schools we undertake to teach literature, and we certainly do teach it with a vengeance. We have bulky grammars, awful and discouraging to the eye; elaborate books, instructive of the art of composition; carefully prepared editions of classical English writings, with explanatory notes, historical notes, glossaries, critical introductions, and so forth. Armed with these, our literature classes are set upon the study of some particular masterpiece –say, a book of *Paradise Lost*. They read it; they declaim it rhetorically; they get it by heart; they analyze it sentence by sentence; they parse it word for word; they study its language syllable by syllable, following each word to its remotest kindred in Latin, Greek, Saxon, old high German, Lithuanian, or Sanscrit; they turn it into prose and back again into verse; they hunt up all the allusions; they make themselves acquainted with parallel passages; they discuss it historically, geographically, critically; they tear and worry and torture the lines of the great poem till they are littered out as dry and innutritive as a worm-eaten codfish. When all this has been done the student's mind is perhaps the acuter for the mental training, but he wishes never to hear the name of *Paradise Lost* again. It is indeed a Paradise Lost for him. And not only have the power and beauty of one English masterpiece been destroyed to his ear, but the chances are that his faculty of appreciation generally has been robbed of its natural freshness and permanently blunted. Whatever may be the merit of this system as an intellectual exercise for the young, it is decidedly not the way to cultivate a book of literature or the power of producing it. Indeed, it seems to me that to teach literature in schools by classes is as impossible as it would be to teach morality in the same way. The love of literature is a natural gift, and if not strong enough to develop itself can only be drawn out by the influence of a certain surrounding intellectual atmosphere and the magic of literary companionship.

12 November 1892

ARCHIBALD LAMPMAN

Some very satisfactory observations are made by the writer of 'Causerie' in the last number of *Arcadia* on the subject of the vacant poet laureateship. Lewis Morris and Sir Edwin Arnold are surely out of the question. Anyone who has ever tried to read the *Epic of Hades* could have no doubt whatever of the impossibility of the former; and equally certain in the case of the latter will be the unfortunate one who has been left alone for an hour or two with no other reading than 'The Light of the World.' Sir Edwin Arnold is not only, as the writer in *Arcadia* says, 'one of the most over-rated and over-advertised poets of the time'; he is one of the most elaborate poetical frauds that ever worked up a reputation by palaver and puffery. He is an instance of the harm that may be done to a man at some little distance above mediocrity by the modern passion for notoriety and money-making. His one respectable poem, *The Light of Asia*, got him into the mischief. It won him a certain measure of fame and spoiled him. Since then he has poured forth stuff less genuine and more hollow in its ring year by year. His last book, *Potiphar's Wife*, bears the stamp of meretricity in every line.

Alfred Austin is a very good poet, and, to those who do not look at the matter purely from the poet's point of view, has more to recommend him than any of the others. He is, I understand, an irreproachable person, loyal and orthodox, and his laureate verses would certainly do the nation no discredit. William Morris, a noble poet and most interesting man, might put forth a claim to the vacant office were it not that in the first place he does not want it, and in the second that he is not anyway exactly the stuff that laureates are made of, either as regards his opinions or the quality of his genius.

Mr Swinburne, as the writer in *Arcadia* urges, is the man for the laureateship. It should be offered to him, and he should accept it. In the present mingling of aristocratic relics with a powerful and increasing democratic life, there is no need to consider the laureateship anything but a purely national office, to be held by the man most honoured and beloved by his countrymen, and to be served simply under patriotic impulse. He need not be bound to sing hymns to royalty; all that is necessary is that he should celebrate his country and make some occasional poetic record of the momentous incidents of his time. This no man is better qualified to do than Mr Swinburne.

ARCHIBALD LAMPMAN

In the death of Mr Paul Peel at Paris, Canada lost one whose name was linked with hers in honourable distinction. This promising painter, who had taken up his residence permanently in Paris, was a native of London, Ontario, and was still a very young man. We have all of us seen some of his large canvasses in the annual collections of the Royal Canadian Academy exhibitions; and although they did not appear to give evidence of any strikingly original gift, we remember well the pleasant impression they left upon us.

WILFRED CAMPBELL

I have often imagined, in the face of the high place now accorded them, that if the English poets of the latter end of the last and the first of this century had been fated to live in the present age, what a hard time they would have had to make the position they now hold. I am afraid that the high-class magazines which give these immortals a prominent place in the subject matter of their text and illustration would be rather backward in accepting for publication some of the verse that they so highly extol. The question to me is, why this condition of things should be? Should a young poet of today send such a poem as 'The Ancient Mariner' to the magazines, he would get a quick return with regrets. And if he persevered for a reason with the critics he would be showered with advice as to lack of form and length of matter. I am afraid poor Coleridge would have had a hard fight for existence. Wordsworth would be shut out completely, unless 'We Are Seven' and 'Lucy Gray' got squeezed into the juveniles. But fancy the reception 'Resolution and Independence' would have today! I can hear lots of my readers say, 'That is not so; its remarkable qualities would be recognized at once.' But with that I cannot agree, and the very men who now worship him the most would be the first to find fault with him for his weaknesses. We hear a great deal about the finish of Keats's work, but, judged by the standards of today, much of his work is mere archaic doggerel. If a young writer writes a number of strong poems today and publishes them in a book with more work scarcely up to the finish of these, the critics one and all ignore the good work and hunt up all the weak points for especial damnation. And the wonder of the matter is that they cite those old poets as our ideal in finish. They won't go to the utter trash written by all of these men, but they go to their few gems, and balance them against the weakest work of the man of today. I am sure that I will call anathemas down on my head, but I must here express my strong conviction that the greatest genius, and the one that bids most for immortality, is the genius that is the most uneven in flight and finish. Nature requires contrast, and the greatest and strongest poetry is that which is at times rugged and even bold. To spend years polishing down a man's thoughts and visions into a certain glittering monotony is just as though nature would level her hills and fill up her valleys into one immense plain. My idea of verse is that it should be as near nature as possible. The very charm of those old poets was their entire originality; they did not write to sell or suit the times, but each man worked out his genius in his own way, and it was recognized. Today the man who uses the file because his talent lies that way is the successful man. And why? Because polish seems to be the fad. The result is that the books of verse floated on the markets by the big houses are chiefly noted for quaint conceits and fancies, but well polished into perfection of brilliancy. Or else they are crystalline masques, containing monotonous and wintry verses, from which all life and originality have been extracted.

DUNCAN CAMPBELL SCOTT

At the very opening of Henrik Ibsen's drama, *The Lady from the Sea*, he epitomizes the circumstances by which his chief character is surrounded. Ballested, who is a whilom scene-painter, a barber, a horn player, and a linguist, is exercising his talents upon a marine canvas, when young Lyngstrand approaches him. The subject he is working at is a view of the fjord, and he explains that a mermaid, who has wandered in from the sea and who cannot find her way out, is to lie dying upon the rocks. But his picture is incomplete, as he cannot find a model for the mermaid. Ballested says that the subject was put into his head by the 'mistress of his house' – Ellida Wangel – and in the opening of the play she is found in just the situation of the mermaid, heartsick for the sea. Ballested's picture is never completed, and similarly Ellida does not die in her captivity. To thoroughly understand the subtlety of the art by which this curious character is portrayed, one must read the play. It contains other characters which are just as firmly and finely drawn, and there is an element of longing for change, for a wider horizon, for a knowledge of life, which actuates at least two of them, Bollette and Lyngstrand. Ellida desires only those surroundings which she has before known, and which are bound up for her in the strange character of the man from the sea. But Bollette wants to see beyond the little town, and expects everything from that; to gain her end she betrothes herself to Arnholm, a commonplace individual, who is to take her out into the 'great, strange world.' But one feels how fallacious the hope of the young girl is, for her betrothed, who is to guide her and who has seen this same world, has returned from it as he went. We feel that this change will not bring her the happiness she expects, for travel and a knowledge of the world may bring to a few souls greater control and therefore greater happiness, but to the many it is only an excitement which changes for a little while the circumstances of their lives. Young Lyngstrand is a type of the artist who has imagination but no creative energy. The Rome towards which he is constantly looking is really the shadow of accomplishment which he pursues. If he could have accomplished one little piece of work he would not have thought so much of Rome, and one feels anew that, relatively, so little depends on the externalities of life and so much on the spirit.

19 November 1892

ARCHIBALD LAMPMAN

Vision

Down a narrow alley blind,
Touch and vision, heart and mind,
Turned sharply inward, still we plod
Till the calmly smiling God
Leaves us and our spirits grow
More thin, more acrid, as we go,
Creeping by the sullen wall
We forego the power to see
The threads that bind us to the all,
God or the immensity,
Whereof on the eternal road
Man is but a passing node.

Subtly conscious, all awake,
Let us clear our eyes and break
Through the cloudy chrysalis –
See the wonder as it is,
Too blind we are, too little see
Of the magic pageantry,
Every minute, every hour,
From the cloud-flake to the flower,
Forever old, forever strange,
Issuing in perpetual change
From the rainbow gates of time.
But he who through this common air
Surely knows the great and fair,

What is lovely, what sublime,
Becomes in an increasing span
One with earth and one with man.
One, despite these mortal scars,
With the planets and the stars;
And nature from her holy place,
Bending with unveiled face,
Fills him in her divine employ
With her own majestic joy.

WILFRED CAMPBELL

A charming book, and well got up as to letterpress, is Dr George Stewart's *Essays from Reviews.* The subject matter, the four great New England poets, Longfellow, Lowell, Whittier, and Holmes, has found a kindly and appreciative treatment at the hands of the genial pen of our well-known essayist. Though much has been written concerning this famous quartet, yet all who take up Dr Stewart's little book will be charmed by the style and treatment of these interesting studies. The most notable fact to be drawn from these pages is that independence as to livelihood and ease from the cares of life are certainly helpful to a literary career. They cannot supply the place of genius, but they certainly give genius a chance to develop so far as the artistic side of literature is concerned. It is a grave question whether Longfellow would have attained such signal success if he had had to struggle for his daily bread. Would not his naturally sensitive and effeminate nature have sunk under the strain? It is interesting to notice that all of the most noted poets who have produced a great bulk of work and have lived to a good old age have been comparatively independent as to means of livelihood. Longfellow, Holmes, and Lowell in America, and Tennyson, Browning, and Swinburne in England are good examples of the result of ease from care in its influence on a literary career. On the other hand, there is no doubt that in most cases while these men gain on the artistic side, and in the bulk of work, they lose on the human, and fail to impress with that strong lyrical quality, that deep, passionate originality that perhaps after all is the supreme quality of genius. A certain amount of suffering is essential to all true genius, the mark of pain is found on all the greatest work, and it would be wrong to say that these men did not suffer; but it was not the dread reality that shrouded Poe, Burns, and Coleridge, the awful loneliness that separated Byron, or the necessity that pinched poor Hood. After all, every man is in accordance with his own inner nature. So it is hard to judge. Meanwhile Dr Stewart can be congratulated on his charming addition to the study of the lives of the poets.

WILFRED CAMPBELL

Another interesting addition to our essay literature is Mr J.E. Wetherell's *Over* [*the*] *Sea*, a brief account of his impressions gathered from a trip to England and Scotland, with special reference to the localities made sacred by the memories of Shakespeare, Burns, Wordsworth, and Tennyson.

There is a simple directness of touch about Mr Wetherell's style and matter, as of one who was his own guide, and not as of one who might have written as well before he started. The chapter 'In Westminster' suggests Irving, but is perfectly free from any likeness more than a kinship of spirit. Without any great pretence, Mr Wetherell has given us a sincere addition to that Canadian culture and literary refinement which is, we are glad to say, slowly but surely growing in our midst.

ARCHIBALD LAMPMAN

There is a term in the loose literary criticism of the day which has become hopelessly hackneyed, and that is the word 'singer' as applied to a poet. Even in the beginning it was an exceedingly namby-pamby expression, but, now that every skimble-skamble sentimentalist who takes to stringing verses dubs himself and is dubbed by his admiring friends a 'singer,' the word has become simply preposterous. It is impossible to apply it otherwise than in derision. Let us, therefore, respect the feelings of the poet, and refrain from shocking him with a sudden sense of the absurdity of his position by calling him a 'singer.' Let him be plain, sensible 'poet' or nothing.

ARCHIBALD LAMPMAN

In the Christmas number of *The Dominion Illustrated* we find one of Professor Roberts's patriotic outbursts. It is eminently well done. Where Professor Roberts undertakes anything seriously in verse he rarely fails to do it well. Many of the lines in this poem are very grand lines in a way. They have a kind of bold, broad-browed strength that is admirable, yet they seem to come shouldering up with a conscious and premeditated effort. In the midst of our present political conditions Mr

Roberts in his patriotic vein is a voice crying in the wilderness, and he seems to have set himself in a premeditated pose to cry there with all his might. He is like one who has said to himself that there ought to be a prophet, and he will be that prophet at whatever cost of effort. It seems to me, however, that the times can hardly carry patriotic verse, particularly of a boastful character. Satire would appear to be the species of verse most applicable to the present emergency.

DUNCAN CAMPBELL SCOTT

One is constantly surprised by the ideality of the men and women who sometimes pride themselves upon their matter-of-factness, but oftener repress any expression upon the subject of their 'feelings,' leaving one to think that the sentiments play no part whatever in their lives. But sooner or later, if you watch them closely, or perhaps you may discover it by chance, you will find them cherishing some little piece of sentiment, some ideal treasure of experience, which they bring out of that casket of the heart which they imagine is clamped with iron, and turn over with a lingering fondness. We are all possessed of the springs of feeling that never run dry, and which assert their presence by keeping our lives more or less green, as they are ample or meagre. I was reminded anew of this rather trite observation on human nature by discovering one of the springs of feeling which was keeping the life of one of my acquaintances green. He is a man who has a family 'growing up,' as the phrase is, and he had been telling me of the difficulty of living on his income, the one good quality of which was that it was sure. He was devoted to his family, but he confessed to not being quite happy, as he had not been as successful in life as he had hoped to be. I may remark that he had the appearance which a conscientious paterfamilias with a limited income who has daughters 'growing up' always wears – an appearance which seems to say for him, 'It makes very little difference how I look.' 'But,' he said, 'I have one source of never-ending pleasure in life, which seems to be mine, I mean especially mine, as distinguished from any pleasure I have in my family and in which they can have no part. I mean the friends of my youth, or rather the memory of them. They are away now; some of them are dead; others, God knows where they are. But they are as near to me now as if they lived in the next square. You know the world is a very wide place, indeed, to the man who always stays at home, and I never could keep track of them, where they went or what they did. I think at one time in my life I forgot all about them, but lately they have been coming back to me, as it were, and I have been living over again those old days and taking a real pleasure in them. When I am bothered about things and a little worried it is curious how the memory of those old friends of mine comes in and gives me some comfort. I am getting old, I suppose,' he closed with a short laugh. I ventured to express the hope that he might see some of them again, but it was not in his mood to think of that; he had idealized them, and he wanted to cherish his memories. 'No,' he said, 'I think it is better so.' And it probably is. He had done his duty by his family and by society in the most matter-of-fact way, so he protested; and he had told me but a moment before that life had no illusions for him, and yet he had shown me the little blade of grass that was greening in his heart, from which I could argue to the whole boundless savannahs of ideality and love which stretch through human nature.

26 November 1892

WILFRED CAMPBELL

The advent of a new story by a Canadian author has a certain interest for those of our people who care about out literary development. We have two or three strong and promising prose writers, and now and then a clever story is published, as for instance Miss Duncan's popular book. I have just had the pleasure of reading a new story by Miss Machar, entitled *Roland Graeme, Knight*, which is probably the best bit of work that she has ever produced. Miss Machar's story is more than clever, for it has a purpose, and a serious one at that. It is a study of a well-worn problem, the labour question, and the relation of the classes in society from a Christian woman's standpoint. The book is readable, well written, and not so intense as many of its kind, owing to a good substratum of common sense and a broad human sympathy that save it from mere sentimentality. But, with all its strong points as an earnest attempt to portray the influence of religion as a social lever, the book falls below the ideal as a literary achievement, and there is not a spark of genius from cover to cover. I would not accuse Miss Machar of plagiarism, nobody would do so, and I believe her religious attitude is her own, but anyone who reads *Roland Graeme* will at once revert to

Nicholas Minturn and other similar stories by the late Dr J.G. Holland, which no doubt strongly appealed to her sympathies and helped to form her social and religious attitude. There is also a suggestion of *Felix Holt* in the hero, with the exception that Miss Machar makes *Roland Graeme* accept the cardinal truths of Christianity, and that without giving us any analysis of his journey in that direction. Miss Machar shows a woman's literary weakness in being unable to keep her own individuality out of her favourite characters, and in a contempt for, and almost hate of, at least one of her evil characters, whom in one place she verges on the hysterical in denouncing. One would almost think that she had some person in mind when she wrote. At the same time, what helps to spoil the book's literary merit is valuable in giving us the characteristics of a woman who will always be more human and more interesting than any book she will ever write, and whose work in prose and verse will be appreciated and felt in so far as she puts herself into it. Miss Machar, as far as I have seen, has no original creative genius, but she has the literary desire strong within her, and she has something else that goes with it, and it is often more looked for in the passing literature of today than mere creative ability, namely, a strong and abiding interest in the social and religious problems of our present humanity, which she has worked with some force into verse and prose. In spite of these evident limitations, Miss Machar's work will compare favourably with much of that of the American didactic school, and as a personality she is a woman whom all Canadians will contemplate with respect and pride.

[ANONYMOUS]

Anyone who possesses a copy of the shorter poems of Robert Bridges has a source of pleasure which is sweet and which will not soon run dry. It is a grateful thing to find in these days, when verse is compelled to contain so much of turgid personal experience, so much that should have remained forever unsaid, a poet who has a pure and simple heart and a winning accent, who charms by his idyllic grace and his unpremeditated happiness. Such a poet is Robert Bridges, and to anyone who wants to spend a pleasant hour with feelings similar to those which the simpler pleasures inspire, I would say secure a copy of this volume, which is published by Geo. Bell & Sons, London. In the atmosphere which fills its covers he will not meet with anything to startle or confuse, but only tranquil shadows and quiet deeps of thought. It is a country which reaches Landor's ideal:

Where every voice (but the bird's or child's) is hush'd
And every thought, like the brook nigh, runs pure.

Sometimes the reader discovers a quaintness which reminds him of William Blake, and often some passage which it is not possible to scan, which does not conform to the usual metrical laws. But if sometimes one can find a little fault from over-sensitiveness of ear, the blemish can be readily forgiven. Upon the very same page will doubtless be some harmony that will chime the faulty line into silence. I wish I had space to quote for the lovers of poetry the two spring odes, 'Invitation to the Country' and 'The Reply.' About the first there is a sort of homely joy in outdoor life and in the beauty of growing things and things commencing to grow that makes one feel the ardency of spring and the ideality of it. It leaves the conviction which the poet himself expresses:

Content, denied
The best, in choosing right
For nature can delight
Fancies unoccupied
With ecstasies so sweet
As none can even guess,
Who walk not with the feet
Of joy in idleness.

In 'The Reply' the dweller in the town contrasts his pleasures with those of his brother in the country and finds himself also contented. But the poet's heart is with the pleasures of the field, and he writes of them with a sort of trust in their power to please; as if, too, his words were not meant for any but himself, but only intended to remind him that the world is yet young and the heart can be kept so. And the essence of his verse is that unexcited pleasure in life which is the more lasting because it is contemplation, and is based upon the eternal truths and upon nothing shifty or compromising. So we get back, as it were, to the springs of poetry, and see the beauty at its source where the water is clear and flows limpidly with a small, pure stream.

I have loved flowers that fade,
Within those magic tents
Rich hues have marriage made
With sweet immemoried scents.
A honeymoon delight,

A joy of love at sight,
That ages in an hour:
My song be like a flower!

I have loved airs that die
Before their charm is writ
Along a liquid sky
Trembling to welcome it.
Notes that with pulse of fire
Proclaim the spirit's desire,
Then die and are nowhere:
My song be like an air!

Die song, die like a breath,
And wither as a bloom;
Fear not a flowery death,
Dread not an airy tomb!
Fly with delight, fly hence,
'Twas thine love's tender sense
To feast: now on thy bier
Beauty shall shed a tear.

This is one of Robert Bridges' most perfect lyrics, and there are not a few of them as perfect. For such things we will love him, and for such things he will be remembered long after the work of many who now receive unstinted praise for performances which cannot be ranked with his shall be forgotten.

ARCHIBALD LAMPMAN

We are reminded frequently in the customs of everyday life of the survival of ancient ineradicable instincts, which bid defiance to the influences of popular religion and even to the actual articles of faith. One case – and the commonest – is to be found in the ceremonials connected with the burial of the dead. We profess to accompany our dead to the grave in the hope of a blessed resurrection, and the assurance of a future life of perfect and eternal happiness; yet in actual practice we surround death with every emblem of utter horror and despair. Nothing can be more hideous or more dreadful than our common paraphernalia of burial – the coffin, the hearse, the palls, the black trappings – everything but the pure white surplice of the minister.

Surely it is not necessary in a philosophic age, when people are beginning to realize with a sort of poetic clearness their true relations with nature and life, that all these horrors should be kept up. Whether we accept with the mass of mankind the belief in a happy immortality of the soul, or whether we refuse to busy our thoughts with that great after-blank into which we cannot see how we shall penetrate with profit, in neither case will the sound-hearted man and the true lover of humanity and life look upon death as in anywise a hideous or desperate thing. The ceremonial of burial might be simplified, and our emblems of ugliness and despair exchanged for beautiful ones, indicative simply of love and a hopeful sadness.

It seems to me that the whole practice of burial, ancient and universal as it is, might well give way to the much more beautiful one of burning. I do not know whether the burning of the dead is as old a custom as burial; but, at any rate, the Greeks practised it largely at all stages of their history until the triumph of Christianity. Moreover, there ought to be no offence in it to those who desire that their bodies should be committed to the earth, for it seems to me that the body reduced to a handful of light ashes may be much more fitly buried than the body in its entire and corruptible state.

WILFRED CAMPBELL

Now that the rude season has wrinkled the barren earth, and the tide of nature's life has ebbed lower with the downward sap, the heart of man pulses with renewed heat, as if he felt the need of the inward warmth that nature has withdrawn. Here in our strong and bracing northern land there is a glow and thrill in the sense of snow and ice that is very gladdening to the heart of boyhood. And I think that many a Canadian will echo the sentiment found in the following song of the bleak months, which the author dedicates at this season to the Canadian boys, old and young:

The Song of the Bubbling Pot

O sing me the song of the bubbling pot
When the weather is cold and the kitchen is hot,
And winds outside are moaning;
When the summer is gone and the birds are fled,

And the leaves are shrivelled that late were red.
And the beehives are hushed of their droning;
O the crackle of wood
Does a boy's heart good
When the snowflakes the haycocks are hooding;
But better than all is the bubbling sound
That comes from the pot when the plate goes round
And rattles down under the pudding.

O the keen, clear days of the chill-nipt fields,
Of the ponds all hidden in silver shields,
And orchards too naked for robbing;
When all the red blood of the frozen year,
That is shrunken in meadows and woodlands sere,
Through the heart of one urchin is throbbing;
As he whistles and lingers,
And blows on his fingers,
Schoolward, when snow clouds are brooding;
But his steps grow quick and his heart gives a bound,
As he dreams of the pot and its bubbling sound,
Of the plate down under the pudding.

Manhood has fame and knowledge and love,
The wide, wide wisdom of heaven above,
The lore of the rich earth under;
And the soul of the poet is wide in its range,
The spirit of woman surpassingly strange,
But the heart of the boy is a wonder;
In the chillest November
The years can remember
The boy-heart with blossoms was budding;
And we all look back to the old kitchen joys,
And the song of the pot and its bubbling noise,
Of the plate down under the pudding.

ARCHIBALD LAMPMAN

Tennyson is said to have done a very wise thing some time before his death. Warned by the fate of Carlyle in the hands of his biographer, Froude, he set to work and destroyed everything amongst his papers and letters that it might not be quite safe to place in the hands of an unwise historian. The biographer of Tennyson will accordingly have plain sailing. There will be nothing to perplex his imagination or mar the perfect beauty of the structure which he proposes to raise.

This is only another example among many of the manly wisdom which seems to have distinguished the great poet in all relations of life – that wisdom which made it so very difficult for newspaper men, portrait painters, and sightseers to get within shouting distance of him. All that kind of people he abhorred, and it was not altogether safe for them to approach his neighbourhood.

There is only one circumstance that detracts in the least degree from our regard and reverence for the poet and the man, and that is 'the lord.' It is a pity that they could not have abstained from marring the noble simplicity of Tennyson's fame by decking him with that incongruous relic of decadent vainglory. It was somewhat ridiculous, and his reputation slightly suffered from it.

3 December 1892

DUNCAN CAMPBELL SCOTT

A few snowflakes were falling, but there was no danger of a storm. The clouds were thin, but sufficiently strong to hold the sun, so there was no glare from the ice. The wind was altogether dead or rose softly now and then with almost a warm stroke in it, blowing loose snow and little particles of ice and wisps of straw across the smooth surface. Fifteen miles away a farm house stood on a bluff overlooking the canal, and we knew good cheer was there, and a Canadian welcome and clear ice every stroke of the way. Or the clear ice was only a rumour; it might be open or shaly or porous, or we might have to walk around the rapids of the river or – a hundred other things that those bent on staying at home fling in the path of one determined to go abroad. When the ice holds, a man is almost sure to find good skating if he will look for it; so we started. Out of the city, where the barges are frozen in, the cheery smoke yet pouring from their red-curtained cabins; where gangs of boys are playing confused games of shinny, where a youth will stand a whole hour to get one whack at a rubber ball, but what a whack! and how he glories in it for two days after, breaking every conversation with a – 'but did you see the swipe I gave it! Then under the bridges, where the cinders from the engines hold you back for a second or two; then down the bends, where you meet solitary skaters speeding away, or whole parties circling slowly about; then through the cut where every breathless urchin roars at you that the ice isn't safe above; then a whole stretch where you meet no one until you reach the first lock. There you are likely to find a pioneer returning from the wilderness and bringing good news with him. Hail fellow-enthusiast! who, with one skate bound on with straps and the other with a piece of rope, hast ventured, Columbus-like, into the unknown, led on by thine adventurous spirit, and with no companion save thy trusty 'shinny'; we will take thy laconic advice to 'hug the bank and look out for shales.' So we go clumping over the locks, never waiting to take off our skates, but rushing at the mile of clear ice, mellow as velvet, coloured like sea water, with the overflow yellow like cream. Then over another lock and out onto the river. Close under the bank, dodging the overhanging trees, and edging away from the black ice, black as night and full of little starry bubbles. What a pace our leader is cutting out! You hear him go crashing into the shale, and before you well know it you are into the place yourself and by it. You hear the long, snarling rip when he strikes the ice frozen from the overflow, and before anyone can stop everyone breaks through and goes hopping along like mad to keep from falling. And now he has found the black ice holds, and we go swooping out on it as if we were flying. Mile after mile. Not a stroke lost; past huge butternuts straggling on the shore, and whole groves of maples standing closely together, wrapped in the pinkish lustre from their own stems, and lonely pines, set high on the frozen shore. Then the sun sets and the air grows colder; we feel it on our thighs as we force them through with the stroke, and it blows a long, surging wraith of snow with it. The ice gives a long boom and splits under our feet. The clear lemon-yellow flares in the west. One star comes out. There are lights on the shore. Then voices hail us, and, taking off our skates, we discover how hard it is to walk, and go stumbling up the bank to the house. We had skated fifteen miles, and this is what we had for supper: baked pike, stuffed with spices; baked potatoes, homemade bread, cider-apple sauce, pumpkin pie, sage cheese, currant loaf, and fritters and maple syrup.

3 December 1892

WILFRED CAMPBELL

Now and then, when I meet in any of our literary journals that hysterical shriek, 'Have we a literature?' I turn in my despair to that elaborate compendium, *The Songs of the Great Dominion*, which is regarded by many as containing the canon of the Canadian Parnassus. And if I do not emerge therefrom quite as comforted and refreshed as I ought to be, I do not need to be asked why, save by those who have not perused the volume. So far as heroic labour is concerned, Mr Lighthall deserves the place he has made for himself as the latest patron of all persons living in the Dominion who at any time or other have been ambitious to express themselves in rhyme, the most important of which, at least judged from his patriotic standpoint, he has collected into a volume. No one knows now better than Mr Lighthall does, that not more than a dozen of the sixty names mentioned in his anthology have ever laid serious claim to real poetical achievement, and that certainly not more than half that number have any title to lengthy remembrance even in Canada. The serious objections to be taken to this work, and they are grave objections, aside from the utter lack of literary standard observed in the volume, are that true Canadian literature as it now exists is neither represented nor even foreshadowed in its pages, and that Canada is represented as a crude colony, whose literature, if it could be called by such a name, is merely associated with superficial canoe and carnival songs, backwoods and Indian tales told in poor rhyme, and all tied together by pseudo-patriotic hurrahs, which are about as representative of our true nationality as they are of literature. Now, it is far from my purpose to cast any slur on a Canadian literary undertaking, and Mr Lighthall, as a sincere and high-minded patriot, as a literary man of lofty ideals, commands our respect and serious consideration, and it is not in any carping spirit that I approach his work at this date. But, at the same time, we have a serious question to consider, if Mr Lighthall's anthology is to be considered of any importance at all, and that question is, the fair representation of our best literature both abroad and in our own country. As far as Canada is concerned, Mr Lighthall's anthology might even at this day be regarded as obsolete, in the light of the remarkable strides our literature has taken. But when we remember that this work is being sold in England and goes into the hands of cultured English men and women as representative of our best work and our claim for rank in the literature of the day, we cannot help but feel that we are being imposed upon, if such a term is not too hard under the circumstances. No wonder that Sir Charles Dilke, on reading the book, set Canadian literature down as even inferior to that of Australia, while the truth is that as far as culture is concerned alone we rank with the best young writers today in the language. If editors of anthologies only knew that it is no compliment to an author, and often a serious injury to his prospects, to be represented by his poorest work, they would be more serious and unbiassed in their selections. It is very unfair to a number of authors to judge them all by the subject matter, as Mr Lighthall has done. The writer who has no mere local interest has no prominence in this book. The result is a false basis for judgment and a general foreign misunderstanding as to our literature. To give one instance of the peculiar misrepresentation, the one writer who is sufficiently accentuated to raise him from the promiscuous heap is spoken of as 'poet and canoeist,' while the fact that he is a professor in a college is cast altogether into the shade.

ARCHIBALD LAMPMAN

How painfully we take our amusement and how many intolerable things are done in the name of enjoyment. A room full of whist players is a spectacle to make a philosopher weep, and a progressive euchre party will turn the head of a sensitive man grey in a single night. More misery can be got out of a common dancing party than from an hour's outpour of one of our popular preachers. How little genuine enjoyment is afforded by these things even to the young people who most assiduously cultivate them is apparent to anyone who will sit composedly for a few minutes in a quiet corner of some crowded drawing room and mark the medley of mechanical noises about him – the unreal laughter and fantastic gibberish that fill up the intervals of conversation. As a matter of fact, most of our everyday amusements are merely the result of a blind and hysterical desire to keep going, to be on the move, and have nothing to do with heartfelt pleasure at all. Most of the enjoyments that we really have we find in those unregarded and unsought for hours which we profess to consider the most tedious – hours of quiet and useful activity, when we are not thinking in the least of pleasure – hours touched with the tenderness of friendship or domestic love, with spirits kindled to a crystal flame by the earnestness of quiet and undemonstrative converse. These are the things that feed and succour the soul and redeem the melancholy of life.

WILFRED CAMPBELL

The failure of Mr Mansfield's adaptation of *The Scarlet Letter* in New York shows the utter impossibility of producing objectively the subjective drama. No one who has read Hawthorne's greatest story can fail to see the masterly dramatic power of the book in its subtle analysis of the processes of a soul in its relations to one of the most tragic conditions of human life. And yet, the very act of putting such a work on the stage has the effect of robbing the drama, for a drama it is, of all its higher qualities as a life study, with which Hawthorne has invested it, and to accentuate for stage effect what is necessarily morbid and even coarse in such a picture.

ARCHIBALD LAMPMAN

Mr Swinburne, the heir proper to the laureateship, is beyond all other poets a lover of the sea. He carries his devotion almost to the point of madness, for he bathes in all seasons and all weathers, and is a most daring and persistent swimmer. There is a newspaper tale that not many years ago the poet while bathing on the coast of Normandy got into a dangerous current and was carried far out to sea. He was observed by a French fishing boat and picked up when at the very point of drowning. After he had recovered himself he sat in the bow of the boat and began chanting verses of Victor Hugo with a tone and aspect so weird and uncanny that the fishermen fell to consulting together whether they had not better throw him overboard again, as he might be the devil. Mr Swinburne also makes it a boast that he never carries an umbrella. An old lady neighbour of his recently averred that there was something wrong in his 'ead, and it transpired that the reason for this conjecture was that she had seen him more than once standing uncovered in the middle of the road in a rainstorm, his face wearing an expression of perfect quiescence and placid abstraction.

ARCHIBALD LAMPMAN

Tennyson is said to have expressed a dislike of Venice, and the reason was that he was unable to get any good, honest English tobacco there.

ARCHIBALD LAMPMAN

In the December number of *The Cosmopolitan* are contributions from two Canadians – a poem entitled 'The Yule Guest' by Bliss Carman and an article on the poetry and personality of Alfred Tennyson by Dr

George Stewart of Quebec. Mr Carman's poem is not by any means up to his standard, although there are lines and phrases in it full of the peculiar quality of his best work. Dr Stewart's article is very interesting, the more so as it is written by one who had the rare advantage and satisfaction of knowing Tennyson personally.

10 December 1892

ARCHIBALD LAMPMAN

Just now no book can be more interesting to lovers of literature than a life of the late poet laureate, and the demand for such a book is admirably met by Mr Arthur Waugh's *Alfred, Lord Tennyson: A Study of His Life and Works*, published by the United States Book Company, New York. Mr Waugh relates the scanty incidents of the laureate's life, linking together in an easy narrative the particulars of his outer fortunes and inner development, and traces from their utmost sources through every grade of influence the growth of his distinctive imaginative quality and his technical mastery. We have here for the first time a complete survey of the accomplishment of our poet 'illustrious and consummate.' We follow the course of that long and wonderful life, marked by so few of the vicissitudes of fortune, but full of the records of intellectual effort and imaginative achievement.

This book, which is written in a simple, charming, and instructive manner, is not one of those biographies which are hastily thrown together to meet a sudden rush of curiosity upon the death of an illustrious man. It was begun long before Tennyson's death, was very carefully compiled from every source of information available in the case of a man so hard to get at as the late laureate, and the writer's critical estimate of the poet's work is manifestly the result of intimate study and careful thought. In one of his most interesting chapters he shows how Tennyson not only concentrated in himself the widely differing artistic impulses of his immediate predecessors, but disbursed again from himself the germs of the peculiar qualities of the poets who rose after him. Keats, Wordsworth, Shelley, and Byron each of them contributed something to his style, while Rossetti, Swinburne, Morris,

Patmore, and others followed out impulses which rayed forth from the larger master's work like so many beams of variously coloured light.

The writer gives brief, simple, and in most cases perfectly satisfactory analyses of Tennyson's longer poems. Perhaps the only thing I would object to is the prominence given to *The Idylls of the King* as his greatest work. This is a disputed point, for recent critics have pointed out serious weaknesses in the conception and execution of these poems, which the laureate himself no doubt designed to constitute his masterpiece. Mr Waugh, however, is not one of those who recognize no fault in the master to whom he is devoted, and in many cases he acknowledges undoubted imperfections. He grants the weaknesses of *The Princess* from the larger artistic point of view, while dwelling upon the exhaustless abundance of its beauties; but he combats vigorously the somewhat harsh criticisms of Mr Stedman upon *Maud*. He grants the dramatic failure of *Queen Mary* and makes the most of the success of *Harold.*

A great many interesting anecdotes of the poet, who was singular for his humour, his gruffness, his shyness, and withal his luminous greatness of heart, are scattered about the book, and its pages are made additionally interesting by a number of portraits and pictures of places notable through their connection with the poet's life. Of the portraits, two are of Tennyson himself, one being a reproduction of the well-known painting by G.F. Watts, remarkable for the fullness of the brow above the eyes and the peculiar sloping-downward look of the eyes themselves. There is also an engraving from Watts's exquisite portrait of Lady Tennyson – a face of most gentle sweetness and delicate beauty.

WILFRED CAMPBELL

There is nothing that we require more at the present stage of our literary development than frankness of opinion and proper, unbiassed judgment. In fact this might apply also to our whole national life, as the grave weakness in our literary conditions is the same as that at the bottom of our national existence. Sad to say, we are less a people with one aim and sympathy than we are a bundle of cliques, each determined to get what it calls its rights and caring little for matters outside of its own interests. And be these cliques provincial, racial, religious, partisan, or founded on mere self-interest they are one and all ruinous in the long run to the welfare of the country in its development as a nation. It goes without saying that we will never have a true national spirit until these different elements are, if not totally eliminated, at least so overwhelmed by a larger national spirit that at a grave national crisis the patriotic spirit will conquer them all and show itself to be the dominant idea. Just as, if our destiny is to become a nation in reality, the clique system will be gradually eliminated in our national life, so in our literary conditions there must develop a larger horizon of effort and appreciation, with the attendant result of a fairer and less biassed judgment as to our literary standards. So far the general mass of the people have left the settling of such matters to a few critics, who are often personal friends of certain authors, and there being no general canon, the standing of a literary man or woman may depend largely on the booming qualities of his or her personal friends. Of course, the 'scratch my back and I'll scratch yours' system is beginning to die out in this country, but it was not long ago that a loud and authoritative statement in one of our literary journals was regarded as final in settling a writer's stand in the eyes of the people. Those who see their favourite authors go to the wall in the literary race must remember that it was much easier to make and hold a literary reputation in Canada ten years ago than it is today, when our leading writers have the best of them gone abroad, and in the literary arena of the outside world have won recognition before achieving it at home. What we need, therefore, today is local criticism on the same standards, and not mere senseless gush or brutal abuse or mean insinuations, as we now have it. Under the old system, the friend of a certain writer was not content with senseless gush as to his or her favourite writer, but must needs go out of the way to cast a slur on all other writers in the country, or pick out someone who was looked upon as a possible rival, and, metaphorically, 'jump on his collar,' to use a current vulgar expression. This constituted the old formula to a large extent. And I am sorry to say that this system has not altogether died out. So soon as our literary critics and journals take the trouble to thoroughly study our literature and examine into its real merits, just so soon will they acquire the gift of seeing good in the work of more than one man; and more than that, the gift of judging one author's best work on its own characteristics and not by the characteristics of their favourite author. To generalize, so soon as a man is wild on the subject of Wordsworth, he becomes unjust to Shelley or Byron, and vice versa. The true and unbiassed critic is never a worshipper of any one writer, but admires each writer for what he regards as his best work as compared with the broad sweep of what is best in literature. Literary supremacy in the true sense is something for the future to decide so far as Canada is concerned. To judge our poets as patriotic poets or human poets or nature poets or poet artists, or as disciples of this or that school, is both unnatural and absurd. But so soon as a people gets to be tolerably well cultured it can draw the line between creative genius and mere talent coupled with literary desire, and so soon will it outgrow the mania for this or that favourite author merely because he is local or much talked of, and set itself to the serious and important task of finding out what is best in its general literature. Meanwhile the critic who comes out and makes a calm, unbiassed statement as to the value of the work of this or that author must be prepared for vituperation at the hands of the particular clique affected by his remarks.

DUNCAN CAMPBELL SCOTT

The passion for reading plays is almost as great as the passion for writing them. I have an elderly friend who has already produced forty-eight and is now on his forty-ninth, writing away with all the gusto of youth, as if he hoped to surpass Lope de Vega, who is reputed to have written one a week, and who actually left a mountain of plays behind him, the best numbered at over four hundred. And there my friend sits plotting and planning his entrances and his exits, himself the kindest of men, yet fabricating disaster and bringing his characters to confusion. And yet he has no hope of dramatic success, 'that most tantalising of all enterprises,' as Mr Dobson calls it, in his preface to the *Plays and Poems of Oliver Goldsmith.* The passion of playwright has got hold upon him, and he is quite contented to let those who are successful dramatically go on their way so long as he is allowed to spin his plots in peace. The reading of plays becomes even a greater passion than the reading of novels, and it is a special training for the imagination and observation. In a novel every motive is explained with the most trying minuteness; the author gives no room for the reader's faculty of penetration, but binds him down to a rigid chart of the feelings of his characters, by which he must steer his way through the book. But a play is stripped of all commentary, and every one must put his own interpretation upon the motives of the characters as set forth by their words and actions. An essay, written by every reader, could accompany every play, which would give his conception of the moral structure of the characters and their development. But no two of these essays would be exactly alike; they would differ as widely as the personalities of the readers. To consider the art of the playwright, it seems to be hedged in by a mass of absurd conventions, which in some cases become tricks the like of which no other art can show. How often are we asked to believe that the persons who knew one another in the first act fail to see through the thinnest disguises in the second! How often does a character, sorely needed by the dramatic exigencies, make his or her appearance opportunely, but without any reasonable explanation, from the ends of the earth, and depart again, having said his say and helped the action a step farther! And with what a childlike faith we accept the improbable comings and goings, the halt explanations, the blind reasons! It seems fitting and proper that Hastings and Marlow should talk with Mr Hardcastle without ever discovering their mistake, or that Marlow should fail to recognize Miss Hardcastle in her modest disguise! We are content so long as the solecisms are not too palpable. We are too well pleased with seeing life before our eyes, with the consequence of actions following closely upon their commission, and with the villain punished and the worthy rewarded. But this we demand, the worthy must be rewarded, the villain punished. The playwright would have an empty house if the rewards and punishments were concealed, as they so often are in life. If the wicked prosper in the first two acts they must be brought low in the last two. But this would hardly apply to the closet drama, where the development and dénouement might be as realistic as life itself and still be read with pleasure and appreciation.

17 December 1892

ARCHIBALD LAMPMAN

We must add another, my friends, to the lengthening list of our poets. I have been reading Mr J.H. Brown's *Poems, Lyrical and Dramatic*, published by Messrs J. Durie & Son, Ottawa. Those who have followed the periodicals will remember some of Mr Brown's pieces in *The Week*, especially some of his excellent sonnets. The present volume is a collection of short poems on a considerable variety of subjects, together with a drama, called 'The Mad Philosopher,' which fills the latter half of the book. Mr Brown is a scholar, a philosopher, and a poet, and his book gives evidence of the extent of his studies, the sweetness and delicacy of his natural gift, and the excellence to which he has attained in the workmanship of his art. We have not gone far before we discover that he is not a careless trifler in verse, but a man interested in the deeper spiritual problems of the day, a writer of humane enthusiasms and serious intent. A great many of his pieces are of a speculative and philosophic cast. His 'Mad Philosopher' centres in the effort of an impractical enthusiast to interest the two most prominent leaders of his day, Napoleon Bonaparte and Thomas Jefferson, in a scheme for the regeneration of mankind. His 'Julian,' a somewhat daring bit of dialogue, inspired, I imagine, by Shelley, treats of the subject of marriage. In his poem, 'A Letter,' one of the best pieces of versification in the book, with now a sharp touch of satire, and now a full phrasing of some generous thought, he states his attitude towards life and society, and calls up before us the chief captains of his soul – Shakespeare, Shelley, and Whitman.

Although not what is called in common critical parlance a 'nature-poet,' Mr Brown sometimes strikes in with a vivid descriptive touch, as when he says:

> Last night the lightning flashed in fork and flame,
> And the deep thunder groaned and roared so loud
> As it would rip the timbers of the world,
> And scatter earth to chaos.

Or:

> A new-born breeze comes out unseen:
> Flits o'er the mead on joyous wing,
> The Verdure-lines in motion swing,
> The heart of nature seems to sing.

One of Mr Brown's especial successes, both as regards thought and versification, is the poem 'On Reading the Rubaiyat of Omar Khayyam.' I give the concluding stanzas, which will sufficiently indicate the wisdom and beauty of the whole piece:

> Oh brave and as strong! my Omar, kind and wise!
> Scorner of sophists and their subtle lies!
> Lover of Truth – of Truth without disguise,
> And soul's integrity – the highest prize!
> With thee I hold He plac'd us here to live –

To love the life He found it good to give;
And though the Secret we should never know,
Why life at worst is sweet – and wherefore grieve?

Lo' in the East the light of morning grows;
The curling mists ascend, the crimson glows;
And in the smile of greeting Earth and Heav'n,
The Universe appears an op'ning Rose!

But I think Mr Brown is at his strongest in the sonnet. There are many excellent examples of this form scattered about through his book. Lack of space obliges me to limit my quotation to one. It is entitled 'Greatness':

What most men hunger for yet none achieves,
    Save him who greatly cares not to be great,
    Who knows the loom of time spins not more state
Than that small filament a spider weaves:
Since single barley-straws make piled-up sheaves,
    And atoms diminute the gross earth's weight,
    Nor comes from Sirius, earthward, rarer freight
Than this small taper-beam my page receives.

No greater is the desert than one sand,
The mountain than one dust-speck at its base,
The ocean than one rain-drop on my hand;
    And Shakspere's self, there in the foremost place,
    Hath but in ampler measure at command
    That thought which shines from rustic Hodge's face.

DUNCAN CAMPBELL SCOTT

I must congratulate Mr R.K. Kernighan upon his poem in the Christmas number of *Saturday Night.* It is a skilful and successful piece of work; it has a movement that proves that Mr Kernighan has a true natural gift for verse. We are all familiar with the author's work under the nom de plume of 'The Khan,' and to an extent at least he is our Canadian James Whitcomb Riley when he writes in the vernacular of homely things; but such pieces as the one I have mentioned above show that he can also deal with images and ideas which require artistic treatment.

17 December 1892

WILFRED CAMPBELL

Prominent among the articles in the December *Cosmopolitan* is a fine one on the subject of the Trappist monks of Oka, written by Mr Gorman, editor of *The Ottawa Free Press*. This article ought to be of special interest not only to Canadians, but also to all Americans who have studied the lives and habits of religious orders. Even in this over-practical and worldly age the cloister life, with its peculiar environments, appeals to the consideration of the thoughtful and reflective mind. And while it seems out of place in our modern world of hurrying toil and scientific spirit, yet as an institution the monastic life in its finer aspects still retains for us a certain dignity and sternness of reality that is found wanting in much of our modern religious life. Mr Gorman has performed for the silent monks of Oka what the distinguished American writer, Mr James Lane Allen, did some time ago in *The Century Magazine* for the convent of the same order in Kentucky. While the Canadian convent is not so old as that of Kentucky, it is equally interesting to those who would study the peculiar characteristics of the Trappist order, which is without doubt the most remarkable and perhaps the most worthy of our consideration and respect among all the religious brotherhoods. It is impossible for the modern cultured mind to regard the monastic institution in contemporary religion as other than a survival of medievalism, and so indicate an attitude towards life more in keeping with that of the middle ages than of the present day. History and human experience have also shown that the first homes of all religious orders that grew out of the ascetisicm of the Christian, Buddhist, and Mohammedan faiths, the milder climates of southern Asia and Europe, are still, and always will be, the only localities where such institutions can be successful. Aside from all other reasons, there is no doubt that much of the corrupt life and falling off from the old standards of the monastic life of western Europe was owing to the climate that tempted men to a greater necessity of indulgence in physical nourishment. In southern Asia, where abstinence from grosser food is almost necessary to common existence, the life of lonely contemplation has long been an inseparable part of the genius of the people. Matthew Arnold expresses this so finely in four lines:

The east bowed low before the blast,
  In patient, deep disdain.
She let the legions thunder past,
  Then plunged in thought again.

Whatever may be the future development of religion, there is no doubt that both the severer climates and the restless, practical spirit of the peoples of western Europe and North America will always prove inimical to the success of the conventual system in religion. Apart from all these considerations and our natural repugnance for any order of men who are consciously or unconsciously out of keynote with the spirit of what is best in the age, anyone who recognizes the inner life of these men, who willingly immure themselves within gloomy walls, and, alienated from their kind and in constant contemplation of death, deny themselves all but the commonest necessities of life, cannot but be impressed by the stern reality of these lives where the tragedy of the soul in its striving for the eternal is daily enacted. While we all agree that there are millions of men and women in the world today who by acts and often by lives of heroic self-denial are in their several vocations as wives, husbands, parents, and citizens doing much more for the good of humanity than could ever be done by any amount of silent contemplation, and however we may differ from the doctrines that have originated this peculiar order, yet we cannot but respect the phase of religion which, no matter how gloomy in its outlook on humanity, is almost great in its intense realism of practice.

DUNCAN CAMPBELL SCOTT

It is a most difficult and nearly always an ungrateful task to write poems for special occasions. The greater the occasion the more difficult the task, for what may be a really great celebration of a most important event may not arouse those feelings of enthusiasm which are necessary to the making of a poem. It is gratifying to know how worthily the commemoration ode for the 400th anniversary of the discovery of America has been accomplished. It was peculiarly fitting that this ode should have been written by a woman, for the American civilization gives a larger and larger scope for the development of woman. She has nowhere attained such freedom and is nowhere, excepting perhaps in Canada, treated with such respect and consideration. It was therefore a recognition of this fact perhaps as much as anything else which led to the choice of Miss Harriet Monroe as the poetess who should express in verse the great anniversary which has just passed. She had proved herself entirely able for the task by her ode for the opening of the Auditorium, and her production for the latter and more important occasion surpassed her first effort. Miss Monroe is first of all a poet, and she approaches her subject from the poetic standpoint. She has enthusiasm not only for her art but for her subject, for the future of America, for the outcome of her civilization. It was almost inevitable then that she should make a success of what would have been a task to one who had not her glow of enthusiasm. But her ringing and true-hearted lines prove that she found the production of the ode no task, but rather accepted the opportunity with a knowledge of its import and with a resolve to make the work the expression of her heart towards the life and aspirations of her people. In the development of her subject she has shown true constructive ability, and her lines progress naturally to their inspiring and prophetic close.

24 December 1892

ARCHIBALD LAMPMAN

The chief delight of this Christmas season is that it brings back into the heart the full flavour of childhood. When the shops begin to light up with their Christmas finery, and the sound of sleigh bells to grow louder and merrier, I smell the perfume of cedar and pine boughs; there comes a sense of old-time winter heartiness into the crisp air; the snow-laden depths of leafless woods and frozen pine forests, plumed and bonnetted with snow, appeal to the imagination and allure the feet as if invested with a sort of human sympathy. I remember a lake with the long, mid-winter road running across its frozen surface marked with young cedars fading into the distance, an infinite dotted line, and I remember the jingling teams that would come by this track on the crystal Christmas mornings, bound for the little rough-cast church on the hilltop above the landing. I remember the rough-voiced farmers, bearded white with hoar frost, and the cheerful, ruddy-faced woman, and the good words they had, and the presents they always brought with them for the parson – a turkey, a goose, a side of pork, a couple of bags of oats, some pairs of knitted socks, and many another thing. I remember how the lake roared under the moonlit Christmas night, as if all the northern genii were gathered like Merlin's chained fiends at Caermardin under that gleaming band of ice, and all night long the imprisoned waters groaned and struggled, now with reports as of pistols, and now with a thunder, as of a hundred cannon. I remember the yearly expedition into the silent woods, when some luckless young pine, delicately tufted, or beautiful pointed cedar was cut and pruned for the Christmas tree. Every Canadian who has spent a boyhood in the country where the northern lakes are remembers these things and many more at Christmas; his heart warms to the like dreamers about him; he thinks well of his country and of the people who have made it; and the old words repeat themselves upon his tongue with an especial tenderness, 'Peace on earth and good-will toward men.'

Let us thank God that this old Christmas custom and Christmas heart-opening have become so firmly rooted in the affections of mankind that neither any destruction of creed nor alteration of polity can affect it. So long as the figure of Jesus Christ through every change in the fashion of faith shall stand as the representative of whatever there is in human nature of pure and patient, and pitiful and divine, the recurrence of His day shall produce a certain tender heart-awakening in everyone who has not become so callous as to be no longer human. For so long a time have the noblest spirit of religion, and let it be also well remembered the noblest spirit of art, consecrated the associations of this day that the susceptibility to its kindly influence is stronger than the rooted habits of our lives. The most careless man, if he be still human, remembers the friendships and good deeds of the past, and feels impelled to do something to bring the glow of happiness to those whose spirits have once been in touch with his. The rich man who has brooded all year over his money bags now, perhaps for the first time, remembers the poor, and knows that Christ's day has brought no better gift to him than the rare and saving consciousness of a few generous acts. But nothing is so touching at this season as the innumerable deeds of loving kindness and self-sacrifice which are done among the poor themselves. How much better thoughts we have of our brother men when we consider the multitudes of poor human hands all over Christendom who are brooding and contriving with their scanty time and their scanty means how they may give some joyous surprise to each of those whom they love. Truly our life would be more barren than it is were it not for the new warmth infused into it by this annual heart-revival.

[ANONYMOUS]

The founder of Christianity said: 'Do unto others as ye would they should do unto you.' This teaching is nearly 2000 years old in Christianity; and what are the ethics of human society today? I do not mean as expressed from pulpits and public platforms, but as lived in the practical lives of men. Society expects men to be happy under the most unlucky conditions, and those who dare to 'kick against the pricks' are scowled out of its precincts as pessimists of the gloomiest order. But in the face of this there is today, in the year 1892, too much misery in the world to be ignored, except by the wantonly brutal. And, sad to say, it is owing in a large part to a portion of our humanity which is in many respects unworthy of the name.

Who can go into one of our large cities and see the terrible instances of human misery and degradation; such scenes as those depicted by Jacob Riis in 'How the Other Half Lives,' in *Scribner's Magazine* a short time ago; such truthful pictures as these of lower life in a city like New York make us despair of our civilization as less satisfactory than many of the more ancient attempts – who can go into such scenes and not feel what a hell this world is after all? I can fancy some delicately nurtured lady saying: 'Horrid! Don't speak of it. Can't you write of something pleasant?' But, madam, while amid your ease and splendour you are glutting some brute of a dog with bon-bons, thousands of your own kind, who have just as much right to earth's good things as you have, are dying by inches for want of the commonest necessaries of life. I have walked the streets of New York, where you will find miles of misery, and have seen enough in one block to populate a good-sized lazarhouse. But, at the same time, I have seen many a carriage pass by, the cost of which alone would have materially relieved these poor wretches. I do not need to inform Canadians as to their own cities and towns, and even country places. In any Canadian city you will see more money put into one church spire alone than would relieve the poor of that church for many a long winter's day. I do not advocate the pauperizing of the poor; but I would ask, who make the poor? If the people of any section had been practising the ethics of the founder of the religion they profess to venerate, instead of looking merely each to his own selfish interests for these many years back, would we really have such a state of things today? And is human society of today one whit better in this respect than (or even as good as) that of 2000 years ago? Everywhere around us we see either a far too abundant wealth, as exhibited in glaring extravagance, glitter, and show, or on the other hand a rapidly increasing community of degradation and despair. We hear a good deal about public charity, when there is no greater farce on earth. It, at the best, means men making a pretence at relieving, in a small way, what they have the power to wipe out of existence if they only want to. Hypocrisy winks at fraud, because hypocrisy is but fraud on a smaller scale. Hypocrisy today means nothing more than that everybody who has even the smallest finger in the common bag intends to keep it there at no matter whose expense. Now, this is all very well if we admit that man is, after all, but a two-legged animal, who preys on his species and believes in the creed that 'might is right.' But how about a condition of society which, doing this, pretends to the highest ethical ideals, and would brand as outcast anyone who would dare assail those ideals as impracticable? There is no doubt but that the growing evil of today is the ever widening rift between the rich and the poor. And I, for one, claim that poverty, in its extreme sense, has no right to exist on this earth if men are only even commonly human. Burns, who himself had felt its sting, reached the truth when he sang:

Man's inhumanity to man
Makes countless thousands mourn.

But poverty is beginning to be felt today, not only by the shiftless and dissolute, but there are thousands who are beginning to suffer who have no right to suffer. There are thousands of men and women in this land today who would be glad to be in possession of even the bare necessaries of life and keep out of debt – who are trying to work honourably for their bread and cannot get it; while thousands of families, on the other hand, are living in wordly extravagance, with far more even of life's luxuries than they can properly enjoy. It is a queer dispensation of providence, when a young man, the son of a man who has made a fortune, as we well know how many fortunes are made today, without any more creditable ambition than to indulge his own vices, or at best be a passably negative atom in society, can afford to spend on his worthless pleasures and personal adornment perhaps ten times as much as would, if possessed by many a struggling young artisan or scholar, enable him to not alone attain his ideals, but contribute to the general advancement and refinement of the whole country as well. This condition of things is getting worse and worse every year, till those who suffer are about sick of old platitudes. Anyone who has studied our general life can see where the blame lies. The fact is, there are all grades of the standard of success, from square honesty to plain stealing or robbery, and all tacitly admit that all these grades are practised in business life. And it is here that the real basis of the happiness of the national life is laid, and not in the church or the school. Religion without ethics and knowledge without humanity or honesty are the same thing, and they breed hypocrites and rascals. The millionaire who died lately in New York is a good sample of the extreme grade spoken of – a man who set himself to work to 'fleece' others, even his personal friends. And the best we can say for him is that he never acknowledged any religious profession or belief. While this dreadful condition of things continues to increase year by year, as is acknowledged on all sides, the advent of such a season as Christmas, with its pretence of human hope, joy, and brotherly love, must come as a sort of ironical mockery to the thoughtful and sincere man. Society may raise new spires to heaven, Christmas bells may peal their sweetness on the wintry air, but while beneath their very shadows and within echo of their voice this existent human hell raises its mute misery to the skies, man is no better than, nor even as good as, the heathenism he claims to despise, and his religion is but an empty failure. My plea is not for miserable charity, the most contemptible insult offered by society to society on earth, but my cry is for justice, simple justice, which is the one thing needful. It is in this spirit that I quote the following lines, which are merely inserted because of the cause they advocate, that of the down-trodden of every age, the galley slaves of the centuries:

The Galley Slaves

Beaten, embittered, and baffled and broken
    Under the hate of the heat and the storm,
Daily we toil on, receiving no token
    Of life where its loves and its victories swarm.

Burdened by buffetings long oceans over
    Dreaming no harbor to love as our own
Weak with no moanings for friendship or lover,
    Unloving, unknowing, unloved and unknown.

Ours but to toil and for others the glory
    Ours but to sweat, but for others the prize,
Ours but to fall with our bare bosoms gory,
    To pass with the hopeless, sad look in our eyes.

Who will care, who will note, when the strife is all ended,
And the wild smoke of battle blows out from the wreck,
If the victory won be sufficiently splendid,
For the poor galley slave who lies dead on the deck?

Who will reck 'mid the shouts when the battle's brute Nero
Is crowned with the nimbus of carnage and might
If the toiler between decks was more than whole hero
Who fought with no glory to strengthen his sight?

We drive to the rock-surfs to give others warning,
We sleep in the battle that others may win;
Blind helots of darkness we build up the morning,
That others may enter and triumph therein.

Dreaming no happiness, glory or splendor,
Bound to the chain and the oar from our birth,
Knowing no voice of love winning and tender,
Poor, wretched outcasts and devils of earth.

We are the slaves of all climes and all ages,
Paying with anguish the price of our breath;
Brothers, we toil on and win for our wages
Human brutality, misery – then death.

[ANONYMOUS]

It was Christmas Eve – a real old-fashioned Christmas Eve, with a storm, and frost on the window panes and rime on the latch of the door. But there was a fire in the hearth, and the odour of suppressed cooking pervaded the house. There were guests around the fire and children at their feet staring at the coals. They had had three songs, and someone cried out, 'Now, let's have something for the children, this is their night.' 'True words,' said a stranger, who an hour before had been blown in by the storm. He had got the ice melted out of his long red beard, thick enough for birds to nest in, and his voice had a hearty ring in it that made the children laugh unreasonably, for they had been rather frightened by his strange face. 'True words,' he said, 'for Christmas is the children's time, and will be forever, and so I'll give them a jingle.' Whereat all the children gathered about his knees, for they knew by the sound of his voice that he was a friend of theirs. 'I must explain,' he commenced, 'that when I was a boy I used to move about all over Ontario, and when I came to live in a new place I had to make new friends. Sometimes the lads used to guy me and call out, "Say, what's your name?" and when they were as rude as that I would rejoin, "It's Pudding and Tame, if you ask me again I'll tell you the same".' The children commenced to laugh, for they had often said it themselves. 'So here goes for the rhyme,' continued the stranger:

Pudding and Tame

There was once a boy who lived back of the church,
Whom fortune had cruelly left in the lurch,
For his back was weak and his lungs were poor,
And his legs were not very good, to be sure.
He never could go, he could only stay,
When the boys would play in the parson's hay;
He could only clutch his bit of a crutch,
And when they would cry, 'Hye! hye!
What's your name? What's your name?'
He would shout for an answer, 'It's Pudding and Tame!
Pudding and Tame! Pudding and Tame!
If you'll ask me again I'll tell you the same.'
And when the breath was out of his lung,
He would make ugly faces and stick out his tongue.

The boys didn't mean him to take it that way;
But when they went over to ask him to play
He flew into a very bad temper indeed;
Could he have reached any stones he'd have flung them,
And could he have changed to a snake he'd have stung them.

They thought it was really too bad to be lame,
To have such a temper and such an odd name,
So they thought to read the parson's books
For a cure for odd names and cross looks;
But search as they would the learned crew,
No book would tell them what to do;
And when at last they were quite at a loss,
One boy said, 'Let's try him with pudding and sauce.'

So they went to the parson's sister-in-law,
Who had a wonderful way with pastry,
She was the best cook that ever you saw,
For puddings and sauces and tastry,
(Tho' Newton's was astronomical,
Her genius was gastronomical.)
In fact, it was said,
She made several puddings
Out of her head.

She made a big pudding all stuffed full of meal,
With suet all through it, and plenty of peel,
Just the sort of a thing to make a rat squeal
With delight if he found it while out on a steal.
And the sauce – well, I'm quite at a loss
To tell you the things that went into that sauce;
But when it was finished it really did seem
Like something delicious one tastes in a dream.
It was winter – it may have been New Year's day;
When the pudding was done as brown as a bun
Each boy took his sister to look at the fun,
And they carried the platter along with a run;
Ten little lads each as fine as a whistle,
Ten little maids as sweet as a thistle;
Each one carried the weight (he or she, as the case may be) was able,
And they plumped it down on the lame boy's table.

At first he looked madder than any adder,
He bunched up his fists and curled in his wrists,
Give his eyes a squeeze as if he would sneeze;
His knees went up to his chin,
His lips shot out, his lips shot in;
And just as they thought he was going to be cross,
He drew in his breath and got wind of the sauce;
In a moment his faces were smiled away
From as wild as March to as mild as May;
He turned in a jiffy; well, then, maybe,
He grew as sweet as an April baby.

He took of the pudding a very large slice,
And he poured on of sauce rather more than would swim it;
Excuse him, his manners were not very nice,
He never knew sauce, so could not know the limit.
And the children took hands and danced in a ring,
And the only thing they could remember to sing
Was, 'What's your name? What's your name?'
And the boy looked up with a smile on his face,
And said, 'Pudding and Tame, just Pudding and Tame.'

He left the pudding and joined in the ring,
And one half the children continued to sing,
'What's your name? What's your name?'
And the other half answered, 'It's Pudding and Tame.'

So they got to be very good friends, you see,
And all sat under the parson's tree,
Every one there had a Christian name,
And the boy that was lame they called 'Pudding and Tame,'
Until at last they got tired of that
And shortened it into P–A–T PAT.

31 December 1892

DUNCAN CAMPBELL SCOTT

It may be considered excusable if, upon the approach of a new year, an enthusiastic Canadian, one who believes that his country is the brightest and best on earth, should indulge in a little flaunting of the maple leaf. The time is propitious. Upon the verge of one of those time divisions which serve as milestones of our progress, we may well pause for a moment, not so much to look back at what we have passed, as to glance forward at what is to come. We have, during the past few years, heard much of blame at the slowness of our national development from those who expect a nation to spring forth fully armed like Minerva from the head of Jupiter. Our progress has been, if slow, at least appreciable; to be remarked chiefly, perhaps, in the growth of interest which Canadians begin to feel in their own affairs and in their position amongst the nations of the earth. This is cheering, for, in national as well as in individual life, all strength and power must come from within. To become worthy to share in the commerce of the earth we must show a commercial spirit equal to our opportunities. And how boundless these opportunities are I need not state; the wealth and productiveness of this land cannot be surpassed by any on the face of the earth. We are often confronted by the statement that the geographical position of our provinces makes it impossible that any vigorous national life can exist, and the failure of our Dominion is prophesied because the success of some country similarly situated cannot be cited to cheer us in our difficult task. But do not doubt; we will serve as the example to the world of a people welded by a national spirit and a national love, although separated by natural barriers. When we have surmounted these difficulties it will be wondered why we considered them as blocking forever the road to our prosperity. The racial differences which now seem so definite will in the natural course of events disappear. What we as Canadians need more than anything else is a firm faith in our country and in her ultimate destiny. It is not necessary to imagine that our Dominion must stand or fall by her present constitution. If in the course of time this proves, by reason of events which have not yet presented themselves, to be unworkable we will have secured experience and wisdom sufficient to change our form of government without resorting to the shameful refuge in national disgrace and annihilation. In the life of every people there are years of danger which have to be lived through with hope in the strength and vitality of those principles upon which its security and permanence is founded; and why should Canada abandon at the first difficulty, or at any difficulty, her hope of national unity. In the young men of this country there is growing a sentiment which will sweep any thought of Canadian disgrace or humiliation into the limbo of forgotten and despicable things. This cause, the cause of the Canadian nation, may be assisted by everyone; in this sentiment and in these objects every Canadian can have a part; and to all those throughout the breadth of this land who can throw up their caps and give a shout for Canada I wish a hearty and a happy new year.

WILFRED CAMPBELL

As the present year draws to a close and the new year approaches with the undreamed-of future, which holds for all joy and sorrow, triumph and failure, more or less, it is a good thing for us to take a glance at our conditions, and ask ourselves if we are fairly satisfied at the appearance of things in general. If there is one thing I detest, it is a tendency to self-deception and to avoid grim realities. Now, this is the season of the year when we should especially examine into our conditions and see how the world stands in relationship to its best ideals, if it has any. As the result of a cursory glance at the past year's history, there is one conclusion we will all come to, and that is that in all countries public affairs as regards their management are getting more complicated as the years go on, and that government by the many in lieu of government by the few is not such an unqualified success after all. The problem of nation-building has come into startling prominence in connection with our affairs during this year, and, as viewed from a political as well as from a patriotic standpoint, presents some conditions for our gravest consideration. If we are ever to be a people like the other nations, we must not refuse to meet those difficulties fair in the face, and not shirk our responsibilities.

There is no getting over the fact that we are unfortunately placed, both in time and locality, for the fostering of a national spirit and growth. We have probably more obstacles of an internal nature to overcome than any nation under the sun that ever tried to realize a national unity and independence. In any part of the civilized world it would be harder to accomplish such results than it was a quarter of a century ago. But it is especially difficult here in Canada. In the old days the national prejudice was strong in men. Now it is rather the other way, as the average man rather likes the novelty of a foreign environment if he can do better, and especially when there is no barrier in customs and language. Then this is the commercial age, and the old national barriers are broken down. I speak here as a Canadian and one who loves his country, but who loves her too well to bury the dangers to her progress, that all true Canadians only see too well, in cowardly evasions for the sake of creating a false hope. Canada cannot afford today to fall back on false sentiments, and on an attempt to force a patriotism that might have carried some old-time nation over similar difficulties. The prodding with the goad that would have made the national drayhorse pull harder in the ruts in days past would now likely cause him to jump the patriotic traces. Men think and compare more than they used to, and politicians especially must remember that they have been for years and years past perhaps over-educating the average voter up to a strong sense of his own individual rights, and they must not be surprised if in a national crisis the mine they have been laying explodes under their own feet. If the people today are hard to please and difficult to lash or coax into patriotic contentment and soberness, the politicians should be the last to complain. I will dare to say, apart from all party considerations, that we as a people have been largely sacrificed to ultra-party considerations. Party government is evidently necessary, but it must never usurp and eclipse the national feeling. When it does the result is a condition of things such as we have in Canada today, the grave difference in our case being that party spirit has prevented the growth of this sentiment instead of merely hampering it. All men who know our national life today know that the country is in imminent danger on account of race and religious feuds, and that the most strenuous steps should be taken to canvass the whole Dominion on this matter. The greatest danger to the country lies in trying to smother as inimical what is but the natural expression of this stage of our development. The most unpatriotic course is that which would leave the whole matter to politicians, who are involved in party considerations that obstruct the smooth path of an unbiased patriotism. What is essentially needed is a sentiment that will sweep like a baptismal wave from ocean to ocean and overpower all local, racial, and other influences – not that these need necessarily to be swept out, but which will keep them in the place where they belong in the community. Whatsoever influence is working to this end is loyal and is in keeping with the true spirit of our growth toward the ideal nation. What I would ask all true Canadians today is, are such elements at work? and are our feelings as a nation overcoming mere provincial and racial prejudices? That is the grave question to propound just now. Are we Canadians even a little more in national sentiment than in the days of confederation? What we are in most danger of at present is not so much an open expression towards annexation, but a pseudo-patriotism that for mere self-interest would muzzle the true expression of the national thought at this most critical point of our country's development.

7 January 1893

DUNCAN CAMPBELL SCOTT

No one can meet Mr Gilbert Parker, our young fellow countryman who has been so successful in the London literary world, without feeling that he deserves all his success and will have more. There is a reserve of force which one becomes, somehow or other, aware of, which inspires a feeling of confidence that Mr Parker, with his assiduity, his great ability, and his opportunities, will achieve a yet higher reputation. He has already seen much of the world, and he seems to have the devouring eye which will not let any fact or colour or circumstance escape him. It is an almost absolute necessity to have command of several locales for success in modern story writing, and Mr Parker has Canada, with which he is thoroughly familiar, and Australia and the South Seas, where he has spent some time, to draw upon. The former field has furnished him already with matter for several of his most successful tales, and he is now engaged in the pastoral and arcadian Quebec in collecting fresher knowledge of the ways and speech of the people for future use. Australasia has provided him incidents for a volume of South Sea stories, which is to appear in May next. In the meantime, *Pierre and His People* has gone into its second edition, and in February Messrs Methuen are to publish a novel, *Mrs Falchion*, which will also be issued by the United States Book Company. Mr Parker has also been successful with his dramatic productions. *The Wedding Day* is now being produced in England, and Geo. Alexander of the St James' theatre, London, has accepted a one-act play from Mr Parker's pen. All this means an extraordinary output of energy, and if our young Canadian continues, and there is no reason why he should not, he will soon occupy a place in the literary firmament which many have coveted and but few obtained. There is about Mr Parker a freedom from disguise, a perfect, genial open-heartedness, and a helpful belief in his art and the worthiness of it which stamp him, as I said before, as a man bound to succeed, and these qualities make us wish him success for his own sake as well as ours. It will be a bright day for Canada when men of such ability can find it to their advantage to remain at home and exercise their faculties in helping to build up the country in which they were born and to which they must often turn with longing. Emerson says somewhere that a man being born in a place means that he has some work to do there;

and there is plenty of work for every Canadian to do in Canada. But, at present, it is not the Utopia of authors, except, perhaps, in appreciation – for I hold that there is a great deal of genuine appreciation – and when a man feels that letters is his calling he must depart from our shores and be a sojourner in an alien land.

WILFRED CAMPBELL

One of the most fascinating studies is that of history. To see the past through the glasses of a Gibbon or a Hume, a Hallam or a Froude, is not alone entertaining and instructive, but it is also inspiring. But how much more realistic and important becomes the study when you have a chance thrown in your way to read the past life of a people through its public, everyday affairs. It is like the power of reading between the lines of a letter. We are not only able to see and hear the actors as they strut the stage, but also to discover the secret motives and circumstances that influenced their actions. I have very little faith in biographies as a whole. They are very often but the funeral trappings and trimmings of a life that in its grim realities was a very different matter altogether. So it is with history. Even when that bias is dead which influences contemporary opinion, other public motives and prejudices are at work to prevent a true depiction of the past in its entirety. I am sorry to say that for this reason we have few great historians. And we ourselves know how common a thing it is to have even the greatest historians tampered with in the interests of certain existing institutions. Under this head nothing can be of greater interest to Canadians today than anything that may throw light on the early days of old Upper Canada. It can easily be admitted that we have as yet no important chronicle of that period, with the exception of what Mr Kingsford is doing in that direction. We have been instructed as schoolboys in certain dates and attendant events in connection with old provincial history. But, beyond this and certain patriotic remembrances acquired in a general way, we know little or nothing as a people of our immediate ancestors of old Upper Canada. The U.E. Loyalist and other biographies, for they are nothing more, give us but a small and, for the most part, a false idea of the real history of those days. How interesting, I repeat, is it, then, to be able at this date to see our predecessors, not through any biassed eye, but in the light of their own daily acts and ideals, both as private citizens and through their civil institutions. How different do things appear. The hideous appears in all its unvarnished reality, and if there is anything that strikes us as heroic in the period it appeals to us by its very unconsciousness of being anything out of the common. You can fancy the surprise that would come over a man, who, having perused the biography of a dead man, written by some friend or relative, suddenly comes into possession of all his private papers giving the key to the motives and actions of his whole life. If the student were not already a man of the world and accustomed to accept such things with a grain of salt, how many illusions would there not be destroyed for him under the circumstances? In dipping into the early life of old Upper Canada, the truth of these cursory remarks appears almost at every step. And if plain documents of a year or a decade tell anything of the life of a people, the elements of sordidness and personal ambition played no small part in the general impulse. It is almost laughable to read the long-winded preambles of the commons and legislative assembly of that date, and especially the former, and the extreme iteration of loyalty is remarkable. And the constant recurring phrase, 'Our one desire is the freedom and happiness of man,' which, if we read the people of that period through the utterance of its corporate representatives, seemed to be the one ideal and aim of the age, sounds very funny side by side with the chronicle of the daily acts of the said body, which many of them would lead us to believe to be the acts of those mysterious personages proclaimed in these public documents as the enemies of justice and the freedom of man rather than those of a body whose ideals were so lofty and unselfish in their aim. As today the great struggle is for money, so in those days, when money was scarce and of little account in a colony with little trade and no commerce, land was the one standard of power and position, and the greed for the acquisition of that solid representative of material wealth is quite surprising even to the mind of this most degenerate present age. The rapidity with which public officials acquired large grants, some to the immense amount of ten thousand acres, is shown in contradistinction to unavailing efforts of really deserving families to even acquire the common allotment of from one hundred to two hundred acres. Of course we do not go to public documents to learn the heroic in any age, and I doubt not but that our Upper Canadian ancestors were not devoid of this essential quality in a nationality, but at the same time we must not forget that the acquirement of wealth was no small element in the national inspiration of our immediate past, and that if we are wise today we will not forget in our hunt for a national feeling to rely largely on the practical everyday interests of an intensely practical people, rather than on any amount of gush and mock sentiment, which is of no more importance today, and gives no more true idea of the real life of the age than did those hypocritical and high-sounding documents with their long phrases about 'justice and the happiness of man' give of the real motives and actions of our old Canadian ancestors.

ARCHIBALD LAMPMAN

At a time when literary men are credited with an unusual aptitude for money-making and a most keen eye for the main chance, it is almost a satisfaction to hear that Ernest Renan, a writer surely of great popularity and exquisite charm, died poor. It is even said that Madame Renan is obliged to sell her husband's library in order to maintain herself until the national pension, which it is proposed to confer upon her, has been granted. Renan sold all the copyrights of his books, and lived upon the proceeds of his salary as professor in the College of France and his earnings from occasional writings. Altogether at the time of his death his income appears to have been about $3000 a year, certainly a very moderate sum for a man of his fame. As he was not of a saving temperament he easily consumed all of this, and left nothing behind him. It was Renan who said to the minister of Napoleon III, who offered him a lucrative government post, 'Sit tecum tua pecunia.' Renan was great, and had the poet's sovereign indifference to wealth.

ARCHIBALD LAMPMAN

If a man were to be exiled to some inaccessible island or cast into prison and given the choice of half a dozen books which he might carry with him to be his solace and support, which books do you think would he choose? No doubt every man much given to reading and thought has amused his fancy at one time or another with some such speculation as this. If it were my case I should choose the Bible, the poems of Homer, the plays of Shakespeare, the poems of Wordsworth, the autobiography of Goethe, and the *Don Quixote* of Cervantes; the Bible as the most fervid and fruitful expression of the religious and prophetic spirit, the *Iliad* and *Odyssey* of Homer as the most perfect narrative of human passion and human effort presented in the clearest simplicity of beauty, the plays of Shakespeare as the picture of human life made for us by the world's highest union of intellect, heart, and imagination, the poems of Wordsworth as the noblest presentment of the influence exerted upon the soul by the beauty and grandeur of outward nature, the autobiography of Goethe as the record of the development of an insatiable and most vital mind uniting the scientific and artistic spirits each in an extraordinary degree, and the *Don Quixote* as the world's book of the sweetest and most humane humour. From these six books a man might draw sufficient strength, knowledge, inspiration, delight, and humanity to last him a lifetime, and leave him with a soul fitted for eternity with all its chambers draped and furnished and all its windows open.

ARCHIBALD LAMPMAN

Now that I am upon such fancies as this – and coming down to a subject which is perhaps of interest only to the more curious student of letters – I have been trying to make out which is the most beautiful sonnet in the English language, not from the artistic sonneteer's point of view, but from the purely human one. After passing in review the sonnets of Shakespeare, Spenser, Milton, Wordsworth, Rossetti, and all the other famous ones, I come to the conclusion that that last sonnet of Keats which he wrote on shipboard in the British Channel not many months before his end is the loveliest and loftiest of all. Here it is:

Bright star! would I were steadfast as thou art –
  Not in lone splendour hung aloft the night,
And watching with eternal lids apart,
  Like nature's patient, sleepless Ereonite,
The moving waters at their priestlike task
  Of pure ablution round earth's human shores,
Or gazing at the new soft-fallen mask
  Of snow upon the mountains and the moors –
No – yet still steadfast, still unchangeable,
  Pillow'd upon my fair love's ripening breast,
To feel forever its soft fall and swell,
  Awake forever in a sweet unrest,
Still, still to hear her tender-taken breath,
  And so live ever – or else swoon to death.

How tender, how eloquent, how serene! Surely no young poet ever took leave of this troublesome life – this skein of so sweet and bitter destinies – with a purer or sweeter note upon his lips.

14 January 1893

DUNCAN CAMPBELL SCOTT

I was lately struck by the appearance which a volume of Montaigne's *Essays*, which had been a wanderer from a public library for some time, presented when it came into my hands through possibly hundreds of others. It seemed to support a proposition that I have heard defended many times and with much spirit, that these old books lived by the uncleanliness which was in them, for as I looked at the pages of the closed book there was a discoloured streak down the centre, and these pages had, by reason of much thumbing, become loosened from the back and had protruded themselves slightly in advance of their fellows, as if petitioning to be read before their betters or wholly to the exclusion of them. It was a comment on a peculiarity of human nature that these pages had been oftener used than any others in the book, and they contained what Montaigne would perhaps not be complete without, but what is a valueless portion of this incomparable work. I was led to think that hundreds of people had read these pages to their own destruction, and had been led to the great essayist from no desire to profit by his genuine spirit, by his animated sayings, by his inexhaustible knowledge of human nature, but by the very small portion of his work which deals with baser things. Montaigne's work, as I have said before, would be incomplete without the chapters which are pervaded by a license which is inadmissible in our own day. They enable us to see more clearly what manner of man Montaigne was, and they throw a distinct light on the customs of the age in which he lived; but they are not Montaigne in the sense in which one uses the name when one thinks of the force he can be in the modern world, and when one associates it with those stores of wit and human kindliness and rare wisdom which make him forever the refuge of minds which can be touched and won by such qualities. Anyone who reads the old authors out of pruriency, for the delight of what is unclean in them, takes them at a mean and disgraceful disadvantage. If they had provided a tale of obscenity and invited the world to partake, theirs would have been the blame; but when they load the board with all manner of wholesome food it is an act of monstrous ill-breeding for a guest to satiate his unnatural appetite with some special dish, and not to refresh himself with the plain and vigorous fare spread before him. We will always find men who will match what is unclean in themselves with the uncleanliness of the old authors, but these worthies are like eagles who soar away from their befouled nests into their natural element, the clear, universal air. Happy is the man who can follow them, who can enjoy the depth of their wisdom and the penetration of their wit, and who refuses to be misled by the belief that they exist for, and are perpetuated by, those portions of their works which appeal to the baser qualities of human nature. The readers who perused only the discoloured pages of the Montaigne to which I have referred had not communed with him at all, they had left him without a shadow of an idea of what a fine, companionable fellow he was, and will never know until they discover for themselves those qualities which made Emerson include him as one of the world's representative men.

ARCHIBALD LAMPMAN

Some fortunate persons have been given the pleasure in recent years of reading two remarkable poems called *The Lost Island* and *Nestorius*, printed and abound in two very thin little books. The author is Mr E.T. Fletcher, a writer I believe, as a poet, almost unknown to fame. These poems, written in stanzas full of musical and imaginative power, the first printed in 1888 and the second in 1892, treat of old world subjects, and are similar in tone and colouring. In both the writer has succeeded admirably in enveloping his theme in that brooding and mysterious splendour which associates itself in our imaginations with the enormous memorials of far-off antiquity.

The Lost Island is a story of Atlantis. A pestilence rages upon the island, and is removed by Sanadon, a Marut, or lord of the winds, who puts on human nature in order that he may be united to the island queen, Evanoe, whom he loves. Afterward, when the doom falls upon Atlantis, he sacrifices himself for the safety of the people, who escape in a fleet which he has taught them to build. Evanoe and her two adopted children, Eiridion and Thya, voluntarily share his fate. The description of the journeys upon which Sanadon carries the two children over the whole earth for the purposes of their education affords Mr Fletcher an opportunity for the exercise of the Miltonic picturesqueness of his imagination:

Such were the lessons which the Marut taught,
Lessons of pity and of hardihood.

Then rose the four from that green solitude
And floated westward over Hadramaut,
Region of death; and passed Canopus hoar,
Fresh as a vision of the morning then, and sought
The silence of the lonely western sea
Unknown and vast, with wild waves rolling free,
Beyond Pyrene and the sunset shore.

Through the dim shadows of the moonlit night
What phantom comes? The winds have sunk to sleep,
There is no sound or motion on the deep;
Wrapt, as a bride, in veil of gauzy light,
What galley, slow and ghostlike, parts the foam,
With labouring oars and shredded sails of white,
Battered with storms? 'Behold,' said Sanadon,
'Girt with his friends, Ulysses wanders on.
Adventurous, forgetful of his home!'
The large-browed chieftains from Scamander's plain,
Sages and warriors, kings of oldest time,

Sitting as gods – Ulysses with the rime
Of years upon his beard – the sails – the vane –
Were seen a moment through the gloom; then passed
Beyond their ken, and all was night again.

In the poem *Nestorius* a young Arab girl comes to the aged and banished patriarch, as he broods by the bank of the Nile, and devotes her life to him. The two go forth into the desert, and after many days reach an oasis which had once been the retiring place of the Mizrite pharaohs, and the last refuge of the worship of the ancient deities. Nestorius exorcises and banishes the spectres of the old religion forever. On their returning journey his little companion starts from her sleep to defend the old man from the threatened attack of a lion, and, in consequence of the shock, she sickens and dies. The return and death of Nestorius are recorded. The poem is not very strong as to 'motif,' but the descriptions of the desert, the oasis, the strange, forsaken palaces, the ghostly throng within them, and the vision of the ancient deities and their worshippers, all lend themselves to that gift of high imagination and sonorous and beautiful versification which Mr Fletcher possesses. How rich this versification is my readers may judge from the following stanzas:

And down the highway, like the ceaseless course
Of some majestic river, swept along
A multitude past numbering, a throng
Of strange-clad, many-nationed worshippers;
Priests in rich panther skins and robes of white,
Princes uraeus-crowned – and sceptred queens.
Brown Abyssinian girls, with tambourines,
Slaves, warriors in cohorts infinite,
Bejewelled Khita, and wild Hagarines.

Far in the van, King Ramses Miamon,
The lord of victory, the eagle-eyed –
A tawny lion stalking by his side –
Stood in his car, and seemed to lead them on:
Still in his hand he held the mighty bow,
Which none but he might bend, of mortal men;
The quiver still he bore, whose arrowy rain
Showered death, like Amun's lightning, and laid low
The hosts of Syria on Khadesh plain.

It will be a surprise to my readers – those of them who do not know Mr Fletcher personally – to know that he is an old man, more than seventy years of age. He was born an Englishman, came to this country when very young, and was an architect and surveyor in the service of the crown lands department at Quebec until his superannuation some years ago. Since that time he has lived in British Columbia, where one of his sons is post office inspector. Among his friends he is distinguished as an excellent scholar and accomplished man.

It seems strange that amid the numerous company of verse-makers whom our reviewers delight to honour with sounding paragraphs, and whose work is, much of it, such very indifferent stuff, a writer capable of *The Lost Island* and *Nestorius* should have reached old age almost unknown as a poet beyond a limited group of sympathetic friends. Let us do honour to such a poet, who has maintained a reserve so fine and so unusual, who has run so far counter to the clamorous custom of his age as to live out a long life in the tranquil love of books, wisdom, and poetry, without caring whether the public buy his photograph or the reviewers blow all their penny whistles in his praise.

WILFRED CAMPBELL

The New York Critic of January 7 is an especially interesting number and contains over half a dozen able reviews of important timely books. A notice of Lowell's *Old English Dramatists* heads the list. This collection of essays, which has been edited since the author's death by Professor Eliot Norton of Harvard college, is ranked by *The Critic* as even superior to that of Lamb on the subject. The reviewer says: 'In these lectures the American shows himself the more charming idealist of the two, unlocking the chambers of poetry with a golden key, and turning them into delightful whispering galleries for the spirit.' These essays, outside of their perennial charm and value, are interesting to us as an example of Lowell's personality in his latter days, as shown in his work. The young Lowell was great as an American, who was both a poet and a patriot. But the man was fated to outlive the era and its dreams for which he wrote and struggled. He lived to change his mind, and with the death of his old enthusiasms his foreign residence toned him down into a delightful cosmopolitan man of letters. Though Lowell never ceased as an American to live in the present, yet it was not the fiery Lowell of 1843 who penned those delightful essays.

The next review is a long and appreciative one of the late Sir Daniel Wilson's *The Lost Atlantis. The Critic* says with regard to this work, which ought to be of especial interest to Canadians and graduates of Toronto University: 'The most striking quality of the essays which make up this volume is what may be called their judicial quality. They are the productions of a clear-sighted and conscientious instructor.' This review, I should not doubt, has been contributed by a Canadian. The late Sir Daniel Wilson has done much in his *Prehistoric Man* and his later works for the study of ethnology. But while he was a hard and close student and a man of eminence, he was too conservative to be a genuine discoverer in any field. Then he was too old a man to come into touch with the growth of science during the last two decades. As a classifier and as a collector of knowledge he has done his part like many other able and painstaking students. But when it comes to a large sweep of the intellect, unclouded and unbiassed for the purpose of free comparison, a broader and more modern type of mind is necessary. There are many men in the world today whose minds are storehouses of knowledge in detail, but who have never grasped the whole at a quick sweep, so as to really own it for themselves or others. This is one of the grave weaknesses of our modern life; a man is regarded as an authority on a subject merely because he has got a lot of technical knowledge with regard to it. I do not say that the author of *Prehistoric Man* was not a scholar of large calibre, or was not a thinker. He was a thinker, but he thought within certain limitations. I rather think that if Dr Wilson had been born thirty or forty years later he might have done more for the advancement of science than he has done.

Another interesting review is on Sydney's *Social Life in England, 1660-1690.* Such a work should be of the greatest importance to all students of our own times. We are, the most of us, too much inclined to live in a mist of tradition as regards the past, and we have a foolish idea that we are much advanced as social beings. After all, when we come down to solid reality, this age is just as sordid and brutal as any that has preceded it. We fancy that all the misery of our time is relegated to the Siberian mines and the poor of London. But if we only want to look we will find enough at our own doors. As for the immoralities, so-called, of Charles II's reign, the less we say of them the better. Idle wealth will produce such a condition in any age or country, and the form of government or of religion does not matter one iota. It is a well-known fact that there is as much vice today in high-class society, so-called, of New York, London, or Paris as there was in the worst days of the Roman empire. The revelations of Stead and others in London alone are revolting in the extreme. Any man who wants to get good reading and who can afford to buy good books should take *The New York Critic* for a year, and buy the books, or a part of them, that are reviewed in its columns, and if at the end of that time he had not gained in knowledge of the thought and culture of his own times, it would not be the fault of that excellent paper.

21 January 1893

DUNCAN CAMPBELL SCOTT

Amongst the most interesting of the publications which appeal to the antiquarian are the issues of old English parish registers and constables' accounts. From these we can to some extent construct the past, discover the manners and customs of our forefathers, their amusements and what they paid for them as well as other things, the fines they were liable to, and the laws to which they had to bow. Such documents have preserved the knowledge of local customs and traditions, and have thrown much light upon the original application of words and phrases which have gained a currency wider than amongst the gossips of the district in which they first arose. One of the latest of these books is the transcript of *The Constable's Accounts of the Manor of Manchester*, edited by J.P. Earwaker and published by Blackburn & Co. of Manchester. The originals of the documents are in the possession of the corporation of Manchester. One of them was bequeathed to it, the other purchased for it, and they now form part of the city archives. It is related of a former owner of one of the manuscripts that he saw it in a bookseller's shop, and, knowing that he had discovered a prize, carried it off under his arm and left a friend to arrange for the price. From the accounts themselves we learn that the authorities in Manchester long ago practised the art, which some of our city corporations have brought to such perfection, of getting rid of objectionable paupers and mendicants by passing them into the next municipality with as great expedition as possible. It is a question of some interest what in the end becomes of these unfortunate individuals. Are they passed on constantly, never resting, with a mayor's pass always in their hands, until at last death thrusts them out of the world with a chuckle, giving them the passport which he never denies to anyone? But if our city officials have retained these habits they no longer wear the gorgeous plumage which their predecessors wore. Beadles were the show of the town in those days, with their utter magnificence and the importance of their duties. Scourging offenders of all sorts – thieves, blacklegs, idiots, beggars, dissolute persons, and nondescript vagrants – was one of their chief duties, as well as applying the municipal tortures for scolding and bewitching. The bellman also was a functionary of more than ordinary importance, and on Shrove Tuesday we are informed he had to take particular precautions against 'lifting,' a practice which consisted of groups of women catching hold of and lifting from the ground all the men they met, and the men doing the same to the women. We could imagine a group of these Manchester dames descending upon and 'lifting' the bellman, bell and all, much to the alarm of municipal authority in general and of that functionary in particular. But *The Constable's*

Accounts contain less pleasant items than these, for there is, amongst other things, a small payment for fixing the heads of two rebels, Thomas Deacon and Thomas Syddall, upon their spires on the Exchange, and Deacon's father, who was a non-juring clergyman, 'never passed under the Exchange without uncovering his head.' What a picture of the times that one description calls up; the son's head on the spire, held aloft between heaven and earth, a warning to rebels and malefactors, and his father, with uncovered head, passing beneath!

ARCHIBALD LAMPMAN

The Canadian reading public are not likely to meet with anything more interesting than a new publication by Professor Charles G.D. Roberts, our master workman in verse. Such an event is unfortunately too rare. In the present case it comes to us in the brief shape of the 'Ave, an Ode for the Shelley Centenary.' In these beautiful and strenuous stanzas Professor Roberts enrolls himself in the special band of the Shelley worshippers, who attribute to that poet a degree of divinity which I, for one, am hardly inclined to allow. But whether the reader be a follower of this cult or not, the beauty and fervour of the 'Ave,' and the sonorous pomp of its versification, can hardly fail to possess his imagination. The poem opens with an address to the poet's beloved Tantramar marshes, always a theme upon which he warms into his finest vein, and the following stanzas will serve not only as an example of his vivid and luxurious delight in splendid landscape and the richness of his gift as a word painter, but also will indicate how he connects the Tantramar marshes with his view of the character and fate of Shelley:

And when the orange flood came roaring in
From Fundy's tumbling troughs and tide-worn caves,
While red Minudie's flats were drowned with din
And rough Chignecto's front oppugned the waves,
How blithely with the refluent foam I raced
Inland along the radiant chasm, exploring
The green solemnity with boisterous haste;
My pulse of joy outpouring
To visit all the creeks that twist and shine
From Beauséjour to utmost Tormentine.

And after, when the tide was full, and stilled
A little while the seething and the hiss,

And every tributary channel filled
    To the brim with rosy streams that swelled to kiss
The grass-roots all a-wash and goose-tongue wild
    And salt-sap rosemary – then how well content
I was to rest me like a breathless child
    With play-time rapture spent,
To lapse and loiter till the change should come
And the great floods turn seaward, roaring home.

And now, oh tranquil marshes, in your vast
    Serenity of vision and of dream,
Wherethrough by every intricate vein have passed
    With joy impetuous and pain supreme
The sharp fierce tides that chafe the shores of earth
    In endless and controlless ebb and flow,
Strangely akin you seem to him whose birth
        One hundred years ago
With fiery succor to the ranks of song
Defied the ancient gates of wrath and wrong.

These stanzas are an excellent specimen of Professor Roberts's diction, which, although at times a little heavy in its movement and wanting in flexibility, has always the charm of an exceedingly broad and full-vowelled flow, with a sort of determined strenuousness of accent. There is, moreover, the indefinable individual touch which marks all of Professor Roberts's best work as his own. The following is one of two very beautiful stanzas in which he skilfully refers to some of Shelley's greater works as figurings of various aspects of the poet's own soul:

Thyself the lark melodious in mid-heaven;
    Thyself the Protean shape of chainless cloud,
Pregnant with elemental fire, and driven
    Through deeps of quivering light, and darkness loud
With tempest, yet beneficent as prayer;
    Thyself the wild west wind, relentless strewing
The withered leaves of custom on the air,
        And through the wreck pursuing
O'er lovelier Arnos, more imperial Romes,
The radiant visions to their viewless homes.

There are other stanzas as fine as these which I would that I had space to quote, but I shall have to content myself with some instances of our poet's gift of descriptive phrase-making – an art in which he is a master:

The flicker of sand-pipers in from sea
In gusty flocks that puffed and fled . . .

Hither and thither in the slow, soft tide,
    Rolled seaward, shoreward, sands and wandering shells
And shifting weeds thy fellows . . .

In that unroutable profound of peace,
    Beyond experience of pulse and breath,
Beyond the last release
Of longing . . .

We have heard from time to time of a forthcoming volume of collected pieces by Professor Roberts, and we trust that its publication may not be long delayed.

WILFRED CAMPBELL

It is rarely that we meet with good religious verse today. Even in the hymnologies the gems are among the oldest. The late Cardinal Newman's 'Lead, Kindly Light' is probably the most human and the greatest among modern hymns, containing as it does in itself the whole circle of modern faith and doubt. The poet Whittier was the greatest hymn writer of this century, chiefly because of his large faith in the infinite and his wide human charity linked with a pure lyrical genius. After all, if a writer is allowed to express an opinion, my choice would fall on the 'Te Deum' as the greatest religious hymn ever written. There is a largeness and majesty in the style and the language that is simply glorious, and one of the greatest punishments one can endure is to hear this great hymn murdered by bad music and a poor choir. It is also a prayer, and such a chant or prayer can only be truly delivered where all is in keeping. Among religious poems not found in rituals Milton's superb hymn to the 'Nativity' is by all odds the greatest. In the Christmas number of *The Owl*, the Ottawa college paper, there appeared a 'Christmas Hymn' by Mr Waters, whose 'Water Lily' has already given him a place among Canadian poets, though I understand he is not a Canadian by birth. This poem is no doubt one of the finest religious poems ever written in Canada. The theology is Roman Catholic, which fact will to a large extent prevent outsiders from appreciating many beauties of expression. But the literary reader cannot but realize many beautiful passages in the poem, as the following:

And down the asphodel-flowered lawn
Of opening heaven the angels tread
With folded wings and eyes serene,
To where the ever-virgin queen
Low o'er the infant droops her head.

The finest lines in the whole poem are those describing how

He empties heaven of all his might
And bides within a little span.

Mr Waters is a true poet, who without any idea of fame has written for the pure love of his art and the enjoyment it has given him. But nevertheless he has done work of a quality that might easily outshine that of others who are more ambitious for literary honours.

DUNCAN CAMPBELL SCOTT

Mr George Meredith is reputed to have nearly finished his new novel, but its name has not been announced. Mr R.D. Blackmore is to publish his new novel as a serial in *Macmillan's Magazine*. It is called *Perlycross*, and is said to be equal in interest to Mr Blackmore's best work.

WILFRED CAMPBELL

If the author of the poem 'Life,' which was sent to this department, will kindly send his address a private opinion will be given.

28 January 1893

WILFRED CAMPBELL

At a time when the Canadian critics have softened their asperity towards our more ambitious songsters, when Mr Roberts is called a master, and when special beauties are being found in the works of John Henry

Brown, Bliss Carman, and many others of our deserving and painstaking poets, I hope that the Canadian people will forgive me for introducing them to another aspirant, who in his own place is not unworthy of public recognition. The poet in this case is Mr James Ernest Caldwell, who has rightly earned, if he has not gained, the distinction of being the poet of the Ottawa valley. Mr Caldwell is also by right the singer of the Canadian lumber woods and farm life. He is a young man of about thirty years of age and most of his verse (for much of it has the right to that title) was written before the age of twenty-three. He has worked all his life on a farm, and is now engaged in that most unpoetical vocation of milk-selling, which he adds to his other rural activities. I do not mean this as an advertisement, but I believe he has a most successful trade in that line and gives good satisfaction. He has had no other education than that afforded by a country school and not too much of that. But I should say, from the evidence of his literary efforts, that he has tried to read, and has thought not a little.

Though Mr Caldwell's work abounds in many crudities and immature strains of thought and style, yet there is much of his work that is both dignified and poetical, and showing a strength of imagination and creative ability that is scarcely credible in a young Canadian farm lad. His two principal poems are 'Cecilia,' a poem of the Ottawa valley, and 'The Marketing,' both written in rhymed couplets after the style of Scott. The first is a story of over 2000 lines, and is a tale of love and treachery, the scenes being laid in Ottawa and the lumber woods of the upper Ottawa. After taking into account the lack of culture in the author, much dramatic force will be found in the poem. Though written at that formative age when a young poet would be liable to imitate, the poem shows a rugged and quaint simplicity of style that makes it his own, and almost leads one to forget that the style of the romance writers is scarcely adaptable to the relation of life episodes in a lumber shanty.

There are many really good descriptions of nature, and all are quite Wordsworthian in their direct simplicity, such as the opening lines of Canto I:

The sky was all a crimson glow
Where the August sun hung rich and low;
The air was still, and the dying day
Like a spent, ensanguined warrior lay

Breathing out its latest hour,
Conscious of its spirit's power.

The description at the commencement of Canto II of the shantymen leaving Ottawa for the woods is a quaint word picture, and is worthy of reproduction:

The clock is pointing round towards four,
The bus is at each tavern door
In Murray street, where flock together,
To spend their hours of summer weather
The hardy reapers of the woods
The nimble riders of the floods;
Now many a farewell glass is taken,
And many a farewell hand is shaken;
And many a bag and box is stored
Within the 'bus; then, 'all aboard!'
Joe, Jacques, Baptiste, François, Xavier,
Dave, Peter, George; yes, all are there.
Fresh from the barber's unctuous hands,
Fingers bedecked with jewelled bands;
A massive chain hangs from each vest,
A soft slouch hat, with care compressed
Poised far and deftly on one side;
Shoes of the calf's soft, supple hide,
High heeled and neat for merry dance,
So step they forth, their play-time o'er,
Gay as the cavaliers of yore;
Bold, reckless hearts that know not home
Joy in a life that bids them roam,
And love the freedom of the woods,
And all the perils of the floods.

Here we get not only the seeing eye and the poetical imagination but also the pathos which is depicted in the last lines. There is also further on a fine song which contains some strong and tender lines.

What is more suggestive of outdoor freedom than –

Pull, boys, pull, leave home and friends behind;
Pull, boys, pull, this life is to our mind;

In the pine woods deep,
Our camp we'll keep,
Where never care will find.

And the lines,

To-night the murmuring pines shall steep
Our dreams in music while we sleep.

have the beauty of true poetry.

I only wish I had more room to quote some other fine descriptions.

'The Marketing' is less tragic, but is a Canadian pastoral, and opens with these simple yet truly poetical lines:

The moon was breaking, dull and drear,
In that cold month which ends the year;
Deep, soft and pure the fresh snow lay
In woods and fields and broad highway.

There is a true homeliness and tenderness in the description of the daily toil and lives of the farmer's home, and some delicate descriptions, such as:

Tardily the pale light falls
Upon the dusky cottage walls,
And through the frost-enamelled pane.

Likewise the description of the preparation for the market is realistic in its quaint verity:

Jessie must see the eggs well packed
In bran, so that they be not cracked;
The butter prints so deftly made
In snowy napkined baskets laid.

There is also a graphic and terse depiction of the rural butcher, at one time an institution, who comes to examine the family cow, and who:

To a shade the weight could tell
And handled knife and steel right well,
And knew who'd fed the heaviest steer,
The fattest hog, for many a year;
And now he view'd his latest case

With grave and calculating face,
And felt her brisket, ribs and flank,
And then pronounced her 'good' point blank.

I have not space to quote any more of this genuine homespun poetry. Sufficient to say it is true Canadian pastoral of the people and for the people. I do not claim for Mr Caldwell that he is a poetical artist. Much of his work abounds in crudities and marks of immature inspiration. It is the work of one who has lacked culture. But he is something more than a mere writer of doggerels. As I have shown, he has the poetical gift in thought and imagination. And what he has done, if of no further value, has at least shown that there can be thoughts of beauty and inspiration drawn even from the everyday toils and privations of Canadian farm life.

I will end this review with one more instance of this Canadian rural verse, which may not appeal to the worshippers of Keats and Shelley, but which in its simple limitations bears evidence also of the singing heart that is aware of the beauty of nature and the pathos of human life:

O, sing me a song, sweet sister,
    A song of the olden time
When hearts were full of music,
    And lips were full of rhyme.
And a song shall bear me backward
    To happier times than these,
When flowers were in the pastures
    And birds were in the trees;
And the robin's song at morning
    Awoke from happy dreams,
As into the attic window
    Came the sun's first ruddy beams.

Gone now are the happy songsters,
    And gone from the fields the flowers;
And few the trees that sigh for
    The gentle summer showers;
And never a juicy berry
    To colour the finger tips,

And dust in hillside fountains,
Where we drank with eager lips.
Now never from out the greenwood,
In the days of blooming spring,
Like the roll of distant thunder,
Comes the throb of the partridge wing.

Over the world the shadow
Of Mammon slowly rolls
And a sacrilegious humour
Hath seared uncounted souls;
Nothing too pure and holy,
Nothing too fair and sweet,
To earn the scornful gibing
That comes from the jester's seat!
Then sing me a song, sweet sister,
A song of the olden time,
When hearts were full of music,
And lips were full of rhyme.

ARCHIBALD LAMPMAN

It is a strange fact that, although seventy-one years have elapsed since the death of Keats, no monument of any sort to his memory has been erected upon English soil. Other poets of less power, but greater worldly fortune, have been crowned with every species of honour, and a corner of Westminster Abbey packed with the memorials of their genius. Yet the fame of this poet, almost the brightest of all, has been curiously neglected. We learn, therefore, with satisfaction that a very beautiful bust of Keats, by Miss Anne Whitney, an American, is about to be placed in the parish church at Hampstead, London, where Keats lived and wrote many of his best pieces. The expense of this memorial is being borne by a number of American literary people, who have thus undertaken a duty which should have been performed long ago by the poet's countrymen.

ARCHIBALD LAMPMAN

The madness of Monsieur de Maupassant is as singular as one might expect from the character of his genius. For some time after the power to compose left him he was haunted by the pathetic sense that he had lost his ideas, and presently he imagined that he saw them floating about in the air in the shape of variously-coloured butterflies, one colour representing one sort of feeling or passion, and another another. Then he fell to work picking these butterflies out of the air with his fingers, and carefully setting them down and arranging them in imaginary patterns on sheets of paper, thus, as he supposed, fashioning works of fiction in a new and symbolical way. But we are told that recently even this curious mode of imaginative activity has been slowly deserting the unfortunate novelist, and he is falling into that condition of stupor and total vacancy of mind which is ominous of the end.

ARCHIBALD LAMPMAN

The doctrine – not a new one, indeed, but a very old one – revived by certain contemporary philosophers, that genius is simply one form of madness, is a very comforting one for those who do not possess it. The men of genius, if there are any existing in our day, might well turn upon these wiseacres and maintain the exactly opposite view – that men of the world are the real madmen, and people of genius the only sane. I think they could adopt this position with all the best of the argument in their favour.

ARCHIBALD LAMPMAN

Prince Bismarck seems to be bent upon supplying the world with another proof that a man may be brilliant, astute, creative, and forceful to any degree without being great. Even the vastness of his immorality in matters of statecraft, which could not have escaped the search of the future historian, would, perhaps, be condoned by a people still flooded with the light of a victorious epoch and prone in any case to take the epic view of its master minds. But what fame might still have left him, despite his want of fine principle, the violence and vindictiveness of his temper have destroyed. His recent declaration in regard to the famous Ems despatch, which could only have been made for the purpose of humiliating his enemies and inflicting the subtlest and most poisonous sort of revenge upon the authors of his downfall, has filled all Europe and the world with wonder at the man who could thus coolly crush with his own hands half his claim to the admiration and respect of mankind.

28 January 1893

DUNCAN CAMPBELL SCOTT

Nothing can be of greater importance as a factor in the education of our youth than a good Canadian history for the use of the schools, in their education as future citizens particularly, as the mass which will before many years commence to form public opinion. Any movement which may result in the possession of such a book must receive the interested attention of anyone who has the welfare of Canada at heart, and any plan which has that in view should be fostered by all those who are in positions where their influence tells for or against such a project. The future of Canada will to a great extent, in so far at least as the national spirit is concerned, be determined by the school children of the next thirty years. If they are taught that they have reason to admire and love the country in which they live, for the great deeds that have been done in it and for the heroic sufferings of those who laid the foundations of its peace and prosperity, they will be fired to maintain the national integrity at any cost. If they can be made aware that this land of ours has had a development from small and arduous beginnings and that men and women great enough to have overcome difficulties and dangers are buried in their midst, we may hope for the upspringing of a genuine national pride. I cannot think of any task more difficult or any more worthy of all the labour and care that a writer could expend upon it than this 'History of Canada,' and if a man comes forward who can give us what we need we will be in truth a fortunate people. Judged by results, anything we could do for him would be too small for his deserts. Nothing could be more dreary than Canadian history as I remember it taught – a mass of cold facts, unanimated by any spirit of historic insight, administered to the pupil as a matter of necessity, like those household remedies which are held to be good for the children whether they like them or not. Now nothing can be more interesting than Canadian history, which has its roots, if I may so express it, on two continents, and which has all the romance of adventure and all the heroism of pioneer effort. To attempt to teach the early history of Canada without showing how all its life flowed either from the old world or New England, and how its development was retarded or advanced by the intrigues and cabals of the old empires, is worse than folly, it is lost time. So our historian must have such a grip of European history that he can refer back to its old world cause the effect which transpired under our skies. And his history must be a record of the

Canadian people and have a constant reference to their social condition, their aspirations and how these were gradually transformed, and the deep waters through which they passed. It should not presuppose any historical knowledge whatsoever on the part of the reader, and each event or actor should be explained or characterized as if they had never before been heard of. For instance, when we come to Lord Durham's mission to Canada, we must learn what manner of man he was, what his antecedents were, why he was chosen for his mission, and what became of him after it was over. In a word, our history should be based in sympathy, a sympathy which should extend to every province of the Dominion, and which should give as true a picture of the special characteristics of maritime province life as that of Ontario, Quebec, and British Columbia. It may be argued that this would make too long a history, but do we want a short history? I think not. It might rather be too long than too short. We want a book in which the scholar can read, and not a mere skeleton of parched and confused facts where he may become utterly confounded. We want a book full of spirit and colour and liveliness, one that will tell us not only the date of the battle of Lundy's Lane, but of the condition of the people who lived in the province at that time; a book that will tell us of Laura Secord and Dollard, and of the thousand picturesque characters which have played upon our stage. I would not attempt to conceal the difficulty of writing such a book, but we should not be satisfied unless something of the kind is forthcoming. Would it not be better to wait until such a book was written than to accept the lesser of a number of evils and choose some production which might be only a little better than what we have at present? In the meantime any power making for the development of a Canadian sentiment must largely reside in the hands of the teachers of our schools. Unaided they can foster it, but they should have that most desirable of all assistants – a Canadian history.

4 February 1893

WILFRED CAMPBELL

The young writers of today who are determined to be true to themselves and have a greater ambition than to be merely the creatures of our current literary combines, cannot but feel keenly the bitter truths spoken by Mr W. Blackburn Harte in his 'In a Corner at Dodsley's' in the February number of *The New England Magazine.* If ever a man were hampered on all sides it is the sincere literary man of today who is determined to write his own work and be original. Mr Harte has evidently discovered the inner workings of things, as most of us have. But it is getting pretty bad when he has to say, speaking of the profession of letters: 'A man can only become honored in the community by being dishonest, for men love not qualities but the appurtenances of power.' And yet this is too true. There are men today who get into literary prominence as a politician gets into power. They affect a sort of mock modesty, but furnish themselves with an army of sycophants and parasites, who occupy all sorts of contemptible positions in the slime of current book-making and journalism, who are glad of the doubtful honour of being associated with a name a little above them in the climbing scale. A private letter of carefully veiled flattery, written as these men make it an art to write, binds this class of creature to them forever. One would think that writers who had certain gifts would not stoop to such contemptible methods of procedure, but the fact remains that there is too much of such 'machine worth' in so-called literary circles today. I have been approached at different times by these rings, who through one of their members propose an attitude of 'defence' or of 'offence' against some imaginary enemy of their affected ideas, or against some person like myself, who persistently refuses to enter into a fraternal system of back-scratching among themselves and back-biting of outsiders who refuse to accept their disgusting overtures. Sad to say, this condition of things runs like a dry rot all through our system of literary toil and ambition. It lurks in corners of some of our best critical journals, it haunts the doors of great city editors, worms its way into great publishing houses, until even Homer does not stand on his own merit, but must enter as an abashed second to the patronage of his modern literary ring-master, who has deigned to reintroduce him. Shakespeare is inaccessible because of the mighty wall of rubbish concerning his worth that surrounds him. It is Shakespeare no more on the stage or off it, but it is somebody else's Shakespeare or his opinion of Shakespeare that confronts the startled reader. It is not the original Wordsworth that the Wordsworthians worship, but Arnold's Wordsworth. They don't even allow the poor old poet to give his own idea of himself or his work, but say he was too much of a simpleton to see his own greatness. It is the same with the Shelleyites. They follow some miserable critic, who ought to have been hanged ere he dared to misinterpret genius in the face of its own words. No wonder, then, in an age when even the great ancients are snuffed out by their patrons, that original work of today has no chance. Mr Harte has hit the truth when he says: 'The abolition of thought is one of the effects of the complete commercialization of literature in these days.' This is the secret of the whole matter. The growth of large publishing houses as commercial ventures has turned literature into a trade. A certain class of clever-mediocre men have usurped the place of the old literary men, and genius is being gradually driven out. Even poetry is regarded as a business. Sonnets are all the go, until I wonder why some ingenious American does not invent a systematic rhymster after the manner of the rapid calculators. They could have a Keats or Shelleyian attachment for variety. The remarkable fact that the respectable part of America's literary men were constantly apologizing for poor old Whitman is evidence of what I have said. They would have done the same for Longfellow or Emerson had they lived today. They were out of keeping with this spruce, matter-of-fact age, when America's laureate keeps himself like a military diner-out. Even Lowell, who tried to adapt himself to the times, used to carry about manuscripts in his pockets; and Whittier, long before his death, was relegated to the past as far as literature was concerned. Everything is style and appearance in letters as well as in everyday life; the chief idea is to be successful, and to be successful one must be popular. The great magazines and the great publishing houses are the stairways by which one must climb to the literary heavens, and to do so the aspirant must conform to their ideal, which is a purely commercial one. It is only mediocrity that will bow to the yoke and condescend to study the 'wants' of even a widely read magazine or the 'catechism' of a popular publishing house. 'Thus,' Mr Harte says, 'we have produced the interesting spectacle of our contemporary literary world. The publishers offer the public the crystals of sugar loaves, but they refuse to give currency to diamonds. Genius is more one-idead, and it cannot surrender its individuality even in the interests of conventional morality.' Mr Harte adds:

> But it is absurd for the publishers to be so desperately anxious to pass all their authors through a moulding machine, that turns them out like children's pop-guns, which will all make exactly the same

> report upon discharge. Of course, the indiscriminating do not weary of these small noises, but once you give boys or men the chance to handle genuine pistols and artillery, pop-guns lose their hold upon their imaginations. The popular writers and the popular critics have always prevented the popularization of the great authors; for pop-guns lose their significance the moment great field pieces are brought on the scene.

The reader cannot help but admire this vigorous writer, not only for his wide and deep knowledge of contemporary literary affairs, but also for his remarkable daring, as when he says:

> The fact is, the position of the publishers is an impertinence. They should rightly be middlemen, authors' agents, who put forth and distribute literature without any power of interference in its character. Only fools buy books for the imprints of publishers. Thinkers buy books to add thinkers to their circles – not publishers. We buy books, and even magazines, to learn the authors' opinions, and to get their opinions expressed in their own fashion. It is very good of the publishers, no doubt, to attempt to exclude from circulation any opinions which from their point of view we may not agree with. But it is precisely the people we differ from that we desire to meet.

Mr Harte is rapidly making for himself a continental reputation as an able and strong writer of an aggressive character, and his truthful unveiling of humbug is making its influence felt in more than one quarter. What is to be particularly noted in his style is its rugged and direct simplicity, where language is powerfully used for the conveyance of thoughts that burn for utterance, in contradistinction to the too abundant affectation of style and lack of sincerity that infest so much of our current criticism.

DUNCAN CAMPBELL SCOTT

The publication of the fourth volume of the correspondence of Gustave Flaubert brings that writer to the notice of the world once again. The personality of Flaubert is to a great extent hidden from the readers of his novels; his artistic sense, morbid in the search after the essential form which ideas should take, would not allow him to live in his books, which remain models of art and of his artistic aims. Founder, as he was, of the modern realistic school in France, he surpasses his followers in the eagerness with which he sought perfection in expression. This passion, which consumed his whole mind and which came to be almost a madness, a madness of discontent at the stubbornness of the vehicle by which he was compelled to express his thought, distinguishes him from every other writer of his time. It arose from a supreme development of the artistic sense overshadowing and dwarfing his capacity for his art, so that he demanded for the expression of his thought some form as absolute and as inevitable as the thought itself, and would not be satisfied with less. Nothing could be a more unfortunate possession for the literary artist who at the same time has the creative desire strongly developed; he is between the Scylla of production and the Charybdis of expression. His happier brother who has the sense of form and the capacity for production evenly balanced will know more of the joys which spring from the creative effort. The musician Mozart will be forever the example to all workers in any art whatsoever of the perfect balance of form and context. All art, as Walter Pater points out, is constantly striving towards the condition of music, and perhaps Flaubert was born with a musician's idea of form and was constantly searching for the absolute fusion of form and context which is found in no other art. This implies that he might have been challenging the impossible. But it is better to do that than to deny the existence of any power in form and to battle for the native might of ideas in themselves. And so Flaubert becomes an admirable figure, although we may be willing to trace his nervous, irritable, almost desperate desire after perfection to his morbid bodily condition, and he takes his place as a type of the artist who will not be distracted by the intractableness of his material, but who works at his God-given task without despair. As he describes himself – 'sick, irritated, the prey a thousand times a day of cruel pain, I continue my labour like a true working-man, who with sleeves turned up, in the sweat of his brow, beats away at his anvil, never troubling himself whether it rains or blows, for hail or thunder.'

ARCHIBALD LAMPMAN

A writer in *The Canada Presbyterian* draws attention to the lack of humour in most of our public speakers, and it is true; a great deal of our public speaking is unutterably long-winded, unutterably tiresome, unutterably uninteresting. Our orators have plenty of ability of a sort – the ability of the hard-headed and successful man of business, with an interminable flow of language; but what they lack is imagination.

There is certainly no inherent wane of intellectual flexibility or vivacity in the Canadian people, for I believe that this country, as soon as every impediment is removed from its free development, will produce the ablest people in every way upon the continent; but there is a general mental and spiritual depression which necessarily results from the maintenance of an inferior colonial position. Beyond a certain point – that point, viz., when the national spirit begins to show itself, as it is now distinctly doing with us – it is impossible for a people to remain in the attitude of colonists without intellectual deterioration – especially deterioration in all those activities of the mind which call into play the imagination and the finer emotions dependent upon the imagination. As long as the status quo is maintained we must be prepared for an unusual degree of dullness in an unnecessarily large proportion of our public speakers. It is a noticeable fact in this connection that the most brilliant, amiable, and vivacious of all our orators, the Honourable Mr Laurier, is an advocate of independence.

ARCHIBALD LAMPMAN

I have often been tempted to sing the praises of Ottawa – this city from which I write – not as a commercial city or as the seat of government, but as a site, as a most picturesque and wholesome foundation for the dwelling of men. It is a city which need not excite in the least degree the jealousy of its greater sisters of the Dominion, for as a centre of traffic it can never rival either Toronto or Montreal. But it has certain advantages – I should say subtle advantages – which are not enjoyed in the same measure by either of those cities. I venture to say that Ottawa will become in the course of ages the Florence of Canada, if not of America, and the plain of the Ottawa its Val d'Arno. Old Vasari said that there was a certain 'air' in Florence which possessed a magical potency in exciting intellectual and imaginative energy. The great Florentine artists found that they could only produce their best at Florence. In other cities – even in Rome – they experienced a decline of power, which they could only attribute to the inferior quality of the atmosphere. I have noticed the same thing in Ottawa. Perched upon its crown of rock, a certain atmosphere flows about its walls, borne upon the breath of the prevailing northwest wind, an intellectual elixir, an oxygenic essence thrown off by immeasurable tracts of pine-clad mountain and crystal lake. In this air the mind becomes conscious of a vital energy and buoyant swiftness of movement rarely experienced in a like degree elsewhere.

Another advantage which Ottawa enjoys is that of uncommon and romantic beauty of situation. Viewed at a distance of two or three miles, from any point of the compass, bossed with its central mass of towers, its lower and less presentable quarters buried behind rock or wood, it is one of the loveliest cities in the world. It is so placed that it can never be anything but beautiful, and as the years go on, bringing with them the spread of a finer architecture and a richer culture of the surrounding country, its beauty will be vastly greater than it is even now. It will become an ideal city for the artist.

11 February 1893

DUNCAN CAMPBELL SCOTT

My Dear Francesca: If like Epimenides you could sleep for fifty-seven years you would find the world changed, but would you find it much better? There would be a chance of your being taken for a goddess, which chance is not so remote even now, I fancy, and you might be worshipped; for, despite the croaking of our philosophers, I know that it will take more than a term of fifty-seven years to persuade the race that it is folly to venerate what it thinks divine. By such a sleep you could escape the irritations of the present, and you might escape those of the future if you were protected by your divinity; but the troubles of life would still exist for your devotees, although they might find them lightened by your worship. For them much the same struggle would be going forward, the weaker would be ground against the wall and the idealists would suffer. The friend for whom you utter such a heart-felt complaint would find himself overwhelmed in the same way, and unless I very much mistake he would also find another spirit as sweet as your own to mourn over him. But are you sure that he has real cause for complaint in the inattention with which the world seems to receive his work, or rather has he not become for the moment confused by what is really only a cloud of dust upon the highway raised by the careless trampling of the hasty throng? Of necessity the world must have something to talk about, and quite carelessly it selects not the best or most worthy, but just the subjects that come uppermost with the turn of the wheel. If your friend knew how most of the literary fame which he envies had been made he would redden to have coveted it. So if his name is left out altogether from the lists of poets which are so commonly ludicrous, and if he is not called the Shelley of Canada, he may perhaps begin to think that there is something in him after all. Perhaps the true test of poetic greatness in our time would be complete neglect, if not contempt. For the great poet always belongs more to the next age than to his own, and instead of the plaudits of the multitude he must listen with fortitude to the approbation of his own spirit. He will be understood by the few, and some of these who believe in him the most fervidly he will draw into immortality with him, and they will be remembered because they gave him comfort when he needed it. About this desire for notoriety Whitman has a sane remark, 'If no one is aware I sit content, and if each and all be aware I sit content.' I quote from memory and may not have all the words in place, but that is the substance of it, and a most excellent utterance it is; one with which any artist who truly values his art will agree. But let your friend be sure that he has done well, and if he has the right spirit in him no one is a better judge of that than himself.

WILFRED CAMPBELL

From the publishing house of William Briggs, Toronto, comes a little book of verse bound in delicate, pale blue covers, and bearing the title, *This Canada of Ours and Other Poems*, by J.D. Edgar, MP. Though Mr Edgar's verse is not unknown in Canada – his 'The Canadian Song Sparrow' and 'The White Stone Canoe' being already well known to readers of verse, the former being incorporated in *Songs of the Great Dominion* – yet it is an agreeable surprise to lovers of Canadian letters that a leading politician, amid the hard toil and stress of public life, should still find time to cultivate those more sensitive and more refined moods that are necessary to the production of verse.

It might be hard to classify these few poems among the many productions of our past and present literary development. The author of 'The White Stone Canoe' and 'The Canadian Song Sparrow' has made literature a pastime or recreation from the sterner toils and cares of everyday life. Such as it is, it shows scholarly refinement and some literary power, with a good deal of the patriotic spirit which this country so sadly needs. 'This Canada of Ours' and 'Arouse, Ye Brave Canadians' have evidently been written from the heart, and there is terse strength and an awakening power in

Let every man who swings an axe,
Or follows at the plough,
Abandon farm and homestead,
And grasp a rifle now.

'The Canadian Song Sparrow' is a genuine nature lyric, and the production of one who has a loving eye for our everyday nature, and makes one wish that the writer had done more work in this direction:

Where the farmer ploughs his furrow,
Sowing seed with hope of harvest,
In the orchard white with blossom,
In the early fields of clover,
Comes the little brown-clad singer,
Flitting in and out of bushes,
Hiding well behind the fences,
Piping forth his song of sadness.

Such lines, by their genuine, simple, and truthful beauty, bespeak for themselves a place in our permanent Canadian literature. 'The White Stone Canoe' is finely written and can scarcely be called an imitation of 'Hiawatha,' but the use of the Longfellian style of stanza and the manner was, to say the least, unfortunate, and takes from the poem even that charm that Mr Edgar has added to it. Even 'Hiawatha' has suffered from the extreme facility of the verse in which it is written, a kind of verse that does not generally adapt itself to any depth of thought or feeling, and is certainly unfitted for the best kind of nature description. It is a kind of wordy chant, that flows from the mind as fast as it enters. Mr Edgar's poem, however, shows a fine, pure choice of language, and a certain vigour of style that makes it more than readable, and leads one to believe that had he taken a less hackneyed form of verse he might have produced an original poem of power worthy of the subject.

There are some good translations in the book, but the other good thing, to my mind, is 'Nunc est Bibendum,' which suggests a poetical power, even in a translation, not common in our literature:

The daughter of a hundred kings,
She spurned the Roman chains,
And sought to spill the fiery blood
That swelled her ruby veins.

In her ears the chariots rumbled,
In her ears the shouting rang,
Then she bared her snowy bosom
To the serpent's poisoned fang.

This is not verse to be sneered at, or tolerated merely because it is Canadian. True lovers of verse read for enjoyment and inspiration, and in this little book both will be found, if to a limited extent. Mr Edgar has done wisely in publishing. And in this simple and unaffected volume he has materially added in a scholarly manner to that rapidly growing store of patriotism and love of nature with which our literature is becoming endowed.

ARCHIBALD LAMPMAN

The letters of Heinrich Heine to his mother and sister from a very early period to the time of his death have been published in Germany in a book called *The Family Life of Heinrich.* The collection is made and edited by Heine's sister's son, Baron Ludwig von Emden, 'in order that the character of the poet might be estimated with more exactness.' A translation by Charles de Kay is to be published shortly by the Cassell Publishing Co. This book is said to represent Heine in a much more amiable light than anything which has hitherto appeared in regard to him. His affectionate attachment to his mother, and that little sister Lotta whom he declared to be 'all music, all proportion and harmony,' and the patient tenderness of his relations to his wife, who sometimes tried his temper a little with her extravagant ways, give us a pleasant impression of the poet which we are grateful and delighted to have. Many of these letters were written in the last years of his life, and we are told that the wit and gaiety which they display would be remarkable under any circumstances, but are infinitely more so when we consider what Heine's health was at that time. There is something very magnificent about the attitude of Heine, who, in the midst of horrible sufferings, in the course of a lingering and torturous death, had the stoic power to play upon all things with that titanic lightning flash of his wit.

ARCHIBALD LAMPMAN

It seems to me that Canadian painters have a great and comparatively unbroken field before them, if they will only take advantage of it, in the colour effects of our midwinter landscape. On some of these splendid February mornings it cannot but occur to one that there is some wonderful painting to be done, which has perhaps not yet been even attempted. In the winter dawn, with every gradation of red and gold and blue; even in the early forenoon, when the towers of our northern capital stand westward, pale luminous, touched with rose, against a pale, greenish-blue sky, when every roof fronting the sun is a sheet of dazzling cream, and every roof not sunlit and every shadow a patch of the clearest crystalline violet; in the coming of the winter night, with its gorgeous changes of colour, subtle and indescribable, what an infinite variety of choice there is for the hand of the painter, and how simple in many cases, yet always how perfect, the beauty with which he would have to deal. No doubt there would be extreme difficulties in the way of painting landscape from nature in a temperature of twenty degrees below zero, but the artists will probably devise some means of making it possible. I can imagine nothing more beautiful in nature than some of our winter scenes, and if they could be imaginatively reproduced by the brush I can conceive of nothing more beautiful upon canvas.

18 February 1893

DUNCAN CAMPBELL SCOTT

If there be any one quality more than another in Miss Harriet Monroe's verse which distinguishes it from that of the American poets of her own sex it is the spirit of intense longing for liberty, liberty of life and art, as well as government. This spirit pervades the whole of the drama which occupies a large portion of her new book of poems, and throughout the lyrics and sonnets which follow it quickens and breathes. There will always be one or two poems in the works of every writer which will seem to epitomize the character and aim of his genius, and the sonnet 'With a Copy of Shelley,' seems to contain that desire for liberty, for advancement, for truth, expressed in a characteristic manner, with something of the intensity and rapture of the poet, in whose volume it was written, which may be taken as the main tendency of Miss Monroe's work. I can recall the utterance of only one woman which is infused with the same spirit of ideal liberty; in this quality the work of

Mrs W.E. Hamilton King is akin to that of Harriet Monroe. But the former writer, who is so little known, has greater picturesqueness, a finer eye for the richness of landscape. In common they have the fault of diffuseness, which is noticed in Mrs King's 'The Disciples,' and Miss Monroe's *Valeria*, and in this as well as in many other points they both resemble Mrs Browning. If Miss Monroe had been possessed of that constructive ability which goes to the making of a drama her *Valeria* would have been a splendid success. That adjective might be applied to it with perfect truth as it stands, for it contains some rare energetic and imaginative writing, and is splendid as well from these qualities as from the spirit which animates it. But if the drama is a trifle too gigantic for Miss Monroe's constructive power, in the sonnet she has found a form for which she seems to have an intuition, and in which she expresses herself with a natural force and freedom. The sonnet is a form which will never grow old, and which will be revivified so often as a poet with something to say uses it, and no matter how many bad sonnets may be written the ideal form remains. When a poet has such a perfect feeling for the completeness and perfection of this form as has Miss Monroe it would almost be worth while to cultivate it alone until the outcome became something more perfect, sweeter, with a richer and more limpid harmony than anything which our day has seen. When over-production is plainly the demon with which our modern writers are possessed it would be an achievement to cast him out and give only the best moments of one's life to the perfecting of some sincere work. And already Miss Monroe has produced several sonnets that are perfect. I wish I could quote them entire instead of giving only their titles: 'To a Beautiful Lady,' 'On Reading a Modern Romance,' 'Time's Perversity,' 'To W.S.M.' The perfection of at least two of Miss Monroe's lyrics, 'Unfulfilled' and 'A Hymn,' outstrips the genuine quality of their companions and leaves them unique in the collection. Altogether, Miss Monroe's book, which is published by McClurg & Co. of Chicago, announces that she is capable of perfect things, which is a sufficient distinction in these days when form seems to be the slave of mediocrity and not the handmaid of genius.

ARCHIBALD LAMPMAN

The practice of snowshoeing is one which every man should cultivate, wherever the conditions are favourable to it. It is an easy, exhilarating, and very thorough way of getting exercise. The free, swinging stride, which the use of snowshoes necessitates, has the effect of awakening the blood in all parts of the body to a full and natural activity. To anyone who is at all accustomed to it, the motion seems to be an exceedingly easy and unwearying one; and it is an undoubted fact that if the snow is in a satisfactory condition a man can go much farther with snowshoes, and much more swiftly without weariness, than he can walking in the usual way upon the travelled road.

But the supreme charm of this delightful exercise lies in the fact that, as in the case of imagination as compared with logic, or the poet compared with the scientific philosopher, the snowshoer is freed from all rules of any absolute system of procedure. Whereas the ordinary wayfarer must follow slowly and ploddingly the worn paths and beaten highways, he sets all guidance at defiance, and marches at the bidding of any whim over fields, over marshes, down valleys, wherever he will. He crosses or follows the level breadth of rivers, finding in them the smoothest and freest floorway for his feet. He strides into the depth of forests, where, but for his shoes, he would be buried to his waist in snow. He climbs upon the tree tops and looks abroad over the world; in imagination the monarch of all he surveys. His tracks are everywhere but along the common road; that, like the artist-Bohemian, he sedulously avoids.

ARCHIBALD LAMPMAN

A Canadian writer whose work is continually gaining in strength of imagination and fulness of tone is the Reverend Frederick George Scott. We are reminded of him by a very vigorous and interesting poem called 'In Via Mortis,' in *The Week* for February 10th. The imagery of this poem, the picturing of the dead and their hidden land, and the emotions stirred within the poet's soul by the voices and shadows of the after world are given to us in the large and vague forms suggestive of all indigenous northern poetry. The workmanship of the stanzas is of a high order, and marks a continued advance upon the quality, already in some cases fine, of such previous work of this writer as we have seen. As a piece of writing it would be hard to improve upon the following stanza:

I know you not, great forms of giant kings.
  Who held dominion in your iron hands,
Who toyed with battles and all valorous things,

Counting yourselves as gods when on the sands
Ye piled the earth's rock fragments in an heap,
To mark and guard the grandeur of your sleep,
And quaffed the cup which death, our mother, brings.

25 February 1893

WILFRED CAMPBELL

It is quite interesting to notice the different attitudes with regard to such poets as Wordsworth and Tennyson assumed by the general public and the cultured poetical critics. And it is strange to note how much the former have been imposed on by the latter. The general public regards a poet to the extent that he thrills and pleases. The poetical critics have a different standard of judgment. The general public cares little or nothing about the evolution of nature or morals, or spiritual intuition. It accepts poetry for its great human qualities, its grasp of or sympathy with the general pathos of human life. And here I must say that to a great extent I agree with the general public. With all due regard to those who would lay so much stress on the inner consciousness, it is not by straining the inner ear for the voice of the Nameless that life is made great, but by clothing the realities of existence with that grandeur and divinity that belong to it.

It was his mastery of the humanities that made Shakespeare the greatest poet of modern times. Wordsworth says:

For I have learned
To look on nature, not as in the hour
Of thoughtless youth; but hearing oftentimes
The still, sad music of humanity.

It is a pity that Wordsworth did not 'look on humanity' more than he did. He had too little affinity to the common toiling souls; he lived apart and brooded too much. Wordsworth was too self-centred to be a great human poet. The great human poet must feel within the common love and the common joy, and be ever aware of the pulse of humanity as human. He must not write of men as beggars and gentlemen, but as men. Now the cultured critic is not at all an appreciator, he rarely discovers a new poet, but is, on the other hand, such a blind worshipper of the poetical god he adores that his first aim is to find in new work some affinity to his idol. He judges verse by what he calls the 'quality' in it, which means nothing more than a certain vague finish. His eye and ear are all wrapped up in style, and he is keen to discover any sin of omission or commission in this regard. He is always talking about the file, and did he have his way would attenuate all modern poetry to a thin flute note of twilight melancholy. The truth is that this idea is perfectly fitted for the guidance of minor poetry, which, devoid of great imagination and creative gift, can afford to spend the time in tuning its gentle and mellow reeds to the required softness that is pleasing to the sensitive ear of the modern critic, who is himself generally a minor poet. But the larger and more sublime landscapes – the rugged skies, the woes and battles of earth – are not for it.

The general public are not yet tired of life, even if the critics are, and they still are interested in the storm and stress, the hopes and despairs, of human life. The true worth of the poet, or rather the joy of the poet, is to dwell on and depict the divinity that is everywhere existent in our common humanity. As he does this, so does he succeed in or fail in being great.

DUNCAN CAMPBELL SCOTT

In the 'Imaginary Conversation' between Bishop Burnett and Humphrey Hardcastle, Lauder makes the bishop say that Mr George Nelly (who is intended for Lord Byron), after certain rather daring performances, began to lose ground rapidly, when on a sudden he cried out at the Haymarket, 'There is no God!' It was then surmised more generally and more gravely that there was something in him, and he stood upon his legs almost to the last. It is a fact that it is only necessary for a writer to be heterodox or even a trifle blasphemous, and to maintain at the same time a show of profundity, to arouse a degree of curiosity which many a writer of real value to the world could never claim as his own. The explanation is not far to seek, for there is nothing about which the mass of humanity is so interested as its religious opinions, and if a writer, either from conviction or with an eye to the 'market,' will early aim a blow at these convictions, provided he will aim it so as to reach the popular intelligence, he may be sure of a monetary success. Robert Elsmere is an example of success so won, and Mr Robert

Buchanan has earned for himself a similar success by his 'Wandering Jew,' which is called by some of the orthodox 'blasphemous' and by others 'a valuable and instructive poem.' The Reverend Hugh Price Hughes says that 'it will do endless good to ponder and remember the attack upon historic and ecclesiastical Christianity which this poem utters. I say that nothing better could be done than that Robert Buchanan should rub these facts into our ecclesiastical skins.' I am sure we will all wish that Mr Hughes had revised that last sentence, no matter how valuable Mr Buchanan's poems may be as an ecclesiastical embrocation.

ARCHIBALD LAMPMAN

I have been reading another of Mr Bradford Torrey's charming and helpful books, *The Footpath Way*, published by Messrs Houghton, Mifflin & Co., Boston. Almost everybody has read some of the writings of Thoreau and John Burroughs. Mr Torrey, although not yet as well known as either of these writers, is, I think, a finer and more suggestive thinker than Burroughs, and a more pleasing, if a less brilliant one, than Thoreau. I can scarcely promise anyone who is a reader, and at the same time a true lover of nature, a greater delight than an excursion through this simple, thoughtful, humorous book, whether the author conduct him to the top of some bird-haunted mountain of Massachusetts, lead him a chase after killdeer plover about the beach at Nahant, loiter with him among the healthy hollows of Cape Cod, or interest him in the family operations and moral qualities of the ruby-throated hummingbird.

Mr Torrey is not only a most minute and patient observer, after the persistent modern manner, of the habits of plants and birds, but also a literary artist, who possesses you with his simplicity, sweetness, and charm, a poet-philosopher, swift to perceive and reveal the parable in every commonest operation of nature, and a humorist of that tenderly reflective sort whose jesting – if that is not too rude a word for anything so delicate – leaves the mind in a gentle and genial sunshine. I think that a writer of this kind does mankind more good than all the weighty system-builders and nine-tenths of the professed poets. He introduces the minds of his readers to inexhaustible sources of innocent and pleasurable activities, puts them upon the watch for innumerable delightful suggestions, and prepares them for a world of tender and humanizing influences.

I quote below a passage from Mr Torrey's essay 'In Praise of the Weymouth Pine' as a specimen of the sort of work he does. I would, however, have my reader read the whole of this article, which is the last in the book. It is a true poem in prose, nobly thoughtful and excellently expressed. It is the best thing that has ever been said about the white pine, a beautiful and inspiring tree, which is to the woody growths of forest and plain what those rarer spirits are to human kind, who write the characters of priest and poet.

> But the pine forest, dark, spacious, slumberous, musical! Here is something better than beauty, dearer than pleasure. When we enter this cathedral, unless we enter it unworthily, we speak not of such things. Every tree may be imperfect, with half its branches dead for want of room or want of sun, but until the devotee turns critic – an easy step, alas! for half-hearted worshippers – we are conscious of no lack. Magnificence can do without prettiness, and a touch of solemnity is better than any amusement.
>
> Where shall we hear better preaching, more searching comment upon life and death, than in this same cathedral? Verily, the pine is a priest of the true religion. It speaks never of itself, never its own words. Silent it stands till the spirit breathes upon it. Then all its innumerable leaves awake and speak as they are moved. Then 'he that hath ears to hear let him hear.' Wonderful is human speech – the work of generations upon generations, each striving to express itself, its feelings, its thoughts, its needs, its sufferings, its joys, its inexpressible desires. Wonderful is human speech for its complexity, its delicacy, its power. But the pine tree, under the visitations of the heavenly influence, utters things incommunicable; it whispers to us of things we have never said and never can say, things that lie deeper than words, deeper than thought. Blessed are our ears if we hear, for the message is not to be understood by every comer, nor, indeed, by any, except at happy moments. In this temple all hearing is given by inspiration, for which reason the pine tree's language is inarticulate, as Jesus spake in parables.

4 March 1893

WILFRED CAMPBELL

The editor of *The Canadian Magazine* has given us in his first number a sample of a periodical which ought to be a credit to the whole country. It is quiet and dignified in tone and appearance, and evidently intends to lay more stress on good letterpress matter than on a gaudy exterior and over-illustration of a poor and superficial type. To say that the magazine is perfect would be ridiculous; we cannot expect a magazine got up in Canada to be equal in appearance and artistic finish to three or four high-class American magazines. But what we do want, and what Mr Mowat is aiming to give us, is a periodical representing as far as is possible what is best in Canadian development and refinement. And I think, as far as a first number can be judged, that he has succeeded. There are four or five short and well-written articles in this first number that are up to the tone of the best English or American reviews. In 'The Manitoba School Law,' by Mr McCarthy, and 'The Anti-National Features of the National Policy,' by Principal Grant, we have two strong and intensely interesting articles as the commencement of a series on subjects now of grave importance to the Canadian people. Mr McCarthy gives from his own standpoint his opinion of the Manitoba school case, and Principal Grant in his desire to have the duty removed from books will have the sympathy of all Canadians who are interested in the intellectual development of their country. Professor Clark contributes a scholarly and thoughtful article on 'Conduct and Manner.' But from a literary point of view, to my mind, the best written and by far the ablest article in the number is 'Some Modernisms of the Stage,' by H.W. Charlesworth, who is, I understand, one of the editors of *The Toronto World.* There is a maturity and charm of style, added to a dignified sincerity, in this article that is irresistible, and one who starts in at the first must read it to the end. It is more than mere splendid criticism of 'things Thespian.' We feel not only that we are listening to a man who knows thoroughly what he is talking about, but we are carried into an atmosphere of one who looks on one of the greatest of the arts from the noblest and most human standpoint. Without going any further, I think that these articles already mentioned make this first number of *The Canadian Magazine* worthy of the hearty support of all sections of the Dominion. Turning to the illustration, the editor is to be congratulated on the beauty of the bit of landscape chosen for his frontispiece. But he is wise in limiting the illustration, as most people would prefer no illustration at all to a profusion of bad pictures.

DUNCAN CAMPBELL SCOTT

In a late number of a well-known American journal there was an article with the caption, 'Does Poetry Pay?' and the question was considered with all seriousness whether poetry can ever be a paying investment from a monetary point of view. The answer to this is so obvious that it is hardly worth the while to have asked the question. But the asking of the question is a fresh instance of how literature is viewed, and how its success is gauged. By a successful book we now mean one which has reached its fourteenth edition, although anyone with a true conception of what merit in literature consists must know that in ten years he could not find a copy of the said 'successful' book in existence in the world, it having gone to the pulp mill to be ground into substance for other 'successful' books, which in turn will meet a like fate. But nowadays there is a sort of sliding scale of perfection in literature or book-making, which corresponds to the different intellectual levels of the reading public. It is but another instance of the old law of supply and demand, and whereas in the last century the educated and aristocratic only had a literature designed specially for their perusal, now each class has its inspired prophets and seers. While this is so there is bound to be some confusion in the terms of praise or blame, and a consequent perversion of the word 'successful,' as applied to literature. It is not in the nature of things that poetry should ever 'pay.' In the first place it is so easy to write verse that is not poetry at all, and this is heralded with as great applause as if it were inspired by the Nine, and so we have a constant stream of mediocre verse which tires and misleads the public. Then the demand for poetry is necessarily limited, and as it never provides for that insatiable thirst for the startling or novel which consumes and parches modern life it must only appeal to those who are clear-hearted enough to be influenced by what is purely spiritual and intellectual. Poetry and the arts generally are mainly useful by being practically of no use at all, and by this quality they may help to save the world. So in the wider sense, in the sense which is alone of importance, poetry, or any other art, does 'pay.' Its return to the artist who practises it is incalculable, and as well to him who enjoys and appreciates it. Art persists by the same force that leads a man to do good, because it is true and beautiful to do so, and from no mercantile reason whatever, and thus art and religion are fed by the same translucent springs.

ARCHIBALD LAMPMAN

The Canadians are like the Scotch of old times. Finding little to do, and small prospect of advancement in their own country, they are obliged, or at least irresistibly tempted, to carry their force and enterprise of character elsewhere. They also had to hew out their fortunes in foreign lands; and they do it. Every now and then some new name of our countrymen becomes prominent in an honourable way in Great Britain or the United States. We have latterly had reason to be proud of the Honourable Edward Blake, whose triumphs in oratory in a land full of the memories and present examples of trained statesmanship and great speaking have exceeded even our expectations. There are other names which are, or are becoming, familiar to us. Grant Allen is a well-known figure in the English literary life of the day. Setting his novels aside – which are, I believe, bad enough – he has done a great deal of interesting and valuable literary work of many sorts. He is most famed, and no doubt properly so, for his sketches and articles descriptive of out-of-door nature. Mr Gilbert Parker has recently become honourably known in London as a novelist and story-teller, and there is a busy future before him, bright with the promise of success and fame. We have all heard of Miss Sara Jeannette Duncan, now Mrs Cotes, and have read more or less of her entertaining and popular work. Her success has been phenomenal, and her name meets the eye in almost every newspaper.

In the United States, Canadians have been universally successful in every line of life. Scattered thickly over the northern states, they have everywhere secured an honourable position, and sometimes risen to prominence. A recent instance is the promotion of Dr Schurman to the presidency of Cornell University – an honour deeply merited, it is said, by his uncommon attainments in philosophy. Dr Schurman is a Nova Scotian, like so many of our able men, who appear to have grown particularly sturdy, in both mind and body, under the breath of the sea. Erastus Wiman, another Canadian in the United States, has managed to appropriate to himself a good deal more than his proper share of the world's wealth, and has made himself conspicuous enough in other ways during the last few years. Mr E.W. Thomson is increasing his reputation in Boston as a writer of short stories. We occasionally see something of his in the New York weeklies, or in 'Two Tales.' Bliss Carman's name floats about in the literary worlds of New York and Boston, now connected with one periodical and now with another, and always carrying with it a suggestion of genius and poetry. W. Blackburn Harte we cannot count as a Canadian, although we feel a special interest in his fortunes owing to his former connection with our journalism, and his brief sojourn in this country.

No doubt a time will come when the more populous life and increasing interests of our own country will keep a larger proportion of its enterprising spirits within its own borders. For the present, however, it is quite natural that those who seek the widest field for their abilities should wander abroad. Let us find no fault with them on that account. They probably bring more honour to their country in the fields which they have chosen than they would if they had remained at home. Here their energies might have withered away in petty and fruitless occupations, and their talent have evaporated in the thin sluggishness of a colonial atmosphere.

11 March 1893

ARCHIBALD LAMPMAN

Canadian scholars and literary folk should thank the Reverend Principal Grant for striking a blow in *The Canadian Magazine* at the absurd and iniquitous duty on books. This tax is so strange and indefensible that its continued existence must be due not to the deliberate intention, but to the thoughtlessness, of the people in power, and if the matter were brought very forcibly to their attention it would doubtless be removed. Why should our rulers take away with one hand what they give with the other? Why should so much care and money be spent upon our educational institutions while a heavy tax is laid upon the intellectual material necessary to render those institutions effective and to mature the fruit of their effectiveness? Putting aside the case of the poorer students in the schools and universities to which Principal Grant calls attention, and turning to that of the mass of the reading public, everyone knows that those people who have just means enough to purchase a few books each year are gradually discouraged in the practice. Finding every purchase so unnecessarily costly they give up altogether the attempt to form libraries of their own. They either rely upon the newspapers for their intellectual pabulum – and none of our journals are fitted to meet the need – or they buy and read those books which are published in cheap editions, a practice which leads to the consumption of much rubbish, and owing to inferior qualities of paper and print to impaired eyesight and a deterioration in the esthetic sense of the reader; or, if they happen to be in the vicinity of lending libraries, they use borrowed books, an unsatisfactory expedient resulting in hasty, superficial, and confused reading.

In this country more than any other we have need of the means of a fine intellectual development for the whole of our people. We look forward, or ought to look forward, to the establishment of a commonwealth freer and nobler than that of any other land. To accomplish this all our people must be educated as no other people are educated, and the best instruments of education must be made as easily obtainable as possible.

Every man in this land, whose occupation calls for the exercise of intelligence, or rather every man, whatever his occupation, should have in his own possession before he has grown old a selected library of 300 or 400 volumes. There are certain books which he should have on his shelf in order that he may read and reread them, until he has mastered them, and so collected together a compact body of important facts and ideas, which may serve as the sure starting points for such logical processes and currents of emotion as must direct his influence upon the social and national affairs about him.

If the 15 per cent duty on books were removed there would be a considerable increase in the book trade, and the booksellers would doubtless be able to sell books somewhat cheaper than if the volume of trade were less. A book which sells in England for 3s 6d could perhaps be sold in this country for 90 cents, instead of $1.25 as now. This difference would be more than sufficient to tempt a great many people into the habit of occasionally purchasing books, and a great and fruitful work would be begun.

Surely there are some members of the House of Commons – themselves readers of books and filled with a fellow-feeling for the great popular hunger for knowledge – who could spare some of the time so liberally given to the subject of binder twine in order that this matter may receive the consideration which is its due.

11 March 1893

WILFRED CAMPBELL

A writer in *The New York Critic* complains of the injustice of a writer in an English review who passes over Mr Aldrich's *Queen of Sheba* with the remark that it was 'no better than the author's other poems.' Now everyone knows that the book referred to is one of the author's most delightful prose tales, and not a poem at all. The conclusion that we arrive at in consequence is that the reviewer in question was either labouring under a temporary insanity or else that he was 'no better than he ought to be,' and, to use a substitute for a plain Anglo-Saxon phrase, he was prevaricating, and grossly deceiving the public by pretending to pass a harsh judgment on the contents of a book which he had never opened. There is, I am sorry to say, too much of this sort of immorality in current criticism today, until a man who possesses any practical knowledge of the making and circulation of books soon grows to hold in utter contempt much of the current jargon on such matters which is found inside columns of sundry newspapers. Much of it is the outgrowth of the childish ambition of would-be littérateurs to foist themselves upon the notice of the public. Many of their readers would be perfectly astounded did they know what windbags many of these men are, and the extent of their ignorance on the very matters that they pretended to treat in such a lordly manner. To watch how these men will review a book that they have merely glanced at, or pass a sweeping charge on one they have never read, is extremely interesting to the professional writer, who can see through all the little pretences and affectations.

DUNCAN CAMPBELL SCOTT

If I were asked to give advice to a young man who desired to form a prose style by a study of the best models of English composition, I would direct him to Shakespeare, Walter Savage Landor, and Matthew Arnold. In them he would find whatever aid example could give him, and I would have to advise him to depend upon his own native taste and his ear for cadence, assisted and confirmed by the study of these great writers. But first of all he must be taught to depend upon what nature has given him as his most valuable asset; whatever he can add to that by study, self-criticism, and research is so much capital gained, but by far the greater portion of his success must be laid to his native gift, his 'ear,' as they say in music. I am writing now of style, of the way of putting a thing so that it will live by reason of the vital force with which it is uttered as well as by the inherent strength or beauty of the idea expressed. And from this point of view I would select Landor as the prototype of all that is excellent in English prose composition; Landor, who, as Mr Lowell has said, 'leaving Shakespeare aside, has furnished us with so many delicate aphorisms of human nature.' He has said himself, 'poetry has always been my amusement, prose my study and business,' and, if for no other reason, it would be safe to consult a writer who had spent as much time over his prose as another man over his poetry. Landor gathers up in himself all the excellencies of the prose writers of the seventeenth and eighteenth centuries, he can be gorgeous in his imagery, ponderous in movement, delicate in fancy, and tender in expression; his instrument has all the stops and registers. But with this variety of power he has his faults, and they are so easily distinguished that they are not dangerous; the want of complete continuity and an imperfect sense of progression mark him as vulnerable in the mass of his work, if the weak spot in his single sentences or paragraphs cannot be found. The study of this great artist should be joined with that of another who put his great gift of expression to more popular uses and who perhaps injured a style which has directness and lucidity as its foundations by controversial writing. Arnold oftentimes irritates his reader by insistence, by repetition, which he finds necessary in order to satisfy himself that he has made his point; but he makes it oftener unconsciously, by a clear, direct sentence that expresses the thought with the bareness sometimes of a conversational statement. In fact, this is a well defined characteristic of Arnold's prose – its conversational tone, like the utterance of some mind stored full of the graces of learning and the love of humanity. And all good prose is never far from this accent of converse as of one mind speaking without effort to another. You find it in Landor, in Sterne, in Thackeray, in Arnold, and, above and before all, in Shakespeare. The latter, supreme in poetry, is also unapproachable in the prose fragments in his plays which are like nothing written either before or since. So our student must go to him for his perfect model of accent as he would come to Landor for his model of form and to Arnold for his model of directness and force.

WILFRED CAMPBELL

For the benefit of those who have not seen it I will quote some stanzas from a very beautiful poem by Mr Edmund Clarence Stedman, the distinguished American poet and critic. The poem is called 'Ariel,' and is the finest I have seen among the Shelley memorial poems. It appeared in *The Atlantic Monthly* for last August and was written by Mr Stedman in May 1892. It contains fifteen stanzas of eight lines each, and is filled with the very spirit of the poet whom it commemorates in these masterly lines:

Thyself the wild west wind, O boy divine,
Thou fair wouldst be – the spirit which in its breath
Woos yet the seaward ilex and the pine
  That wept thy death?
Or art thou still the incarnate child of song,
Who gazed as if astray
From some unchartered stellar way,
With eyes of wonder at our world of grief and wrong.

Not ours to parley with the whispering June,
The genii of the wood,
The shapes that lurk in solitude,
The cloud, the mounting lark, the wan and waning moon . . .

For thee the last time Hellis tipped her hills
With beauty; India breathed her midnight moan,
Her sigh, her ecstasy of passion's thrills,
To thee alone.
Such rapture thine, and the supreme gift
Which can the minstrel raise,
Above the myrtle and the bays,
To watch the sea of pain whereon our galleys drift . . .

In such exquisitely beautiful language the poem is sustained from beginning to end. In the ninth stanza the elfin character of Shelley's power is given in the lines:

The slaves of air and light obeyed afar
Thy summons, Ariel; their elf-horns wound
Strange notes which all uncapturable are
Of broken sound.

Then the poet turns to the present and alludes to the poetical followers of the 'poet's poet':

But now with foolish cry the multitude
Awards the throne,
And claims thy cloudland for its own
With voices all untuned to thy melodious mood.

After this magnificent stanza describing his death and cremation:

Oh, the swift wind, the unrelenting sea!
They loved thee, yet they lured thee unaware
To be their spoil, lest alien skies to thee
Should seem more fair;
They had their will of thee, yet aye forlorn
Mourned the lithe soul's escape,
And gave the strand thy mortal shape
To be resolved in flame whereof its life was born.

The poem ends with an acknowledgement of Shelley's lasting fame:

The century wanes – thy voice thrills as of yore
When first it fell.

I am astonished that such a beautiful poem written by a distinguished American should not have been noticed by the Canadian devotees of Shelley.

18 March 1893

ARCHIBALD LAMPMAN

It has been a common complaint in regard to courses in literature, not only in the universities of our own country, but in those of other lands as well, that they do not produce the effect upon the literary output of the people nor accomplish the great general advancement in culture that is expected of them. Of course, one of the principal reasons for this is that the study of literature is carried on in many universities and higher institutions of learning in a very stilted and academic manner. The courses of instruction, including as they do grammar, philology, the study of the growth of modern languages, the history and analysis of literary masterpieces, conducted mostly in a spirit of barren ingenuity, produce scholars simply – too often pedants – rarely men of original energy or even of true literary taste. This is particularly so in the case of universities like our own, whose endowment is not sufficient to admit of the division of the main branches of study into many branches and the placing of specially qualified men in charge of each. In the English courses one professor has usually to cover the whole ground, and in order that a man may be found properly equipped for the position from an academic point of view a sacrifice has generally to be made on the side of critical and artistic attainment. The study of literature has, therefore, like all the studies which are not what are commonly called practical, a tendency to fall into a sterile and depressing, however thorough, routine.

A remedy for this would be some system, the reverse of university extension, whereby new blood and a regenerating energy might be infused into the university courses from the more vivid literary life without. In all the universities courses of lectures in English literature might be arranged apart from the regular system – lectures which would be delivered by literary men, not connected professionally with the universities, but known to be specially gifted as critics and essayists. Each lecturer might deliver a certain number of lectures at all the universities, passing from one to the other, and there might even be an arrangement among the lecturers whereby their work might all fit together into a complete and symmetrical scheme, the result being the formation and maintenance of a sort of lecturing guild, in touch both with the inner work of the universities and the activities of the literary world. A moderate payment allowed to each lecturer by each university would suffice for the support of such a body of men and enable them to devote the best part of their time to this work.

I imagine that if any such plan as this could be carried out it would give an immense impetus to literature and the higher culture. The students at the universities would benefit by being brought into closer contact with the actual life of literature, and be receiving instruction and stimulus from a great variety of sources; while the men of letters employed as lecturers would be given opportunity to devote their energies to the work for which they are by nature best fitted. I speak of English literature as the study to which a system of this kind would best apply, but the same idea could, of course, be worked out with advantage in some other branches of university work.

18 March 1893

DUNCAN CAMPBELL SCOTT

If it be a fact that humour in literature is on the decline, there is certainly no doubt that this world is as anxious to laugh today as ever it was. I was reminded of this fact the other evening by the conduct of an audience we had assembled to hear a lecture that was not advertised as humorous, but which they succeeded in making so, subjectively, before the somewhat surprised lecturer recovered from the usual vote of thanks. There were some pleasantly facetious remarks at the opening, which may have misled the willing audience, but it let the lecturer know at once that it was willing to meet him half way if he wanted to be funny. And after that every pleasantry was greeted with audible titters, every semblance of a joke was rewarded with laughter. I did not quarrel with this; but the plainest fact in the whole matter was the eager, the desperate desire of the people to laugh. One good fellow who sat before me and who was built for mirth, like Falstaff, had such a merry time of it that no one could have denied that laughter was a gift of the gods. Covering two chairs with his bulk, he commenced to shake early in the evening, and was in a state of eruption, as they say of volcanoes, until the close. He laughed at everything he could find to laugh at, and as he had no friend with him to poke with his elbow, an action that seems to carry some relief for the paroxysm with it, he was transferred from one point to the next in a state of commotion. I was reminded of James Whitcomb Riley's exquisite description of laughter, and only wished that my Falstaffian friend could have had room to 'pelt his thighs and roar again.' The wages of humour have always been high, but the world will open its hands today with infinite generosity to the man who will make it 'hold both its sides.' There is no decadence in the desire to laugh, but the humorous is disappearing from fiction. We have a sort of scientific substitute for it; we have Mr Hardy's rustics and Mr Meredith's whimsical creatures, but we have no humour like George Eliot's or Charles Dickens's or Sterne's, spontaneous and gusty, driving ill tempers before it like clouds before the wind. But the desire is just as strong for laughter, and our modern life has even developed a class that think it quite proper and edifying to laugh in church.

WILFRED CAMPBELL

I do not pretend to be of those who make a special study or worship of the sonnet as a form of verse. I have often thought, as many others have, that this form of verse has been done to the death, especially by our minor poets of the last two decades. We all admit that there are a number of beautiful sonnets, but the few gems are no excuse for the myriads of poems of this sort that have poured forth in England and America during the last twenty years. Anyone who picks up an anthology of sonnets will perceive the truth of my remarks. You may in such a collection note the clever conceits of the corps of mediocre verse writers, young and old. But you soon grow to realize that the greatest poets have paid the least attention to the sonnet as an art. There are some extremely clever sonnet artists in America and England, especially in America, who have wrought hard to perfect this form of verse. But what does it all amount to? After all is said and done, the reader goes to an anthology of these poems, and he finds at the most half a dozen in hundreds that appeal to him and haunt him as true poems, and it is not strange to say that these half dozen are not found among the delicate word artists who have wrought so hard in this direction, but exist among the few sonnets of the greater writers in both countries who made use of this form as a lyric interlude between more ambitious flights of creation.

In England we know that the half dozen or so highest creations in this form are from the pens of Shakespeare, Wordsworth, Keats, Milton, and Tennyson. In America the case is similar, the few good sonnets being the productions of our leading poets. In my estimation the three or four greatest American sonnets have been written by Gilder, Longfellow, and the Canadian Heavysege. Their sonnets which I will quote were not written with the premeditated idea of producing a fine sonnet, but show on their faces suggestions of power that are not found anywhere else in this form to the same extent. Gilder's sonnet, 'On a Life-Mask of Abraham Lincoln,' is, I believe, the greatest by an American, and one of the few great sonnets in the language. It is a little epic:

This bronze doth keep the very form and mould
Of our great martyr's face. Yes, this is he;
That brow all wisdom, all benignity;
That human, humorous mouth; those cheeks that hold
Like some harsh landscape all the summer's gold;
That spirit fit for sorrow, as the sea
For storms to beat on; the lone agony
Those silent, patient lips too well foretold.

Yes, this is he who ruled a world of men
As might some prophet of the elder day –
Brooding above the tempest and the fray
With deep-eyed thought and more than mortal ken.
A power was his beyond the touch of art
Or armed strength: his pure and mighty heart.

Longfellow's 'Nature,' though less powerful, is, next to the one quoted, a great American sonnet; like Gilder's, it shows 'a power beyond the touch of art,' beginning, as it does:

As a fond mother when the day is o'er
Leads by the hand her little child to bed.

The sonnets by Heavysege are 'Annihilation,' 'The Dead,' and 'Night.' In the first occur the lines:

All round about him hanging were decays,
And ever-dropping remnants of the past.

In 'The Dead' are lines of great power and beauty, as:

Even as gigantic shadows on the wall
    The spirit of the daunted child amaze,
So on us thoughts of the departed fall.

He speaks of 'Night' as:

Like a nude Ethiop 'twixt two houris fair,
Thou stand'st between the evening and the morn.

In all of these sonnets we get glimpses of the power of great poets. They are not little frameworks, so polished and overwrought as to make the critic wish the idea framed were a little more prominent and the adornment a little less clever. But they lead us by a few lines into the presence of the holy of holies of genius itself. This, to my mind, is the office of the sonnet, which has been over-much abused in these latter days of artificial writing.

25 March 1893

WILFRED CAMPBELL

The New York Critic has at last formally acknowledged Chicago's importance as a growing literary and art centre. The great commercial capital of the nearer west henceforth ceases to be noted merely for pork packing and corners in corn and is to be honoured by a special department for its literary and art correspondence in the pages of the leading American critical journal. In *The Critic* for the 18th March the Chicago letter takes precedence of the Boston correspondence, a fact which helps to fulfil Mr Howell's prophecy concerning the western development of literary enterprise and culture, but which must be a painful blow to the over-sensitive feelings of the effeminate representatives of the whilom American Athens. Unmindful of the sneers and scorn of many eastern critics, the capital of the interior has for many years back been coming gradually to the front as a centre of culture. Some of her leading dailies are unrivalled outside of New York for editorial power and general tone, and on their staffs are found some of America's brightest and most cultured journalists. It has long been recognized on this continent that the best critical ability is not confined to the back pages of some of the monthlies and to the few critical journals; but that these authorities are themselves often rivalled and surpassed by much of the literary ability attached to many of our ablest dailies and weeklies. Among the foremost papers on the continent are *The Inter Ocean* and *The News.* The editor of the latter journal is, I think, Mr Eugene Field, who is not only one of the ablest editors, but also one of the most versatile and charming of our contemporary American poets. His verses for children are only equalled for pathos and delicacy of touch by those of that other now famous western poet, J. Whitcomb Riley. In Miss Harriet Monroe, the laureate of the World's Fair, Chicago has another poet of whom she may well feel proud. There are passages in her 'Ode' of a quality and power unusual in the work of women writers today on this continent. In *The Dial*, edited by Mr James Morton Paine, also a leading writer and critic of fine sensibilities and keen power, Chicago possesses perhaps the ablest critical journal, after *The Critic*, in America.

These are only a few names among the many able and accomplished journalists and men and women of letters who are helping to build up the more practical and human culture of the west. There is no doubt that the influence of the World's Fair has done much to forge Chicago ahead in culture as well as in material importance. But it is safe to say that the impetus given in this direction, that of higher culture, is one that is liable to be lasting and healthy. As far as we know there seems to be a fine, large spirit of development all through the west, therefore we can safely prophesy that the literary development of the near future will be one worthy of the people and the spirit that is fostering it. *The Critic* says of its new Chicago correspondent: 'Miss Lucy Monroe, who has been enlisted in our service as a regular weekly correspondent, is an accomplished littérateuse who has made a special study of the history and practice of art. As a prose writer she reflects no less credit on the city she lives in than is reflected thereupon by her sister's achievement as a poet.'

ARCHIBALD LAMPMAN

What a superstitious value many people attach to hard work – mere sordid labour. Most people seem to think that the mass of mankind were only made to be 'worked,' to be kept at the mill from dawn till sunset. The idea of recreation, or any period of idleness, is shocking to them. To grant a holiday is almost to overturn the world. Truth to say it is chiefly in our northern lands that this monstrous puritanical notion of the necessity of toil holds sway. The light-hearted Greek wisely consumes one-third of the year in holidays, and the Italian is not long held to his work when the festival bell is ringing. The Florida cracker takes a whole day to drive his load of oranges eight or ten miles to the nearest shipping point, and his life in the fields is not our idea of a life of labour. But even among us the opinion is growing, and growing fast, that it is not absolutely essential that a man should have to work laboriously for six, eight, ten, or even fourteen hours out of the twenty-four. Shrewd persons begin to think that production is being forced on in an extravagant and wasteful way, and that while a certain portion of the people are compelled by an irresistible force to carry out this production, a large other portion sits by in comparative idleness and enjoys the spectacle. The new idea is that every man shall work, that the work done shall be no more than necessary, and that in consequence the whole may be divided up into very moderate apportionments for each citizen. It is safe to say that the time will come, no matter how many generations from now, when every man on earth will be obliged to do his share of the world's work, but no more than his share, and that share will probably keep him employed for three or four hours a day, with frequent holidays. Then we shall develop a race of men indeed, men who shall have time to get knowledge and think – a race of philosophers and kings.

I am led to these extravagant reflections by the extraordinary brilliancy and beauty of the weather. The snowbanks are vanishing away with a swiftness that is rather heard than seen, and all the ruts are running with earth and water. I think that the people should rise up and demand one immediate measure of reform. It should be made law that whenever the weather rises to a certain grade of excellence (the fact might be announced by the running up of a flag on the tower of the meteorological bureau of each city) all places of business should be closed and all workers permitted to go forth. Not only this, indeed, but those who persist in working, if such there should be, should be driven out with scourges of knotted cords. What blessings would result from such a measure! How the race would benefit in beauty, health, lightness of heart, knowledge, and wisdom!

DUNCAN CAMPBELL SCOTT

A letter from Mr George Scharf to the London *Atheneum* of the 11th instant brings to light a most curious circumstance in connection with a series of portraits which he has ascertained were painted by Sir Peter Lely in 1672, but which had become scattered and misnamed in their different locations. They were all portraits of the first Lord Clifford of Cudleigh, high chancellor of England under Charles II. They were exactly alike, representing a young nobleman 'seen only to the waist, wearing a crimson velvet tunic, a broad ermine cape, a square white lace band and long fair hair.' In November 1865, one of the pictures was purchased by the National Portrait Gallery and entered in the catalogues as Henry Jermyn, Earl of St Alban's. Some years afterwards Mr Scharf, in visiting Ham House, discovered another of the portraits, which was named 'Lord Maynard.' Another was one of the nine portraits in the official residence of the first lord of the treasury in Downing Street, but this one was unnamed. At Euston Hall there was another called in the catalogue, 'The Duke of Monmouth.' Mr Scharf discovered in a catalogue of an engraver called Harding the missing name of the portrait in Downing Street, 'Thomas Lord Clifford,' and upon application to Lord Clifford of Cudleigh it was ascertained that in his collection of family portraits was a picture of the first Lord Clifford exactly similar to the one in Downing Street. This established the identity of the portraits, but the scattered works might have been forever called by their fictitious names if it had not been for the discernment of Mr Scharf.

ARCHIBALD LAMPMAN

A writer in *The Nineteenth Century* for March on the classical poems of Tennyson says: 'The lovely passage in the "Passing of Arthur," which describes:

> The island valley of Avilion
> Where falls not rain, or hail, or any snow,
> Nor ever wind blows loudly,

was obviously suggested by the prophecy of Proteus to Menelaus in the fourth book of the *Odyssey*, thus translated by Abraham Moore:

> Thee to the Elysian plains, earth's farthest end,
> Where Rhadamanthus dwells, the gods shall send,
> Where mortals easiest pass the careless hour.
> No lingering winters there, nor snow, nor showers,
> But ocean, ever to refresh mankind,
> Breathes the shrill spirit of the western wind.'

Why should Tennyson's lines be supposed to be 'obviously' suggested by this passage? Is it not an idea which could have arisen quite naturally in Tennyson's own mind? Nay, is it not probable that the fancy, together with the movement of the verse, was indeed perfectly original. The man who really understands poetry can have no patience with this ridiculous genealogy-hunting for everything that a great poet writes. The blind bookworm never realizes that it is possible for two strong imaginations even at a distance of many centuries to happen upon the same image without ever having communicated with one another in the remotest way.

1 April 1893

DUNCAN CAMPBELL SCOTT

There is one question in which the Canadian reading public and the Canadian writer have a common interest, that is the art of book-making in Canada. Every one knows what the Canadian book of a few years ago was like. I have had something to do with the publication of a few Canadian books, and I know with what a pained surprise the suggestion that the old-fashioned Canadian book was not a perfect example of the art was received by one of our publishers. 'What!' he exclaimed, 'do you want anything better than that?' at the same time producing a copy of somebody or other's speeches bound in that peculiar cloth that seems to have broken out into goose pimples. The cover was warped and fitted the pages like a charity coat, and it was labelled like a grocer's cannister, but to the astonished publisher it was a sample of the best he could do, and he was satisfied with it. But there has of late years been great improvement in the art of book-making in Canada, and although there is room yet for advancement I hope it will not be long before we can show as well made a book as our neighbours. Not that I would advise our publishers to take American books as models of what books should be. The Americans, it is true, print attractive books, and occasionally beautiful ones, but they are too fond of what is merely pretty, and often the attractiveness of their work wears off speedily and leaves one with a sense of the commonness of the design. Their ordinary work will not compare with English work of the same class, and the best English work remains unrivalled in the world. There is a style about the issues of a good English house that one can see nowhere else. It is the result of experiment and experience since the fifteenth century; and it is not to be wondered at, when one thinks of the thousands of handicraftsmen who have been trained during these centuries, that English books are the best in the world. So it is rather to England that our publisher should look for his models; it is from them that he should study the nice distinction which governs the way in which the type should be set upon the page, the balance of margins, the manner of lettering, and all of the many nice points which go to make a perfect book. The use of cloths for binding which have smooth surfaces and pleasant tints, and papers which are neither hard nor brittle, will add much to the pleasure of a lover of books. It is a pleasure to own a book whose cover will not scream owing to its roughness as you take it down from your shelves, and whose print will not appear after a half an hour's reading to be so many points of sand pricking the eyes and fatiguing the brain.

ARCHIBALD LAMPMAN

New Zealand appears to be the paradise of the philosopher and the poor man. It is said that there are no rich men there, and no poor, and the labouring man is king. They have a prime minister, Mr Ballance, who is taking every measure possible to confirm and perpetuate this admirable state of things. The sale of public land has been stopped, and it is law that no more of it shall pass from the public ownership forever. It may be let only upon leases of short duration. The premier is endeavouring to carry a land bill under which no man may possess more than 2000 acres of land, under penalty of five years' imprisonment for false declaration. 'With the exception of a short line from Wellington to Palmerston, all the New Zealand railways are in the hands of the government, and it is the premier's ambition to see the state in possession of all mines, factories and steam transit lines.' Of the two houses of parliament, the lower is purely democratic, the members being elected on the 'one man one vote' principle. The upper house is the only place where the plutocrat holds any vestige of power, and Mr Ballance is taking measures to 'fix' that by getting some stout democrats and workingmen added to the present number. On the whole, what with land acts, coal mine acts, factories acts, lands income assessment acts, and many more acts, it seems to be rather difficult in New Zealand for a man to line his pocket with very much 'unearned increment.' I think we had better emigrate. The continent of America is getting too full of practical politicians and railway magnates to be a fit place for any simple and honest man to live in.

WILFRED CAMPBELL

In Miss L. Munroe's Chicago letter to *The New York Critic*, she mentions the following amusing and also pathetic condition of things in connection with the selection by the local committee of pictures for the fair:

> The fact that seven-eighths of the paintings submitted were rejected foretold a large amount of discontent, but, for the most part, the

disappointed have remained discreetly silent. A large proportion of them hailed from small western towns, where the opportunities for study are somewhat restricted, and I am told that great was the merriment of the jury during its three-days' session. Ambitious farmers' daughters sent in their greatest efforts, painted entirely by hand, and teachers of drawing in Podunk contributed landscapes which had been the admiration and despair of their pupils. There is a touch of pathos, which Mary Wilkins alone has probed, in these restricted lives – hopeful, industrious, ambitious, plodding along in ignorance of the fact that their labor is fruitless. If they would only be content with the applause of their neighbors, the average of happiness in the world might be a trifle higher.

From a ranch in Texas comes a picture which showed a genuine honest endeavor on the part of the painter to reproduce something that he knew and loved. A note accompanied it, in which the man wrote that he had never had the opportunity for instruction, but that he had worked conscientiously for many years in the hope of achieving an end worthy of the effort. But this picture fell below the standard, and the plucky Texan will have to endure rejection. Another case which appeals less forcibly to one's sympathy is that of a man who has the true American push. He sent in a picture 20 feet long of the capitol at Washington, painted from a photograph, as the creator of this masterpiece has never seen the building. His modesty also commends him to our admiration, for he valued this amount of paint at the meagre sum of $10,000.

The most amusing phase of the controversy resulting from the selections connects itself with a prominent Chicago painter who was on the jury. No less than six of his works were among those accepted, and no other artist, with the exception of one from Minneapolis, who was also a member of the jury, approaches this number. When asked for an explanation of the discrepancy, the Chicagoan replied that 'the members of the jury were of course exempt' – exempt, with their laurels still to win – exempt and not ashamed to take advantage of the privilege! Naturally it is only the small men of the jury who would lay themselves open to such a suspicion, but it leads one to ask why men of that calibre should be honored with such a responsibility.

Though we may smile at such a picture, the facts of the case go to show that no matter how crude the standards may be in the rural west, there is a strong impetus toward culture of some kind, which will blossom some day into something worthy of the new world. Miss Munro's letter is a clever one, and interesting, though her remarks on Mr Field's new volume of verse savours perhaps too much of the critical for a correspondence column.

Turning to the London (England) letter in the same periodical, we also get another picture. This time it is contemporary literary conditions across the water. The picture is drawn by Mr Arthur Waugh, who appears as London correspondent for the first time, and shows, indeed, if it be a true one, but a sorry outlook for English literature of the near future. He says:

> It is proverbially easy to deal in paradoxes, and proverbially futile. Yet, at the risk of being accused of facile futility, I firmly believe that the winter from which the literary world is just emerging has been at once as stagnant and as suggestive as a student of development could desire. Little has happened, but much is astir. 'A storm is coming, though the woods are still.' The books of the season have been uninspiring enough. No great creative work of fiction has been issued for months; readers who, during the corresponding weeks of 1891-2, were indulged by three vastly engrossing novels, *Tess of the D'Urbervilles*, *The Little Minister* and *David Grieve*, have been forced to content their imaginations with captivities in the Mahdi's camp, or jogging journeys through Connemara in a governess cart – things good enough in their way, but still not literature.
>
> The fact is that the whole field of literary activity has been paralyzed by the death of Tennyson. Authors themselves are probably unconscious of the cause of their want of alacrity; but the cause is there all the same. Literature is left leaderless; there is a sort of restless discomfort in the air; we have not yet settled down after the blow. Memory and attention are still centred on the loss which the world of letters has sustained. Throughout the winter the demand for Tennyson's work has kept printers and booksellers busy; the monthly bulletins of a certain literary journal show that the interest of the reading public has been almost entirely retrospective – everyone has been opening once more the familiar green covers to whose contents the first 'Finis' has been written. For a few weeks after the laureate's death the air was full of suppressed excitement and animation; it seemed as though the prospect of a change in the literary

> kingship were to give a new impetus to poetry. But the moment passed; no new laureate was appointed; a calm followed, but it was the calm of stagnation. Literature seemed at a standstill, and a new home rule bill was far more interesting to the man in the street than the reminiscences of a country squire or a rural dean. I recently saw a letter from one of our leading publishers, complaining that during the week in which Mr Gladstone moved his bill the sale of books declined to one-third of its normal quantity. Small wonder, then, that the book of the season was the confession of a political spy.
>
> And yet, I think, it has been a suggestive season, if a stagnant one. Literary activity must be fed by current events; if the home life is dull and inanimate the inspiration is certain to be sought abroad. And so the past winter has found English literature turning to the continent for aid, and the latest movement is, I think, rather ominously un-English.
>
> 'When shall we hear an English song again?'
>
> says one of our youngest singers, and something may, perhaps, be urged in support of this rather querulous complaint.

Mr Waugh goes on to say that 'the minor poets have been full of movement.' 'But their tone is so imitatively French that they can scarcely be regarded as a phase of English literature at all.'

DUNCAN CAMPBELL SCOTT

Mr Gilbert Parker has had a most gratifying success in the United States with his novel, *The Chief Factor.* Over 30,000 copies were sold in three weeks. His new novel, *Mrs Falchion*, which will shortly be published, will have a similar success, to judge from the interest which is being taken in its issue.

ARCHIBALD LAMPMAN

People are generally a good deal interested in the habits of famous authors as regards the act of composition, and almost every writer has some peculiar trick of method in composing which a biographer has studiously recorded. We are told that Addison, in the old days, wrote as he paced up and down a long room, where there was a decanter of wine at each end, and the decanter may perhaps account for the liquid mellowness and abundant good humour of some of his pleasant passages.

Wordsworth made verses as he walked, and particularly as he paced the length of a secluded path near his house at Rydal. Many of his lines and stanzas must certainly have taken form out of doors, for no indoor atmosphere could have inspired their magical freshness and sunny purity of vision. Tennyson did some work in his rambles, but probably more as he sat with his pipe over the fire. He was sometimes too lazy to write down what he composed, and many things that might well have been preserved slipped from his memory and were forgotten. 'Many thousand fine lines,' he declared to a friend, 'go up the chimney.' Poe, when the verse-making fit was upon him – and it did seize him like a sort of convulsion – roamed about his house biting his nails, muttering half aloud, and fretting like a caged beast. Keats wrote easily, without much exertion, and generally, if it was summer, in the open air, lying upon a grassy bank or sitting under a tree. I do not know whether it is really possible for a man to sit squarely down to a table with a sheet of paper before him and write poetry, but I have never heard of anyone who was in the habit of doing it. The commonest habit with imaginative writers of all kinds is that of pacing backward and forward like Wordsworth or Addison – minus the decanters. The gentle exercise of walking relieves the restlessness of the nerves and enables the imagination to concentrate itself upon its subject.

8 April 1893

WILFRED CAMPBELL

The revival of the national sentiment or feeling is again becoming popular, as evinced by the successful dinner given by the new Canadian Club at Hamilton. Mayor Balcher's remarks were to the point, and will be appreciated by all true Canadians. The time has now come when many of these clubs ought to be organized all over the Dominion, making the national idea paramount in the hearts of the young men, and killing in the bud any attempt to foster on our soil old country feuds of racial, religious, or other origin. I think I may say, as a Canadian, in a Canadian paper, without any disrespect to the classes referred to, that we have altogether too many St George, St Andrew, St Patrick, and St Jean Baptiste societies in this country for the national good. They may be all very well for the men who were born on foreign soil. I can respect the feelings of the man who looks back to the country of his birth with feelings of love. But it should stop there, and I for one firmly believe that the young Canadian, who is necessarily practical, should save all his sentiment for his own country as a whole. This is where he was born, and where his children have been or will be born, and he cannot afford to import foreign feuds, to the detriment of the national future. I have noticed that the men who sneer at any idea of a young Canadian having any national sentiment or feeling will not forget to honour or dishonour the natal day of one of the saints above mentioned. A great deal has been said in abuse or laudation of our respected neighbours across the line, but they have long taught us a lesson to our discredit, which we have failed to profit by, and it is this, that, whatever be their merits or demerits, they are first and last Americans, and intend to remain so, and woe be to any foreign influence, of whatever kind, that dared to place itself before the national sentiment in any section of her people.

ARCHIBALD LAMPMAN

Someone has said that life is one long disease, and this world nothing but a gigantic hospital, and Heine added that the great doctor is death. This is one of those terrible sayings that may be uttered either by the egotist who has pursued life's pleasures to the utmost, and found therein in the end nothing but emptiness and spiritual annihilation, or by the philosopher who has sat all his life long with a raw and sensitive soul in the midst of the concourse of men, and brooded upon the desperate obliquity of human institutions and the hopeless inaptitude of human character, the vileness and instability of the average, and the hideous blackness of the worst. You, too, reader, who are a thinking man, having before you an ideal of the human form and human soul divine, if you should stand at some unfortunate hour in a busy street of one of our thronging cities, and should watch the crowd go by you, the multitude of faces unceasing in their variety, but all marked with the struggle and care of the crooked propensities of life – faces, some of them weary unto death, some worn with bodily sickness, others hardened, withered, or distorted with the countless maladies of the soul, greed, ambition, lust, drunkenness, and many another; and, lastly, some even that will fright you with a nameless suggestion of vileness and loathsome degradation – you, too, will be willing to say in that unfortunate hour that life is one long disease, and this world nothing but a vast hospital, and, moreover, that the great physician is death. But, patience! Even in a time when these things are becoming most apparent to us may we not perceive the dawning of a new hope? Have we not already noted the beginning and spreading of a new conception of the higher life – a conception which has not yet reached the masses of mankind, but we certainly hope may do so eventually, though not in our day? This conception is the child of science, reinforced by the poetry that is inherent in the facts of the universe and all existence. Thus reinforced, the conception is a religious one. It is independent of the ancient creeds, for it does not trust for its effects to any system of post-mortem rewards and punishments. It is different from the old stoic virtue of the philosophers, which at bottom was merely prudence, a utilitarian quality. This modern conception is not a materialistic one, although at first it may seem so; it is, as I have said, poetic and intrinsically religious. It comes to those whom the new knowledge has made acquainted with the vast facts and secrets of life, arming them with a breadth and majesty of vision which withers away from the soul the greeds and lusts and meannesses of the old, narrow, and ignorant humanity. The small ambitions and petty passions of this world seem infinitesimal indeed to him who once enters into the new conception and lives, as it were, in the very presence of eternity. As yet this new spiritual force only acts upon the few, for it is a modern thing, but its growth is sure. Spreading downward, with the steady extension and dissemination of culture, from mass to mass, it may in the end work its way into the mental character and spiritual habit of all mankind. Then, indeed, the world will become less and less a hospital, and the old cankerous maladies gradually decline and disappear.

DUNCAN CAMPBELL SCOTT

That it is impossible for a journal to succeed in advance of the general culture of the society to which it appeals is illustrated anew by the failure of *Arcadia.* In very many if not in all respects that paper was the best which has been issued in Canada. In its general style it was better printed and had less of the provincial air about it than any journal or magazine that has attempted to gain the sympathy of the Canadian public. But it was in advance of the general culture of the mass of our people, and it failed, as every such attempt must fail, in creating an interest in artistic work outside the circles which are already interested in art and matters pertaining to art. These circles are, in our Canadian cities, restricted, and in the towns and country they do not exist at all, so that the failure of such an excellent paper as *Arcadia* was almost a foregone conclusion. I doubt if it would be possible to support in the United States even a journal of similarly high aims, which would depend upon the interest of a cultivated class of readers for its success, unaided by any of the great piano firms. It has not been accomplished yet, and the musical and artistic papers of the States depend largely for their success upon subventions from the manufacturers of musical instruments and of artistic goods. At the same time, it is to be regretted that such a valiant attempt to foster and advance the culture of the country has met with such indifferent treatment, and Mr Gould must have the very warmest thanks of all lovers of art and literature for his attempt. He has already done work of lasting benefit and importance for music in Canada, work that will live after him, and his life is but another example of how much may be done by a single man of high ideals and broad general culture. Music in Montreal would not be what it is if it had not been for Joseph Gould and his disinterested effort. It is, I say, wonderful what a musician of broad views and with an interest in all the arts can accomplish, not only in the sphere of his own but in the cause of art generally. Such a man, Mr J.W.F. Harrison, succeeded in transforming the musical life of Ottawa, and, with his genial interest in everything artistic, he gave an impulse to culture which cannot be exaggerated. It is fortunate for a Canadian city to have its music in the care of a man who is more than a musician; and I daresay that every Canadian city has likewise a man who has been the means of fostering the small beginnings of what will some day be a great and useful impulse in our national life.

15 April 1893

DUNCAN CAMPBELL SCOTT

Raphael Joseffy, the pianist, says: 'Hasty attempt without sufficient preparation is the bane of all American effort in the realm of art.' Again: 'His [the American's] rapidity of apprehension too often gives him a distaste for the slow, patient labor and study absolutely essential to the thorough elaboration of every great thought in art. The slow-thinking, plodding German, and the tenacious, bull-dog Englishman have thus a very great advantage over him in their efforts to achieve the highest art perfection.'

Life in America has bred an unrest that looks for results and expects them without the labour and care that make them valuable. In consequence we have a principle at work in art which has developed the smart and 'taking' to the disadvantage of the higher and nobler qualities. The magazines are great and powerful nurses of this principle; it is recognizable in the illustrations and literary work which they often present, which cannot be classed with any known forms of art or literature. They exist for the magazines and by reason of them, and they follow the demand for the merely pretty and ephemeral upon which many of the periodicals exist.

ARCHIBALD LAMPMAN

Success is in most cases not the result of ability only, but of the mercy of chance – the happy fortune of youth which has guided our feet into the right path. How often do we find men in every walk of life who are universally credited with great gifts, yet who have never really succeeded. The labour of a lifetime has been wasted; they are like one who has been wading in sand. Youth, in the beginning, did not set them at the right task, and they had neither pluck nor the good fortune to recover themselves. The lives of such men are more or less unhappy. Their souls inevitably take on the crookedness and ill health of everything that is forced into a shape for which it is not intended. Well is it for them if life has given them so many of its smaller compensating joys that their unhappiness is never anything more than a gentle, sluggish melancholy. Often they are less fortunate; all the circumstances of life have made them raw, and death finds them raving in savage bitterness. This is the commonest and one of the most pitiable of the tragedies of life – the sickness of the soul that had the ability and the yearning to accomplish much but got astray in the world's confusion and found no outlet for its distinctive power. The deeper, the more brilliant the natural gift, the more terrible the wreck which its disappointment must entail. Very often this life ruin is due to the fact that a special gift has not been recognized by its possessor till too late, or that the merciless needs and constraining circumstances of his environment have forced him to deliberately set it aside. Oftener still, however, it is the result of the awful blindness or shortsighted obstinacy of parents. Long before their children have reached manhood or womanhood they have planned for them their lifelong pursuits, in many cases paying no heed to the indications of natural bent, but allowing themselves to be guided solely by some fanciful preference, or, worse still, a narrow solicitude for what they imagine to be the child's material welfare. If such parents were permitted to see into their children's hearts in after years and mark the evil growths, the maladies, and distortions that have grown up there like the fungi and creeping things in cellars hidden away from the sun and never used for any healthy purpose, they would perceive, as they seldom actually do in life, how tragically wrong they have been. I call to mind a woman whom I once knew, who had an undoubted natural genius for the stage and the opera. She had never married and had grown old before her time, body and spirit eaten away by the flame of the poetic longing which she could not gratify. Her life was like the rose which has never spread into blossom, but remained withered and stunted in the bud because its root was buried in a barren and innutritious soil, denied water and denied the sun.

Parents should watch their children's growing minds for every indication of natural aptitude, and when any natural aptitude is discovered every facility should be offered for its development, not, indeed, to the exclusion of the development of other faculties, but so that it may take the lead and all the other faculties by their acquirements may minister to its strength. People often discourage the development of certain talents in their children because they consider the callings towards which they lead them undignified, not respectable, or dangerous to morality. In this case, too, they make a mistake. There is always a much greater moral danger to be apprehended from a thwarted ambition, a native mental energy curbed and repressed, than from any amount of freedom given to any natural and legitimate desire for action. The yearning for artistic expression in any form is a particularly dangerous one to repress; it will find its proper outlet or it will explode and destroy the vessel that contains it.

WILFRED CAMPBELL

Among recent volumes of Canadian verse one of the most worthy is *Poems, Lyrical and Dramatic*, by Mr J.H. Brown. It is not our intention to criticize the work more than to point out some of its qualities in passing. It is rarely that the reviewer is justified in making sweeping assertions for or against a work. And sad to say this is only too common today in Canada. A reader may be struck with the beauty of a bit of verse by a certain writer, but it should not lead him to bar out all other writers, after the fashion of a critic in *Arcadia*, who, in a late review of a poem by a Canadian poet, said: 'Only one other Canadian poet could produce such a fine bit of work.' Such an assertion shows a rashness unworthy of a critic. How does he know what Canadian poets can do? Probably his knowledge of Canadian poetical literature is limited to his adopted idols. The only fair and legitimate use of a review is to show that the book in question has merits worthy of the attention of the public. The mere disparaging of literature that is so common in contemporary so-called criticism seems to be more the output of bitterness and spleen than anything else. No book of verse ever published in Canada or anywhere else has been devoid of faults. And the duty of the reviewer is not to hunt up the faults which all sensible men know do exist, but to point out that the book has an original keynote of its own, which marks it out from the literature around it. If the book does not show such a keynote then it were best to leave it alone.

In Mr Brown's book I recognize a distinct note that marks his work out from that of others. Though not as intense a lover of nature as some of our poets he has the true poetical sympathy for external nature in her great moods. He appreciates the eternal beauty ever present in the universe. But his muse loves to ponder most of the great drama of mankind, with a special interest in the freedom or liberation of human society. In this he is akin to Shelley, whom he calls:

> A prisoned soul, new-thrilled with life's desire;
> All tears, all smiles, despairs and eager yearning.

Anyone who has read Mr Brown's book in a thoughtful manner, as the true critic should, will observe that he has made a faithful study of many of the great poets, and that he has consciously or unconsciously learned much from them. In his dramatic work we see a knowledge and love of Shakespeare, and in his other work we get an appreciation of Omar, Browning, and Walt Whitman. But Mr Brown is not a mere imitator. He has a soul which is intense in its discernment and its love of the lofty and wise. What he has read he has digested well and has made it his own. I think that among Canadian poets he is distinctly the poet of humanity and its problems as approached from a philosophical standpoint, and in this sense hs is the most thoughtful of all our poets. He is decidedly lacking on the side of creative imagination, or at least he has given us no sign of it in his book. But he has gained on the side of philosophical meditation. At least this is as far as my understanding of his work would teach me. I have no right to say what others might find in his work. I do not think that Mr Brown's book has had that proper consideration that it deserves at the hands of those who take upon them to introduce our authors to the Canadian people. At some future time I will give some examples of his verse in this column.

DUNCAN CAMPBELL SCOTT

In these latter days, when everything in the earth and under it is being subjected to scientific inquiry, it seems strange that the venerable myth of the sea serpent has not before this met its deserts in the shape of a careful sifting of the evidence as to its probable existence and a comparison of the accounts of its various appearances. But some person has at last been found with enthusiasm enough to discuss this abstruse subject. He has even digested the sober descriptions of the serpent written by journalists of the great American republic, and this part of his subject was certainly worthy of some consideration. It is a curious fact (is it not?) that the American sea serpent usually appears off the coast of Maine and then in colossal proportions. You will recollect that Maine is a prohibition state. This fact, however, did not find its way into Mr Oudemans's book, but many other strange and interesting things did. He disposes of the false sea serpents which have been thrust upon a confiding public really interested in the original monster, and he finds that the great republic is responsible for two-thirds of these canards. If his researches had extended to the serpents of inland waters Canada could have swelled the record of lies on this subject; for many of our countrymen have seen strange things from fishing smacks on the lakes. Our author, after weighing all the evidence carefully, comes to the conclusion that the sea serpent 'is a long-tailed pinniped, a member of the carnivorous order which includes the seals and walruses.' It is to be hoped after all his trouble that Mr Oudemans, who is a Dutchman, will be rewarded some day by a sight of the serpent which he has so thoroughly investigated and settled so far as such a mythical creature can be settled. His book is written in English although he is a foreigner, and is published, moreover, by a Dutch house – Brill of Leyden.

22 April 1893

ARCHIBALD LAMPMAN

I do not know whether very many people outside of New England read Emerson's poems, but, if they do not, they ought to. There are few poets who are more bracing reading. In Emerson there is the freedom, the vitality, the fertility, the inexhaustible permutation, the god-like optimism of nature herself. His mind is like the heaven itself – cool and infinite, with its stars – and it is fed from a heart like the ploughed earth, sunny and fecund, and full of perpetual chemic change. Emerson is sometimes charged with being obscure, but, in spite of his tendency to condensation, he is not really often so. His pieces are, indeed, so packed with pictures, suggestions, and luminous thoughts that they must be attentively read or much will escape the grasp of the reader, simply because there are so many things. Emerson should have a special attraction for the impatient reader, or the reader who has not much time to give to his books. His work is so well adapted to piecemeal reading. One can open his books anywhere, and take up the thread of some inspiring current of thought. He was like his own bumblebee, voyaging hither and thither, in 'Syrian peace, immortal leisure,' collecting only the purest honey of reflection, gathering it wherever he found it, and stowing it away in separate cell upon cell, with little regard to form or the symmetry of the whole.

Emerson was in the fullest sense a nature poet. He identified himself with nature. He was not so persistent and hardy a roamer of forest and lake as Thoreau, but his faculty of penetrating into the methods and moods of nature was as fine as his. He had, of course, the prevalent New England austerity, that quality of mind that may be likened to the cool and cloudy freshness of an early spring day, where, through the scattered clouds, golden sunbeams break with an especial gladsomeness and charm. When Emerson does yield himself in a line or two to an impulse of luxury, he is irresistible. Hear how he addresses the bumblebee:

When the south wind, in May days,
With a net of shining haze
Silvers the horizon wall,
And, with softness touching all,

Tints the human countenance
With a color of romance,
And infusing subtle heat
Turns the sod to violets,
Thou in sunny solitudes,
Lover of the underwoods,
The green silence dost displace
With thy mellow, breezy bass.

Emerson's sympathy with nature is not, however, in the main that of the observer, the student, or the artist; it is a sympathy of force, a cosmic sympathy. He is drawn to nature because in the energies of his own soul he is aware of a kinship to the forces of nature, and feels with an elemental joy as if it were a part of himself the eternal movement of life. His voice is like the voice of the pine, whereof he says:

To the open air it sings
Sweet the genesis of things,
Of tendency through endless ages,
Of star dust and star pilgrimages,
Of rounded worlds, of space and time,
Of the old flood's subsiding slime,
Of chemic matter, force and form,
Of poles and powers, cold, wet and warm;
The rushing metamorphosis
Dissolving all that fixture is,
Melts things that be to things that seem
And solid nature to a dream.

DUNCAN CAMPBELL SCOTT

The other day I was attracted by a reproduction of one of the late Paul Peel's paintings, the original of which is to hang in the art gallery at the World's Fair. I am not sure what name the artist had given it, but it might naturally be called 'Before the Bath,' as his other picture on a similar motion is called 'After the Bath.' It represents an interior, with more than half of an ordinary bath seen beyond the edge of a screen; an old nurse is leaning over the edge of the bath coaxing two little children who are holding back mischievously. One is hiding in the angle of the screen, you can fancy her holding her breath; the other is in full view of the nurse, and the figure is drawn with every appreciation of the delight which the youngster has in teasing her old 'nurse.' You do not see her face, but you can tell that she is laughing. Her sister is not yet discovered in the angle of the screen and considers herself safe drawn back out of view. The whole conception is so natural and so charming that it seems to open up a new view of the uses to which the commonest domestic incidents might be put by a master, especially the incidents of child life. There is nothing in the world around which tender and human feelings gather as the everyday life of children, and there is hardly an incident which, properly treated, might not serve to show some touch of character. And what an effect such poetic reproductions have upon the mature spectator! They renew in a profound way the associations of childhood, and mingle them with a regret for the disillusionment which life and a sordid experience have given. They bring a longing for the days when we were owners of something which 'a man who was really a carpenter made'; for the days when our familiar habitations which seem so confined now were palaces, when it was a day's journey to the stream a stone's throw away, and when over the neat pasture fence was the world, unexplored, even unthinkable. My feelings were stirred anew with regret upon looking on Paul Peel's picture; regret that he had not lived to work out to the end that strain of tender and poetic feeling which had commenced to make him famous.

29 April 1893

WILFRED CAMPBELL

Mr A. Stevenson of Arthur, Ontario, has a very able and interesting article on 'The Speech of Children,' in a recent number of *Science*, which ought to be appreciated by all who are interested in the development of the young. Some of the expressions which Mr Stevenson has noticed are common to many children, though there is a wide diversity owing to the capabilities of the child. Some children have very little of what is called 'baby talk,' and seem to emerge (almost at once) from muteness into fairly good English. Others, more often found among boys than girls, appear to develop the linguistic powers more slowly. The tendency to shorten words and drop hard consonants is similar to that of primitive or deteriorated races. In fact it seems that the child in its early development passes through all the stages from the lower to the higher, as represented by the animal as well as the human species. It may jar on some loving mothers to be told that their darlings are merely little human animals, but it is largely true, all the same. Of course there are ages of race-culture heredity behind the child, that separate it from the mere animal. But we have all seen how a dog or a cat can be refined up to modern tastes as to its diet and creature comforts. It is when the child begins to think and wonder that the great void between the beast and the human becomes evident. And there is nothing on earth more beautiful and refreshing than the innocent thought and wonder of a thoughtful little child. If a child is at all thoughtful it seems to get farther than the sagest mind ever got. It is a pity to fill one of these pure individualities with all sorts of unnatural facts. For my part I would prefer to prolong their ideal world, where every field is a universe undiscovered, and every bird or squirrel a fairy or genii. After all, the ideal writer is the one who has the children for an audience. The present writer has such an audience, where he reigns more supreme than Howells or Stevenson in both realism and romance. He has no rivals, though he has the severest of critics, for, the natural child, being an acute philosopher, can see through humbug and nonsense quicker than many an adult mind, for all its love of the wonderful and the unknown, and 'Now, papa, that's silly, that's not a nice story at all; tell us a nice story,' greets the unfortunate author whose imagination has not been up to the usual requirements. If the audience is allowed to choose its own subject the general cry will be 'a cat,' or 'a dog'; the adventures of a cat or a dog being as interesting as those of Sinbad if related rightly. Perhaps a small boy shouts out, 'No, a bear! a bear!' Children like to be frightened just a little, not too much; so the bear story is voted unanimously. The present writer, who some time ago ran out of the whole stock of nursery epics in prose and song, has had since to draw largely on imagination. The epic with the traditional hero, be he feathered, quadruped, or human it matters not, but interesting must be his history, this Ulysses of the primitive folk. Prose is their favourite, as it allows directness, and the mind of the child is all set on the action or incident. Everything is presented as a picture. In poetry the child first catches the rhythm and sound. Tragedy is a favourite. They realize also pathos, and have a strong sense of a humorous situation, even when they cannot tell why.

The present writer seldom falls into verse when catering to this pigmy literary world, as he feels it easier to please the adult mind than compete in a sphere where 'Mother Goose' is both Homer and Shakespeare. I find, however, that my child public enjoys the epic, which really means the adventures of a hero or a set of heroes, and the tragedy. In the former the Homer must not dare to nod for an instant, and in the latter the action must be simple and direct.

ARCHIBALD LAMPMAN

Huyia Yeddo, we are told by *The Chicago Tribune*, came to Chicago from Tokyo, the city of the gentle and the exquisite, to arrange for the Japanese exhibit at the World's Fair. He and his assistants have found the easy and natural manners of this intelligent America too much for them, and they have resolved to go home as soon as possible. 'Too much crowd; no can stay,' said one of these innocent old-world persons to a reporter. It seems as they walked up State Street one evening they were beset by a mob of young hoodlums who pushed them off the sidewalk, punched their faces, assailed them with insulting epithets, and finally left one of them insensible. 'These youths,' said the Japanese narrator, 'were perfect strangers and quite unknown to me,' and he added that they were supposed to be of the gentlemanly class of Chicago. Anyone who has qualified himself to live in imagination in decorous and beautiful Japan will realize the sorrow and amazement of these poor souls, exposed to the tender mercies of such a crowd. Let them take this experience as a warning, and when they return to Japan let them use their best endeavours to stem the tide of Americanization and Anglicization, which will certainly in the end sweep away all that is gentle, all that is lovely, all that is exquisite in their ancient and inimitable habit of life. The Japanese may perhaps be ignorant of some useful things which we know, but the lessons which they have to teach to us are of vastly greater importance.

DUNCAN CAMPBELL SCOTT

One of the most interesting articles in the April number of *The Fortnightly Review* is that by Sir Archibald Geikie, FRS, upon 'Scenery and the Imagination.' The author deals first with the ancient conceptions of the physical phenomena of the world, and shows how the legends of gods and demi-gods arose from an attempt to explain the disturbances which it was plain to be seen had taken place in the face of the earth. He then contrasts with these the new ideas which modern science has brought to the appreciation of natural beauty. He says: 'It will not be hard to show that in dissipating the misconceptions which have grown up around the question of the origin of scenery, science has put in their place a series of views of nature which appeal infinitely more to the imagination than anything which they supplant.' This is certainly true and the writer sets about to prove it. It is almost impossible that a man should be too learned if with his knowledge and acquirements he brings the right spirit towards life. If he has a genial soul and wealth of sympathy every new fact or perception which he makes his own is just so much pleasure added to life. It increases his power of comparison and generalization, and enables him to call upon every fact in nature and life for illustrations or correlations which will throw additional light upon the subject in hand. We can form some idea in reading the works of Darwin what a pleasure in life his must have been, as with profound knowledge he compared, observed, and sifted. Sir A. Geikie quotes these lines from Lowell, which express very beautifully the attitude of a poet towards the new and profounder science:

I grieve not that ripe knowledge takes away
　The charm that nature to my childhood wore,
For, with that insight cometh, day by day,
　A greater bliss than wonder was before;
The real does not clip the poet's wings;
　To win the secret of a weed's plain heart
Reveals some clue to spiritual things,
　And stumbling guess becomes firm-footed art.

It would be as useless to argue that the knowledge of the convulsions and transformations which have made the world what it is cannot add to our appreciation of the beauty of the world as to maintain that a musician gains no pleasure from a knowledge of the structure of the sonata he plays on, the sculptor from a knowledge of the anatomy of the statue which he admires. There is one part of such a pleasure in natural scenery which everyone can enjoy, and that is the perception of its ancientness. I can never look on any portion of the old Laurentian range without an added feeling of wonder. I shall never forget what a sensation of loneliness and awe came over me as from the Isle aux Coudres (itself haunted with the oldest historical associations for

Canadians) I watched the sun go down behind the mountains that gather over Baie St Paul. There was not a cloud in the sky, and as darkness came on the presence of the mountains seemed to grow vaster. They wrapped themselves in darkness and stood aloof, obscure in their ancientness.

6 May 1893

DUNCAN CAMPBELL SCOTT

Sister Ste Colombe

There was one person in Niger who believed that he had seen a vision. It was old Pierre Moreau. He was a fisherman, at least he spent most of his time in fishing, and lived on the edge of a little marsh near the Blanche. He had built his hut from slabs and untrimmed logs, and he lived there utterly alone. He had come to the village when he was already old, and because he had pulled two fish out of the deep pool under the bridge he thought he could not do better than stay for the summer. He ended by staying altogether. He had grown so old that in the winter he lived by charity as he could do no work. No one paid much attention to him, no one thought of his being sick; but one winter he lay in his hovel and would have died if someone had not noticed the untrodden snow piled around his cabin. It was then that he had seen the vision. He was never tired of telling the story, and once some boys who had stolen on him unnoticed heard him repeating it to himself as if he was saying his prayers. He would tell it to anyone who would listen, as he leant against a pier of the bridge with his line dangling in the water, or sat before his door smoking. This is what he would say: 'I'm old now, but when I was young you couldn't hold me, so I ran off and did nothing but tramp round. But I got tired, anyone would get tired, and I brought up here. I never did any harm to anyone, but I never went to church, and that is why the good God sent His angel to save me. One winter I would have died. I could see the snow getting higher and higher on my window, and one night I expected to die. All of a sudden I was walking in one of the places where I had lived, and the bells were ringing. Crowds of people were going to church, and I went to church; but then I saw the sea before me; then it changed and I knew nothing. Soon I thought I was back home, and my father was playing the fiddle and keeping time with his foot. Then everything got dark, and I thought I was going, when the place seemed bright as day, and I looked up and saw one of the angels of the good God bending over me. I thought I was dead at first, but I saw that I was in my own hut and the good angel of God made me better, and I have never been sick since.' This was the story as he at first told it, but he added a clause afterwards which he raised his voice in delivering: 'You say that this one lived on the earth before and that she is still here. I know that she is still here, but she came first to me and she may stay, but she is the good angel of God all the same.' This good angel of God that came in a vision to old Pierre Moreau was Sister Ste Colombe.

'Hush, child!' said Madame LeBlanc to her granddaughter; 'hush! here comes Sister Ste Colombe.' 'What makes her so pale?'

'She sits up all night with the sick.'

'Why do they call her Sister Ste Colombe?'

'I don't know; perhaps it is because she is so quiet.'

'I know; old Pierre Moreau told me; it is because she flew down from heaven like a dove.'

'Well, who knows? God is good.'

'If I got sick would Sister Ste Colombe come to nurse me?'

'If you had no one to take care of you she would.'

'When I grow up I'd like to be like Sister Ste Colombe.'

'Well, not everyone can be good like her; but who knows?'

'But I'm better than Tertulien.'

'Yes, but Tertulien is a very little boy.'

'Well, if he was to grow up naughty, if I was as good as Sister Ste Colombe, I could pray for him.'

'Perhaps it is so with Sister Ste Colombe; who knows?'

The next afternoon the small Tertulien Dorion rushed in to his mother. He had been wandering away from home all the morning, and now came in full of some marvel to soften the fact of his return.

'Come, look here; there's a man in our yard.'

'Mon dieu, the boy has come back! Tertulien, where have you been?'

'And he's lying down,' said Tertulien, ignoring the question.

Sure enough, when his mother went out to see, there was a man in the yard, and he was lying on his back, with his hands over his eyes to keep off the sun. He could not speak when she asked him who he was, and for very pity she had her husband carry him in and lay him on a rough mattress beside the kitchen stove. (to be continued)

WILFRED CAMPBELL

To me it is a great privilege to be able to live in the country. There instead of acres of wood, brick, and stone walls your horizon is limited by woods and fields and skies alone. Instead of monotonous plank sidewalks your foot feels the yielding turf or the cool and cleanly earth. Everywhere the eye wanders or the foot goes some new object of interest or some new beauty comes into view. The skies are always changing, or the woodlands or pastures putting on new variations of form or colour. Though the glory of autumn is my favourite amid the beauties of the round year, yet there is an ever-abiding beauty and mystery in the spring. Everywhere the one note, the one hint, is reviving life. On every bush, field, and tree hope hangs out her banners, and joy fills both morning and night with her exhilarating music. What voyagers you will meet on a bright May morning in the span of a child's walk to the nearest fence. From the quick, vanishing butterfly that is lost while you look in the misty sunlight to the drowsy brown caterpillar curled up on the gravel walk, all life is astir, or at least dreaming about it.

Even on the coldest and wettest of spring days, when the season of bud and blossom would seem to be simulating her sister autumn, she can scarce hide her identity. For she ever carries about her unconscious evidences of her true character. She may muffle in grey, veil herself in misty rains, and coax the north-east wind, who is but a surly lover at best, knowing her true love to be the soft southwest, but somewhere a peeping spire of green or a looped, white, curling bud like cream from under the matted leaves will betray her. Even in Canada, where she acts most scandalously in her flirtations with bluff winter, spring is spring, the season of returning life. People who live in the country rise earlier than their kindred of the cities and towns, chiefly because their cares and duties call them out often before the peep o' dawn. While the city man lies abed and waits to be called about 8 or 9 o'clock the rural dweller needs no monitor, but is up betimes, brushing the dews from the grassy lawn, helping to provide the city man's breakfast. Each seems resigned to this strange partnership. But the balance is met when the city man sits up worrying or carousing into the small hours, while his rural cousin is sleeping the sleep of the weary. As to which is the happiest life depends on temperament. Men as a rule like to be what they are, especially if they smoke and have a good digestion. But there is no doubt as to which is the healthiest and most natural. If all things were fair and equal in this much-deranged world according to the philosophers and theologians the rural life would be an ideal one. It is over-toil and lack of culture that degenerates the husbandman into a clodhopper. Some of the most intelligent men I ever talked to were New England and Canadian farmers, and I know that in all instances they were enjoying, especially in the New Englander's case, the advantages of a heredity developed in close contact with outside nature. I thoroughly believe that this same class of men would deteriorate in a city or town, though they might put on some of that miserable gloss which is falsely called culture. All the fine outward deportment and manners in the world won't change a brute into a kindly, gentle man. This is where the country has the advantage in the long run, given she has the proper material to work on. The city attends to the manners and clothes, the country acts on the heart and intellect. This is the difference between the going to sleep at sunset and at the going out of the electric light, or the waking to the sound of horse cars or to the song of a meadowlark – all the difference in the world. It is the difference between pinchbeck and pure gold, the difference between a cellar plant and one grown out in God's pure air. Let men talk about religions and theologies, but the greatest and best church ever built is walled by nature's horizon and roofed by the great dome of sky, at night or morning, summer or winter, where the liturgies are eternal in runeless books of earth and sky, where the choirs are never desecrate or out of tune, in the endless chancels of wood and meadowcroft, where the preachers are eternal, unconscious influences forever at work. Out in such a temple as this for a man to be irreligious, in the loftiest and holiest sense, is to bespeak him as less than a clod, for even the clod blossoms or girdles itself with green if left to the influences that nature has linked it to.

DUNCAN CAMPBELL SCOTT

We are all interested in the pursuit of the ideal. There is no one of us so prosaic or so matter of fact that he cannot match his neighbour with something to which he aspires, something which is apart from all other things and above them, like the flag on the citadel, which is pulled down last of all by the enemy, if we allow him to get that far. But even after it is pulled down and some false flag floats there for a degenerate ideal, there stands the pole certifying to something which was there and has departed. How often do we see men who have failed in life still flying a rag of bunting to let us know they have not capitulated, that they have the ideal still. I am not given to thinking that the world is becoming materialized, and that we are forgetting our social ideals in the general posture before Mammon, but there are some things which make one pause to think whether we have not forgotten some ideals which it would be well to recall. Is our sense of justice as fine as it used to be, or rather as it should be? Are we as true to the disinterested motive which should not endeavour to sway judgments? Have we not, partly at least, removed the bandage which blindfolded the goddess and allowed her to look at the scales? Does not society seem willing more and more to allow to the most fortunate of its members immunities which it would deny with rudeness to those less powerful? I think we must answer all the questions in the affirmative; and if so, are we not drifting away from the safe ideals which hold that an offence against society is equally dangerous whether committed by a rich man or a poor man? I am not sure that our ideals of sympathy are not undergoing a change for the worse and are not taking on a mawkish and sentimental tone which, if allowed to work out its course, would very speedily let every rascal who was clever enough to work upon the nerves of the public go free. We are asked more and more frequently to concern ourselves with the woes which have been brought upon the families and friends of people who have thought the ordinary rules of conduct too arduous for them and who have endeavoured to announce a new edition of the ten commandments, specially revised and annotated. But we would do well to keep our sympathies clear, not to let them go too far afield, and to allow the burdens to be borne justly by those who have been thoughtlessly loaded with them. With our daily papers we have everybody's trouble on our breakfast table every morning, and yet I do not find that our humanity has improved or that the millennium is anywhere dawning. Then, as 'Ouida' was saying the other day, we have fallen into too great sympathizings and lamentations over Cain, forgetting Abel altogether, forgetting the agony of the man who loses his life in commiseration for the man who deprives him of it. It would be well for us to remember our ideal of justice here, and at the same time recollect that society is responsible to a very great extent, if not to the whole extent, for every crime that is committed. As social ideals spring from individual beliefs, it would be safe to have a re-examination of these last from time to time to find whether they have not become tarnished with neglect, or whether, perchance, they were only pot-metal and not genuine bronze at all, and need to be cast out and broken to pieces under the wheels on the great roadway of life.

WILFRED CAMPBELL

The exhibition number of *Scribner's Magazine* contains the following exquisite bit of verse by T.B. Aldrich. Among the late fugitive poems by America's most artistic poet, I have seen nothing that equals this little poem. The subject is the pathetic suicide in London some time ago of Amy Levy, the poor young Jewish poetess. Amy Levy was a true genius, and had she lived might have ranked high among current women writers:

Broken Music

I know not in what fashion she was made,
  Nor what her voice was, when she used to speak,
Nor if the silken lashes threw a shade
  On wan or rosy cheek.

I picture her with sorrowful, vague eyes,
  Illumined with such strange gleams of inner light
As linger in the drift of London skies
  Ere twilight turns to night.

I know not; I conjecture. 'Twas a girl
  That with her own most gentle, desperate hand
From out God's mystic setting plucked life's pearl –
  'Tis hard to understand.

So precious life is! Even to the old
  The hours are as a miser's coins, and she –
Within her hands lay youth's unminted gold
  And all felicity.

The winged, impetuous spirit, the white flame
  That was her soul once, whither has it flown?
Above her brow grey lichens blot her name
  Upon the carven stone.

13 May 1893

This is her book of verse – wren-like notes,
    Shy, franknesses[,] blind gropings, haunting fears:
At times across the chords abruptly floats
    A mist of passionate tears.

A fragile lyre, too tensely keyed and strung,
    A broken music, weirdly incomplete:
Here a proud mind, self-baffled and self-stung,
    Lies coiled in dark defeat.

13 May 1893

DUNCAN CAMPBELL SCOTT

Sister Ste Colombe (concluded)

The man was sick and wasted, and he looked as if he was not far from death. Tertulien stopped running away, and commenced to take a great interest in him. 'Look, here,' said he, 'have you got a knife? I know you haven't, because I've got it,' pulling it out of his pocket. 'You dropped it when you were coming in. Do you want it back? Look here, did your mother ever whip you for running off?' The man stirred under the coverlet.

'My sister tells on me sometimes; that little girl that comes in here; did your sister ever tell on you?' The man never answered; he brought his arms over his chest and drew them tight. 'I don't mind that,' said Tertulien. 'How yellow you are, and your face is full of holes. Why aren't you fat, like me? You're just like old Pierre Moreau. Perhaps Sister Ste Colombe might come and take care of you if you haven't been bad?'

The child prattled on, the man watching him with dull eyes, but never speaking. He had not opened his lips since he came in. He kept his teeth clenched so that the muscles of his jaws stood out under his skin. He lay propped up by the back of a chair with a pillow for his head. He never seemed to sleep.

Madame Dorion sent for the curé, but the man hardly looked at him. He would not answer the questions; the grip of his hands and jaws only got a trifle tighter. Father Campeau sat down beside him quietly, and stayed for an hour; neither he nor the man spoke. The neighbours came in by twos and threes to look and wonder at him. The women were half frightened at his grimness and his silence. Tertulien brought in all the neighbours' children one by one and exhibited him to them. 'See his eyes,' said Tertulien; 'this is his knife, he gave it to me; you needn't be afraid. He can't speak, but he's a good old man.'

The third day Tertulien was alone with him, when he raised his arms, and waved them about in the air. Then they dropped on the coverlet, his eyelids sank, he seemed to sleep. His breathing was gentle and regular, his eyes were not quite shut, his hands had relaxed by his side. Tertulien crept close up to him; he had never seen him asleep before, and he peered into his face. The man commenced to talk, in his waking doze. He saw Tertulien. 'You are brave, go and see for youself. Anyone will show you the way. The house has a gable and there is a dove-cote in the yard.'

Tertulien was afraid to move; he was fascinated by the gleam through the half-shut lids. 'There is no need for so much noise. Good-bye, we say, and we never come back.' Then the eyes shut and the man slept. He slept soundly, and when Tertulien came back he had slipped away from the chair and pillow. He went and told his mother. She stooped over the sleeper to raise him. His rough shirt was open. She noticed a sort of little hollow on his breast, chaffed and callous, where something must have pressed; slipping out of sight down his side was a leather cord. She raised him gently and smoothed the hair back from his forehead.

That night, when the sun had commenced to go down, the man woke. Tertulien had just come in and was standing close to him. He reached out his hand suddenly and caught the little boy by the arm and drew him close. Then he kissed him once firmly and let him go. Tertulien did not move; he threw his arms about the man's neck and gave him a child's kiss, full on the lips. Then such a strange look stole across the worn face, that Tertulien in fear ran for his mother.

'Mon Dieu,' she said, 'run, run for someone.' Tertulien ran to the door and his mother hurried after him. 'Run, Tertulien; call Sister Ste Colombe.' She was coming up the street with a bowl in her hands. The sunlight had glorified everything about her; even the bowl that she held was gilded. Her wan, transparent face shone beneath her wimple. Sparrows fluttered across her path. Tertulien, half-abashed, could only point to the door where his mother stood, and Sister Ste Colombe hurried on. Madame Dorion went back to prepare the man. She found him with his head resting on the floor, and, with a cry, she knelt behind him, raising his head and letting it rest in the hollow of her hands. Sister Ste Colombe was coming along the passage. She put down her bowl. Tertulien was pulling at her dress. She reached the door. She saw Madame Dorion holding up the half-dead face. She tottered and sank down, holding her hands to her side. One sharp pang seemed to cross her face, her lips moved. Tertulien, who was lingering at the door, heard some half-articulated name, and the look of pain was transfigured to a smile of ineffable peace.

'Jesu, pity us,' cried Madame Dorion, but added softly, as she dropped her eyes to the head in her hands, and caught the light that shone from the face, 'Hush, hush; he has seen heaven.'

Outside the last light lingered in the sky. The vesper bell rang softly from St Joseph's. The disturbed swallows, eddying far into the glow, swept round the steeple, their sharp twitterings seeming to fall from each bell stroke like a shower of sparks from a whirling torch; until the ringing ceased and they slipped one by one into their vibrating nests. Then the drowsy hum of the bell faded off, with the waning light, leaving the night voiceless and dim.

And Sister Ste Colombe?

She was in very truth a good angel of God.

WILFRED CAMPBELL

If it be true that the Democratic and Republican spirit is doomed in the neighbouring republic, owing to the rapid absorption of the middle classes into the very rich or the very poor, it is time that our neighbours began to consider the form of aristocratic government they would prefer. As long as there is the usual accompaniment of pomp and titles, the wealthy classes will care very little. Some may look upon this matter as a joke, but the love of personal grandeur and family distinction has long permeated the classes outside the four hundred. Today conventionality rules the world; there is no ordinary family in the States, Canada, or England that would refuse ennoblement of some sort. The large number of American heiresses who have placed millions in the scale against a worn out or impoverished lordling have proved the theory to be true. It is all very well to say this only represents the wealthy classes, but as the poorer classes depend largely on the wealthy for their living, they are likely to grow more and more subservient for the sake of material gain, and will be quite willing to pander to the aristocratic tendency so long as their personal interests are ensured. If all this tendency be on the increase, and it be necessary for Columbia to choose a sovereign of some sort to act as crowned head, she could not do better than choose the duke of Veragua, the lineal descendant of the one man who ever had any right claim of sovereignty over this continent. This gentleman, who has been closely associated with all the recent celebration display at Chicago and New York, would probably make as good a figurehead ruler as any crowned head of modern days. He is of noble blood and has the great discoverer 400 years behind him as an impressive background to begin on. Then those wealthy families who have already bought up the most of the junk shop duchies and earldoms that Europe has to spare might bargain with the old world governments for the sole right of the patent. This would give the Columbian empire or monarchy as decent a nobility, as far as numbers and wealth go, as could be found anywhere. This idea might also be a new inducement to Canada in the direction of annexation, doing away with the objection many would have to change in the form of government, and might obviate the difficulty where a knighthood or a CMG might stand between a man and his natural inclinations. I throw out this stray idea as a hint. It is not copyrighted, and the only compensation I would ask of our Columbian friends in case they might at some future time adopt my idea is that they kindly forbear from associating my memory with the suggestion.

ARCHIBALD LAMPMAN

Although a great deal of the glory has departed from Boston, it yet remains and will remain a city of much intellectual importance and much individuality of character. There is still in Boston something which suggests the capacity to originate great intellectual and spiritual movements, a thing which can hardly be said, so far as I know, of any other American city. Emerson, Lowell, Hawthorne, Channing, Longfellow, and Whittier are gone, and there are no great personalities to take their place, but they have implanted in the heart of the city that shared their fame the vital seed of their spirit. In its multitude of sweet and serious minds it carries on the tradition of high thought and noble purpose given by them. There is great good, great seriousness, great humanity, in Boston, and it may be that when the social movement, which the increasing strain of the present condition of things is bringing daily nearer, really begins, it will proceed from Boston, just as the anti-slavery movement did forty years ago. In Boston, even in our day, there is very little of the exaggerated luxury and display which disgrace the wealthy classes of New York, and make the observer tremble for the possible outcome of so colossal a madness, so reckless a taunt flung in the faces of the millions whom their huge fortunes leave destitute. I am told that among the richest and oldest circles in Boston there are many people, first and foremost the women, who set aside the vanities of dress and appearance with an almost Spartan scorn, and that these persons may generally be known by the bareness and simplicity of their garb and manner. With these sensitive and delicate-minded people the very possession of inordinate wealth seems a reproach, and the continual spectacle of human suffering, together with the consciousness of the great difficulty of properly relieving it, breeds in them a sort of melancholy and restlessness, which is becoming one of the hopeful signs of our time.

ARCHIBALD LAMPMAN

I have been wandering recently about the streets of Boston. It appeared to me at first that the people whom I saw were thinner and paler than the people of our Canadian cities, a feebler and wearier generation; but when I came in contact with some of them personally I found myself mistaken. I perceived that there was a degree of strength and energy in them which was not at first evident. What I had noted simply amounted to this: that the aspect of the average Boston face was less robust and more keenly intellectual than the average Toronto or Montreal face. There is a greater quietness and seriousness in the look and bearing of the Bostonian than in that of the Canadian, and there is also, it seems to me, a tenderer kindliness and a quicker sympathy. This must necessarily be so, for he is in the midst of a sweeter culture, breathing a wider intellectual air. The Boston young man of the better sort, for instance, has less exuberant gaiety, developing often into horseplay, than the average Canadian young gentleman, but he has more ideas, he feels deeper, he is more companionable for a thinking man. If what I learned is true, he is also a purer and more wholesome specimen of the race. He has in fact reached a higher level of development. The Boston women are brave, clever, independent, and they show it in the grace and freedom, and I had almost said majesty, of their bearing. I admire this bearing, different as it is from the fine manner of the English or older-fashioned Canadian women. The grace and freedom which we perceive in the bearing of English or Canadian women generally has its source in the consciousness of superior culture and position; in American women it springs from the sense of their own independence, of their own fearlessness, of their own self-control. It is democratic and founded, like every beautiful thing, upon a true and indestructible principle. Something of this fine grace and dignity we are beginning to see in our own women of the young generation, and for the same reason they are being democratized, they are entering consciously upon a new and nobler life – a life of unlimited activities.

ARCHIBALD LAMPMAN

To the eye Boston is one of the most interesting of American cities. In the variety of its architecture, the peculiarity of its situation, the narrowness, crookedness, and irregularity of its streets in the more crowded parts, the curious remnants of age to be frequently met with, the beauty of its great Central Park, the common and the adjoining public gardens, it has abundant charm for the stranger, accustomed to the desperate neatness and uniformity of more recent cities. The roar and confusion at mid-day in the narrow and winding thoroughfares of its congested business portion are a joy to the heart of the loafer, and the unintelligible complexity of its street railway system is enough to turn the head of the stranger who has a number of places to go to, and wants to reach them in a hurry. Boston is said by some people to be a very expensive place to live in; by others to be a comparatively cheap one. The dearness or cheapness of it in reality depends on one's knowledge of the city and skill in shopping.

20 May 1893

WILFRED CAMPBELL

The New York World has just celebrated its tenth anniversary by bringing out an issue of one hundred pages. In its review of the last decade it has a bright but rather incomplete article on American literature. It says, very truly: 'During the last ten years American literature has produced no great masterpieces. No commanding genius has arisen, but only a number of new men and women of talent – men and women of delicacy, insight, refinement – but none of whose present importance entitles them to rank with the immortals.' The modern or present-day school of verse writers is cleverly summed up as follows:

> But during the past few years an extraordinary number of new writers of exceptional cleverness have made their appearance. Never before have the American periodicals been kept at such an even level of excellence. The excellence may be ephemeral, it may not appeal to the future, but to us of the present it has a most grateful flavor. It is an excellence that in the larger number of cases concerns itself with manner rather than with matter. It has no great truth to enunciate, no message from the infinite to convey; it deals in airy nothings and it tricks them out with elaborate felicity. This is especially true of our singers. It is astonishing how many of them have attained to an almost flawless perfection of form. It is a pity they have nothing to say, they say it so admirably. The very forms they affect are rarely original. They have developed a strange passion for the resuscitation of old poetical garbs – the ballads, the rondeaus, the villanelles of the past – and in their very imitations they are imitators of imitators; they follow in the wake of Dobson and Andrew Lang. Yet they are excellent imitators.
>
> Fifty years ago such beauty of expression would have been the gift only of the favored few whom the gods had inspired. To-day the most difficult metres seem to lie within the reach of many sensitive and artistic minds. Edith M. Thomas, H.C. Bunner, Helen Gray Cone, Frank Dempster Sherman, Clinton Scollard, Charles L. Hildreth, Maurice F. Egan and a score of others – what are these, after all, but elegant triflers in verse, and yet does not this very elegance rise to the dignity of an art? To some of us the dainty trick cloys, however, and we turn with something like relief to rougher and more potent voices, infused with a stronger individuality – to Eugene Field and Whitcomb Riley in the west, to Dawson in Philadelphia, to Amelie Rives in the south.

Of course this article is limited to those who have arisen in the last decade. But while Aldrich and Bunner are mentioned, no evidence is given of the high place occupied by Gilder in verse, and no mention is made of such important prose writers as Cable, Craddock, Allen, Garland, and Mrs Catherwood. Nor can I understand why Sherman and Scollard are mentioned among the younger poets when such a powerful writer as Cowen of Kentucky is left out. The same slip is made in the absence of Miss Guiney and Miss Reese from the list of women poets. Apart from this I entirely agree with the writer in his conclusions as to the average school of writers. The great lack seems to be in real genius. Of over-perfect style there is abundance. But of great subject matter, dealt with on a large scale, there is none. It may be that the United States has somewhere genius undeveloped. But it has gone out of fashion in a decadent and over-practical age. The magazines and publishing houses have chained literature with meagre golden links to the triumphal car of an advertising and superficial present. Therefore the keen businessman who is literary has usurped the place of the true literary genius who refuses to be chained, and thus sinks into a condition of neglected outlawry.

ARCHIBALD LAMPMAN

Edgar Fawcett as a poet and novelist is distinctively the product of New York, or, indeed, one might say, the modern metropolis in general. His talent – brilliant, ingenious, productive, but artificial, overstrained, and devoid of tenderness – has developed naturally in the eager and heated air of a vast city, in the midst of its awful material splendour, its spiritual ennui, its perpetual and complex exhibition of all the extremities of human passion and vicissitudes of human destiny. His work is that of a man from whose soul every simple and childlike impulse has been eliminated, who is driven by weariness of every ordinary emotion or natural image to find his material in the fantastic and the intensely far-fetched. The imagery in Mr Fawcett's poetry is often of a most tremendous character, but its effect upon the imagination is that of lurid unreality; it astonishes but very soon surfeits the reader. Nevertheless, some of his pieces are so remarkable for fantastic invention and a certain sensuous verbal exquisiteness of presentation that they must be classed with the most interesting products of American genius. As a novelist Mr Fawcett is less able than as a poet. In verse of a half-lyrical, half-pictorial order he is at home. He does not possess the story-telling faculty, nor the faculty of dramatic expression. His novels have the cumbersome movement and air of over-elaboration common to the writings of imaginative men who are unable to absorb themselves in the characters and situations they desire to create. His dialogue is always stilted and unreal, sometimes quite astonishingly so for so able a man. Yet here, too, as in his poetry, the imaginative power, the abundant, if uninspired, invention, the purely intellectual force displayed, are so great that we cannot refrain from according the work a sort of high praise, though it may repel us with its lack of sweetness, its lack of humanity, its lack of tone.

DUNCAN CAMPBELL SCOTT

In the following words, written in 1887, Wilkie Collins gave an interesting account of his manner of writing and constructing his novels:

> My first proceeding is to get my central idea – the pivot on which the story turns. The central idea of *The Woman in White* is the idea of a conspiracy in private life in which circumstances are so handled as to rob a woman of her identity by confounding her with another woman sufficiently like her in personal appearance to answer the wicked purpose. A clever devil must conduct the conspiracy. The sort of wickedness wanted seems to be a man's wickedness. Perhaps a foreign man. Count Fosco faintly shows himself to me before I know his name. I let him walk and begin to think about the two women. They must be both innocent, both interesting. Lady Glyde dawns on me as one of the innocent victims. I try to discover the other – and fail. I try what a walk will do for me – and fail. I devote an evening to a new effort – and fail. Experience tells me to take no more trouble about it, and leave that other woman to come of her own accord. The next morning, before I have been awake in my bed for more than ten minutes, my perverse brains set to work without consulting me. Poor Anne Catherick comes into the room and says, 'Try me.' I have got an idea; I have got three of my characters. What is there now to be done? My next proceeding is to begin building up the story.

Then the novelist describes his invention of the details of his work:

> I have yielded to the worst temptation that besets a novelist – the temptation to begin with a striking incident without counting the cost in the shape of explanations that must and will follow. In the case of *The Woman in White*, I get back, as I vainly believe, to the true starting point of the story. I am now at liberty to set the new

> novel going, having, let me repeat, no more than an outline of the story and characters before me, and leaving the detail in each case to the spur of the moment.

After working for a week the writer finds he has not yet discovered the true beginning, so he has to recast his material.

> One evening I happen to read of a lunatic who has escaped from an asylum – a paragraph of a few lines only in a newspaper. Instantly the idea comes to me of Walter Hartright's midnight meeting with Anne Catherick, escaped from the asylum. *The Woman in White* begins again, and nobody will ever be half as much interested in it now as I am. For the next six months the pen goes on. It is work, hard work, but the harder the better, for this excellent reason, the work is its own exceeding great reward. As an example of the gradual manner in which I reached the development of character I may return for a moment to Fosco. The making him fat was an afterthought; his canaries and his white mice were found next; and the most valuable discovery of all, his admiration of Miss Halcombe, took its rise in a conviction that he would not be true to nature unless there was some weak point somewhere in his character.

ARCHIBALD LAMPMAN

It is a pity that Mr Arnold Haultain gave to the little collection of poems recently issued by him the very unprepossessing title which they bear, *Versiculi.* It was an unnecessary humility, and the word will be apt to prejudice the reader against the pieces before he has opened the cover. Mr Haultain is a well-known scholar and a critical writer, whom his countrymen value, and in these verses we find, as we should expect, fine thought, deep feeling, and the evidences of a pure and sensitive soul. One recognizes, however, that the author is not at ease in the composition of verse. The thought is generally better than the workmanship, and one of the pleasantest of the poems – that entitled 'Adunaton Eidenai' – is considerably injured by a poor last line. Of the seven sonnets at the beginning of the collection. 'To the Plenitune,' is finely said, although a little obscure. 'At Dusk,' is beautiful, and has a fuller accent than any of the others. Mr Haultain's poem 'Beauty,' which we read not long ago in *The Week*, is the most important of these brief poems. Those who read it will remember its genuine fervour, its abundant fancy, and its many pleasant lines.

3 June 1893

WILFRED CAMPBELL

The offering of the poet-laureateship to Mr Ruskin may be an honour to a man who is famous in letters, but is certainly unjust to the undoubtedly large genius of both Swinburne and Morris as poets. Since Wordsworth and Tennyson the post has become dignified, and has risen from the position of court troubadour to represent the nation's recognition of the greatest living poet of his generation; and if there be two, as in the case of Tennyson and Browning, the one most representative of the popular feeling. It is ridiculous to ignore two such men. And the present action is a childish attempt to ignore the gifts of two writers whose work is abiding in our literature.

3 June 1893

DUNCAN CAMPBELL SCOTT

Now that the season for outdoor walks and afternoon-long rambles is with us, and we can go forth as yet unmolested by that forest robber, the mosquito, it is pleasant to spend hours in the sun under the shadow of a maple whose foliage is yet so tender that the rays reach you only half-tempered by the delicate intervention; or, better, to spend a whole day listening to the first birds singing in some pleasant opening in the bushes, where they have all seemed to wander by common consent, to compare notes, perhaps, and mounting higher up the hills, until noonday finds you on the steepest places, with a tranquil distance below you, and only the poplars and the willows showing veils of green. It is no bad plan to take a book with you on such an excursion. You may not read it. Experience has taught me that one rarely does, but nevertheless it is no bad plan to take a book with you. It is only in perfect moods that one can enjoy whole days in the woods; the pleasure is too intense, it is a wearing tension on the nerves that commonly leaves most people with a headache. We take our sylvan pleasures too ecstatically and come to them with too great a preparation, not with the feeling that we are to be tranquillized, but in some sort surprised and overtaken by a shock of enthusiasm. Having got so far away from our natural state we make an expedition to recover it, too often in groups of tens and even twenties, with a commissariat department, as if the goddess was to be surprised by such an organized incursion. If you should chance then to find that it is one of the days you should have spent in the grooves between the stones and mortar you may find it somewhat of a relief to have a book in your pocket; you may feel tempted to draw it forth and read a little here and there and afterwards imagine that you had read a great deal. But which book to take? That is always the vexed question. It must, of course, be light, for it will never do to feel it tugging at your pocket, and it must be small, to slip readily into it. Be wary of what it contains; here an error of judgment may spoil your walk for you. Only a certain sort of a man makes a pleasant walking companion, and so it is with a book. You want something that will not take you by the throat with an idea; something that will not remind you of the world you are trying for a little to leave behind; something that will not try to teach you a lesson; something that will not excite your imagination beyond the borders of the little copse you may at that time be resting in. I know which sort of a book to take. You are a lucky man or woman if you, for yourself, know, but you are happier if it never comes out of your pocket.

ARCHIBALD LAMPMAN

Every householder, I think, has heard of the servant question. He has heard of it until he earnestly desires some revolution which will effectually remove the trouble. The mistresses of households complain that they can no longer secure servants who are servants in the old sense of the word – simple, honest, sympathetic young women, who will devote themselves thoroughly to the duties of their position and be deferential, contented, and industrious. They complain that such girls are no longer to be found. Indeed no, for the class has disappeared, and it is necessary and right that it should be so. Democracy advances rapidly, and not only liberty, but fraternity and equality also are becoming more and more the sine qua non of a contented human race. The position of a servant, who lives in your house, does your coarse work and is in every respect located as a social inferior, was, thirty years ago, natural and accepted. Now it is an anomaly and will very soon be impossible. There is no longer any sound relation or mutual confidence between mistress and servant. The servant is suspicious and self-assertive, for she feels that no one has a right at the present day to treat another openly as a social inferior. The mistress also is unable to exercise her superiority in the old, confident way, for she, too, feels that the order of things is changed and that it is now a practical truth that one person is of the same dignity as another. In many of the farming districts the difficulty has been removed by actual equalization. The farmer's family and their servants, men or women, dwell together in the easiest manner, treating each other exactly as equals. This is no doubt as it should be, but in the cities other solutions will probably be adopted. Some co-operative plan of housekeeping and food-providing will be discovered within the next ten or fifteen years which will enable certain numbers of associated housekeepers to have their work done for them by contract. It will save a great deal of trouble and moral uncomfortableness, and the sooner people resort to it the better. To the simple, modern American mind, not affected by Anglicism or plutocracy, there is nothing more unpleasant – I would almost say more humiliating – than to have a certain human being in one's house whom one cannot under present social arrangements treat as an equal. It is a dishonest position, and every right-minded person feels it to be so.

WILFRED CAMPBELL

To those who are interested in the progress of mankind it is very pleasing to realize the immense strides discovery has made in the last ten or twelve years. Among the sciences no more wonderful advances have been made than in those of astronomy, geology, and archaeology. By the first the sun has been discovered to be an immense electrical centre. In anthropology the existence of man on this earth for millions of years has been proven without a doubt. And in archaeology we have sufficient evidence of wonderful civilizations on this continent long prior to the mound builders. The unquestioned proof of man's long existence in his present state, even by some supposed to be previous to the anthropoid ape, has caused some persons to doubt the applicability of Darwin's theory of evolution to man. But it is not so easy to overthrow the theory of evolution which is now accepted by many orthodox ministers. Men are but now beginning to dimly understand the relation of the Infinite in nature and human history. It has taken men centuries to gradually work back to the first principles and read aright those pages that tell of the marvellous drama of life and its forces that has been enacted on this planet for millions of ages. Leaving aside the Darwinian theory of the gradual development of the human species from the lower creation, the history of the life of man on this planet is one of wonderful interest and significance. If man has inhabited the earth for millions of years, how infinitesimal is the history we have that stretches through the blurring mists of two or three thousand years back to the Romans, Greeks, and the Egyptians. We talk of developing during this time from barbarism to a modern civilization. But if so, how long has this state of things been repeating itself in the history of mankind. We have just discovered that the ancient Hindus were more scientific astronomers than we are today. According to the ancient temple teaching of the Brahmins as to the origin of man, the great Atlantic races existed for over half a million years and became extinct about 14,000 years ago. According to this account, the Egyptians are descendants of some of the more easterly of these people. This would explain the mystery of the wonderful similarity of the ancient pyramids of Central America to those of Egypt. Only there is no doubt that the ruins of Central America are more ancient than those of Egypt. Dr Brinton of Philadelphia, the most learned archaeologist on this continent, is of the opinion that this is the oldest of the existing continents, and that the present Indians have remained in their present state for at least 5000 years, and that they are partly the descendants and partly the destroyers of a former race, commonly known as the mound builders. It has now been proved that men were alive here prior to and during the glacial ages. One of the most interesting facts to Canadians must be that the present mines at Thunder Bay were worked ages ago by some of these extinct peoples, and that what was until a short time ago a wilderness of wood and water was, in ages prior to the existence of Greece and Rome, a civilized community which time, the destroyer, has long since swept away. To me there is a great fascination in all this wonderful process, and its contemplation is but another proof of the greatness of our existence and of the wisdom and incomprehensible greatness and glory of the Infinite.

DUNCAN CAMPBELL SCOTT

Nearly everyone who reads Dante in English reads him through the medium of Cary's translation; but how little is popularly known of the man who has given the English world the standard translation of the great Italian. Other translations he made, of Aristophanes, and others of the ancients, but they have faded out; his original works had scarcely enough vitality to survive in his own time, and are now unknown, but his great achievement still holds the foremost place among all the translations of the *Divina Commedia* which have appeared since his time.

This is a sufficient tribute to his erudition and worth. There may be translations more faithful in part – we constantly hear that there are – and his cannot be called a faultless one, but it will continue for years to supply the English reading public with its version of the great vision. If Rossetti could have translated the *Commedia* with the fidelity with which he rendered the *Vita Nuova*, and with the same wonderful art could have transferred its charm into our mother tongue, he would have made the greatest, the most incomparable success in translation which the world has ever seen. He had the requisite power, as witnessed by the wonderful transference of the Paola and Frencesca incident – a power that withers the feeble efforts of Cary. The last few lines of the passage in Cary read:

> . . . But at one point
> Alone we fell, when of that smile we read,
> The wished smile, so rapturously kissed
> By one so deep in love, than he, who ne'er
> From me shall separate; at once my lips
> All trembling kissed. The book and writer both
> Were love's purveyors. In its leaves that day
> We read no more. While thus one spirit spoke,
> The other wailed so sorely, that, heart-struck,
> I, through compassion fainting, seemed not far
> From death, and, like a corpse, fell to the ground.

The same portion of Rossetti's translation reads:

> But one sole point it was that conquered us,
> For when we read of that great lover, how
> He kissed the smile which he had longed to win;
> Then he, whom nought can sever from me now,
> For ever, kissed my mouth, all quivering.
> A Galahalt was the book, and he that writ;
> Upon that day we read no more therein
> At the tale told; while one soul uttered it
> The other wept: a pang so pitiable
> That I was seized, like death, in swooning-fit,
> And, even as a dead body falls, I fell.

The task that Rossetti set himself was far more difficult than Cary's, who chose the comparatively simple medium of blank verse. Rossetti's translation is in 'terza rima,' the form of the original, and gains greatly in musical force and beauty through this form. It is needless to point out the superiority of the latter passage. If Rossetti had had the activity of mind which only could have rendered the accomplishment of such a stupendous work possible he might have made a translation of merit equal to this fragment. He had the requisite knowledge and insight, and, above everything else, he had an intuitive feeling for the inner sense, the atmosphere of the Italian's work. We can only speculate upon the potential greatness of such an unaccomplished work, and read Cary with a feeling that he is not winged, but only moves slowly and faithfully, giving us a not inadequate rendering of his sublime author.

ARCHIBALD LAMPMAN

One of the most noticeable institutions (it may almost be called an institution) in Boston, or for that matter in the United States, is *The Youth's Companion*, nominally a paper for young people, but in reality a kind of weekly family magazine. It is an illustrated paper, which has been brought to an extraordinary pitch of popularity and prosperity under the astute management of its now aged editor and proprietor, Daniel Ford. Mr Ford seems by some fortunate intuition to have divined the peculiar instinct of American family life and to have found the precise means of ministering to its needs. It is a paper beautifully printed, beautifully ordered, and delicately illustrated. An immense amount of talent and industry is spent upon its production; talent and industry of a peculiar kind, for the conditions imposed upon its contributors as regards the quality and subject matter of their work are most difficult. Party politics, sectarian theology, and many other subjects are tabooed, and many kinds of writing, as for example all sorts of fairy-tales, are inadmissible. A number of other restrictions, as regards motif, length of article, use of words, etc., weigh heavily upon the intending contributor. It has been said that *The Youth's Companion* has reduced commonplace to an art, and that its pages are destitute of any inspiring influence as it is possible to make them. Nevertheless it publishes vast numbers of stories, poems, and articles of use and interest by many of the best writers of the time, and that it is always readable and suits an immense constituency is attested by its enormous subscription list of 560,000. One of the largest, most comfortable, and best appointed buildings in Boston is entirely occupied by its staff and machinery.

ARCHIBALD LAMPMAN

A good deal of regret is felt by literary people and the better class of theatre-goers on the other side of the line at the decease of the Theater of Arts and Letters in New York. It was an attempt – the first of its kind in America – to bring the drama into closer relations with the realities of life, and make it a vehicle for the conveyance of serious thought. High hopes had been built upon it by those who had been looking for some influence to counteract the degenerating tendencies of the ordinary stage, but its management appears to have fallen by some unfortunate accident into rash and incompetent hands. Its last effort was the production of Miss Wilkins's *Giles Corey*, a drama of a somewhat too sombre character to be very popular. The only dramatic organization of this kind now existing in America – if it can be called an organization – is that of the Hernes in Boston. These people, however, are somewhat too eccentric and too deeply immersed in the fad of extreme realism to promise any great and reasonable success.

ARCHIBALD LAMPMAN

I would like to call attention to the following very pretty sonnet in the last *Week* by Mr Colin A. Scott:

Remembered Love

A weariness of sweet familiar words,
    Of oft-repeated, oft-remembered songs,
    Of duties fingered till they seemed as wrongs,
That cut the aching heart like sharpened swords,
A weariness of tender, binding cords,
    That passion of subtle love, in love so winds
    About his very own, the while he blinds
Their eyes to any but his crested lords.
A weariness that Helen lightly sped,
    For with her magic fingers on the keys
    She woke a sudden stir of memories,
That thronging from the place where they had fled
Burst like a storm of blossoms, roughly shed
    From over-arching, long-forgotten trees.

10 June 1893

WILFRED CAMPBELL

The New York Critic has offered a prize to the first person naming correctly the ten best American books, the ten best books in this case being decided by the vote of the whole, those ten books getting the most votes being accepted. *The Critic* has set a hard task if it wants to be true to the best interests of American literature. If it had asked for the best three or four or five books, from a literary standpoint, the question would not be hard to settle. It is generally acknowledged that from the highest critical standard Hawthorne's *Scarlet Letter*, Emerson's *Essays*, and Poe's *Poems* are the most remarkable contributions to continental literature. Then would come as a second three: Whitman's *Leaves of Grass*, Motley's *Dutch Republic*, and Howells's *Modern Instance*. Holmes's *Autocrat* might well come in as a good seventh, but beyond this there would be no certainty. There are a host of fine works all so worthy of our consideration that it would be hard to decide. Washington Irving's *Legends of the Hudson* would have a foremost place. Among the poets we have Lowell, Bryant, Longfellow, Whittier, and Emerson, all with strong individual claims. On the other hand there are Lanier and Miller, who have characteristics not found in the New England school. In history there are Parkman, Prescott, and Bancroft, the value of whose works is in each case individual, not to speak of Nicolay and Hay's splendid *Life of Lincoln*. Irving's *Life of Columbus* also could not be passed over. Two such fine dictionaries as Worcester's and Webster's could not be left unmentioned, nor could the remarkable *Century Dictionary*. We have also *Appleton's Encyclopedia*, the only worthy rival of the *Britannica*. A great work and one of the most monumental of our times is Kennan's *Siberian Exiles*. In archaeology, Dr Brinton of Philadelphia has done invaluable work. In this department valuable dates have been furnished in Donelly's *Atlantis*, a work no longer despised by scholars. In philosophy, Noah Porter and many others have made important contributions, and in the domain of philosophy, history, and mythology, Professor Fiske of Harvard takes a high rank. Among remarkable humorists, Holmes easily comes first, and Artemus Ward and Mark Twain would follow with especially strong qualities of their own. In fiction, beginning with Hawthorne, Howells, Irving, Cooper, James, Harte, Craddock, Eggleston, and Cable, there is a whole host of strong and clever writers whose ranks are always being augmented. In theology, New England especially has produced such writers as Channing, Freeman, Clarke, Mulford, and Allen. Clarke's *Ten Great Religions* is the one great work on comparative theology ever written in America, and Mulford's *Republic of God* is a work of genius. Able writers like Schaff, Munger, and Abbott are but a few among a great regiment of theological writers. A valuable addition to contemporary culture is Mrs Van Rensselaer's *English Cathedrals.* But I must stop, as I have mentioned enough names to show the great variety we have to choose from. It is interesting to know that nearly all of America's great writers are of the past, and only two of the first dozen, Holmes and Howells, are now living.

ARCHIBALD LAMPMAN

The following very beautiful lines by Mr E.W. Thomson of *The Youth's Companion*, and formerly of Toronto, have been going the rounds of the United States press from St Paul to New Orleans. They are entitled 'The Song Sparrow,' but the mood and cadence in them suggest to me that the author is thinking of the vesper sparrow, whose note is somewhat different from that of the song-sparrow, and is much richer and more poetic.

The Song-Sparrow

When ploughmen ridge the steamy brown,
And yearning meadows sprout to green,
And all the spires and towers of town
Blent soft with wavering mists are seen;
When quickening woods in freshening hue
With bursting buds begin to swell,
When airs caress and May is new,
Oh, then my sky bird sings so well!

Because the blood-roots flock in white,
And blossomed branches scent the air,
And mounds with trillium flags are dight,
And dells with violets dim and rare;
Because such velvet leaves unclose,
And new-born rills all chiming ring,

And blue the sun-kissed river flows,
    My timid bird is forced to sing.

A joyful flourish lilted clear –
    Four notes – then fails the frolic song,
And memories of a vanished year
    The wistful cadences prolong:
'A vanished year – O heart too sore –
    I cannot sing,' thus ends the lay;
Long silence, then awakes once more
    His song, ecstatic of the May!

DUNCAN CAMPBELL SCOTT

It has always been a vexed question what problems or conditions of human life are fit and proper subjects for the novelist's art. We have the disputants occupying all conceivable positions, and carrying on their battle with weapons of every fashion. In the meantime the novelists choose the subjects that suit them, and draw their pictures of human nature as they conceive it to be, and the battlefield of the critic is constantly shifting between the old masterpieces and the new. From the point of view of art no subject is immoral, as the reproduction of any diseased or abnormal condition of life should be so managed as to portray at the same time the hideousness of it, the wrongness of it, and in some measure at least to suggest its antidote. The really immoral novel is the one in which these accompanying forces of life and art are obscured or altogether obliterated, in which we have the glamour of vice without a hint that there is anything more than the glamour. It is not frequently given us in life to trace the results of disobedience to the moral laws worked out to a conclusion before our eyes. These results are often so subtle that they would escape the eyes of the keenest observer, and even when we see them we are prone to attribute the change to some other cause. It is just here that the novel (and I may add the drama) steps in with its aid. Through the eyes of one gifted with no ordinary vision, and with logical and casuistic powers which draw conclusions unerringly from certain premises, we see life laid bare and come to understand something of its complexity and depth. Supposing such a man, his choice of subject becomes a matter of indifference. If it deals with the lurid side of life we can trust him that the shadows thrown will be more terribly black. It is childish to restrict to that which is within the scope of polite conversation in society the powers of a genius bent on searching life. The great problem of existence is worked out far beyond the parlours, and the laws of life are wider than the decalogue by which society steers its empty ship. Every one knows that there is misdoing in the world; the record of it is dumped at our doors every morning and evening like nothing so much as a garbage barrel, through which we have to grope for the little bits of metal we expect to find, and he is at bottom a vicious man and a barbarian who would allow his daughter to read the newspapers and to refuse them the great moral novels which deal with the severer aspects of life. But let us consider: There are two classes of persons whom such books hurt. The first is the white-minded, the pure-souled, the class which cannot bear to be shocked, which lives a life of even tranquillity, which winces at the approach of evil and seeks only the pleasant things of life. This is a small class, but it should not be asked to read books which do not appeal to it. There is a literature perfectly adapted to its needs; it may enjoy the *Midsummer Night's Dream* and forget *Lear*. The other is the class which reads for the love of the mere immoral incident. It carries its own doom with it. We may very well let it gloat, unable to read its own sentences of death in the very pages it cannot appreciate.

ARCHIBALD LAMPMAN

An article in a recent number of *The Week*, describing the beautiful and mountainous reserve which has been set aside at Banff, in British Columbia [sic], as a national park, brought again to my mind a subject upon which every lover of nature and every one who has interest and pride in his mother earth must feel deeply, viz., the rapid and certain destruction of the primeval pine forests. In the older provinces these noble and irreplaceable forests are already nearly gone. While there are still adequate specimens of them left, ought not some reservation to be made, in order that our children and we ourselves in the years to come may have an opportunity of knowing what our country looked like in its natural condition. An ancient and close-grown pine forest is a unique and wonderful spectacle, and its effect upon the imagination is something not produced by any other thing in the world. Once gone they are gone for generations; as far as we are concerned, forever. Is it impossible to expect that any light, any gracious impulse, any ray of imaginative ardour, should penetrate the barbarism of our rulers? Could they not be induced, at the small sacrifice of some pitiful gain, to set aside even a moderate space of the unbroken wild in each province as a national or provincial park? As I have remarked before, all nature-loving people feel strongly on this point. I never see a sawlog afloat on one of our rivers without a pang, not because I would not have logs cut, but because I know that the trees must all go, must all perish irrecoverably.

DUNCAN CAMPBELL SCOTT

I was very glad to learn the other day that Mr Thomas McIlwraith was contemplating a new and enlarged edition of his *Birds of Ontario*. The book is a capital one, and is written in just the form which makes the study of ornithology interesting at once to the scientist and the lover of birds. There is no better authority on the birds of Ontario than Mr McIlwraith, who brings to his subject rare knowledge and a true love for the beautiful creatures he writes about.

ARCHIBALD LAMPMAN

To the credit of our age be it said that acts of charity on a vast scale are not uncommon, and are indeed becoming more frequent. One of the causes of this no doubt is the growth of a feeling of moral uneasiness among people of great wealth. The unflinching directness of modern thought has affected them. They feel that their position is not a just or strictly honest one, and they endeavour to make amends to humanity by giving lavishly of the store which they themselves or their fathers put together in an age of a less delicate sympathy.

Certain people in Vienna have been trying for a long time to establish an asylum for sufferers from pulmonary diseases, but in vain. Just recently Baron Nathaniel Rothschild came forward and offered them his chateau at Reicheran in the Styrian Alps, agreeing to make all the alterations necessary to place it in a condition to receive patients. It will probably be ready for its work by next winter. This property is worth $1,250,000, and there is accommodation in the chateau, which is situated in one of the most salubrious places in the world, for 500 beds. The same nobleman has thrown open his park and greenhouses in Vienna to the public, a small entrance fee being charged, which is devoted to certain charities.

17 June 1893

WILFRED CAMPBELL

A serious deficiency in current literature, and especially in the department of verse, is an utter lack of imaginative creative ability. We have an overplus of dainty conceits and delicately spun lyrics, and far too much of verse of a purely descriptive quality. The magazines and weeklies are stocked with such verse, and it is regarded as the characteristic poetry of the age; but of original conceptions of a high order we are almost utterly destitute. Many have been educated into the idea that Tennyson at his best was a poet of rugged power and original conception, but the fact is that his extremely brilliant and successful poetic career was one of marked decadence in this respect, and few realize that the day of great creative genius went out with Byron. What Tennyson did for English verse was to polish and over-refine it. He made verse-reading possible, and even pleasing, to the strict morality of the average middle-class English household. His 'May Queen' took the place of 'The Bride of Abydos,' as the romantic gradually passed into the prosaic that succeeded it. It is true that he gave us some stirring ballads, but his influence on English verse-making did not fall on this side. The successors of Tennyson are a lot of small men, who owe much of their positions as poets to culture and leisure. These men have many masters; some, the nature school, claim Wordsworth as their supreme idol; but, did the simple old man live today, they would flee in horror from his lack of style. Some follow Keats, and claim for him qualities he never assumed or deserved. Keats was a man who had a sort of archaic madness; but a knowledge of, and an interest in, the real life about him is entirely lacking in his work. Keats will always remain an interesting story in English poetry. But woe to the man of today who tries to build a literary fame with such as Keats as a master. Keats is as evanescent and elusive as his own goddesses, and his imagination is purely of the fantastical order, as would be natural in a man who dares to approach any mythology with an utter lack of the religious genius that gets at the real greatness and human interest that alone can make any mythology important. The man who absorbs Keats gets a sort of honied literature without any comb, and his poems become a series of literary confections. But the brawn and muscle are not there. Such poetry may do well to adorn the current magazines, for gentlewomen to gush over, or to be admired by a certain order of critics, but it never will move or inspire the world. There is another class of poets who make an idol of Matthew Arnold. They swallow all of his literary creeds, and assume his austere melancholy towards life. They strain to think and write as he did, forgetting that Arnold's real power lay not in all this, but rather in the fact that the man was there himself in all he said and felt. Arnold had many weaknesses of style and limitations of voice as a poet. His marked greatness is as a thinker, who had deeply imbued himself with his own ideals and conceptions. His very egotism is his strength. When he attempted to follow Keats or Wordsworth he made an utter failure. It is impossible for this reason for any man to be a successful follower of such a poet as Arnold, and yet be original. Others of the current schools follow Rossetti and Swinburne, while some essay Browning, with little more success than the attainment of the merely grotesque. That they are all followers of Tennyson in reality goes without saying, which is evidenced by the utter lack of any real new thought or creative imagination in current work, coupled with the evident straining after what is called style or finish. One man gets the trick of Keats's phrasing, his peculiar way of building a line, the adjectives he used and their unique effect. Another assumes Wordsworth's simplicity of attitude toward nature, another aims at Shelley's elusive and airy buildings out of nothingness, with brilliant success. Another strains to express some subtle thought, or personal contempt of the great horde, after the Matthew Arnold plan. But they all forget that to be great a man must first and last be himself, and that borrowed clothing, no matter how it may suggest the original, sits as badly on the borrower's back as the skin of the lion did on the body of the ass. To be called the American Byron or Wordsworth or Tennyson is not certainly a compliment to a man's originality, however it may redound to his powers of imitation. Such a phrase concerning a man's work should cause the reader to look up the work so compared and note wherein the comparison lies. But such a state of things is the result of making mere words and their picturesque groupings for artistic effect the first and most important end of the would-be poet. Subject matter seems somehow at a discount, and what is called quality has taken its place. Strip most of the so-called poetry of its borrowed plumage and very little would remain; yea, not even the dignity of a backbone of thought or incident. The day of the great writer is when we have the great creative power and lofty imaginative genius. A very good test of our current writers would be to search their volumes for evidence of original mental qualities and large sympathetic grasp of our common humanity. A writer may drench himself with the form of expression used by Shelley or Rossetti, and then apply the peculiar mannerism to the analysis of his personal feelings concerning certain aspects of a spring day or of a sea picture, and yet not have a great mind. That is one reason why there are so many successful writers of verse today. The fact is that a large mass of college graduates with literary susceptibilities have discovered the trick, and can turn out any amount of the kind of gentle, sensitive verses with a sort of delicate finish that the magazines of today seem to require. A remarkable instance is that the greater amount of this kind of work is done by women. Of course I would not rob all of these poets of a certain amount of even poetic genius, but it is another thing to compare the writers of this sort of verse with the minds that conceived such poems as Byron's 'Address to the Ocean,' or 'The Dying Gladiator,' Coleridge's 'Ancient Mariner,' Shelley's 'Cloud,' Keats's odes to a 'Grecian Urn,' and 'To a Nightingale,' Burns's 'Lines to a Mountain Daisy,' and 'Tam O'Shanter,' Hood's 'Bridge of Sighs,' and the many beautiful poems by Tennyson and Browning, such as 'The Lotus Eaters,' 'The Moated Grange,' 'The Revenge,' 'The Funeral of Wellington,' 'Herve Riel,' 'The Ride from Aix to Ghent,' all of which are poems of great original conception, and show powers that culture alone could not produce. On turning our attention to America, we have Poe's 'Raven,' Bryant's 'Thanatopsis,' Whittier's 'Maud Muller,' Longfellow's 'Wreck of the Hesperus,' all exquisitely rare as poetry, and containing in themselves in various degrees those evidences of the rare mind, with its grasp of humanity in a lesser or greater degree, coupled with the true dramatic capability of being able to crystallize the individual conception or thought in such a way that it could never be improved upon. Now, let us apply this test, and search our current literature for work of this order, and we fail to find it. Many critics who are acute enough to see this lack try to explain it away when writing up their especial idols by claiming that this is not the highest order of poetry, or that the times are changing, and that 'pensive meditation' and 'acute observation' amount to genius of a high order. That may 'go down' with the people who have not taken the trouble to weigh current literature in the balance in which I have just weighed it. But the fact remains the same, that the truest poets the language has as yet produced have ever been deeply interested in the issues of life and death, and these are the paramount ideas with which they will ever dwell. Wordsworth, who has been called the greatest nature poet, has never divorced nature from humanity in any of his work, and it is really, after all, man with whom he deals. The true greatness of Wordsworth lies in his simple, grand emotion, his power of entering into the humanities of the scene about him. He is not and never could be a minute scenic artist, such as the descriptive sonnet writers we have today. Emerson had also some of this peculiar quality. In both men it was a great pressing in, as it were, of nature's impressiveness on their souls. Such men never could write of nature in cold blood. They were too deeply impressed with its reverence to do so. In the highest sense they were impressionists.

Many of our writers of today, on the other hand, are cold-blooded, professional writers for the magazines, who, many of them, turn out any amount of stuff, more from ambition than from a desire to produce what is in them.

They set themselves a task, as many of their brother-writers in prose do, with the result we have just described.

DUNCAN CAMPBELL SCOTT

Nature has at best only a limited number of patterns for days in her workshop. This morning, for instance, how many we have like it in June of every year. A grey but luminous dawn; then a gentle, fragrant rain that seems to draw the odour out of everything; then an hour or two of quiet silveriness, with damp pathways, and the moistened earth with a light wind turning out the white sides of the maple leaves. The snowballs hang drooping, filled with rain. The earth seems to be waiting for some more powerful manifestation. At length the rain comes again, softly at first, then slanting more and more and pouring down unreservedly. Then it stops suddenly, and the landscape takes on that perfect distinctness that rain brings, with the same silveriness, but with a stronger wind blowing the leaves away from the branches of the trees and giving you a glimpse of the bluebird, which has been vocal through the whole morning in defiance of the wet.

24 June 1893

ARCHIBALD LAMPMAN

A little collection of poems, called *The Marshlands*, by Mr J.F. Herbin, published at Windsor, NS, by J.J. Anslow, will be found to afford some charming reading. Mr Herbin is a landscape painter in verse, and he has the power to paint landscape admirably – sometimes singularly – well. All his senses as regards the phenomena of outer life appear to be most acutely developed, and this sensitive faculty of perception has at its command a power of metrical expression which I fancy is yet only in growth, and may some day enable him to make poems as complete in form as they are in pictorial truth. As yet he seldom succeeds in producing work without serious weakness or blemish. His successes are in detached passages, phrases, and lines, but some of these are exquisite. I would make an exception to this statement in the case of the sonnets, 'Haying,' 'Scowing,' 'A Homestead,' and perhaps 'The Night Mower.' The last named is the most imaginative of all, but it weakens a little in some of the lines, and is not as cleanly and compactly made as it should be. The other sonnets I have named are entirely satisfying. They are true pictures, clear and fresh from nature, with the very earth savour in them. Anyone who loves the earth and the things that grow and move upon it will love these two or three sonnet-landscapes, and feel them in some sort as he would feel the originals. Let me quote the best of them, 'Haying':

From the soft dyke-road, crooked and waggon-worn,
    Comes the great load of rustling scented hay,
    Slow-drawn with heavy swing and creaky sway
Through the cool freshness of the windless morn.
The oxen, yoked and sturdy, horn to horn,
    Sharing the rest and toil of night and day,
    Bend head and neck to the long hilly way
By many a season's labour marked and torn.
On the broad sea of dyke the gathering heat
    Waves upward from the grass, where road on road
        Is swept before the tramping of the teams.
And while the oxen rest beside the sweet
    New hay, the loft receives the early load,
        With hissing stir, among the dusty beams.

There are true descriptive lines in many of the poems, such as, for instance:

A solitary mower marks his way
With hissing scythe in the brine-savoured hay.

The tide-deserted creek glows in the sun;
And the wet scows, now stranded on the shore,
Gape dark and empty, near a loaded cart
Drawn by two sturdy oxen, white and dun,
Which, as the evening reddens more and more,
Bend to the driver's word, ready to start.

For years add beauty to a peaceful age.

In the longer pieces Mr Herbin has less command than in the sonnets, but there are some good things, especially in 'Willows,' and 'Change.' Taken in the main, there seems to me high and serious tone in this little collection of poems. I think it is the tone of one who loves beauty, and loves her purely and honestly.

DUNCAN CAMPBELL SCOTT

When Matthew Arnold, in his criticism of the *Journal Intime* of Amiel, pronounced that it was on the side of literary criticism that he was most powerful, he vindicated once more his right to be called the greatest critic of our time. It was in criticism that Amiel was supremely great, and not only in literary criticism. In his journal he sometimes dwells upon music, and whenever he does one feels that here, too, he was supreme, that he understood this art and spoke of it with a sureness and a subtlety which its critics do not often bring to their task. It is our loss that he does not oftener speak of it; that he did not speak of other musicians with the same critical power that he used with Bach, Beethoven, Mozart, and Wagner. I would like to copy here his comparison of Mozart with Beethoven, to my mind the very finality of criticism:

Mozart – grace, liberty, certainty, freedom and precision of style – an exquisite and aristocratic beauty, serenity of soul, the health and talent of the master both on a level with his genius. Beethoven – more pathetic, more passionate, more torn with feeling, more intricate, more profound, less perfect, more the slave of his genius, more carried away by his fancy or his passion, more moving and more sublime than Mozart. Mozart refreshes you like the dialogues of Plato; he respects you, reveals to you your strength, gives you freedom and balance. Beethoven seizes upon you; he is more tragic and oratorical, while Mozart is more disinterested and poetical. Mozart is more Greek and Beethoven more Christian. One is serene, the other serious. The first is stronger than destiny, because he takes life less profoundly; the other is less strong because he has dared to measure himself against deeper sorrows. His talent is not always equal to his genius, and pathos is his dominant feature as perfection is that of Mozart. In Mozart the balance of the whole is perfect and art triumphs; in Beethoven feeling governs everything, and emotion troubles his art in proportion as it deepens it.

ARCHIBALD LAMPMAN

It is strange that in a country like this, where people talk so much about progress and prosperity and so forth, the number of those who count artistic and aesthetic development as one of the things to be sought after is so few. Here we have much material for new and original work in art; all we need is the means of education, and some source of influence which shall act upon the latent artistic talent buried in our midst. The least possible is done in this direction by those who have charge of public affairs, and very little indeed by private individuals of wealth and influence. No doubt many a native gift, capable of adding to the foundation of a national structure in art, is withered away for want of assistance, and does not even appear. It is a pity, for there are certain materials for the artist in the present stage of our country's growth, which will soon disappear, and which might produce work worth preserving.

One of the things which might be done by the Dominion government would be the improvement and increase of the so-called national gallery at Ottawa. If even a few good and valuable works of art were added to this collection, it would furnish an educating influence for young painters and sculptors of inestimable worth. Practically more could be done in this way than by the establishment of hundreds of schools. There is no education for the artist apart from nature, whether in painting, music, literature, or any other like the contemplation of a great and inspiring model. If funds are lacking – and they can easily be found for less worthy objects – let them be secured by doing away with some of the encumbrances now maintained – the Royal Society, for instance, which is a useless and somewhat ludicrous institution. By expending $50,000 annually, and so adding fifteen or twenty valuable articles to the exhibit each year, in a short time a very interesting and respectable collection might be made. The purchases ought to be made from all over the world, wherever great art work is done.

DUNCAN CAMPBELL SCOTT

That very day
From a bare ridge we also first beheld
Unveiled the summit of Mount Blanc, and grieved
To have a soulless image on the eye
That had usurped upon a living thought
That never more could be.

Those lines of Wordsworth embody a common experience. By the force of imagination we form ideas of the great natural scenery of the earth, which are usually disappointed when we stand face to face with the wonder. Perhaps ninety per cent of the people who look at Niagara for the first time are disappointed, and feel as if they had been cheated 'of a living thought that never more could be.' Man is anxious to be carried away and awed by something outside himself, and expects this of the ocean, or of the Rockies, or of the Mammoth Cave, but when he confronts the fact he finds it perfectly natural, and that he was greater than it after all, and has only to grieve for 'the soulless image in the eye.' But I find that, as a matter of course and by some generic law, the imaginative idea resumes its place, and is if anything heightened by remembrance. When we look back at the picture we find we were not disappointed, that the fact was as we expected it would be, and that our spiritual intuition was fulfilled. But in the record of Wordsworth's experience during his journey to the continent, which we find in that ever delightful poem *The Prelude*, this is not the only instance of a fact of everyday human nature, if I may be allowed such an expression, transferred into poetry, often beautiful, sometimes sublime. This is one reason why *The Prelude* is so readable as a whole; it is replete with facts of common experiences expressed in poetic form. Another reason is the constant reference to nature as a setting for man's life. Constantly does the poet turn to the open air and the freedom and activity of the life of nature. Constantly does he seek images and comparisons for the life of the soul from the unconscious proceedings of the power which moves in the world about us. He likens imagination rising from the 'mind's abyss' to an 'unfathered vapour that enwraps at once some lonely traveller,' or the soul to 'the mighty flood of Nile poured from his fount of abyssian clouds to fertilize the whole Egyptian plain.' Quotation would be endless were one to attempt to illustrate the varied power of such comparison and simile.

ARCHIBALD LAMPMAN

The awful destructiveness of the human race is exemplified in small things as well as great. Not only are our magnificent pine forests disappearing, not only is the buffalo practically extinct and the wild pigeon rapidly becoming so, but wherever any wild thing of interest or beauty occurs in rare haunts it is instantly set upon and destroyed. I have known some out-of the-way places in my neighbourhood where rare wild flowers could be found not long ago in considerable numbers: now they are gone. People could not be content to look at them, admire them, pluck a few, and leave the rest to renew their kind, and yield us the yearly service of their beauty. They must bear them away in armfuls, pull them up by the roots, and make an end of them in the momentary pride of securing a greater display than anyone else. They have killed the goose that laid the golden egg. Recently I was told of a place where I might find the golden lady's slipper, the moccasin flower. The knowledge was imparted to me as a secret. I went there, and found many of them blossoming in bits of deep wood that the crowd had somehow missed. They stood in little companies by the pools in the moist, rocky soil, and shafts of the afternoon sun shining in upon them made them wonderfully beautiful. I carried only two or three of them away, and neither persuasion nor torture shall draw from me the knowledge of their secret abode.

1 July 1893

DUNCAN CAMPBELL SCOTT

Mr Frank Yeigh has given us an opportunity of glancing back at our provincial history, and of comparing what Ontario now is with what she once was. The result is inspiriting, and one is irresistibly led to make forecasts of the future, to turn prophetic, and to promise a greatness and a power for our beautiful province transcending anything which she has at present reached. Mr Yeigh's book, *Ontario Parliament Buildings, 1792-1893*, is an historical record of the four buildings which have been successively occupied by the provincial house. It is a valuable record; but it is more – it is a readable one. Anything which Mr Yeigh would undertake to do would be well done, would be carried out with spirit, taste, and judgment, and his record of the many interesting and important occurrences which have gone to make our provincial history is written in a pleasant and entertaining style. Moreover, there is a selection of the things one would want to know, and, in very many instances, notes and striking descriptions of the times which went before our present civilization, and which made it possible.

The book is filled with pictures of the old buildings, which are in themselves very important and well worth preserving and making readily accessible. The portraits are for the most part good and well chosen, but, if such have been available, portraits of some of the old worthies would have rendered the collection still more valuable, but there may have been difficulties in the way of obtaining them which could not be overcome. The illustrations of the new building are somewhat marred by the presence of scaffolding and pulley ropes, but they give a sufficient idea of what must become a more beautiful structure. I say must become, for every building needs time to develop its beauties, and that the new building has beauties, and great ones, no one can deny. I do not think the word grand can be applied to it, but it has a charm which satisfies and inspires – the view of it gives delight and kindred impressions.

When time has gathered about it countless associations for every Ontario man, it will seem the fitting centre of his provincial life. The most interesting of Mr Yeigh's chapters may be 'Famous Scenes in the Old Chamber,' and 'Then and Now.' I say 'may be,' because my own reading has hardly satisfied me that they are, and the reader of this review will have to satisfy himself by reading the book, a process which should involve buying it, and he will not regret doing that. The book is well printed and bound by Hunter, Rose & Co., and published by the Williamson Book Company.

1 July 1893

WILFRED CAMPBELL

We notice that the term 'quality' is used today in connection with our current minor verse. And, while I would object to it as an unfair and misleading expression as applied to true poetry, yet it comes in very handy as a sort of apology for the kind of pseudo-poetry that is marking these times, and which, in the absence of real poetic imagination and creative ability, has taken to pensive musings and landscape painting in words. The real critic when he meets this article, which is as easy for some men to make as it is to whittle a stick, he passes it over with the slight mention it merits. But there is another class of critic, who, bearing the same relation to true criticism that this kind of verse-maker does to poetry, and stumbling up against a sort of poetical miracle of this kind, he is dumbfounded. Of course, it is a sonnet, and is possibly called –

At Even

I sit me moanless in the sombre fields,
The cows come with large udders down the dusk,
One cudless, the other chewing of a husk,
Her eye askance, for that athwart her heels,
Flea-haunted and rib-cavernous, there steals
The yelping farmer-dog. An old hen sits
And blinks her eyes. (Now I must rack my wits
To find a rhyme, while all this landscape reels.)

Yes! I forgot the sky. The stars are out,
There being no clouds; and then the pensive maid!
Of course she comes with tin-pail up the lane.
Mosquitoes hum and June bugs are about.
(That line hath 'quality' of loftiest grade.)
And I have eased my soul of its sweet pain.

(John Pensive Bangs, in *The Great Too-Too Magazine* for July)

The critic stumbles, I repeat, on this remarkable effusion, and this is what he remarks: 'This is verse of a high poetic quality. It is Millet-like in its terse realism. Mr Bangs is not one of your common flabgasters in rhyme. He is a monk in literature, and wears the hair-shirt of realism. Mark his delicate touches, his firm hand. No laying on with a whitewash brush for him. Oh! It is rare; it is restful. It makes me –w–. No, the disciple of realism and Arnold does not weep; he only groans. I will hang on to myself.' He then consigns all of the other poets who may be standing around stopping up Bangs's literary way to early poetical graves, and black oblivion, while he notes the mellow moon of this his particular poet radiating the heavens with its beams, and rising higher and higher into universal favour. But the funniest part is that the critic should give Mr Bangs so much praise for his realism. He surely would not have Bangs make the cows drive the landscape, the dog do the roosting, and get the hen, the maid, and the June bugs mixed up promiscuously. Hardly! John Pensive Bangs has too much horse sense for that since he went to college, read Matthew Arnold, cut his hair, and got toned down a bit. Nor should the critic expect that Mr Bangs ever did sit thus, 'moanless,' in the fields, a martyr to blackflies and damp grass, in order to capture this most rare and fleeting glimpse for the uplifting of his lesser human brethren. Not by any means. John Pensive has a patent on this sort of business, and ten to one he wrote it in his back office, two flights up, with a cigar in his mouth, and the spittoon two points on the weather-bow. Nor should the critic think it anything remarkable to rig or hitch such a landscape together, so as not to forget even the June bugs. This is simple enough. We might give him some more examples. They need no lofty thoughts or wide knowledge of nature and man. This is another, called

Pitching Hay

Hitched to the waggon by the grimy hands
Of the horny-fisted farmer, stands the team,
Filling the drowsy air with languid dream
Of gone, last-winter oats. Aloft there stands
The lusty farm-hand, and he mops his brow,
And says, 'We'll hustle in this last load now.'

Or these lines of 'singular discernment,' says our critic:

Far up the road, where once a waggon was,
Lies all deserted where the toilers sped,
    The foot-path leading to the dun cow's shed
Has but a solitary hobbling toad.

Fancy such a picture of desolation and bleakness, and so on.

We have no space here to quote from many such landscapes as 'Raking Chips,' 'The Lonely Clam,' 'Morn,' 'Beetles,' 'Hoeing Potatoes,'

'Bunch-Grass,' 'Tadpoles,' 'Sharpening the Bucksaw,' and other equally interesting and peculiar subjects for word-landscape, and all found in John Pensive Bangs's new volume of poems, called *Red Top and Radishes*, and all containing that remarkable attribute called 'poetic quality' in a marked degree.

WILFRED CAMPBELL

I have just discovered a passage from Frederick Harrison's article on 'The Decadence of Romance,' which backs up my article of the week before last. Here it is:

> We come, then, to this, that for the first time during this whole century now ending English literature can count no living novelist whom the world consents to stamp with the mark of accepted fame. One is too eccentric and subtle, another too local and unequal, a third too sketchy, this one too unreal, that one far too real, too obvious, to prosaic, to win and to hold the great public by their spell. Critics praise them, friends utter rhapsodies, good judges enjoy them; but their fame is partial, local, sectional.

Not only in romance but in other branches of art is there this dearth of genius, or even talent of the first rank:

> With a very high average of fairly good work, an immense mass of such work, and an elaborate code of criticism, the production of brilliant and inimitable successes is usually arrested in every field. Having thousands of graceful verse-writers, we have no poet; in a torrent of skilful fiction, we have no great novelist; with many charming painters, who hardly seem to have a fault, we have no great artist; with mises-en-scène, make-up, costumes and accessories for our plays such as the world never saw before, we have no great actor, and, with ten thousand thoughtful writers, we have not a single genius of the first rank. Elaborate culture casts chill looks on original ideas. Genius itself is made to feel the crudeness and extravagance of its first efforts, and retires with shame to take a lower place. We are all so fastidious about form, and have got such fixed regulation views about form, we are so correct, so much like one another, such good boys and girls, that the eccentricities and idiosyncrasies of the inventive spirit are taught from childhood to control themselves and to conform to the decorum of good society. A highly-organized code of culture may give us good manners, but it is the death of genius.

All the men who have made the Victorian age of literature bright with their names had done their best work by 1865. 'We had already got all, or all that was best, of Tennyson, Browning, Carlyle, Ruskin, Lytton, Thackeray, Dickens, Trollope, George Eliot, Disraeli, Kingsley and others who lived after that date.' The trouble today is that we have 'overstrained our taste, we are overdone with criticism, we are much too systematically drilled, there is far too much moderate literature, and far too fastidious a standard in literature.' We are so terrorized with the bugaboo of 'correctness' and 'finish' that we sacrifice any originality we may possess.' Says Mr Harrison:

> If another Dickens were to break out to-morrow with the riotous tomfoolery of Pickwick at the trial, or of Weller and Stiggins, a thousand lucid criticisms would denounce it as vulgar balderdash. Glaucus and Nydia at Pompeii would be called melodramatic rant. *The House of the Seven Gables* would be rejected by a sixpenny magazine, and *Jane Eyre* would not rise above a common 'shocker.' Hence the enormous growth of the 'Kodak' school of romance – the snap-shots at every-day realism with a hand camera. We know how it is done. A woman of forty, stout, plain and dull, sits in an ordinary parlor at a tea-table, near an angular girl with a bad squint. 'Some tea?' said Mary, touching the pot. 'I don't mind,' replied Jane in a careless tone; 'I am rather tired, and it is a dull day.' 'It is,' said Mary, as her lack-lustre eyes glanced at the murky sky without. 'Another cup?' And so the modern romance dribbles on hour by hour, chapter by chapter, volume by volume, recording, as in a phonograph, the minute commonplace of the average man and woman in perfectly real, but entirely common situations. To this dead level of correctness, literary purism has brought romance.

Fielding, Scott, Dickens, Thackeray, Trollope lived full lives, they 'drank with both hands from the cup of life'; but 'George Meredith, Robert Louis Stevenson, Howells, James, look on life from a private box. We see their kid-gloves and their opera-glass, and we know that nothing could ever take them on to the stage. There is no known instance of a great novelist who lived obscure in a solitary retreat, or who became famous only after the lapse of many generations.' Life is growing dull. 'Comfort, electric light, railway cars and equality are excellent things, but they are the death of romance.'

Index

LITERATURE OF CANADA

Poetry and Prose in Reprint
Douglas Lochhead, General Editor

1 *Collected Poems*, Isabella Valancy Crawford
Introduction by James Reaney

2 *The St Lawrence and the Saguenay and Other Poems, & Hesperus and Other Poems and Lyrics*, Charles Sangster
Introduction by Gordon Johnston

3 *Our Intellectual Strength and Weakness*, John George Bourinot
'English-Canadian Literature,' Thomas Guthrie Marquis
'French-Canadian Literature,' Camille Roy
Introduction by Clara Thomas

4 *Selections from Canadian Poets*, Edward Hartley Dewart
Introduction by Douglas Lochhead

5 *Poems and Essays*, Joseph Howe
Introduction by Malcolm G. Parks

6 *Rockbound: A Novel*, Frank Parker Day
Introduction by Allan Bevan

7 *The Homesteaders*, Robert J.C. Stead
Introduction by Susan Wood Glicksohn

8 *The Measure of the Rule*, Robert Barr
Introduction by Louis K. MacKendrick

9 *Selected Poetry and Critical Prose*, Charles G.D. Roberts
Edited with an introduction and notes by W.J. Keith

10 *Old Man Savarin Stories: Tales of Canada and Canadians*
E.W. Thomson
Introduction by Linda Sheshko

11 *Dreamland and Other Poems & Tecumseh: A Drama*, Charles Mair
Introduction by Norman Shrive

12 *The Poems of Archibald Lampman (including At the Long Sault)*
Archibald Lampman
Introduction by Margaret Coulby Whitridge

13 *The Poetical Works of Alexander McLachlan*,
Alexander McLachlan
Introduction by E. Margaret Fulton

14 *Angéline de Montbrun*, Laure Conan
Translated and introduced by Yves Brunelle

15 *The White Savannahs*, W.E. Collin
Introduction by Germaine Warkentin

16 *The Search for English-Canadian Literature: An Anthology of Critical Articles from the Nineteenth and Early Twentieth Centuries*
Edited and introduced by Carl Ballstadt

17 *The First Day of Spring: Stories and Other Prose*
Raymond Knister
Selected and introduced by Peter Stevens

18 *The Canadian Brothers; or, The Prophecy Fulfilled: A Tale of the Late American War*, John Richardson
Introduction by Carl F. Klinck

19 *Saul and Selected Poems including excerpts from 'Jephthah's Daughter' and 'Jezebel: A Poem in Three Cantos'*
Charles Heavysege
Introduction by Sandra Djwa

20 *New Provinces: Poems of Several Authors*
Introduction by Michael Gnarowski

21 *At the Mermaid Inn: Wilfred Campbell, Archibald Lampman, Duncan Campbell Scott in 'The Globe' 1892-3*
Introduction by Barrie Davies